THE PORTLAND CHRONICLE

A Jamaican Novel

By

Denis G. Dun

PUBLISH AMERICA

PublishAmerica
Baltimore

ISBN: 978-1-61546-730-3
PUBLISHED BY PUBLISHAMERICA, LLLP
www.publishamerica.com
Baltimore

Printed in the United States of America

CHAPTER 1

Thirty years before the discovery of the headless corpse an old woman sat on her stool, legs crossed, a shawl over her head that barely revealed wispy strands of gray hair and wrinkled features beneath. Back and forth she rocked, mumbling incantations to her native deity in a language not now understood by anyone in her family. It was not the season for rain yet it had rained hard for several days. She squatted on her haunches fanning a smoky, smoldering fire that once in a while responded to her efforts, but so often her hopes were extinguished in a puff of smoke. The piece of soggy cardboard that served her as a fan began to bend and give way to the constant stress of supplying air to the unwilling fire. The firewood, so carefully preserved, was drenched through and refused to burn, and the old woman cursed her unhappy fate. Then she bent over and blew hard on some small glowing embers, and, as if in answer to her prayers, a flame leaped up and it did not vanish in a puff of smoke. At last! The fire was blazing; there would be cooked food for her family that night.

She had come to Jamaica from India with her husband almost sixty-four years ago as part of an experimental agricultural program expected to grow rice for the increasing Jamaican population. The program succeeded in Trinidad where the equatorial rains in the hot season nourished the crops. But Jamaica lacked the constant mid-year rains and the crops did not thrive; the program failed. Instead of a passage home the coolie workers were paid off and induced to remain in Jamaica. The old woman had never learned to speak English; she had relied entirely upon her husband, an educated and intelligent man, for any necessary translations. When he died the old woman became isolated and alone, having in large measure, lost the ability to communicate with other people in the village.

They had not spawned a large family; only two sons and a daughter, but they all still lived in the village settlement. The old woman lived with her eldest son, his wife and their only child, a boy. Her son had become a Christian and changed his name to Hutchings, to honor his English teacher in India. He married a native woman from the mountain settlement, and when his son was born, the child was christened in the small Anglican Church. Fancying the Biblical character his father named him Daniel.

Daniel's parents were proud of the fact that their son had a birth certificate—one that showed he was their "legitimate boy child." Only three people in the village—the minister, the schoolteacher and Hutchings—could make such a boast. But Daniel was a small boy, of slight, thin build—almost undernourished—not much of a physical specimen to brag about. His long thin arms and legs—mere extensions from his well-worn 'hand-me-down' oversized shirts and pants, were like the stick-limbs of a scarecrow. He was nevertheless, a handsome boy—smooth light brown skin and thick curly hair, indicative of a mixed Indian-African heritage; fine angular features, a romantic, classical, almost angelic visage.

Daniel's father worked for James 'Squire' Henderson on the Manor House Estates, a large banana, coffee and coconut plantation that began at the coastal plane and extended several miles into the hills and mountains. At times Daniel accompanied his father to the plantation and was greatly impressed by the Squire—a man who seemed to be the most powerful man in the world! He wore boots that ended just below his knees! The Squire too noticed the handsome boy, often standing quietly behind his father. He asked about him—whose boy he was. And when the Squire learned that he was the son of a trusted worker, he called to Daniel and questioned him. The Squire was impressed by quick and intelligent answers, so much so that he spoke to his father and insisted the boy be sent to a school. In school Daniel learned quickly, and by the age of eight he could read, write and calculate, which placed him much above other children in the school, and even above most adults in the mountain settlement.

School had a lasting affect, not only from the lessons taught, but also in moral and religious matters. Many times he read the story of Daniel in the Bible, and he resolved to be like the Biblical Daniel, God fearing and brave in the face of danger. He was ambitious too; when he became a man he vowed, his children would be more fortunate than he was, and he would see to that. They would not walk bare-foot on the roads—they would be like the Squire—they would wear shoes! And one day, he resolved, he would be the busha, and manage the Manor House Estate. But school was not a luxury to be endlessly enjoyed, and at the age of ten, when more fortunate children were anxiously contemplating their first visit, Daniel had already left and started out to work, along with his father on the Estate.

Towards the end of that year there were natural disasters. Several days of continuous heavy rain had seen the rivers turn into raging torrents, so much so that it was difficult to move about and impossible to continue work on the Estate. It had rained for the last ten days—heavy downpours, without stopping. The rains had confined everyone to their houses and huts, some of which were perched precariously in the valley above the river. Every available household pot and pan was being used to collect the water dripping through the leaking roofs. The banana and coconut leaf thatched structures were saturated and could no longer prevent the water pouring through. The unfortunate occupants covered themselves with coats, sacks upon their heads and shoulders, and banana leaves over their heads for those not possessing a coat or sack. Some sat huddled together, the sacks wrapped about them in futile efforts to keep dry and warm. Each family, suffering their own particular discomforts, remained isolated in their huts, not knowing how their neighbors were faring. Most fires had been extinguished days before, and many had lost their precious burning charcoals used to conjure warmth and light. In any event, there was not a dry stick or twig for miles around that could have been put to that use. The deluge had flushed all kinds of strange creatures from their usual lairs and haunts; lizards, crabs, frogs and insects—stinging ants, nipping beetles, cockroaches, scorpions and spiders—all were seeking refuge and freely crawled about the huts. Misery had descended on every living creature.

As the night went on, the floodwaters began to rise, and the water coming down the mountainside began to flow through the huts. Suddenly, without warning a wall would collapse, or a roof would fall in, and the swirling water would take the pieces away—along with the unfortunate occupants. Their shrieks and cries for help went unheard, and one by one the little houses and huts were demolished and swept into the raging river. By morning the little settlement of Swift River had been devastated. There were a handful of survivors and over fifty missing, washed out to sea, including Daniel's parents and his aged grandmother, but miraculously he had survived. Some of the bodies washed away were later found, some on the shore and some out at sea, totally unrecognizable, ravaged by crabs, fish and decomposition.

Without hesitation, his surviving uncle claimed his father's property and took in the orphaned boy, and very soon it was made it clear to him that in spite of his loss, he must earn his keep and pay his way; his meager wages were seized.

Later that year a hurricane added to the misery and destroyed much of what had been left standing. But on the Estate the job of replanting began, although many of the workers were discharged for lack of work. Fortunately for Daniel, he was among the few retained. The Squire, sympathetic to the tragedy virtually adopted the young boy and arranged for him to live on the estate, in the personal care of an older employee.

As the youngest employee on the estate, he was assigned the most menial tasks, to fetch and carry the water for the men, or to take messages back and forth. He was not strong enough and certainly not big enough to tackle the strenuous work normally required of the men, although he was often put to the test. Initially he assisted the men in their work, but gradually more and more of the real work came his way. Many of the coconut trees destroyed had been replanted, and although not yet mature, were growing well and prospects revived.

The workweek usually ended at noon on Saturdays, that is unless essential work was being done, and then everyone was obliged to work the extra hours. On one such Saturday afternoon, produce was being loaded on a ship anchored in deep water some distance from the shore. The loading took place some distance from the Estate itself where the ships could anchor conveniently, and where the produce could be stockpiled in advance. At noon, everyone was down at the waterfront when the men stopped for the noontime break. Some were resting on the beach, some reclining and smoking. It had rained during the night, but the day was clear, bright, and hot. Someone wanted coconut water to drink. There were several palm trees on the beach, and all it needed was for someone to climb the trees and pick the nuts. Most of the men had been working hard and steadily from early that morning, and were disinclined to climb the tall palm trees.

"Ah! Daniel.—Daniel, come 'ere, bou'y," one of the men called. "Come pick coconut."

Daniel had climbed the tall palms before—it was something that every boy had to be able to do—a sort of 'coming-of-age' was the ability to climb coconut trees and pick coconuts. And Daniel was a willing boy. Carefully he selected a palm tree with several large clusters of the half-green nuts that would be full of water. The palm grew on firm ground a short distance off the sandy beach, and with a gentle slope towards the open sea it was an easier climb. Still it was a strenuous effort for the young boy, and with the nuts picked, he rested and with the men drank coconut water.

8

Daniel had not quite finished eating when the foreman arrived on the scene, standing almost beside Daniel as he entered the small circle of reclining workers. Daniel knew the man well and had a number of times felt the end of a 'cowcod,'—a cane made from the stretched, dried penis of a bull—that the man always carried with him. It was used primarily by the foreman as a sign of his authority, and as a prod, to intimidate, and sometimes to inflict punishment on those he did not like, even though such treatment of the workmen was not allowed. The foreman looked about disapprovingly, at the scattered shells and opened nuts and sized up the situation immediately.

"Wher' fe me jellydoe?" He demanded. The man was universally disliked and no one answered. "Y'u all tek de Squire coconut an' y'u doan leave none fe me?" he asked indignantly.

There was no answer from any of the men.

"Who pick de nuts dem?" He demanded but not expecting an answer, and without warning he vented his disapproval on the person nearest. He struck Daniel a sharp blow across his backside. "Y'u mus' be de culprit!"

Daniel jumped out of reach and almost started to cry—the pain was intense, but he did not cry. He rubbed the injured parts and kept out of reach in case the man had it in mind to strike him again. A man protested the act of unprovoked cruelty; "W'at y'u li'k 'im for?" he demanded. But the foreman was not about to apologize.

"Daniel, bou'y," he called, "Y'u goine pick jellydoe fe me."

"No sur." The voice came from the man in the circle. It was the man who had earlier called to Daniel. "Him already climb."

"Well 'im goine climb again."xxxxxx

The man was indignant. "'Im is a li'kle bou'y, an' 'im not fit to climb palm tree two time," then turning to Daniel he said, "rest y'uself Danboy. Ah will pick."

The foreman did not like to be contradicted nor have his authority questioned in any way. "If 'im know w'at is good fe 'im he will climb palm tree two time," he said angrily.

The man ignored the foreman and continued to ready himself for the climb. "Y'u rest y'uself, bou'y." he said quietly to Daniel.

The foreman was enraged. "If 'im know w'at is good fe 'im 'e goine climb two time!" He repeated, shouting. "An' if 'im doant climb, I'se goin' bust 'im arse good!"

The man was outraged and indignant. "'Im balls doant drop yet an' y'u goine mek 'im climb palm tree two time?" He looked about the circle for support as the men grumbled their agreement.

"Ah say if 'im knows w'at good fe 'im 'e will climb palm tree two time!"

There was a very threatening tone to the man's voice that was not misunderstood by anyone, especially Daniel. The gathering voiced their objections and misgivings, but to no avail. The man offering to climb was already standing at the base of a tree, but seeing that it would be worse for Daniel if he continued, he reluctantly sat down again.

The foreman called to Daniel again, "Daniel!"

Daniel was still feeling the pain; he knew what to expect if he refused. Timidly he approached the man. "Yes sur."

The foreman looked about for a tree; he was impatient and quickly made his choice known. "Dis one, bou'y," he said, striking a tree several times with his cane. "Dis one!"

It would not be an easy tree to climb—it went straight up without a helpful slant so often found on palms growing on the shoreline.

"Tek y'u time, Dan bou'y," said the man who had offered to climb in his stead. "Jus' tek y'u time," he encouraged him.

Daniel took a deep breath and started his climb, and almost reached the top. At that point he was exhausted, so he paused to catch his breath again before continuing. He went up a foot higher but at the top the tree was still wet from the overnight rains. He held on and tested his grip. Instinct told him it was not safe to continue and that he should descend, but then he was almost there; he was fearful but determined. He wrapped his arms about the trunk, held on and raised his legs once again to a new position. That too was wet and slippery, and his feet did not hold. Again he locked his arms tightly about the trunk, hugging the trunk to his chest, trying desperately to gain a secure position with his feet. Neither position held—his arms were slipping and there was no hold with his feet. He slid down the trunk three or four feet before his arms and feet could no longer stand the abrasive bruising from the rough trunk. He made a desperate attempt to maintain his hold but could not. He swung around the trunk before loosing his grip completely and letting go. His fall was perhaps twenty feet, and he hit the ground half on his back and side. Fortunately the ground was sandy and soft, or his injuries could have been immediately fatal. Nevertheless, he was severely and seriously injured—he had broken his hip.

The first man to reach him was the man who had opposed the foreman, and he was kneeling beside the still body. The men quickly gathered around including the foreman, all gaping at the unconscious figure.

"Y'u bust 'im arse good!" Shouted the man looking up angrily at the foreman, and within a second he was on his feet and had grabbed the foreman about the neck attempting to throw him to the ground. The two men wrestled for a short while, throwing futile blows at one another until they were separated and held apart by the other workers.

The men picked up the unconscious boy and carried him to the pier. Someone produced a bottle of rum and splashed it about his head and face until he opened his eyes. At least he was not dead—yet—although he well might be in a few hours. He was placed on a dray, taken to the Estate House where he was put to bed.

It was a day later that the accident came to the Squire's attention, and he wanted to know why Daniel was climbing the palms—a task usually assigned to the men. Soon enough he had the complete story and was incensed by what he heard; the foreman was summoned and discharged immediately. The Squire knew that firing the man would not improve the condition of the injured boy, but at least such a thing would never happen again.

The Squire gave his personal attention to seeing that Daniel had proper care, and visited him frequently for the weeks following. For more than a month Daniel was unable to leave the bed; his recovery was long and painful, but slowly he regained his strength. Three months later he was able to walk with the help of crutches, and for the next year he was still an invalid having to rest frequently, and unable to work. The broken bones mended, but he would always be crippled and suffer the effects of his near fatal fall.

The Squire often visited with the promise of a job as soon as he was able, and when at last he rejoined the workmen at the estate, it was as assistant to the headman, who was only too glad to have the able help keeping the accounts and adding up the time sheets. In time the position gave him some authority, and in spite of his age and his physical handicap he acquired a certain respect amongst the workers.

A few years later he was appointment headman—a promotion that was not unexpected. And four years later he married Sapphire, a young woman, like himself of mixed East Indian heritage. Within a year they had a daughter, Opal, and two more daughters, Jewel and Ruby, arrived in the next three years.

During those years the Squire had come to rely on Daniel, especially when his business interests compelled him to be in Kingston for long periods of time. And some years later when he went to England, Daniel was left in complete charge of the estate. On his return the Squire was very pleased to find everything as he would have wished.

CHAPTER 2

Alice Barnham had lived most of her life at Chivers Estate, which bordered the Manor House property on the West. She was the only child of Charlie McIntire, a long line of McIntires whose family had owned the plantation for over two hundred years. When the British Government abolished slavery, and decreed that all slaves were to be set free, there was considerable resistance from plantation owners right across the island. The McIntires who were slave owners, led the opposition to emancipation in that part of the country. The ingrained opposition to freeing the slaves came from Jacob McIntire, a retired sea captain who had made a fortune in the slave trade, and even after the British Government outlawed the practice, he continued to harvest Negroes from the West African coast and trade to the American South. It was the near capture by a British frigate off the Carolina coast that convinced him to stop. His ship, loaded with human cargo, had been pursued off and on for several days, and by the evening was about to be taken. Darkness and a dense fog enveloped the two ships and he very narrowly escaped capture. Family historians represented him as a benevolent, caring landowner, who showed only deep concern for his slaves, but that couldn't have been further from the truth, for in fact he was a brutal and sadistic man, having less regard for slaves than he did for his dogs. He frequently scheduled Saturday floggings, strictly for his entertainment, and "to keep the niggers in order." It was an activity in which he eagerly took part until forced to stop when slaves became too expensive and too difficult to replace. That realization came following the death of a Negro slave—also called Jacob— Jacob's 'virtue' was his tendency to sing, even when being flogged! As the lashes fell he would sing some native hymn—to the endless amusement of Jacob McIntire. Consequently the unfortunate man was often whipped, and once too often it seems; he succumbed to the ill treatment, and McIntire was unable to obtain a replacement at any reasonable cost.

When the day for freeing the slaves arrived, most chose to abandon the estate, although they had nowhere to go except to scatter into the hills. Some chose to remain on the Estate and receive nothing more than their food and shelter in return for their hard labor, the living conditions being no better than before. The day of retribution for Jacob McIntire did finally arrive when he fell from his horse; his boot caught in the stirrup breaking his leg so badly that the bone was exposed. He never recovered. Someone, it was suspected, had placed a sliver of broken glass under the saddle of his horse. His wife Rachel remained on the estate, a bitter and lonely woman. Nevertheless, the McIntire family retained the plantation despised by the general population and with a tainted reputation that lingered on into present memory.

When Charlie McIntire died his daughter Alice inherited the plantation, and she continued to live at Chivers with her husband Hugh Barnham. Hugh, a government official, had met his wife while traveling in the country, and although both were near middle age they had a daughter, and it was a very happy marriage. Sadly, it lasted only a few years; Hugh died from a 'growth'—they called it. It was a lingering and painful end—"a merciful release," the doctor said, but that was not much consolation. Maud, Alice's nursemaid from childhood, was a comfort and help to end the grieving; she pointed out that Alice still had much to look forward to in life; that she was a wealthy middle-aged widow with a delightful infant daughter, and she had a large estate to attend to. As a result Alice set out to find an overseer—a 'Busha'—to manage her estate. Searching produced many disappointments, but she finally employed Major Henry Barclay-Thomson to be the Busha of Chivers Estate.

CHAPTER 3

Henry Barclay-Thomson was the third son of a one-time wealthy and prominent Jamaican family from Upper Kingston. Now in his early thirties, in spite of a somewhat wasted life, he retained much of his youthful good looks and charm. He had been schooled in England at an upper class Public school, where he excelled in sports, especially football and boxing. In football it was his sense of timing and his ability to anticipate the maneuvers of the opponents; in the ring it was his ability to counter-punch with telling speed. After leaving school he accepted a lieutenant's commission in one of England's foremost regiments, the Berkshire Hussars. As a junior officer during the First World War he was posted to the Middle East, and returned with decorations for courage and bravery in action. In point of fact these were not acts of courage and bravery—they were impulsive acts of rash stupidity and bravado, but they happened to be the right steps to take under the circumstances, and without thought for his own safety Henry Thomson had taken those steps.

These achievements—if they could be called such—came easily to the handsome, wealthy young man, and they added considerably to his reputation and prestige. In the Regiment he met Marjory, the daughter of the Regimental Commander, Brigadier Sir Francis Digby, and after a brief courtship she became his wife, even without the approval of the Regimental Commander or the Digby clan. This was further testimony to his impulsive and rash bravado—no officer in the regiment would have dared to even contemplate such action—but he was ambitious—he had thoughts of one day replacing his father-in-law as regimental commander!

The anticipated birth of their first child brought about a reserved, conditional, acceptance by his wife's family, but as the war was over and normal life in the army was dull and boring, he needed excitement to stay alive. Consequently, things were always happening around Captain Thomson, and he soon acquired a following of likeminded fellow officers. Very quickly he earned the reputation of a troublemaker, a fighter, and the nickname "Basher Thomson," but as his notoriety spread it drew the unfavorable attention of his father-in-law. Sir Francis was decidedly unimpressed with behavior so unbecoming to a gentleman and an officer of the Regiment; Thomson became an acute embarrassment, and as a result he was encouraged to 'retire'—preferably to South Africa, the West Indies, or some other distant place. As he had risen to the rank of Captain, on 'retirement' he was offered a generous gratuity of two thousand pounds, a small pension for life and complimentary promotion to the rank of Major, including all the entitlements of that rank. The offer was too tempting to refuse; he resigned his commission and with his wife returned to Jamaica.

In the years that followed they were restlessly back and forth to England in search of what might be called 'their place,' but mostly, this amounted to aimless wandering and the dispersment of what was left of the Thomson fortune. Time and alcohol took its toll, and with a declining income, it combined to awaken them to the realities of the world—the need to find gainful employment. The realization did not come quickly; old habits were hard to break, and it was not easy to adjust to the life of the employed. The expensive tastes persisted; the vaulted airs and attitudes were indelibly imprinted on their personalities, making any real philosophical acceptance quite impossible. Nevertheless, the position of Busha at Chivers Estate gave Barclay-Thomson full authority on the Estate—he had sway over all, and could delude himself with this false mantle of power, and the notion that it was all his. And when this delusion failed, he could wash away disturbing thoughts with copious amounts of rum, and he could find solace in the company of some woman from along the coast, or from some distant mountain village.

Married life for the Barkley-Thomsons therefore traveled a rocky road; after ten years, two adorable children, innumerable squabbles and fights, countless infidelities, financial stresses and strains, the marriage had survived in name only. And yet each expected of the other that appearances be maintained, and that to the outside world their life should reflect blissful harmony. In the company of family or friends she addressed him as "Love!" And the answer would come back, "Yes, my Sweet!" So it went most of the time, until alcohol blinded discretion, caution and propriety were discarded, and each again engaged in some outlandish and scandalous affair. Sometimes these affairs were hidden, sometimes they became known only to the other infuriated spouse, who would swear reprisals and vengeance. And then sometimes they were common knowledge to everyone. The sum total was that a kind of balance had been reached, neither one accepting or forgiving the sins and transgressions of the other. The feelings of hurt and betrayal were very real on both sides, but they never acted as deterrents to further indiscretions, and they continued to live sometimes together, sometimes apart, but still as 'man and wife.' The children, a boy and a girl—mercifully—had been sent to the care of the grandparents in England, and from there were shuffled off to boarding schools. Visits between parents and offspring were few and far between, and each were strangers to one another.

The facts of their existence at Chivers Estate did not appear to bother them very much as they went about their essentially idle and vacant lives. Henry would sober up each morning with several cups of hot, very strong sweet coffee, mixed half-and-half with piping hot milk. This mixture would bring back a mild alcoholic jag, and give him impetus to face the day. Marjory would rise somewhat later, shake her stupor with several cups of strong tea taken very slowly—almost unconsciously—with two slices of hot buttered toast and English marmalade, all served to her in the cool of the morning on the well shaded veranda.

Her days at the Estate were spent mostly reading, tending the small flower garden surrounding their house but populated mostly with weeds, or taking a stroll about the estate grounds. Occasionally she would have a horse saddled and would ride off into the plantation, or down along the seashore. Some mornings she would be up very early before the daylight had broken, and be off in her little car along the winding coastal road to Buff Bay. There in the early morning light she would watch the naked fishermen pulling in their nets and beaching their boats. Often she was tempted to strip off her clothes and join them—naked, to splash and frolick in the very warm sea. Only twice did she yield to the urge. But she never failed to bring back fish for their supper that night.

On Saturday mornings the maid would accompany her into town to do the weekly shopping at the local market. This expedition into town was something of a highlight to the week's events; there was always something new or interesting to see or to hear about, and the market people knew her well. Her notoriety came from her obsession to get her money's worth, always demanding her 'brata.' Amongst the market women she was known as 'Missus Brata,' who would then alert each other to her arrival at the market.

"Missus Brata da'ya. See—she come," the words were passed along. The women would then reduce the size of their bundled offerings so that when the 'brata' was granted, as it always was, it amounted only to the right amount for the price asked. But it satisfied the purchaser, and the vendors too, who would then loudly complain about the woman who drove such hard bargains. "Lawd Missus!" They would complain, "Y'u done mek poor people poor! How y'u come so?"

From time to time, however, boredom got the upper hand, and she would, without prior notice to husband or maid, impatiently pack her suitcase, throw it in the back of her car and take off to Kingston or Montego Bay. She never seemed to know in advance when the urge would strike. The only notice that anyone got were her shouted orders to the yardman to fill the gas tank, see that there was oil in the engine, water in the radiator, and that the tires were good.

In similar fashion her friends were never given advance notice of her intentions; her arrivals were unannounced, and quite often unwelcome. The cool receptions never dissuaded her, or caused her the least embarrassment—she knew where the spare rooms were, and she knew the servants by name, one of which might even be called to take the suitcase from the car and put it in the spare bedroom. Later, she would explain to her often unwilling hostess, "My dear, I simply had to get away from that place—I'm sure you can put up with me for a day or two—can't you my dear?" There it would end, and no one ever probed for reasons—everyone seemed to understand completely.

Jamaican Lore—Y'u can't stop bud fly over y'u head, but y'u can stop 'im mek nest in y'u head.

CHAPTER 4

Following her husband's death Mrs. Barnham was for a time very restless, finding it difficult to settle either in Kingston or at Chivers Estate. The Estate under the management of Henry Thomson was doing very well, and she was quite satisfied to leave matters in his hands. She knew of his unsavory reputation, but despite that he was a good manager, and she had decided long ago that his personal life was none of her concern. Two years passed and she was tired of the long drives back and forth between her two residences, and she settled down to live in Kingston.

Chivers Estate was neglected for the next three years, although it remained fully staffed and ready. During that time the Estate House was made use of occasionally, only for brief periods each year, on holidays and some odd weeks, and when the mood took her, which was not often. For her, getting there was the difficulty; counting every twist and turn, the distance by road was a little less than sixty-five miles. As the crow flies—over the mountains—it was less than one third of that. The trip was a tiring, daylong journey, not the sort to be undertaken frequently, or by anyone with the least inclination to be carsick.

Six years later though, Mrs. Barnham had her own reasons for wanting to move back to Chivers. Her daughter Bridget was eight years old and hardly knew the place. If Bridget was ever to succeed as a property owner, it was not too early to begin her education in that regard. Furthermore, the plantation needed her personal attention; things at the house, for which she had great concern, had not been quite right for some time, and she was never really sure—there was nothing that one could put a finger on—it was more feeling than fact, and Mrs. Barnham was known to be guided by her instincts.

The housekeeper at Chivers, Constance—Constance in name only, Mrs. Barnham always said—had taken over the place in the absence of its owner, and was keeping it for the entertainment of her friends and relations. Once or twice to test the theory, Mrs. Barnham arrived at the plantation house without giving prior notice to the housekeeper—just to catch them in the act. What Mrs. Barnham did not know, however, was that Joseph, her chauffeur, got wind of the plan from the table maid, and sent word to alert Constance. Mrs. Barnham arrived to find the place as spick and span as anyone could wish, and Constance on the veranda awaiting her arrival. How Joseph accomplished the feat is not known, and remains a mystery to this day, but the result did not allay Mrs Barnham's suspicions—she just knew what that woman was up to!

The move to Chivers was well planned; three mule drays would be required, which were to be loaded with furniture and baggage, covered over with good tarpaulins, and firmly tied down in case of rain—almost a certainty during the passage through the mountains. Each dray would be drawn by two strong mules supplied by Henderson's Trading Co. , Ltd. , driven by their best dray-men, and with a foreman in charge. Altogether the journey would take two days and thus an over-night rest-stop for men and mules had to be arranged. Mrs Barnham would depart from Kingston shortly after seeing her possessions safely on their way—and she would arrive at Chivers a day ahead, in time to supervise the safe unloading.

The move was executed precisely as it was planned. The three drays came rumbling up the long driveway late in the afternoon and were greeted by a throng of expectant and excited onlookers from the Estate. The draymen, who had been driving since the early morning, through pelting rain and blistering heat, were exhausted, and wandered off, somewhat unsteadily, to find their feet with a bottle or two of rum divided up between them. They were not needed any more for the time being; there were many willing hands able to unload and take baggage and furniture to its appointed place. In short order the drays were emptied, and the mules led off to be stabled and fed.

Mrs. Barnham was once again ensconced at Chivers. It was a move to repossess her property and to assert her authority where it was badly needed, and it really did not matter to her who knew her real reasons for being there. Shortly after arriving Mrs. Barnham found that an additional maid was needed to help run the household. The servants in Kingston remained there at the big house, with the exception of Old Maud who was not really a servant, but more a companion and confidant to Mrs. Barnham, and who, for that reason always followed Mrs. Barnham from one place to another. Her nominal task was to take care of Bridget, but this amounted to little more than overseeing a nursemaid who in fact performed the real work. It was therefore necessary to find a suitable housemaid from what was available in the country. Given the nature of the plantation owner, this was not a task to be delegated—Mrs. Barnham intended to do the hiring herself. Constance was instructed to pass the word around that there would be a position open at the plantation house, and those considering themselves suitable and desirous of such employment should present themselves within the next week at the Estate House for interviews with Mrs. Barnham.

The move to Chivers duly accomplished, Mrs. Barnham settled in—not that much 'settling in' was necessary. What it amounted to was a probing and a searching into every crack and cranny for missing or broken articles, of which there were a number. After a week, Mrs. Barnham had not quite vented her anger and annoyance at these discoveries; everyone had received at least two or three proper reprimands, and she had stopped a few shillings from wages here and there, and there might yet be more to come.

During this time no applicants appeared for interviews, and neither did anyone appear in the week following. Another week passed, and still there were no applicants. This was by all accounts, most unusual; work in the country was hard to come by, especially a job that offered the perquisites of domestic employment at Chivers Estate.

After the passing of another week Mrs. Barnham could not contain her frustration and annoyance. Recollection of the family history as slave owners returned to her. Even fifty years ago a boycott would not have been justified. Slavery has a long memory, she thought, but surely all that was in the past. She summoned Constance—had she passed the word about? Yes. Indeed she had, but no one had answered the call. In fact, the word had also been quietly passed that no one should dare apply, unless Constance first approved of them. Constance was widely revered—almost as much as Mrs. Barnham, not only for what she could do for you, but also for what she could do to you.

This was not the coveted domestic situation that it appeared to be; none had the courage to apply without Constance's approval, and Constance had approved no one. In fact there was a deeper conspiracy; Constance was saving the position for one of her relatives, and the relative in question, to whom word had been sent, had not yet appeared for reasons unknown. In the meantime Constance discouraged other prospective applicants through veiled threats and dark suggestions of dire consequences for anyone daring to appear without her consent. She made it abundantly clear that the housemaid would be under her direct control, and if they wished to enjoy any part of their life in domestic service, they had better meet with her approval, which of course, would not be forthcoming. The conspiracy was enjoined by the other domestics; the cook, the washerwoman, the yardman and estate workers all knew where the power lay, and without being active participants they acquiesced and co-operated.

Mrs. Barnham knew that her reputation as an employer was not an enviable one. From time to time in the past she had hired and fired a goodly number of her servants, but a total boycott was not justified or warranted, and she was quite determined to defeat it. The following morning she summoned Major Henry Barclay-Thomson. They had met a number of times since her return to discuss plantation business, and although they knew each other well, they did not socialize—in fact the relationship was strictly a business one.

It was on a Friday morning that Barclay-Thomson was summoned to the Great House at Mrs. Barnham's bidding. They sat down at the far end of the veranda in large wicker chairs, away from Old Maud sitting at her usual place. This was to be a private meeting, and Mrs. Barnham wasted no time in getting to the point.

"I need to find a maid. The people, for some ridiculous reason have not come in looking for work. I want you to find me a good girl—someone who is clean, and can be trained to do the housework. You are sometimes in the country parts, and you could have her come in for an interview."

"Certainly," said Thomson. He never refused to do anything that was asked of him, which made his bad habits much the easier to overlook.

Henry returned the next day with news of a likely prospect. The address was as inexact as it possibly could have been. This girl was the relative of a plantation worker, and she lived in a settlement somewhere up in the hills, near Fruitful Vale, about six miles along the coast road towards Port Antonio and then into the hills another six or eight miles. Thomson had met the girl, and he had a keen eye for attractive women, and she would be his immediate choice. It would take a determined search to find either the settlement or the person in question, but if one traveled the road in the right direction, making inquiries as one went, sooner or later they should be successful. Early the next day he passed this information on to the impatient Mrs. Barnham.

Mrs. Barnham immediately made plans. On Sunday afternoons Mrs. Barnham usually went for a drive in the country, but this Sunday it would be a special trip, and she would leave early enough to carry out a search. Casually she told Constance that her departure time would be three o'clock rather than at the usual time an hour later. She would be going to Port Antonio, she explained. She had not been there for some time, and perhaps would have late tea at the hotel. Joseph was told to be ready to leave at that time, and Bridget and Maud would as usual accompany her.

Sunday morning was, by all accounts, a beautiful day. Joseph spent the morning washing, polishing and grooming the car for the weekly excursion. Mrs. Barnham had her lunch as usual at noon. Lunch on Sunday was always special, and there was always rice and peas. The meat dish was often a chicken or a duck selected from the plantation flock, stuffed and roasted to perfection. Constance arranged the meals and this Sunday it was roast beef—rare, swimming in rich brown gravy—and the rice and peas of course. Constance always saw to it that enough food was cooked to feed all the servants, any number of her 'guests,' and at the same time there be enough left over for supper in the evening.

Prior to Mrs. Barnham's return to Chivers, Constance's 'guests' had arrived after the morning church service, all in their best Sunday clothes. Their journey to the Estate was usually accompanied by loud conversations and gales of happy laughter echoing through the estate, and the greetings were likewise loud, in gay and festive fashion. Since Mrs. Barnham's return however, things had changed, and the 'guests' now arrived very quietly through the back entrance; there were no loud salubrious greetings. Sometimes latecomers would hurriedly make their way up the main driveway, very quietly, with furtive, anxious glances in the direction of the Great House, and then disappear quickly down the pathway, behind the outbuildings.

At half-past two Mrs. Barnham rose from her afternoon snooze, took her bath, splashed herself liberally with 4711 Eau de Cologne, and dusted herself generously with Colgate's body powder. She chose one of her freshly washed, starched and ironed, white Sunday dresses. To match she wore a broad-rimmed white hat trimmed with a wide, pink satin ribbon, and shoes to compliment her hat and purse. At three o'clock she had a cup of tea, a cucumber sandwich, and was ready to leave. With Joseph in his clean, well pressed khaki uniform and peaked cap, Maud and Bridget sitting beside her, they were off in a cloud of dust, on the road to Port Antonio, to interview, and expectantly to employ a maid. Had anyone mistaken her for Her Excellency, the Governor's wife, then it would have been an honest and excusable mistake.

They drove along the winding coastal road for about fifteen minutes passing through several small road-side settlements. At this point Mrs. Barnham instructed Joseph to stop at the next settlement and get directions. In Jamaica there may be at least half-a-dozen or more places with the same name, with perhaps only two or three ever being important enough to be noted on a map. It was therefore important to be in the vicinity of the place being sought in order that one be properly directed by the local inhabitants. Joseph did as instructed, and soon was driving off the coastal road into the foothills, along narrow, winding, country roads. Along the way the people at the road-side were dressed in their Sunday clothes, and as the vehicle slowly passed, they gave the passengers curious, questioning looks. Some of the children standing at the road-side waved respectfully, some stood at attention and saluted as the lady in white drove past, quite indifferent to their existence in her big, chauffeured automobile. This was not a sight frequently seen in that part of the country—in fact it might be safe to say that it had never been seen there before.

Several times they stopped and asked directions, and once they took a wrong turn, but a few miles further on they came to a clearing where the steep banks leveled out. A number of houses were spaced along some narrow, winding paths that disappeared into the surrounding mountains. There was a small, one-roomed road-side shop, evidently the center of activities for the settlement, where a small group was gathered. There was a little church, sitting on a gently rising slope, the small grave yard with toppling headstones surrounding the small, white-washed, mildewed building. People were milling about, some in small groups talking and generally socializing following the afternoon church service. Joseph stopped the car at the small shop at the corner of the road with the footpath leading up to the church.

As the car stopped, so did a young woman descending the path towards the corner. In a fresh, white dress, a small brimmed, tattered hat, that had obviously seen better days, she was nevertheless confident and proud of her appearance. She was the nearest person to the car, and she stood there looking curiously at the vehicle and its occupants, hesitant to approach any further. Mrs. Barnham eyed the young woman; the woman lifted her chin in the air and took a slow, self-conscious step forward and stopped. A small group gathered quickly to look at the car, and to satisfy their curiosity about its occupants. As the numbers grew, so did their courage and they pressed closer.

Mrs. Barnham leaned out of the window, "Good afternoon," she said. No one answered—and then again, "Good afternoon. Young woman!"

The woman did not reply; she hesitated, uncertain. Mrs. Barnham repeated her call, "Young woman! Good Afternoon."

The woman looked about her, from left to right, as if wondering to whom the call was made. A few moments passed by, and then suddenly, as if she had just realized that she was the young woman spoken to, she mumbled some inaudible words, and a weary sigh, but it could have been interpreted as "Yes, Mum."

Someone in the gathering crowd said in a low voice, "De lady callin' to y'u." Still the woman did not respond.

"Young woman, I am speaking to you."

The woman again looked around her as if in doubt, although it must have been perfectly clear to her just who was being spoken to.

"Me, Mum?" she asked, in a low voice, a hand pointing to her bosom, the other hand clutching her hat and skirt.

"Yes, I am speaking to you. —Come here," she ordered.

The woman looked about her again, up at the sky and around in several directions. Very slowly she took one step forward, stopped, and then looked straight at her questioner without replying.

Mrs. Barnham's patience was being tested. She was not used to that. "Young woman," she called again. "Come here!"

The woman, once again slowly looked about her, and once again took a slow, deliberate step forward, and stopped, still looking straight at Mrs. Barnham.

Mrs. Barnham's temper was rising. "Young woman, I told you to come here!" She almost shouted.

A few moments went by. "I done come dere," replied the woman, this time looking down at the ground around her, and then defiantly at her questioner.

"Young woman! You are impertinent!" snapped Mrs. Barnham.

"Yes, Mum," replied the woman quite politely, her gaze again wandering about, but still she did not move towards the car.

"I told you to come here! You are very impertinent."

"Yes Mum, I knows I'se 'pertinent, Mum."

Again someone in the crowd spoke to the woman, "De lady callin' to y'u. Why y'u doan answer polite? Go speek to de lady."

"Young woman, I told you to come here," again Mrs. Barnham ordered, with utter exasperation. "You are very impertinent."

. "A'h knows dat, Mam." The woman again paused to look around her still considering whether to comply. She took her time in thinking it over, looking up at the sky, around, and then at her questioner again. A few moments went by. She took a deep, wearisome sigh, two small steps closer, and stopped.

The voice that had spoken appeared from out of the crowd, took the woman by the hand and dragged her unwillingly towards the car.

"Good afternoon, Mum," said the voice still tightly holding the young woman's hand.

'Well that's better,' thought Mrs. Barnham. She looked the woman over for some time before continuing. "What is your name?" she asked strictly.

"She name is Lilly, Mam," said the woman from the crowd. "She is me niece, Mam." And turning to lecture Lilly, "Speek to de lady—why y'u doan be polite?"

Lilly pouted, and did not answer.

"Haul in y'u mout' gal," whispered her aunt strictly, hoping not to be overheard.

"I am Mrs. Barnham, from Chivers Estate. I am looking for a maid."

There was a murmur from the crowd. "It Mrs. Barn'am! Mrs. Barn'am—Chivers! De plantation. Oh—oh!"

"Yes, Mam," replied the woman. "Oh yes, Mam!"

"I need a maid to come work for me, and I was told there was a Williams here who could work at Chivers."

"Oh yes Mam!" exclaimed the woman, "Well dis is Lilly Williams, Mam. W'at a t'ing! Dis is Lilly Williams, Mam!"

"Well, I'm not so sure that she would do," said Mrs. Barnham. "She is not an obedient girl, and I must have obedience, and proper behaviour. I do not put up with any rudeness."

"Lilly is very polite Mam, She just shy, Mam," and added cautiously, "Jus wid strangers, Mam, but she a very good girl, Mam. She can wash, Mam, an' she can cook, Mam."

The girl did have a neat, clean appearance thought Mrs. Barnham, and she did need a maid. In fact, Mrs. Barnham had a feeling about the young woman—she was a good-looking woman, and would be suitable if trained and taught. Lilly was now standing demurely with hands behind her back, the picture of politeness and obedience. Mrs. Barnham pondered the situation. She must get someone, and show that she was in control in her own house, and she wasn't going to make the trip for nothing.

"How old are you?" she questioned.

"Well, Mam, I'se nineteen years, an' t'ree mont' now Mam."

"Have you worked in domestic service before?"

"No, Mam," shaking her head.

"You know that you will have to sleep on the premises?"

"Yes, Mam."

"The pay is three shillings a week when you start—and four shillings after a month. You get three meals every day, and a nice clean room for yourself. Is that satisfactory?"

"Yes Mum."

The questions and answers continued for some time, but in general they satisfied Mrs. Barnham. So it was arranged that Lilly would start working for Mrs. Barnham beginning the next day, or as soon as she could find herself at the Estate. But Mrs. Barnham was impatient.

"I need to get someone right away," she continued, "Can you come with me right now?"

"No, Mam," said Lilly. "Yes, Mam," said her aunt, both speaking at the same time. "We needs to fetch some t'ings, Mam." Turning to Lilly, "Y'u can go right now. Y'u mus' go wid de lady."

Lilly's expression changed to that of bewilderment and dismay. Her feeling of near panic must have been close to that of her distant ancestors when they were suddenly taken into slavery, deprived of their freedom, and shipped off in chains to a strange land. Nevertheless, she retained her composure with only mild protestations. "But—Auntie. But—But—Auntie," as her aunt made arrangements for them to fetch her personal items and some clothing, and return to the car in half-an-hour.

But it was almost an hour later that they were seen hurrying down the mountain path towards the waiting vehicle and the impatient Mrs. Barnham. Joseph had left the car some time earlier, and was fully engrossed in conversation surrounded by a small gathering of admirers at the other end of the shop. As the two women approached, he hurriedly left to open the car door to the front seat, and taking the small parcels placed them on the floor. He ushered Lilly into the front seat, and slammed the door.

The crowd that had dispersed quickly gathered again to wave farewell to the departing Lilly. Auntie left the crowd ran to the car as Joseph started the motor. She threw her arms around the girl's neck and kissed her fondly on the cheek. Lilly did not respond. She looked straight ahead, not even turning to look at the waving crowd as the car started down the road. Little more than an hour earlier she was a carefree, happy person—now she was bewildered and confused, uncertain of what would happen next. The speed of these events had completely overwhelmed her. Darkness was gathering and the mountain air was turning on its usual nighttime chill. As the car cautiously wound its way down the narrow mountain road, the tears gathered and rolled down her cheeks. In the darkness no one could see or sense the depth of her despair.

When they arrived at the Estate it was quite dark. Constance was at the front steps anxiously awaiting their return. They were unusually late, and the supper would not be edible if kept hot much longer. She was intensely curious about the additional passenger, and directed whispered questions at Joseph whenever an opportunity presented itself. Mrs. Barnham, as soon as she had made herself comfortable, told Constance about the new maid. Constance could scarcely conceal her annoyance and irritation, but dutifully agreed to arrange for an evening meal and accommodation in the servants quarters. The full details of the encounter between Lilly and her employer she later learned from Joseph as he recounted events with considerable embellishment.

Early the following morning, Lilly presented herself to Constance.

"So. —So y'u is Lilly," she started off, looking her over critically. "So y'u is Lilly! Ahem!" She folded her arms and silently continued to look over the young woman standing before her and fidgeting in obvious embarrassment.

"Yes, Mam." replied Lilly.

"Well," she said, at last. "Y'u come 'ere fe work!—an' work is w'at y'u goin' do!" She was not about to make things easy for the newcomer, and her authority had to be established right from the start. "Y'u is to call me Miss Constance."

"Yes, Mam, Miss Constance."

CHAPTER 5

The servants' quarters consisted of six identical, separate rooms, and a washing room connected with a narrow, open, broad walk. These quarters, some distance from the main house, were over-hung and shaded by several very large trees that must have been there since the beginning of time. Lilly was assigned the last room in the row, as the one having the lowest status of the household help.

The days passed quickly as Lilly acquired the art of being a maid for Mrs. Barnham. It started with work in the kitchen, cleaning the pots and the lampshades, polishing the floors in the Great House, and any number of other menial tasks. The cook, Clara, was delighted to have a young and able helper to whom she could delegate tasks. Lilly was a quick and willing helper, and soon earned the goodwill of her teacher. Constance in the meantime kept a jealous and watchful eye on the new maid's progress; every now and again she would interject her authority over activities in the kitchen to disrupt the air of placid co-operation—her displeasure directed at Lilly. After the passage of a few weeks, a firm bond of friendship developed between Clara and Lilly, and Constance knew then that a change had to be made; she would transfer Lilly to household duties under her direct control and supervision.

Constance was a person with instance likes and dislikes; as she saw it, her authority had been undercut by the manner in which the new maid had been employed, and this placed the unfortunate Lilly in the category of dislikes. Close supervision would give her the chance to find fault with the trainee, and perhaps even bring about her dismissal—the opportunity to introduce her relative to the position had not been abandoned, even though as yet there still had been no reply.

Lilly was given a maids uniform, a white apron and cap, which was to be correctly worn at all times, and she assumed her work in the house as directed by Constance. Constance selected the most difficult and distasteful jobs for the new maid, the first of which was to empty and wash the chamber pots and replace them under each bed. The oil lamps were to be refilled, the shades cleaned and polished, and if a shade was broken the cost of replacement would be taken out of wages. And when those chores were completed, there were always floors to be waxed and polished.

The first few days passed without incident until noticed by Mrs. Barnham, who decided then that some close inspection of her newest employee might be in order. The cap was certainly not placed correctly—the problem was the hair—and that would have to be set right. The appropriate instructions were given on the proper way to set her hair, which must be washed, combed, kept clean and tidy—and then her eyes were lowered to observe bare feet! No one was allowed to work in her house in bare feet! Everyone must wear shoes when in the house. Mrs. Barnham had a strict aversion to the servants wandering about the yard with the chickens and ducks in their bare feet, and then coming into the house without washing their feet and putting on their shoes—droppings from the chickens and ducks were not to be brought into the house on bare feet!

"Where are your shoes?" she demanded.

"Me doan got none, Mam"

Constance was summoned. "This girl does not have any shoes. She cannot be in the house without shoes! She will have to get some before she can work in the house."

This was an opportunity for Constance—not a good one, but an opportunity nonetheless. She turned to Lilly, "I did tell y'u to put on y'u shoe. Why y'u doan do as I tell y'u?"

"But Miss Constance! Ah did tell y'u I doan got no shoe."

Constance was not going to take any back-answers. "Get out'a de house! De Missus doan allow y'u in dere wi'd out shoe." Lilly quickly withdrew. "Dat gal! Mam, she is so disobedient, Mam. I doan know w'at I'se goin' do wi'd her."

Mrs. Barnham was not taken in. "We'll have to see she gets a pair of shoes," she said quietly.

Lilly did not go directly to the kitchen, but waited in the pantry listening—and when she arrived in the kitchen she was in tears. "Why Miss Constance tell lie 'pon me?" she asked Clara.

"Doan't mine Miss Constance," Clara consoled her. "She doan't fool de missus."

Later, in the afternoon Mrs. Barnham went upstairs to her bedroom. She was about the same size as Lilly, and knew that in her closet there were several pairs of old, unused shoes, one of which must be suitable to give to the new maid. Mrs. Barnham made a selection—a well worn, but comfortable-looking pair of black shoes—and took them downstairs with her, placing them out of sight behind Old Maud's sewing basket on the veranda. In the late afternoon, Mrs. Barnham picked up the shoes and wandered out into the garden and then towards the servant's quarters. She knew that she would find Lilly somewhere near the kitchen or the rooms, and she knew that her presence would not attract attention, as she often went for a walk in the yard and garden in the afternoons. Soon she saw Lilly in the kitchen with Clara.

"Come here, Lilly," she called. Lilly stopped and presented herself promptly. "Yes, Mum."

"I have found these for you," said Mrs. Barnham, handing her the pair. "See if they will fit you."

"Oh! Mam! T'ank y'u Mam. T'ank y'u." Lilly was overcome.

She placed one shoe on her foot. Feet that have not 'grown up' in shoes tend to be much wider than those that have, and Lilly tried several times without success to get her foot into the shoe. The shoes were too small, but she was not going to admit defeat. Again she pushed her toes into the shoe and then stood to force her foot into the shoe. Nothing in the world—least of all the pain— would prevent her from wearing them.

"Oh! t'ank y'u Mam!"

Mrs. Barnham had watched with some concern—the girl may injure her feet, she thought. "The shoes are a little too small," she said somewhat nervously.

"Oh no, Mam. Dey is jus' rite, Mam," Lilly said with some evident satisfaction despite the discomfort she must have been suffering. She took a few steps back and forth. "Dey is jus' rite, Mam!"

"Well, if you can wear them make sure you just wear them in the house."

"Yes, Mum. T'ank y'u, Mum! T'ank y'u!"

Mrs. Barnham resumed her stroll about the garden. There was something about the woman that affected her; the determination, the desire to please and the excessive gratitude over an old pair of shoes that would be so painful to wear. The next time she was in the shop, she thought, she would buy the woman a comfortable pair of shoes.

The following morning, Lilly appeared dressed in her maid's uniform ready for her usual chores in the house. She placed her newly acquired shoes alongside the other maids' shoes at the doorway ready to be worn when entering the house. For a few moments she stepped back to admire them, and then she went to the kitchen to have her breakfast. When she returned the shoes were not there—someone must have removed them. Constance was engaged in the pantry and dining room attending to Mrs. Barnham's breakfast, and Lilly waited until she could call to her.

"Miss Constance. Mornin' Miss Constance."

Constance ignored the calls for fully five minutes, and then, finally, "Yes. W'at y'u want? Why y'u have on y'u apron? Y'u 'ave to work in de kitchen."

"Miss Constance, me shoe—me shoe gon'. S'mady done te'k it up."

"W'at y'u mean—y'u shoe gon'? Y'u doan got no shoe girl."

Constance had not been told about the unexpected gift from Mrs. Barnham the evening earlier. Lilly attempted to explain.

"So it y'u who te'k de Missus shoe? Y'u tief de shoe! I'se goin to de Missus—right now—an jail is waitin' fe y'u! I 'ave to tell y'u dat jail is waitin' fe y'u, Miss Lilly!"

"No! No! Miss Constance— " Lilly tried again to explain. Constance did not wait for explanations. She went to the dining room, and reported the 'theft' to Mrs. Barnham.

"I have to tell y'u, Mam," she started off, "dat new girl Lilly, she is a tief, Mam. She tief y'u shoe, an' I ketch her wid it, Mam." Constance produced the pair of shoes as evidence of the theft, holding them in front of her mistress, turning them this way and that, so they would be clearly seen.

"No! No Constance. I gave her the shoes," said Mrs. Barnham, somewhat impatiently. Constance was sometimes very tiring thought Mrs. Barnham, but she probably means well.

The explanation was grudgingly accepted. It was an angry and irritable Constance who replaced the shoes at the doorway.

"Y'u mek' it dis time, girl!" she muttered, as she went into the pantry.

The following Saturday morning Mrs. Barnham made good on her resolution; she took Lilly with her to the market and bought a new pair of shoes that were comfortable and fitted well.

As Lilly became accustomed to the fancies of her employer, and because of the gift, was determined to show her gratitude and to please her mistress, and she did so much to the annoyance of the housekeeper. Constance too, became accustomed to the new employee, and being angry all the time took too much energy. Several weeks later Constance had finally regained her composure, and in spite of the anger, the days passed uneventfully. Her attitude softened somewhat, but she had not given up the notion of replacing her with the relative.

But there had been little opportunity to find fault, and she was now more cautious in assigning blame. Furthermore, no immediate plan presented itself by which she could have the new servant dismissed.

CHAPTER 6

Every second week, beginning on Saturday at noon, there was a day and a half off from work. The servants alternated their days off in pairs so that the house was always staffed. On her first weekend off, Lilly had gone back to her home in the hills, but the distance was more than a few hours hard walk each way, and she decided not to make the trip any more than was necessary. On days off then, there was not much to do at the plantation. The estate workers, those still on the job, left on Saturdays at noon, and generally headed to the nearest rum shop to get an early start on Saturday night revelries, and they did not return until the Monday morning. Lilly, used to having her friends and relatives about, found that her days off were dull and lonely, in spite of the Sunday gatherings hosted by Constance, and she longed for the familiar social contacts of the settlement at Fruitful Vale.

On one such Saturday in the early afternoon, Henry Thomson was returning to his house. On the way he had stopped his horse at the citrus grove some distance from the Great House. The picking time was approaching, and arrangements would have to be made—fruit had to be picked 'green' for the long journey to England; it must not be allowed to over mature. The trees were laden with fruit and he picked some large tangerines, one of which he had sampled as he made his way home, the others were cradled in his lap. As he passed by the out buildings, Lilly was leaning sullen and bored against a tree. He had seen her several times since she arrived at Chivers, but had not spoken to her. His path took him within a few feet, where he slowed the animal to a stop. He smiled a greeting, and picking up a tangerine, held it up as though to toss it. Several times, with a questioning look, he made the motion as though he would throw it, as if to ask, "Would you like it?"

Lilly returned the smile and nodded her acceptance, holding up her hands in anticipation and readiness to catch. The tangerine was tossed, and caught.

"T'ank y'u, Sur."

"I'm glad to see you got the job here," he started off. "How are you getting along?"

"Me is doin' good, Sur."

"You know, I told Mrs. Barnham about you. I recommended that she get you for the job."

"Yes, Sur? Me didn't know dat, Sur. You did tell de Missus to tek me on?"

"Yep, that's right," he confirmed.

Lilly pondered the information and slowly peeled the tangerine.

"But how could dat be, Sur? How could you tell de Missus 'bout me, Sur?"

"Well, I spoke to Williams about you—you know he works here sometimes. And anyway, I had seen you before. Don't you remember?"

"Ah! Yes Sur. I 'member now."

"So, how do you like working here?"

"Well, Sur, I'se doin' good, Sur."

"I'm glad to hear that," he said. The horse was getting restless, and stamped a front foot, but Henry held the animal steady.

"I'm glad to hear that," he said again. "I want to see that you get along well. If there's anything that troubles you, come and see me about it, and I'll try to see about it."

A large fly was buzzing about the horse's head and the animal was showing its impatience.

"You remember, come and see me if you want something," he said, and turned the animal towards the house. She was quite an attractive woman, he thought. Yes, she was indeed a good-looking woman. She could quench the fire in his groin!

Lilly leaned against the tree and ate the tangerine, pondering the events of the last few minutes. He was a nice man, she thought. But why had he recommended her to Mrs. Barnham? That was strange—how did he know her? Maybe he liked her? She liked the idea!

>From time to time, over the weeks, they met and talked. Occasionally too, he gave her fruit that he had collected. Meeting with him broke the boredom of her workdays, and excited her for some strange reason. It might have appeared too, that their meetings were not always accidental, but the weeks passed uneventfully. The citrus was taken in and shipped out.

It was a good time of the year—no one ever went hungry, and with the approach of the Christmas Season, everyone took on a happy, expectant mood; the weather was cool and comfortable.

Jamaican Proverb—No matter how good y'u nyam, Duppy ah watch y'u outa de carner of 'im yeye.

CHAPTER 7

Old Maud had been around longer than anyone could remember. Charlie McIntire had employed her to take care of Alice, his young daughter soon after his wife died, and over the years Maud became firmly placed in the McIntire household. She was devoted to her young charge, and might even have been seen to sacrifice her interests and desires to those of her employer and his little daughter. She never married or ever became romantically involved with anyone, although there was ample opportunity. In character she was mild and soft-spoken—almost innocuous, and yet she was full of reasonable, sound and comforting advice. As time passed, Old Maud was elevated from servant to that of companion and confidant to Mrs. Barnham, a situation that no one ever expected would change, or would ever have wanted to change.

One evening at dinner Maud was suddenly taken ill. She stood clutching her throat with both hands, choking, and gasping for breath. For a few moments Mrs. Barnham was unable to move. Maud gasped for breath, looked about with a vacant, expressionless gaze, and then she collapsed. Constance rushed to her side supporting her until she was gently put to lie on the floor. Mrs. Barnham fetched a glass of water from the table and tried to force the stricken woman to drink. Constance got a fan, which she waved furiously in her face. When this had no effect, she grabbed a bottle of rum from the side table, and splashed most of its contents over her cheeks and forehead. Had there been any life left in her body the strength of the liquor would surely have made her regain consciousness, but she remained quiet and lifeless. Lilly and Joseph, came running from the kitchen in response to shouts from Bridget. They carried her senseless to her bed, where she appeared to be sleeping comfortably. At some hour during the night, Old Maud drew her last breath and quietly passed away.

The following morning Joseph was dispatched with a letter to Dr. Morris in Port Antonio. Dr. Morris lost no time in coming; he returned with Joseph by mid-morning. He made an examination and wrote up the certificate. He was invited and stayed for lunch, and agreed to notify Mr. Jackson, the undertaker, and the Reverent Meeks, just as soon as he got back to Port Antonio.

The undertaker made his appearance late in the afternoon. In the back of his old car he had transported a coffin, which with the help of the yardman, they unloaded and carried to the bedroom. Two varnished pine boxes with stout padlocks containing the tools of his trade were taken from the car to the bedroom.

In the early evening it started to rain and continued in a steady downpour throughout the night. The sound of rain upon the roof, on the trees and bushes was somber commentary on the day's events. The man was alone with the body for several hours, working silently by lamplight well into the night. It was close to mid-night when he emerged to say that everything was done, and the body was ready for viewing. Mrs. Barnham and Bridget went upstairs, spent a few minutes, and emerged together with bowed heads, wiping away the tears. A few minutes later Constance, Joseph, Lilly and the other servants, who had waited patiently in the kitchen, went up stairs. Shortly after, the undertaker was given a stiff glass of rum to see him on his way back to Port Antonio. He left, and everyone went to bed. Two lamps were left burning beside the coffin, resting on two chairs in the upstairs bedroom. The funeral had been arranged for the following afternoon, at two o'clock.

Mrs. Barnham was fully awake very early the next morning—she had hardly slept a wink the whole night. She had lain in bed half awake, sometimes sobbing quietly, sometimes dozing until remembering recent events brought her back to full consciousness. The morning light had not yet appeared when she decided that sleep would no longer be possible and she got up.

Two days after the funeral Mrs. Barnham was still deeply mourning her companion and confidant, and two weeks later she still had not recovered. A change in scenery might help, she thought, and she decided to return to Kingston.

Jamaican Proverb—It hard to keep out de devil, but harder to drive 'im out!

CHAPTER 8

It was some weeks after Maud's unexpected death that Marjory had been away on one of her unannounced journeys. She arrived back at Chivers late on the Friday afternoon, and for most of the evening not a single word was exchanged between the man and his wife. The following morning Marjory went to the market as usual, and came back home to find that Henry was still not back at lunchtime, which was unusual for a Saturday afternoon. She ate her lunch alone and then wandered out into the back to make inquiries as to his whereabouts. She did not have to go far, because down the pathway she could see Henry on his horse talking to someone under a tree. She watched, and recognized Mrs. Barnham's maid, and as he started towards her, she turned about and returned to the house. Henry spent the afternoon making up accounts—he never asked where she had been, or what she had been doing, and she never volunteered the information.

As the evening drew on, the bottle of rum opened at lunchtime was empty, and he opened another. Marjory did not drink rum, but had already mixed gin with lemonade taken from the icebox. By the late afternoon, both, still silent with their thoughts, were well on the way to intoxication.

It was the maids week-end off—there would be no prepared or served evening meal—they would have to fend for themselves from the remains of the lunch put aside for that purpose. Marjory helped herself, ate at the table and returned to her gin and lime. After an hour or so, Henry stirred himself and did the same. When he had eaten, he strolled unsteadily onto the unlit veranda, and after a few minutes, out onto the pathway, into the darkness and disappeared. Marjory did not pay much attention, and soon fell asleep in the comfortable armchair, her feet resting on a low stool.

It was after midnight when Marjory awoke. The oil lampshade had become badly smoked and the light was very dim. At first she just opened her eyes and looked around. The night was giving out its usual sounds; the infectious, rhythmic beat of a calypso band could be heard echoing through the mountains. A night lizard from somewhere in the rafters was croaking, tree frogs were chirping, and bats were flitting about from tree to tree. The fact that she did not see Henry did not alarm her, he had probably gone to bed, she thought. She finished her gin and lime even though what she really wanted was just a glass of cold water. Soon she was up—it was late—time to be in bed. As she went unsteadily towards the bedroom, she looked out on the veranda to see if Henry was there. He was not there. She returned to the dining room to light another lamp and look in the bedroom. There was no sign of her husband, and there were none of the usual indicators of his having been there. The clock said twenty past one—that was pretty late. He must be somewhere, and she would like to know where. Then a sense of panic surged through her—"Damn it!" She said to herself—"the Bastard!"

Hurriedly, she found the hurricane lantern kept on the pantry shelf, and hurriedly lit it, turning the wick down as the flame leaped up. Using it to light her way, she took off in the direction of the servant's quarters—she knew exactly where she was going and where she would be looking for her husband. At the last room of the building, she stopped and listened. There was no sound that would have raised the suspicions of anyone else except those of Marjory Barkley-Thomson. She knew he was inside.

She turned up the wick on the lantern and mounted the broad walk outside the maid's room. Without hesitation, with clenched fist she banged on the closed door.

"Henry!" She shouted at the closed door. "Henry!"

There was no answer. Someone in the room next door was moving about.

"Henry!" she shouted again, banging still harder on the closed door. "Henry! I know you're in there!" She tried the door, but it was latched from inside.

There were sounds of the servants being aroused, and doors were opened one by one as the occupants appeared, holding lamps high, to see what the disturbance was about. Marjory continued to hammer on the door, quite oblivious to the gathering audience. Everyone by this time was out observing the drama.

Constance appeared from out of the gathering. "De Busha not here, Miss Marjory," she volunteered.

"Oh yes he is," snapped Marjory. "I know damn well where he is."

"But no body is here, Miss Marjory," Constance insisted, and as if to prove the point, she approached the closed door intending to knock and have the person inside open the door. Before she could knock, sounds of movement came from within, and slowly the door opened. Marjory grabbed the handle and violently jerked it open. Henry appeared in the doorway, sleepily pulling up his trousers. He staggered and swayed from side to side as he stepped out of the doorway into the dim light.

"Thank God you've come," he said in a low voice, sheepishly. "Thank God you've come!"

"You Bastard!" shrieked his wife. "You dirty Bastard!" Her voice echoed through the night.

For a moment he did not reply, but continued to fumble with his trousers. He ran his hand over his head combing down his hair with his fingers, swaying unsteadily back and forth.

Then he found words again, "Thank God you've come," he repeated. "I didn't know how I was going to get out of there."

"You filthy beast! You dirty—filthy—beast!" Again her shrieks sounded through the night, as anger and disgust was giving way to hysteria.

He disappeared into the darkness of the room, and returned in a moment holding his shirt. "Thank God you've come," he repeated. "You've saved me!"

"I'll save you all right! You filthy bastard!" She shouted through a flood of tears. She raised the hurricane lantern and swung it at his head. As stupefied as he was, the attack was anticipated, and he caught her arm while still in motion, but he did not hold her arm for more than a second. He let go to return to the matter of his trousers, which had slipped further down.

"My dear," he said, slurring the words, leaning unsteadily towards his wife, "It's time we were in bed. Let's go to bed."

Swaying from side to side his head lurched almost into her face. For a few seconds he looked into her face, and then turning slowly, still trying to adjust his trousers, he stumbled off into the darkness.

The estate was fully awakened. There were hushed, animated expressions of amazement from those gathered around, and Marjory suddenly became aware of their presence, and the impact of her actions entered her consciousness. Suddenly she was acutely aware of her situation, acutely embarrassed and humiliated. Quickly she gathered herself and rushed towards the shelter of their house.

Marjory was awake very early the next morning. Remembering the events of the night shocked her into full consciousness, and she got up immediately.

Quickly she dressed and packed her suitcases, carried them out and threw them onto the back seat of her little Standard. She found the gas storage drum in the garage and filled the gas tank, spilling more than she managed to get into the tank. Long before Henry was awake she was well on the way to Montego Bay. Somewhat earlier, with everyone still asleep, and long before the sun would be up, Lilly gathered up her few possessions, stuffed them into a small bag, and left Chivers on the long trek back to Fruitful Vale.

CHAPTER 9

James Henderson—'Squire'—as he was called, was the owner of the Manor House Estate. Manor House was a very old plantation house dating back to the time when the Spaniards held the island. The building had been constructed like a small fortress to withstand earthquakes, hurricanes, attacks from marauding pirates and English privateers. When the English captured the island in 1655, the Spanish owners hurriedly buried their treasure somewhere on the estate, drew a map, and then killed the two unfortunate slaves that had helped them. They then abandoned the property and slaves and fled across the sea to find refuge in Cuba. The remaining slaves promptly looted the house and set it on fire. The English rebuilt the house and through the centuries it survived in remarkably good condition. The wealthy Henderson family acquired it many years later.

The Estate was the Squire's abiding interest, pride, and joy, where he would spend as much of his time that his business would allow. Although he was easygoing and agreeable, he was an astute man who did not tolerate dishonesty or unwilling workers. But he was considerate and generous, and that allowed a kind of family relationship to develop between the employer and his workers. Most of the workers had been many years on the plantation, and he knew everyone by name. He did not employ a Busha, as did most of the other plantations and estates—James took a personal interest in the daily activities and liked to see to things himself. During his necessary absences from the estate, he put the day-to-day management in the hands of a Headman, and he had been fortunate for the most part, to have had capable men to rely on, although as he discovered, some may not have been the most honest.

Some years later when he returned from a lengthy visit to England, he was very pleased to find everything in such good order. There was not a single item that could have been better handled or which he would have done differently, and he realized then that Daniel was a considerable asset to his business. He began to think of ways in which he could reward the man and ensure that he remain permanently employed at the Estate. He knew that good, honest and intelligent men were difficult to find, and he was determined to retain him on the estate. Although he thought about it off and on he had no definite plan in mind and none came to him, and as the weeks passed he did not think about it very much. However, six months later he became quite ill with a fever that left him very weak, and he was unable to visit the plantation for several weeks while recovering in Kingston. It was during this period of recovery that he once again had to rely completely on Daniel, and his thoughts again turned to the matter of retaining him on the estate. It was then that he decided what should be done.

Along the eastern border of his property there was a mountain survey road—little more than a narrow footpath suitable for animals, but well used by the market women, their hampers and head-baskets fully loaded with yams, pears and breadfruit, on their way to market. Over a mile from the Manor House itself there was a mountain spring that flowed from the property across the roadway, making it an ideal place to build a small house. There was good clean water and convenient access to the property from the roadway. The market women often rested at the spring to drink and water their animals, and it had become a transient gathering place on Fridays afternoons, and on Saturday nights when the market women were returning home.

The Squire decided that an acre or so could be severed from the main property, and the title given to his Headman, free of cost. Also, the Squire thought, he would give the Headman sufficient lumber, nails and 'zinc' from his hardware store in Kingston with which to build a house. The land would be a gift, free of cost, but the costs of the building materials would be recovered by a small interest-free loan repaid from wages over an extended period. Indeed, it was a generous thought, and he would even waive the mortgage payments if the situation warranted.

As soon as he was well enough the Squire set about putting his plan into effect. He did not want to create a situation where other workers would feel envious and thus create animosities, but he did want to make the gift something of an occasion. He had a lawyer prepare the deed, and called in the surveyor from Port Antonio to set the boundaries. He rode out to the place several times to give instructions to the surveyor and to satisfy himself that it was where it should be. The plot was large enough to allow the occupant to grow vegetables and plant fruit trees. There were already several mature fruit trees growing, but the land would have to be partially leveled and cleared of the underbrush for the building and other trees.

It took several months to accomplish, but by the end of November everything had been done. The time of the year was right for making this gesture, and it could be explained that he wanted the Estate Headman to live close by and be available at all times. In carrying out his plan though, he made the mistake of discussing it with his wife Harriet, and she was most vociferous in her objections.

"Why do you have to give him land?"

"What has he done for you to deserve land?"

"You are making him a neighbor of ours, and he is not the sort of person I want to have as a neighbor!"

"The land is too close to our house."

And the objections continued whenever an opportunity presented itself. The Squire though, had already made up his mind, and was quite sure it was the right thing to do.

"He is an honest, loyal man," he countered. "We do not find men like that every day, and I need him. Besides that, he is partially crippled and has worked many years for me, since he was a boy. I want to keep him here, and I want to reward him."

"Where else could he go to get work? He has to stay here!" and still the objections continued.

A few days before Christmas the Squire called Daniel to his office. It was the time to give out Christmas gifts to the workers, and tradition dictated that each should receive an additional week's wages. If it had been a good year and the men had worked well the Squire would add again to the annual bonus. He did not as a rule hand out weekly wages, but again, tradition dictated that he personally hand out the Christmas presents. At the appointed time, the workers gathered outside his office, and one by one as their names were called, they were given their presents with a handshake, and best wishes of the Season. It had been a good year, and the bonus had been doubled. Everyone was in a happy, jovial mood, and they thanked him, wishing him good health and a long life. The Headman was usually treated in like fashion, but on this occasion there was no envelope for Daniel.

The ceremony over, the men dispersed and the Squire took a somewhat puzzled Daniel aside. As he had not received his bonus, Daniel wondered if this had not been just a memory lapse on the Squire's part, but he was not about to mention it.

"Come with me," the Squire said, "I want to show you something." The two men took off slowly walking to the eastern boundary. As they went, the Squire engaged in casual conversation, inquiring about the Headman's family, how they were doing, and if they were thriving. When they arrived at the severed land, he turned to Daniel, "What do you think about this piece of land, Daniel?"

"It is very nice, Sur," Daniel replied, looking about. "Yes Sur, it is a very good piece."

"What do you think about building a house here? Would you like to build your house here?"

The question was greeted with amazed silence; he had not grasped the significance of the question. The question was unexpected and it caught him off guard; he could not find words to answer. He looked at the land again and then back at the Squire with a puzzled expression.

"Well,—how would you like to build your house here?"

"Well—Sur?" Daniel was dumfounded; he could not find words. .

"Well? How would you like to build your house here?" The Squire asked again.

"Sur?—I doan k'no w'at fe say."

"Yes Daniel. I am going to give you this piece of land for your own, to build yourself a house! It's a Christmas present to you and your family."

Daniel could hardly contain himself and thanked the Squire repeatedly. Together they walked the boundaries as the Squire gave him details of his plan, and as they returned towards the Manor House, the Squire handed him an envelope containing the usual Christmas bonus along with the deed and the survey. The following week the lawyer appeared at the Squire's office and transfer papers were signed to make Daniel the sole owner of the plot.

With a generous loan from the Squire they built a modest house; it had three bedrooms and a kitchen, a raised wooden floor—a source of endless pride for his wife and elder daughter. They took turns in polishing it with beeswax and a brush made from the husk of a dried coconut. The land about was intensively cultivated with a little bit of everything; yams, sweet potatoes, sugar cane, bananas, and caliloo—all grew in abundance. There were also orange trees, mango trees, pear trees and breadfruit trees. The entire property was fenced high with odd pieces of board, galvanized sheeting, kerosene tins cut open and flattened into sheets, and any other piece of wood or metal found suitable. The fence was kept in good repair, and the gate kept locked—a small fortress to keep out prying eyes and pilfering hands, but still insufficient to prevent occasional violations of privacy and property. And all his children wore shoes.

Jamaican Proverb—Before y'u marry keep y'u two yeye open; after y'u marry shut one!

CHAPTER 10

The Squire's wife, Harriet, was a 'simple country girl' from St. Ann's Bay. When they first met, she was a shy, quiet, petite creature, demure and intensely feminine—qualities that attract a particular type of male—the kind of man that seeks a mate unequivocally female—a woman to be cared for, loved, and nurtured. And even though there were difference in their ages and education, they seemed to be a perfect match for each other.

Harriet was not a person given to much conversation, serious or otherwise, and to strangers, she often seemed to lack what was deemed to be common knowledge—by some, she was dismissed as 'simple,' or unintelligent. This veneer of reserve, however, disguised much of her real character. There were people quite close to her who should have known her well but never really did, and they were certainly unaware of her obscure character. Perhaps this was because Harriet herself was quite unaware of the forces that motivated her and guided her behavior. The worst of her hidden characteristics were intense jealousy, suspicion, and selfishness. She had a primitive disregard and disinterest in the needs or the suffering of others—unless, of course, these people were useful to her, and thus, in her mind justified her tolerance and their existence, and possibly, in extreme circumstances, her assistance. These latent characteristics did not appear until after the birth of their son, some six years after they were married. James, for his part, was oblivious to her faults for many years, and held his wife in high esteem; he showed his deep affection by indulging her every possible whim and fancy. She was indeed, thoroughly 'spoilt' by his attention. He seldom failed to grant her every wish, even though at times it was against his better judgment, costly and inconvenient.

Their son William was born a year before the headman's first daughter, Opal, and for several years each family—the estate owner and his headman—had the pleasure of watching their children grow and develop. But for the Squire, this contentment was not to last. Harriet always jealous and possessive towards her son, was resentful of his father's attentions, and would often circumvent contacts between them. Whenever association was possible, she would intervene and change arrangements so that any close and prolonged contact between them was prevented. By the time William was ten years old a rift had developed between husband and wife; they would openly disagree over the simplest things concerning their son, and a wedge had been driven between father and son.

The quarrels however, had deeper roots—Harriet's ingrained jealousy had raised her suspicions about her husband's faithfulness—she suspected he had a lover—or at the very least, must have had a lover. She did not have the least bit of evidence to support her suspicions; she did not know whom, where, or when, but her over-active imagination convinced her that 'like all men' he must have at some time, been unfaithful to his marriage vows—and for all she knew, he still had a mistress! As a result, and quite without foundation, she withdrew all normal connubial relations with him. James, at first, was bewildered by the false accusations and by his wife's rejection, but as time went by, he was embittered and angry. The most hurtful to him remained the exclusion from meaningful contact and influence with his son. Harriet's influence was so possessive and domineering, that the young boy began to see his father as an outcast—someone who was not relevant to his needs or to his existence, and perhaps, for all he knew, never had been.

James continued his struggle against his wife's influences, hoping that as William grew older, he would begin to think for himself and see through his mother's scheming character. Regrettably, that was not to happen; Harriet, over the years imbued in her son an unusual degree of conceit and arrogance, which could not be overlooked, not even by a caring father anxious to be a friend.

During the time when William was in school the family took up residence in their house just outside Kingston. His mother had strong objections to her son boarding at the school, and this arrangement suited James too, because it allowed contact as he drove his son to school each morning and back again in the afternoon. It was not from the lack of trying that these daily meetings had little influence on the thirteen-year-old boy. William was at the stage when self-interest was a preoccupation, and he was completely disinterested in the daily quarrels that erupted between his parents. Discussing family difficulties every day on the way to school only pained him. After all, he thought, his mother provided whatever he wanted, and there was little to be gained from his father.

The second year that William was at the school, the weather was excessively hot; there seemed to be no relief possible. If only it would rain—perhaps it would cool a bit. James did not lunch in town; more often he returned home at noon, to relax, and have the kind of meal that he preferred. It was on such a day that James, hot and irritable, returned home. The usual noonday spat with his wife did not improve his mood, and he took his drink to sit on the veranda and await the dinner bell calling him to the table. He did not feel well, but then, it had been so hot, and indigestion had nagged him all day. The dinner bell sounded and as he rose to go to the table he was seized with a cramping pain in his chest. He staggered a few steps towards the dining table, but within seconds he was unconscious on the floor.

The maid still at the table, screamed for her mistress and Harriet came running. They placed a cushion under his head, loosened his tie and shirt. The maid ran to the bedroom for Bay Rum and smelling salts. In a minute or so, consciousness returned, but the pain was still there, as severe as ever. It came in waves, and each time it came he contorted and lapsed into near unconsciousness. The doctor was sent for, but it would be some time before he would be there. As the spasms of crippling pain engulfed him, he sought some comfort, and held out his hand towards his wife.

Harriet hesitated, extending her hand for a few seconds to clasp his, and then suddenly pulling back, extending it again to hold his shaking hand. He gripped the ends of her fingers tightly as a wave of unconsciousness came over him and his mind went blank. As it subsided, he opened his eyes.

"I'll be all right if you hold my hand," he said. "Please—hold my hand." And after a long pause, "I always loved you," he whispered. "I always loved you—I was never—unfaithful—to—you."

Harriet's hand snapped sharply back. She looked at him with disgust, annoyance and disbelief. She exhaled in exasperation—that he could have said those words in the hearing of the servant, but she did not speak. He returned her gaze, "Hold my—hand," he pleaded, and another spasm choked off the words.

Harriet did not comply. His eyes were closed, but not now tightly shut as if in the throws of a spasm. The maid had been wiping his face and forehead with a small napkin soaked in Bay Rum. Quietly she moaned all the while, "Oh! Mister James! Oh Mister James."

Sensing the inevitable, the maid began to splash the Bay Rum liberally on his face, to bath and rub his temples. He did not open his eyes, and his breathing, which had been up until then deep but regular, now came less frequently, in deep and labored gasps.

The maid splashed more Bay Rum, and wiped his forehead vigorously, hysterical and agitated. "Oh! Mister James, Sir," she sobbed, "Oh! Mister James!—Lawd 'ave mercy!" She cradled his head rocking back and forth, and began to cry uncontrollably.

Harriet watched without speaking. A minute or so passed before she took the maid's hand. "Don't waste the Bay Rum," she said calmly. She retrieved the half-empty bottle from the maid's shaking hand and replaced the cork, pressing it firmly into the bottle. The maid covered her face in her apron and began to sob hysterically. Several minutes passed; Harriet remained silent. She took a deep breath—and then another. She looked calmly at her dead husband's face—she could not stand the maid's sobbing a moment longer.

"Go to the kitchen," she ordered strictly, without a trace of emotion.

The prospect of widowhood did not affect her. The Doctor would soon be there, she thought. She must change from her housedress into something more presentable, and she must put on some rouge and lipstick. It wouldn't do for him to arrive and see her dressed like that.

CHAPTER 11

The Squire's untimely death had its greatest impact on his business in Kingston, but there was also a great sense of loss among the workers at the plantation. It had taken a day for the sad news to reach the plantation, and when it did work stopped immediately. It was stunning news indeed, and everyone was shocked—in a state of disbelief and deep mourning. Mrs. Barnham was quite overcome at the sudden loss of such a good friend and neighbor, and she made plans immediately to attend the funeral in Kingston. Daniel, for his part, maintained his composure as long as there were people about, but as soon as he could he went off alone into the bush, rested his head against a tree and cried uncontrollably for a long time. And then he sat against the tree, his face buried in his arms, remaining there for several hours until once again he could control his emotions. He returned home late that night, and was the first to break the news to his wife. Both broke down at the telling with the tears streaming down their faces. For weeks after whenever he thought about the Squire, the tears would weld up and he would turn his face away. And for months he was still deeply mourning the death of the man he dearly loved.

The funeral service was held in Kingston, and was a most spectacular affair. Hundreds of friends and acquaintances sent wreaths and flowers, and large crowds of interested spectators gathered as the hearse made its way to the Parish Church in Half-Way-Tree. And there were genuine signs of grief and sorrow; in the church many were openly weeping and drying their eyes. Following the early morning service, the coffin was transferred to an open car and a small procession of cars immediately made their way over the mountains on the long journey to the Manor House Estate. Internment was to be in the family crypt on the Estate.

The crypt itself was many years in existence, and had not been opened for almost fifty years—not as far as anyone was aware. The last time the doors were opened was to allow the body of the Squire's father to be placed inside. The crypt was off to the side of the house, some distance away, in an isolated section of a large area designated as 'the garden.' The area was shaded by some enormous trees, and was heavily overgrown with shrubs and vines that hid it completely from view. From time to time the area was cleared, but that too had not been done for several years, and to all appearances, not ever. Realizing that the Squire's body would be placed in the crypt, Daniel immediately set about having the area cleared. With three of his best workers, they began to chop at the overgrown vines and bushes, but the small structure was hardly cleared by the late afternoon when the coffin and entourage arrived from Kingston.

Family and friends gathered about as the coffin drew up to the crypt. With very little ceremony, the doors were opened and the coffin placed inside. The gathered mourners left flowers and wreaths and then withdrew to the Manor House to have a small supper before returning to Kingston. After their departure, Daniel and several of the men went to the crypt. He inspected the doors and made sure that they were secure and locked. He was angry and resentful that he and the Squire's devoted men had been excluded from any part in the funeral arrangements; they had been ordered to keep their distance and to stay away—Mrs. Henderson did not wish to see them there.

He gathered some of the scattered flowers fallen from wreaths and placed them at the crypt, and then he sat on the step at the entrance, still mourning, and deep in thought. He would take care of the crypt and remember the day the Squire died. He wondered how the Squire's death would affect the estate and how it might change his life on the estate—the only life he had ever known. But he knew that the future held changes.

After the funeral Harriet and William remained at the Manor House for a while. William was just fourteen years old—hardly able to manage an estate at that age and still in school, and Harriet, who had a distinct dislike for Daniel could not accept his advancement to the position of manager. She informed him that a manager would be hired as soon as possible. That, however, was not unexpected—Daniel knew Harriet and was aware of her views—he expected that a manager would be hired.

It was something of a relief to Daniel and the workers that for a while at least, they would not have to deal directly with William or his mother; neither were held in high regard. But several weeks passed by without a suitable busha being found, and Harriet began to get anxious—she wanted to return to Kingston so that William could go back to school. Daniel was managing the Estate very well as he had done in the past, but Harriet did not consider him suitable for the job, and resented the idea; she just couldn't bring herself to accept him as the busha. She approached her friend Mrs. Barnham for advice. Mrs. Barnham suggested that Henry Thomson could probably manage the two estates with the assistance of Daniel until another manager was hired. Harriet knew Mrs. Barnham very well—ostensibly they were close friends—but true to character Harriet did not like the somewhat older Mrs. Barnham—that is until there was a need to do so, as she had done on previous occasions. But now there was a need the friendship was again cultivated. Until she could hire a busha Harriet had to depend on her headman Daniel, and on Mrs. Barnham's busha, Major Henry Barkley-Thomson.

Mrs. Barnham was devastated by the untimely death of her close friend and neighbour. Remembering her own sad loss years earlier, she imagined that Harriet would be similarly affected, and she extended all the consolation and sympathy of which she was capable, somehow seeking a return of the same for her own grief and sense of loss. But Harriet was not similarly affected—she accepted the sympathetic attention because she needed assistance and advice in running the plantation, not because she was in need of consolation or sympathy, and she offered none in exchange.

While James was alive Harriet had been completely free of restrictions, and always did much as she pleased. His presence gave her a certain sense of security, that even with their estranged relationship she knew that he would protect her. For some strange reason now that he was dead, she did not feel the loss of that security. In fact his death gave her an unusual sense of freedom—of relief—she no longer had to concern herself with a husband.

The reading of her husband's will did not change her sense of security. The Manor House property was willed entirely to their son William and to his heirs. The Trading Company was willed to his wife Harriet, leaving her with a very large business and substantial income. The Manor House Estate was to be held in trust by Harriet until William reached the age of twenty-one. In the event of William's premature death, the Estate would go to Harriet, or be equally divided between William's heirs should there be any at that time. In the will there was a significant omission—the word "legitimate" did not define William's heirs; it did not exclude illegitimate offspring, and consequently it would included any and all of William's children, legitimate and otherwise. That omission, however, did not present any difficulty; the possibility that illegitimate children would appear and claim their inheritance was very remote, and the omission was ignored.

As he got older William began to take an interest in the operation of the estate, but at the time he was still a schoolboy, and the estate was not his only interest.

His involvement in the affairs of the Estate was more interference than assistance, and the workers without exception, resented him intensely. Their resentment took the form of ignoring him and his instructions, even if the instructions came directly from his mother.

Nicknames were often assigned to owners and managers, and these names were indicative of the respect—or lack of it—that the workers had for their managers and the estate owners. In the same way that his father had been dubbed 'Squire' as a term of respect and even affection, William was called 'Cockey'— like a rooster—indicative of his immature and authoritative manner. William soon learned of the nickname although he was never called 'Cockey' to his face, but quite often behind his back and within his hearing. It always produced the desired effect; it made him very irritable and angry.

The various businesses in Kingston required good management, and Harriet was determined to see that William would later on provide that good management; she was determined to see that he develop the necessary skills— after all, he was her son, and would have to meet her expectations. Shortly after he left school she made arrangements for him to go to England and stay with an uncle, the purpose being that he further his education and get business experience. She bought his passage on one of the ships that regularly brought goods to the Trading Company in Kingston, and prepared herself for his absence. As the day for his departure drew closer, she packed his cabin trunk, and then repacked it a day later. The following day she again unpacked his clothes, only to repack them once again. This preoccupation continued for almost two weeks, until there was no time left. Many concerns were entering her mind, and she began to give him advice—some helpful, but mostly trivial, and all in great quantity.

"Watch your manners," she told him. "Do not pick your nose. Keep your bowels open—remember that blocked bowels are very bad for your health. Blocked bowels are what caused your father's death. Remember to bathe every day—English people have some bad habits that you must not pick up—they only bathe once a week."

The advice was endless, continuing even until the early morning when she tearfully watched him board, and the ship slowly move out to sea. Initially she was satisfied that it was the right decision to send him away, and even though she missed him, she considered it a necessary step in his own—and her—best interests.

Harriet continued to live alone at the Manor House, and as the months passed she missed him more and more, and then she began to regret having sent him away. With her son away and few people to talk to, she began to feel quite lonely—very lonely.

She had often ignored her husband and other people around her, not realizing just how important it was to have people about, even if it was only to ignore them! For the most part Harriet despised the servants with little understanding or appreciation of the effect it had. The feelings of dislike—even hate—were quite mutual; her dislike, and at times her spiteful acts, were quite often repaid in kind. Never did she know how many times someone spat in the food she was being served, and only once did she find a broken toenail in the rice and peas. It was difficult to have conversations with them; she was not a good conversationalist at the best of times and never found anything to talk to them about. As time went by though, she yearned more and more for some kind of social contacts. She was not an imaginative person and it was impossible for her to entertain herself, and there was little in the house to interest her and to occupy her time. Mrs. Barnham had returned to Chivers, and they often visited back and forth, several times during the week, and they usually went to the market together on Saturday mornings, but there was a limit to how much time she could spend with Mrs. Barnham; the woman bored her, and somehow did not satisfy her needs in that way.

Although she knew Henry Thomson quite well they had never socialized. Harriet never approached anyone she considered beneath her, and while her husband was alive, Henry fitted into that category. In fact she even despised him for his seedy reputation, but now that she was alone and very lonesome, she would have welcomed even a brief conversation with him. Their business meetings were few and very brief, but she watched him coming and going during the weeks, and decided several times to be out walking whenever he was expected to be passing by. These efforts had produced only a few very casual meetings, but at least they had exchanged brief compliments of the day and there had been some acknowledgement of each other's existence.

Henry usually took Mrs. Barnham's car over to the Manor House, especially so if the weather was threatening. Occasionally he used his horse or a mule if he had to ride into the property. One morning he took his horse even though the weather was uncertain and rain very likely. For the last hour the distant rumble of thunder could be heard and he was anxious to be getting back, but before he could be on his way it broke and the rain came down in torrents. He was passing the veranda when Harriet, who was pulling in the chairs from the blowing rain, called out to him.

"Major. Major Thomson. Come in. Take shelter."

At that moment there was a flash of lightening and a crack of thunder that jolted them both. Henry, who was already pretty well soaked through, would normally have declined the invitation, but the lightening made him change his mind. He quickly tethered the horse in the garage and ran over to the house onto the veranda.

"Thank you," he said removing his hat and shaking off the water.

"My! You are soaked—right through. I'll get you a towel. Come into the drawing room."

The wind had picked up and the rain was blowing on to the porch where everything was getting wet. Harriet disappeared into the house and soon returned with a large towel. She handed it to Henry in the drawing room.

"Thanks," he said, wiping his face and head. There was another flash and a tremendous crack of thunder. It made them both jump.

"I'm terrified by the lightening. Doesn't it scare you? It scares me silly!"

"Just a bit, but the chances of being struck are not very great, you know. But it is frightening."

"Take a chair—please sit down."

Henry found a chair near by and sat on the edge still wiping his hands and face. His shirt was soaked and he wiped it with the towel.

"Would you like to change?" Harriet asked. "I have one of my husband's shirts that should fit you. I can get it for you."

"Oh. No thank you. It'll soon dry off."

There was silence while he wiped the shirt again and Harriet watched closely.

"Can I offer you some tea?" she asked after a while.

"Thank you, no. I'm really fine. It's just a little water," he said smiling and trying to make light of it.

Again there was silence.

"Can I offer you a drink? It will take the chill off."

"I'd better not. Not right now, thank you."

Harriet ignored his refusal. She knew he was a hard drinker and if there was an opportunity for social engagement, then here it was.

"I have some very good whisky? Straight from Scotland! Haig and Haig!— Pinch!"

Henry's thoughts were about getting back to Chivers. He was hoping the rain would soon let up and he could be on his way. He did not like the woman, never had, and he never found her attractive. He was beginning to feel uncomfortable. Again there was silence, only the distant rumbling sounds of thunder, the wind and rain beating heavily on the roof. But he paused thinking it over. It was some time since he had some really good whisky. Then he decided against it—he did not want to get involved with Harriet, and at that moment taking a drink would not be a good thing to do.

"No, no thank you. I'd better not. Maybe some other time. I am anxious to get back. I have things to do."

Harriet sensed the hesitation in his reply.

"I very seldom take a drink," she said. "It's not that I don't like it, but there has to be an occasion to have a drink. And then I only have a light wine. You know, like some port or sherry."

Henry did not answer. He began to regret—just a little—his refusal. He was beginning to feel a bit cold too. The air in the house was very damp, his clothes were very wet, and the wind made it feel much colder.

"My husband used to have brandy every now and again," she continued. "He kept a very good Cognac—or so he told me, but I wouldn't know the difference. I tasted it once, though. I still have some here." She paused. "James used to import a case at a time—from France—every so often." She paused again. "Maybe I can tempt you to change your mind?"

French brandy! How long since he had tasted a good French Cognac? That was temptation beyond his power to resist, and he gave in.

"Well, if you insist."

Harriet produced the bottle and two brandy glasses. She filled one with a large portion, and handed it to him. In the other she poured a normal amount and sat in a large chair near by.

"Cheers!" he said, lifting his glass towards her.

"Cheers!" And the glasses touched.

"Ah!" He sighed. That was indeed a fine brandy. Soon he felt the warmth circulating through his body. He emptied the glass and Harriet refilled it. In half an hour he had downed another and was beginning to feel the effects. He had already had enough to make most men have double vision, but he was a hardened drinker and was only in the early stages of intoxication. Harriet had only one more drink but the effects on her were noticeable. She was tipsy, and had started to laugh without reason at everything that was said. It began to irritate him—he did not like silly women that laughed at nothing—or couldn't hold their liquor—but he was not about to say anything. There was a pause in the conversation when they both sat staring at one another without speaking. The rain started to pound heavily on the roof. Suddenly Harriet jumped up.

"Oh my God!" she exclaimed. "I left the windows upstairs open. Help me get them shut." and she hurriedly made her way up the stairs.

Henry followed her into the first room at the top of the stairs. The window was indeed wide open and the rain had soaked the floor around. He shut the window and made his way into another bedroom. The windows in the next two rooms were also open and he closed them down. He went into the next bedroom.

Harriet was already there and had closed the window. She was leaning against the doorway breathing heavily to catch her breath. The darkened room, the wind, the rain beating on the roof, the flash of lightening and the roar of the thunder gave the place a strange and mysterious atmosphere. Harriet had been transported to a different world—she was walking on air! As Henry passed her hands went up and grasped his shoulders pulling him close to her. She held him tightly and pulled him closer. Her face was turned up towards his, looking intensely into his eyes. This was an invitation that could not be misunderstood, but Henry was not about to accept. He put his hand up against the doorframe to keep from being drawn closer. Harriet changed her hold to the collar of his shirt, and pulled him close. Their faces almost touched.

"Take me!" She breathed softly almost in a whisper. "Take me, Henry. Please, I'm so lonely."

Her actions surprised him and he had no immediate response. He had been propositioned before, but then he had anticipated it and sometimes it was welcomed, but coming from Harriet it was unexpected and not welcomed. Their eyes met as he looked into her face. For a few moments, still without answering he began to push her gently away.

"Take me, Henry. For God's sake, please take me! I'm so very lonely."

There was a note of desperation in her voice, and for a moment he felt real pity for her. But perhaps for the first time in his life he felt no desire for any woman, and especially not for that woman. He did not want to make love to her—he could not make love to her! It was beyond his understanding; that even through pity, or as an act of kindness he could not make love to that woman. He would have been at a loss to explain it. He pushed her further away.

"What's the matter? Don't you like me?"

Suddenly, perhaps in his anxiety to get away or in panic, he answered without thinking. "No! No I don't!"

"Don't you like me?" She repeated the question not believing his answer.

"No! No I don't." The answer was cold and firm.

"Why don't you like me? Make love to me, Henry."

"I have to like the woman I make love to—I have to have feelings for her, and I don't think of you in that way."

"I can make you like me," she pleaded.

"No. I told you—I don't think of you like that." The answer was firm and final.

"You are a cruel man! I know you have other women. Am I not better than the women you go with?"

"The difference is I like the women that I go with, and I can't go with someone I don't like!"

The hurt was intolerable. Suddenly her dreamlike world turned into a nightmare. She burst into a hysterical rage. "I hate you—I hate you! Get out!—Get out of my house!"

The tears were streaming down; her hands were like hammers pounding at his face and chest. "I hate you! I hate you!"

Henry held her hands and dodged the blows, and seconds later was downstairs. The wind, the rain, the lightening and thunder had not let up, but he did not hesitate. He grabbed his hat on the way out, jammed it on his head and buttoned his shirt in the garage. He mounted the horse and in the raging storm was quickly on his way back to Chivers Estate.

This episode with Harriet did not change anything at the Estate, except that she no longer went walking when Henry was expected to be there. Whenever she had to meet with him it was with very mixed and confusing emotions. She was hurt—humbled—and very angry by his outright rejection of her advances, but at the same time she still wanted him, and somehow yearned for his affection—some affection. In calm moments she fantasized on what would have taken place between them, and deeply regretted the love affair that had never been consummated—it would have been such a wonderful thing—if only—. Even now she would have offered herself again—and if he refused her, she would have happily seen him nailed to a cross and crucified. Henry, for his part tried his best to avoid her, and meetings, whenever necessary, were business-like and brief. For the next two years Henry Thomson and the headman Daniel, jointly managed the Manor House Estate.

CHAPTER 12

William's interest in the plantation might have been an inherited trait from his father, but unlike his father, he had no interest in the lives or well being of his employees. When he returned from England the plantation was under the management of Henry Thomson and the headman, Daniel, but William took it upon himself to interfere without hesitation whenever anything displeased him, and often things displeased him. The intrusion into his affairs frequently angered Henry, and Harriet made matters worse by issuing her instructions through her son rather than by delivering them directly to Thomson herself. Her embarrassing encounter with Henry was far from forgotten, and she was reluctant to contact him any more than she needed. Considerable animosity soon developed between the hired Busha and the young owner, and arguments between them were not easily resolved. Henry retained as much of his dignity and authority as was possible under the circumstances, and was happy, several months later to be relieved of his responsibilities. During his time there though, Henry Thomson had developed a good and close working relationship with the handicapped Coolie, and each thought highly of the other.

William was not the kindly employer that his father had been. He was a stern and profit-minded owner, and he drove the employees, some would say, without good reason. Pleasing him did not bring any rewards, but displeasing him was not the thing to do—unless such was done intentionally, for some ulterior reason. A few brave men had sought to test their new master's resolve and had paid the ultimate penalty—they were no longer employed on the estate, and some had even been dismissed without the pay that was due to them.

Along with the business in Kingston and the operations of the import agencies, William was a very busy man indeed. His mother, who had not taken much interest in her husband's affairs, had of necessity involved herself, but often not in a meaningful or helpful way. She would offer advice, from a distance, and even on the most unimportant matters expected her advice, good or bad, to be followed in every detail.

After William assumed direct management of the Estate, it took several months to delve through his father's accounts and personal papers. One Sunday morning he found the account of the loan made to Daniel. The mortgage was for two hundred pounds, repayable at the rate of twenty pounds per annum, without interest. It was a generous arrangement—too generous—William thought. But then his father had often done things like that, which in his opinion did not make sense. Only sixty pounds had been repaid and the loan was more than fifteen years old.

"Ridiculous!" he thought. "And no interest payable! That will have to end!" He placed the account on the desk to remind himself to get the matter straightened out in the morning.

The next morning he was up earlier than usual. Before breakfast he went to the produce buildings, two parallel open sheds, about thirty feet long used to sort and store produce prior to shipping. Several men were already there, squatting on the floor awaiting the arrival of the foreman and their assignments for the day.

One of the men saw him approaching. "Cockey—he comin'," he whispered.

And before William got there two of the men rose and walked away without looking in his direction.

"Mornin', Sur." The men remaining acknowledged his presence, and then slowly continued their conversation in lowered voices.

"Ah w'at 'im want now? One muttered under his breath.

"Morning," William replied. "When you see Daniel, tell him to come and see me right away"

"Yes, Sur," they answered, almost as one.

William took a look around the sheds. There was little to inspect. The buildings were empty of produce, and would be so for the next month. Bananas would not be cut for at least four or five weeks. The only thing in the sheds was a stack of 'crocus' sacks left over from the last coconut shipment.

"See that these bags are put away properly," he called out to the men. "The rats will be cutting holes in them."

"Yes Sur," replied the senior member. "Yes Sur."

"Now you make sure they're put away," he added, threateningly.

In fact the bags were placed in a pile for the express purpose of attracting the rats, which had a liking for the used bags. Every now and again, for sport, the men armed with sticks would surround the bags, while others cautiously removed bags picking them up with long sticks one at a time to flush out the rats. The men with the sticks, with great excitement, would chase and slaughter the escapees. This activity usually took place on a Saturday afternoon after work, and with their pay in hand, it was undertaken in a carefree and jolly manner, accompanied by drinking, and other activities. Later some would stay to gamble away their week's wages. Every now and again one of the rats escaped its pursuers, but still, some ten or twelve pairs were caught each year. William did not approve of the practice because the rats very quickly destroyed the bags, which then had to be replaced at some expense. He disapproved despite the fact that the rats often did considerably more damage to the stored crop itself. Often too, the rats were put aboard the ships during the loading, where they continued to wreak their havoc, much to the annoyance of ship owners. William knew of the practice, which his father had allowed and even encouraged on occasion, but he had no qualms about putting an end to the frolic.

William made his way back to the house and an hour later he was at the stables preparing to mount his horse when Daniel appeared.

"Mornin' Master William," he said. "Y'u send fe me?"

For a moment William forgot what he wanted to see the headman about. William did not like to be addressed as 'Mister William'—or 'Master William,' especially 'Master'—which to him was indicative of junior status—he wanted to be called 'Squire,' like his father. After all he thought, he had succeeded his father over seven years ago, and was entitled to be called 'Squire,' and given the recognition that came with his position. But what William did not understand nor recognize was that among the workers, his father had acquired the title as a term of respect and endearment, and that the title was to be earned, not inherited, and neither could it be imposed. Yet he hesitated to demand it, even though it annoyed him, and made him angry. In the sudden flush of anger he had forgotten just why he had sent for Daniel. When he remembered he was still angry. Slowly he let go the reins and the horse wandered off.

"Daniel" he said, reaching into his pocket for the account of the loan. "I see from the accounts that you owe money on the land, and no payments have been made for years." He produced the account and handed it to Daniel.

Daniel took the paper—the sudden introduction of the matter caught him by surprise, and for a few moments he was at a loss for the right kind of response. He began thinking back, remembering what had passed between him and the Squire. The Squire had never demanded payment at any time, and when the last payment was made, had told him to take his time in making the payments. In fact, the Squire had even suggested that the amount would be reduced, and part of the loan forgiven, but none of this was ever recorded or noted in the accounts. The amount shown on the account was a hundred and forty pounds—a very large amount.

"Well yes Sur," he said. "I still owes de money. Y'u father did tell me to tek me time and give him de money little-little,—not to mine if I doan' pay it all."

"Well it is a hundred and forty pounds, and it should have been paid off by now. You must pay twenty pounds by year end, and you must pay twenty pounds every year until it's finished."

For a few moments Daniel did not reply, "Dat will be very hard, Sur," He still did not know how to handle the situation, but he knew that he must be careful of what he said. "Now is October, an' me pay is only twelve pound till Christmas, an' me Christmas money is only thirty shillings."

"Well," replied William, "you must remember there is no interest paid on this loan, and that is not right. There should be interest paid. You must find the money. Is that clear?" He strode off in the direction of his wandering horse.

Daniel was left standing, his words cut off before he had a chance to reply. William mounted the horse and Daniel's frustration rose. How would they manage? The best that he could do would be about four or five pounds and that would be a lot. He knew what Sapphire his wife would say—there had been no increase in wages since the Squire died, and she always complained about the shortage of money—it would mean another quarrel. However, he did owe the money and he would pay what he could. Master William would have to be satisfied.

Several days passed before Daniel told Sapphire about the demanded payment. The expected quarrel was not what he had anticipated, and he was relieved about that—at least, he felt, she understood that sacrifices had to be made. Preparations had to be made for shipping out produce, and there wasn't time to engage in useless quarrels and arguments. His attention was soon concentrated on the more immediate tasks.

CHAPTER 13

It was Daniel's practice to eat his lunch in the field or wherever work was being done. As befitting his position of headman, his wife prepared his lunch, and had it delivered to him by one of his daughters, whichever one was available at the time. For several days, Opal, the eldest of the three girls, had been making the journey from his house to the estate carrying the lunch pan and a jug of tea. On her daily trips she had been seen by young Master William, who was not unaffected by the attractive young woman. Her long hair, falling almost to the middle of her back, a most attractive feature, could not be ignored. But that was not the only thing that would have attracted his attention; she was a full figured woman displaying all the classic dimensions of a native Venus.

For several weeks, Opal made the noonday trip to and from the fields. In the field lusty males often hailed her—as long as they were out of earshot of her father. She had often been the focus of male attention, sometimes unwanted and irritating, but mostly accepted as just part of what it meant to be an attractive native woman. She would toss her head and ignore the remarks, unless there was one particular young man there who had caught her attention and interest. And then she would return the idle banter with a smile, toss the flowing hair once again, and continue on her way.

Occasionally, Opal stopped at the estate kitchen to gossip with the maids. Her mother knew the servants employed there, and even though her relationship with them was friendly, it was not close. There was rivalry between them—Sapphire considered herself to be above the level of a domestic servant, and this jealousy colored their relationship. In spite of that though, Sapphire Hutchings would often stop to exchange the latest gossip, which she would then eagerly transmit to her husband at the first opportunity.

Opal was not as adept as was her mother at gleaning the gossip, but her daily visits were beginning to bring results. It seems that Harriet Henderson was anxiously prompting her son to court their neighbour's daughter, Bridget Barnham. And it seemed that Master William was not particularly interested in the idea, even though Bridget was perhaps the only suitable young woman in the vicinity. They had of course, known each other since childhood, having literally grown up together. Bridget was a nice girl, he thought, but she was cast in the role of a sister rather than that of some romantic interest.

With the loan on the land to be repaid, Sapphire wished for her daughter to be working at the Manor House, and approved of Opal's daily visits to the kitchen, hoping that it would bring about her daughter's employment there. Opal too, was eager to continue her daily trips to the kitchen, but for quite a different reason. She too, had seen and watched the Squire's son from time to time racing his horse, and was not oblivious to the fact that he often watched her closely. Typically, she went about her business as though he was merely another feature on the landscape and that she had not noticed him. She did not look in his direction, but made certain that he did not miss her walking by, and gave him every opportunity to look and watch without embarrassment to himself.

As the weeks passed, Sapphire became impatient—Opal had not got the hoped for employment. She urged her daughter to make inquiries, and to ask for work. As Opal's efforts did not bring the desired results she decided to take a hand; she would go the Estate House and solicit work for her daughter.

The following morning the two women went to the Estate House to seek Harriet Henderson. Before going to see Harriet, they stopped in at the kitchen and chatted with the cook, telling her the reason for their visit. Even though the cook said there was no opening and little chance of getting a job, they decided nevertheless to speak to Harriet. On that morning, Harriet was not in the mood to have requests made of her, and without a moments consideration, turned them away. Sapphire was angered by the sharp, terse refusal, but people in her position have always had to gracefully accept these ungenerous denials, and she was not about to break with tradition, no matter how angry she felt. She took her daughter's hand and returned to the kitchen to relate the results of the interview, and still smarting with the curt rebuff they started off right away on their return. They had not gone very far when William was seen approaching from the opposite direction on his horse. As he came nearer, they stopped at the side of the pathway to allow the horse to pass.

"Good marnin', Sur," Sapphire said. "A good marnin' to y'u Sur."

William stopped his horse. "Good morning," he replied. There was the woman that he had so often watched from a distance. He thought he knew who she was, but was not really sure, and he would not have dared to ask. But there she was! He could not take his eyes off her, as he looked her up and down. She was even more attractive than he could have imagined.

Sapphire did not miss the fact that her daughter had made more than just a slight impression on the young man—and if she could she would make use of it, to their advantage.

"Dis is me daughter, Sur," she said. "Dis is me daughter, Opal."

"Good marnin', Sur," said Opal. Often glances can say more than words, and they exchanged glances.

"We'se was lookin' fe work at y'u house, Sur," Sapphire continued, and after a few moments, "We was lookin' fe work jus' fe me daughter, Sur, but dere doan seem to be any."

Opal suddenly regained her senses and was surprised at herself—at the thoughts that passed through her mind. She dropped her eyes, and felt her face getting hot and flushed—the realization that she may have betrayed herself. William was still in the depth of his thoughts and did not immediately reply, and when he did it was in a distracted manner, as though he uttered words of which he was not conscious.

"Yes, looking for work—" and then, "Ah, yes, for work at the house. Well I'll see what I can do. I'll see if there is anything there—I'll do my best," and he meant it; he would do his best to get to know the woman.

Sapphire was pleased with herself—very pleased. The Squire's son was interested in her daughter! That was something that she could make use of, and that she would too—if ever the chance arose. The women continued on their way not speaking until they were almost home.

"Master William, 'im tek after y'u," Sapphire said, laughing and relishing every moment of the meeting. "Him 'ave sumptin' fe y'u!"

A few days went by, and then a week, and nothing had been heard about any work. Sapphire was impatient to see her daughter employed at the Manor House. As she prepared her husband's lunch, she spoke to Opal.

"Dis mornin', w'en y'u tek Pappa 'im dinner, why y'u doan go look for Master William? A'x 'im 'bout de work he done promise fe y'u."

Opal nodded her agreement. During the week past she had not seen him on her morning walks, and she had wondered why—up until that time she had seen him almost every day. It was not the desire to get work that made her wish to seek him out, but that was a good excuse.

As usual, she stopped at the kitchen after delivering her father's lunch and picking up the empty lunch pans. Master William, she discovered, had gone to Kingston for a week or so, on business, and would likely be back in a few days. The few days stretched into a week and more, and Opal had almost forgotten about the purpose of her visits to the kitchen.

The following Saturday work on the estate stopped at noon as usual, and everyone prepared for the social events of the evening and the Sunday day of rest. It was a hot and humid day, so having eaten her lunch, Opal decided to go to the beach for a swim. Her sisters were not inclined to join her and she decided to go by herself. She found a large piece of cloth to use as a towel, rolled it into a tight ball, and headed for the beach, about three miles away. The beach that she would go to was a short distance across the coast road, private and sheltered with numerous tall coconut palms that grew close to the water's edge. Along the coast road, she turned at the sound of a vehicle coming from behind a bend in the road and not yet visible. She stood and waited for it to pass before attempting to cross the road. A motorcycle roared into sight, and was gone in a few seconds, the rider hunched over, his face half covered with driving goggles. She had crossed the road when the motorcycle reappeared from the opposite direction at much reduced speed. The cyclist stopped his machine beside her, and removed his goggles. It was Master William, the Squire's son.

"Well," he said, "what are you doing out here?"

"I'se goin' to tek a swim, Sur," she replied, somewhat coyly, and after a pause, "Y'u 'ave a motorcycle, now, Sur?" she asked.

"Ah, yes, it's new. I just got it in Kingston. What do you think of it?"

"It very fine, Sur. It very fine," she replied, looking it over in obvious awe and wonderment. "It go fas' eh Sur?"

He began to show her the various features, and explain what various pieces of the machine were designed to do. And then, after a while, "Would you like to have a ride?"

"Oh! Yes Sur. Yes Sur!"

William showed her how to sit on the back, and told her to hold on to him tight. She tucked her bundle between her legs and held him tightly around the waist, and in a moment they were off, flying along the road at unbelievable speed. As their speed increased, and they turned along the winding coastal road, Opal tightened her hold around his waist, leaning from right to left as they rounded the turns. They passed people on the road, but no one could be sure who the riders were. One had his face hidden behind a pair of goggles, and the other, with hair flying in the wind, had her head pressed close against the driver's back shielded from the wind.

Away they raced fifteen minutes or so before William slowed. It was again an isolated section of the road, beside a sandy, palm-filled beach. He turned towards the beach and drove into the shelter of the palms. As the vehicle stopped, Opal dismounted, and for a few minutes she could not recover her balance, breath or speech. She stood beside the cycle, holding on to the handle bar to steady herself. The speed had frightened her, it was an experience beyond her imagination, and the excitement of it had taken her breath away, and made her giddy. After a moment or two, she rested her head on his arm, closed her eyes, and breathed deeply, still trying to recover her balance. He looked at her bowed head, and with his other hand held her head steady pressed to his shoulder.

Since their first meeting over a week ago, she had been constantly on his mind, although he did not understand why she attracted him to such a degree. He was fully aware that any such affair was 'socially improper,' but emotion and infatuation had overtaken his reasoning. While in England he had had an affair with his uncle's chambermaid—an affair that might have lasted but for the fact that one day his aunt discovered them together in bed. The maid was promptly discharged and he received a stern lecture, and threats to be immediately sent home—from his enraged aunt, and his somewhat less enraged uncle. But this was very different—this woman held him in a spell—compelling—overpowering— he had to worship this goddess of a woman! She was only his headman's daughter—a servant girl—but she was quite irresistible. His head was spinning, his pulse was racing, and he was almost breathless!

He stood the motorcycle on its stand and took her by the hand, leading her on to the sandy beach into a secluded spot among the coconut palms. He removed his riding jacket and spread it on the ground—Opal watched curiously. He sat on the jacket and held out his hand towards her, but she did not accept his invitation. She watched him for a few moments, puzzled and confused, and then suddenly she turned her back, standing quiet and motionless. He rose to his knees put his arms around her waist and drew her down to lie beside him. With his arms around her she turned her face away, bowing her head down and covering her face with both hands, quivering, and trembling noticeable. He kept his arms around her and slowly took her hands away from her face. For a few moments they were face to face, and then he kissed her passionately. He laid her down beneath him as his hands caressed her breasts—and then her body, moving to her hips and all regions of her body. She reached for his hand and held it, struggling to get up, but he held her firmly beneath him.

"No sur! No! No! Please Sur!" She cried. He did not release her, lifting her skirt and removing her underwear.

"No Sur! Please Sur, don't do dat!" She pleaded in vain. "No! No!"

In a few minutes he lay on top of her recovering his breath while she made several attempts to get up, but he was not yet ready to release her. Finally, he withdrew, and when he did she quickly replaced and adjusted her clothing. She picked up her small bundle and ran off towards the road, determined to get away quickly. William did not stir for several minutes. He rolled on to his side and buried his face in his arms. He was relaxed and calmer now, but feeling deep twinges of guilt. Then he slowly pulled up his pants and tucked in his shirt. Before starting his motorcycle, he looked around for Opal. She was not in sight, but she must be on the road.

He mounted the vehicle and very slowly drove towards the road. About half a mile on the road he caught up to her and stopped just ahead. She ignored him and continued her brisk walk. As she passed he took hold of her arm.

"Don't go," he said. "I'll take you home."

For several moments she struggled to get away, but he held her firmly. "I'll take you home," he said again. "Please—don't go."

She stopped struggling and he pulled her closer to him. He put his arms around her holding her tightly. For several minutes he held her close, and then once again he kissed her passionately. Opal did not resist.

"Come, get on and I'll take you home."

She mounted the motorcycle once again, and they sped off. He let her dismount at a secluded place close to the estate.

"When shall I see you again?" he asked, as he prepared to leave.

Opal did not answer.

"I want to see you again. Will you meet me again?"

Opal still did not have an answer, but she nodded. He took hold of her hand and squeezed gently, and with that he took off at a high speed, down the driveway towards the Estate House.

William drove directly to the house and parked his machine in the garage, a short distance from the main house. He spent a few minutes wiping off the dust and looking over his new motorbike—he was very pleased with it—it gave him a sense of freedom that he had not found in other ways. It was not quite dark when he walked up the back steps to the house. His mother was standing in the doorway—she heard the motor when he drove in, and was waiting for him.

"What took you so long?" she asked. "I've been very worried about you. You should have been here this afternoon. What were you doing that took you so long?"

"It's a long trip, Mother," he answered. "I didn't rush." He was not about to tell her of his meeting with Opal—he was hoping that she would never find out. He could imagine the unending fuss.

"You had better go and clean up for dinner."

CHAPTER 14

The shipping season came and went, and Christmas Day was less than two weeks away. As always at that time, the steady winds that blew off the sea were cool and refreshing, and excitement in anticipation of the holiday filled the air. The people were happy just at the thought of Christmas—their cheerfulness was infectious, impossible to explain in the light of their meager and harsh circumstances, and quite impossible to depress.

As the Day grew nearer, bonuses had to be given out. It went without saying that everyone would get a weeks extra wages, but some, because of their position and efforts, would be entitled to receive two weeks wages. Daniel called a meeting of the foremen to decide on who should be on the bonus list—if any. There had been dissatisfaction about the wages and the bonus for several years—there had been no increases since the Squire's death. After all, it was reasonable to expect more if the year had been profitable, and certainly the men had worked hard and it had been a profitable year. Daniel was expected to deliver the message and to get the men their bonuses.

Very early the next morning with a list in hand, Daniel went to the Manor House to see Master William. He was still in bed when he got there, and Daniel filled in the time chatting to the servants in the kitchen. He was on good terms with all the servants, well liked and respected.

William finished his breakfast and called Daniel into the office. He sat behind his large mahogany desk, and leaned back in the chair. Daniel remained standing awkwardly in front of the desk, like a schoolboy getting a lecture from the headmaster.

Daniel presented his case. "Yes, Sur, Master William. It time f'e de' men dem to get some li'kle raise, Sur."

"The business must be such that it can give a raise," countered William. "And, you should know, Daniel, that the business is not so good right now. Prices are down from last year. No, there cannot be any increase this year."

"It now over four year an' de men doan get no increase, Sur. It time for dem to get a li'kle sometin' extra."

"If any increase was given this year there would be no benefit to the Estate. There must be a reason to give a raise, and this year there isn't any extra to give. That is my final answer," and to emphasize his words, he closed his record book with a sharp snap.

Daniel was not going to give up without pressing the cause further. "Four year is a lang time for no increase, Master William. Your farder, de Squire, would always give even a li'kle brata, even if t'ings were not so good. An' de men dem, dey was always grateful and work hard fe 'im. It good fe keep de men dem grateful, Sur."

William did not even consider the argument. "My decision has been made, Daniel. Tomorrow I will get the money for the regular Christmas bonus, and you can hand it out tomorrow afternoon. That is all for now, Daniel," he said, and motioned him towards the open door.

Daniel stood his ground, and was about to argue the case further. William cut him off. "That's all now Daniel," he said, with a tone of exasperation. "I'm busy now," and he turned his attention to some papers on the desk.

Daniel was left standing, in the middle of the room while William continued to leaf through the papers—it was not a good meeting. He knew William was absolutely unshakable in his decision—the bonus would be unchanged from last year. The men would not be satisfied, and he was in full sympathy with their discontent. However, there wasn't anything that they could do about it—the alternative was to stop working, and well, that wasn't much of a choice. No one had ever stopped working on an estate in order to gain a higher wage. Most of the work for the year was over, and only a few men would be needed for the next three months. There would be many dissatisfied workers when they returned in the new-year.

The year had ended on a sour note. With the workers getting more and more dissatisfied it did not make his job any easier, and Daniel knew that there were some always looking for reasons to complain and stir discontent. He knew who those men were, and even though he was completely in sympathy with them, he felt it was his duty to see that the work was carried out properly, and he was going to do that. As far as he was personally concerned, he too was very dissatisfied with his bonus none of which he would see that year, as it would all go to paying off the loan against his house.

The new-year, despite the cheerful hope and anticipation of the season, did not start well. The weather turned cold, and heavy rains began to fall almost daily, and sometimes continuously for several days. All work on the estate virtually came to a halt, not that that had ever been a serious problem in the past—they always seemed able to catch up. A number of the men became ill, and then in a week everyone seemed to have caught the infection, and many were quite ill. Almost all the servants at the Manor House were sick, and Harriet, unused to fetching for herself at any time, decided to return to Kingston, wait out the weather and the epidemic. William declined his Mother's insistent demands that he return with her, telling her that it was necessary for him to remain there. But for his own private reasons he was very glad to see his mother depart.

Since his first meeting with Opal a month had past, and they had not met again. She had been constantly on his mind and he had been anxiously thinking of some way to arrange a meeting. In spite of the rain, quite heavy at times, he had wandered about the estate, hoping to see her. No work was being done on the estate, and there was little reason for anyone to be about, other than for an occasional inspection or to feed the stabled animals. He was glad to see his mother depart—it would make it easier for them to meet.

With only the cook still up and about and Harriet away, the house was quiet and desolate. A day later while the cook served breakfast, he asked her how she was going to manage doing all the housework by her self. Not to miss the opportunity, the cook complained long and hard about the amount of work that she had to do, and pointed out that it was just too much for one person. William, not known to be sympathetic about other peoples' troubles, surprised the good woman by being just that—he was very sympathetic. He even suggested that she get someone to come in and help—and he suggested who that person might be. He reminded her that the headman's wife had inquired on behalf of her daughter about working there, and he suggested that the cook get the young woman to help.

Opal had not been seen for several weeks and the cook went to search for her, finding her at home with her mother. Opal's reluctance to work at the Manor House puzzled Sapphire, but between the cook and Sapphire, she was persuaded to return to the Manor House with the cook. It was a situation ideally to his liking when returning that afternoon William found Opal at the house waiting for an interview.

He nodded and smiled as he went into his office, but Opal did not follow. He returned to the doorway, beckoned for her to come in, and then she hesitantly, shyly, followed.

The last time they had seen each other he had forcefully made love to her; she had not been a willing participant, and their meeting now was awkward and strained—between the master and the servant—and yet he had made love to her! The feeling of familiarity and understanding that immediately followed the motorcycle ride somehow did not return. William was clumsy—he desperately wanted to divulge his feelings towards her, but could not bring himself to do so. Opal, for her part, was hoping that they would again be on familiar terms, but he would have to make the first move—it couldn't come from her. The meeting was short and businesslike; Opal accepted the offer of work and left his office.

When she left William flopped into his chair. "O God!" he muttered to himself. "What a fool I am! Anyway," he thought, "there'll be another day."

The following night while she served dinner, William used the opportunity to repair the damage of the previous afternoon, and a far friendlier conversation ensued.

"After the work is done outside," he said, "come to the veranda at the side, and we can talk."

On the veranda at the side there was a swing settee, several chairs and tables. It was on the darker side of the house, not often used at night unless there were guests, when lamps were lit and brought out. After dinner William went to his office as he usually did, but he did not stay long. Before finishing his last cup of coffee he went to the side veranda and lay down on the settee. The tree frogs kept up an incessant chanting, almost hypnotic—he closed his eyes and dozed off. It was over an hour later he heard soft footsteps on the pathway, and then on the steps, but he did not rouse himself until he heard a step on the veranda. In the darkness he reached out to take her hand and gently pull her down beside him.

CHAPTER 15

Harriet returned unexpectedly a fortnight later; she arrived early in the afternoon. For several days it had not rained, but the skies were still dark and overcast. Life was getting back to normal although many people were still suffering the effects of the epidemic—at least it was not getting any worse. Both William and his mother escaped the infection, and so did Opal. The lovers had complete freedom in their nightly rendezvous.

Both Daniel and Sapphire were satisfied to see their daughter now employed at the estate house—Daniel, because it would ease the financial strain of repaying the loan—and Sapphire, because she knew of Master William's interest in their daughter. Little did Sapphire know just how far this interest had progressed, and in so short a time, but had she known she might have taken a more cautious view. Opal had returned home only twice since her employment although the trip there and back was about an hour each way. Opal was deeply in love, and her days were like a dream—she hardly understood what had happened to her, and at that point hardly had a care. There had been little time for mother and daughter to talk about anything, least of all about any intimate relations with Master William. And even if there had been more visits and more time, Opal would have kept those matters to herself, at least for the time being.

Upon her return Harriet ignored the young woman, but that was not in any way unusual—Harriet often ignored the servants working close to her—she accepted their presence with disinterest—a fact of unpleasant necessity. But then something began to nag her subconscious mind. At first it was just a restless feeling of unease—that something was not quite right, although she did not know the 'if' or the 'what' of it. And still this sense of unease did not enter her conscious mind for several days. Then quite suddenly, she realized that something was definitely not right, and still she did not know why she should feel that way. But her senses had been alerted, and she just knew that something was not right—it was like a sharp pinprick that suddenly wakes one up and sharpens one's awareness of things around one. Was it William? Was it the new maid? The house? The fact that she had been away? It plagued her off and on for several more days, and then suddenly, like a thunderclap—it came to her—William!—William and the maid!! It was only the fleeting glance that passed between them at the dinner table that brought the message home. The realization hit her like a bolt of lightening. No! Absolutely no! The idea was just too appalling—too revolting—too disgusting—that just couldn't be it!—O God! No!—Absolutely No! But—she was not mistaken—she knew!

In the middle of the meal she suddenly felt as though she would vomit. The knife and fork were thrown into the plate still half filled with food, both hands placed beside the plate on the table, she stared at her son gaping at her, his mouth half open in amazement.

"Mother? Mother? What's wrong?"

She continued to stare at him without answering. And then slowly her eyes shifted—she glared at Opal standing against the wall holding the water-pitcher with both hands, clutching it to her body. Then slowly her glare returned to her son again, still without uttering a word.

"Mother, what's wrong?" Still—no answer. She began to recover, and she began to get very angry. Her face flushed, and as the fury rose within her, the power of speech was completely lost—she could not utter a word. She rose slowly from her seat and stood up.

"Mother, what's the matter?" William gasped and stood up. He left his seat and went to his mother's side. He had never seen his mother in such a state and it alarmed him. He reached her side and took her arm.

"I am perfectly well, William," she said, in a very firm, measured tone. "I am perfectly well. Thank you!"

He recognized the tone—he had heard it before but not often. He knew it meant that his mother was very angry—very angry with him—but he did not know why. As Harriet moved away from the table she plucked his fingers from around her arm, and still holding them firmly, flung them away from her towards the floor in disgust, as though they were soiling her hands. Turning her back she made her way out of the room up the stairs towards her sitting room.

William turned to look at Opal in amazement. The questions sped through his mind—Did she know? How could she? How could that be possible? If she did know, what would she do? She couldn't possibly know for certain unless someone had told her, and in that case, who? Who knew of their affair, if anyone? He turned to Opal with a questioning gesture.

"Miss Harriet," Opal whispered. "W'at tek her, Master William?"

In spite of their close relationship, she still addressed him as "Master"—that was something she had not quite risen above, the master-servant relationship was still a fixture in her mind.

William shrugged, "I don't know, but I'm going to find out." And then he added in a whisper "You fix the coffee. I'll take it up in a few minutes."

He returned to his seat, one arm on the table, thoughts racing through his mind. Silently, slowly he picked up the fork and still in deep thought continued to eat. He sat there for possibly fifteen or twenty minutes and still had not finished the food on the plate. Opal returned with coffee served on a tray, which she placed beside him on the table. Awkwardly she stood there silently for a few minutes, and then still without a word turned to leave the room. At that point William become aware of her presence. He turned towards her, "I'll take it up."

In the sitting room he placed the tray on the center table and poured two cups of coffee, adding sugar and milk as his mother liked it. He placed a cup beside his mother's chair, and sat in the chair beside her.

Harriet had regained her composure and collected her thoughts by the time he entered the room, and she had already worked out her course of action. William, she knew, was involved with the woman—she did not have to be told—and that could not be tolerated. That he would deny it went without saying; that she would have to put a stop to it likewise went without saying. There would be little point to accusing him of an improper relationship and having it end in denials, but it was impossible for her to just leave it alone. She had to ask him!

"Mother—" he began, as he handed her the coffee. He was about to continue when she interrupted.

"What is going on between you and that woman downstairs? Are you carrying on with her?" she asked quite calmly.

"Mother!" he exclaimed. "How could you think such a thing?" He had resolved to deny anything and everything. But his face began to redden. He was not used to lying to his mother and her sudden reaction had caught him by surprise. Each paused to absorb the development—the question—the answer. The pause continued.

"Well," said Harriet, at last," if I have your word."

William did not answer, only nodded his agreement. Now she knew she would have to take the matter into her hands, and that would take a little working out, but work it out she would.

Jamaican Proverb—Ripe mango doant know de danger 'til a hungry neyger fine 'im.

CHAPTER 16

Several days later, Opal, carrying fresh bed linens, entered Harriet's bedroom. The door was open and Opal did not knock. Harriet did not appear surprised—as though she expected the maid. Several dresses and assorted garments were spread on the unmade bed, and Harriet held two dresses taken from the closet. Opal clutched the fresh bed sheets closely to her body, and before she could speak Harriet interrupted.

"Ah! Opal. There you are. I was tidying up a few of my dresses." This was unusually cordial coming from someone who had previously shown only qualified dislike. Opal was taken by surprise; she stood speechless and motionless, not knowing what to expect.

"Some I don't wear any more, and I thought that you could have them." She went to the bed and picked up the brightest frock, a fine embroidered linen. "See this one, I will never wear it again. Do you think it could it fit you?" She picked it up and held it up towards the speechless girl to judge its length.

Opal was at a loss—she could not believe what she was hearing. Slowly she placed the bed linens on a chair and approached her mistress.

"Oh yes Mum!" she murmured. "Oh yes Mum."

Harriet held the dress up close to the astounded girl. It would be a good fit; they were both about the same size.

"Ah, yes," continued Harriet. "That would fit you very well." She looked at it critically, her head to one side.

Opal began to recover her astonishment and she began to have extraordinary feelings of gratitude towards her mistress.

"Well then you can have it!" said Harriet.

"T'ank y'u Mam," said Opal almost inaudibly, and she repeated herself several times. She folded the dress carefully and placed it on a chair. Then she

78

stepped back and looked again at the dress on the chair. "But Mam," she said after a few moments. "Dat is a very good dress, Mam. Are y'u sure y'u doan me'k a mis'take, Mam?"

"Oh no," answered Harriet. "I will never wear it again. You might as well have it."

"But it cost plenty, Mam. It is maybe too good fe me?"

"Oh no! No! It's yours. I'm sure you can use it."

Opal thanked her again many times. She replaced the clothes, made the bed and tidied the room. As she was about to leave Harriet turned to her, "Ah Opal," she said. "There's just one thing."

"Yes Mum."

"There's just one thing, Opal. I don't think you should tell the other servants about it."

"Yes Mum?" And again, "Yes Mum?"

"Well, I can't give them all dresses, you know." There was a pause; "They won't like it if I don't give them all something too. You know what I mean?"

"Oh, yes Mum."

"It might cause trouble between you and that would not be good."

"No Mum."

"So let this be just between you and me."

"Oh yes Mum, I see."

Harriet went to her cupboard and found a small paper bag. "Here, put it in this. That way no one will see it." And as she put the dress in the bag, "Now you promise not to tell anyone?"

"Yes Mum, I doan't tell no one."

Opal decided to return home that night as early as possible. The day had passed like a dream. The unexpected gift from a mistress who up until that day had not shown her any particular affection had filled her head with all kinds of thoughts and fantasies. Maybe she knew about the affair with her son, and somehow approved! Anyway, she was eager to show the gift to her mother and sisters. With the frock tightly wrapped in the paper bag she quickly made her way home.

She was hardly in the house before the bag was opened, her work clothes removed and she was in the frock, excitedly showing it to Sapphire and her sisters. It was indeed a good fit, and what imperfections there were could be ignored in the splendor of such a lovely frock. Sapphire gazed at it in amazement. After the initial excitement had faded they sat at the table excitedly discussing the days events. Soon Daniel arrived home from his long day at the plantation. He eyed the new dress without uttering a word, and sat down. Sapphire quickly placed his food before him on the table, and began telling him about Opal's new dress. He ate his food without comment, quietly listening to the chatter of the women, but he was uneasy and disturbed by the sudden change in Harriet's attitude. He finished eating and took a close look at the new dress.

"Dis is very expensive piece," he said, feeling the fabric between his fingers. And then he returned to his chair. Opal was up on her feet again spreading the skirt and showing the fit. After a while Daniel interrupted.

"Dat is not fe people like we," he said. He was a proud man, not ostentatious, and he did not approve of his wife's tendency to show off and put on airs. Her desire to prove her superiority over the other estate employees had been a bone of contention between them for a long time.

"Dat is fe dem dat lives in the Big House, an' fe dem dat pays fe it."

"Pappa!" Opal protested, "De missus do gi'e it to me!"

Sapphire immediately joined the protest, "A w'at de gal fe do? She to tell Miss Harriet she doan want it?" They continued their objections in chorus.

"Ah buy y'u clothes. From de time y'u born y'u 'ave good clothes an' y'u never walk wid out shoe pon y'u foot. Why y'u ave to tek dese people old clothes now?" But he was not inclined to argue. "Dis piece of clothes will bring trouble—it is fe dem dat have de money." He rose from the table and left the room. He was tired and his old injury had ached him throughout the day, and he would be up again early in the morning. He left the women still talking and admiring the garments and he went to bed.

William and Opal did not meet for several days following the episode at the dinner table. When they thought that it was again safe they were careful only to meet at night on the coast road outside the plantation, or down on the beach on the other side of the road. Their meetings had been brief and they had not yet found a suitable place to meet and to be alone.

William found the change in his mother's attitude towards Opal to be most unusual. He listened carefully when Opal told him about the gift, and he thought it quite strange—he knew his mother did not like Opal, and still harbored deep suspicions about their relations, so why the sudden change? He often thought that his mother acted in strange and unusual ways, and that was nothing to be wondering about, but this was really very different.

Several weeks later Harriet was again in her bedroom when Opal appeared in the doorway to tidy the room and make the bed. There were several pairs of shoes placed together on the floor, and undergarments spread on the unmade bed.

"I am still sorting out old clothes, Opal," she said. "I just won't have any use for them any more."

She picked out several garments and offered them to Opal. "Would you like to have them? Do you think you could use them?" she asked sweetly.

"Oh yes, Mam. Tank y'u Mam." And the young woman gratefully accepted.

"Well then you can have them."

Once again she was cautioned to keep the matter strictly to herself, and she promised not to let the other servants know. In the bag was placed a pair of shoes and several silken undergarments, and when the elated woman left the room she was still thanking her mistress.

"Soon you won't be thanking me very much! You little bitch!" Harriet muttered to herself as the young woman left the room.

The articles were wrapped tightly in the paper bag and taken home, and no one else was ever the wiser.

CHAPTER 17

William was looking forward to the first Saturday evening in February. A tourist boat was expected to call in at Port Antonio, and the town would be filled with strangers milling about, some tipsy on rum punch, some looking for women and for some excitement. There would be calypso bands, dancing and lots of festivities, and the bars filled with strangers, many escorting local women. He would be able to mix and mingle with Opal, and would hardly be noticed or recognized. It was an opportunity for them to be 'out on the town' doing things that they would otherwise never be able to do together, and they would be able to join in as a normal couple. Opal was as excited as he was at the prospect of being able to do something different, and at being able to wear her finest dress—the one given to her by her mistress. It would be her first night out, and the thought exceeded even her wildest dreams.

As the night approached, William told his mother that he would be going out to Port Antonio to 'meet the tourists'—ostensibly, an evening of social encounters with mostly American tourists. Harriet saw no harm in that, and in fact approved, seeing it as a good opportunity for him to meet other people. Nevertheless, she was full of cautionary advice—not to drink too much, and of course, not to be home too late.

Even with the prospect of a night out a conflict raged in his mind. The natural feelings and desire for the object of his infatuation in opposition to his mother's orders and to what he knew to be true—that there was no future to their romance—that it would have to end sooner or later. The thought was constantly in his mind and he could think of nothing else; it gave him the most awful headache. As the week passed though, and he met Opal, his headache seemed to lessen somewhat. He would be using the car that night and arranged to meet her at the gate on the coast road.

The arrangement worked perfectly and soon they were in the town looking for a place to park the car. They drove slowly through the streets past the hotel and found a quiet side road not far away. It was a perfect evening, comfortably cool and very dark, with every star in the sky brightly shining. Out at sea the tourist boat was clearly visible, alight from stem to stern. On the main street the tourists were milling about in pairs and groups, followed by an army of locals anxious to provide whatever they desired, and in so doing earn a few pennies. William knew of a local 'hot spot'—a sailor's bar and dance hall—in the lower section of town. The sounds of several bands could be clearly heard through the night as they beat out their steady rhythms. They made their way towards the music.

The establishment was walled in with a high, stout bamboo fence and closed off with a narrow unlocked gate. They entered almost unnoticed by the small group of patrons, a few on the dance floor, some sitting at tables, and some at a long bar at the furthest end of the building. From what he could see, the crowd was a mixed group of tourists, some crewmen from the ship and local people that he did not know. At any rate, it was not the high society group that he was not anxious to meet, and he was comfortable that they blended in very well. The tables were all lit with small candles in small glass jars, and he found one just off the dance floor on the far side of the room. He ordered drinks when a waiter came.

In the dim light it was the first time that he could see Opal. Up until that time he had not given much attention to how she was dressed, but now he could see that she was wearing his mother's dress. The recognition of the dress shocked him for a few moments when he realized that she did not have another suitable dress to wear. Why had he not thought of that before? He was embarrassed at his own thoughtlessness but did not say anything. A bright red flower was in her hair at the side—she was irristable!

The band played lively calypso tunes and soon they were on the dance floor along with the thickening crowd. Opal knew the latest dance steps and began to teach her partner. The evening passed quickly and after several more drinks, it did not matter to them who might happen to be there and see them. Long after one o'clock the party was still in full swing, but they had been on the floor several hours and were beginning to tire. They made their way off the dance floor toward the bar to get a final round of drinks.

William, holding Opal by the hand, pushed his way through the crowd towards the bar. He reached the bar and waited for attention. He turned to a man at his side half slouched over and was face to face with Major Henry Thomson, the busha of Chivers Estate. They stared for a few moments as they recognized one another. Henry was the only person that he would have been likely to meet in the "Paradise Bar," and was one person that he did not want to meet. They had a mutual dislike—if not hatred—for one another even before his father's death.

"William Henderson! Fancy meeting you here!" He was drunk, or very close to being drunk, and his speech was slurred.

William did not answer. He did not want to get into a conversation, apart from the fact that he did not like the man; he was embarrassed about being seen with the headman's daughter. He did not know just what Henry might say or do, especially if he was drunk. As yet Henry had not seen Opal, and she had not seen him, lagging somewhat behind William as they approached the bar. Opal made her way to the bar and stood between them, still without recognizing Henry. She turned, and in a moment she recognized the Busha—and he recognized her too!

"Oh! My! My!" He swayed backwards on his stool and then forward. "Who have we here?" He paused. "A night on the town?" He paused again. "I did not know you two were together? How nice! How very, very nice!" There was a note of sarcasm in his voice, the meaning of which did not escape William.

William was flustered and embarrassed not knowing quite how to handle the situation. He muttered "Nice to see you again," He turned towards the barman and gave his order.

"We should have a party," said Henry, putting his hand on William's shoulder. "We should have a few drinks together. Come. Let me handle these." He fumbled about in his pocket and retrieved a small bundle of bills.

William was ahead of him. "It's been nice to see you again. We must be off now." He turned to head back to his table.

Henry rose unsteadily, "Don't rush off. Let's have a drink together."

He picked up his near empty glass and followed them uncertainly across the dance floor. They were sitting down when he got there. Dragging a chair from the next table he sat down beside them.

"It's so nice to meet up with friends," he said. "You know," he continued, "it can be very lonesome here." He emptied his glass, putting it down hard on the table.

"Yes sir, William, m'boy, it can be very, very lonesome here. I bet you didn't know that. Even though you're in a big crowd you're still lonesome." He turned to Opal looking intensely into her face.

Opal had never spoken to him before even though she had seen him many times on the plantation. She knew that her father had worked well for him for years, and liked him despite his social shortcomings. She was strangely fascinated by his rakishly handsome and debauched appearance that somehow pleaded for help, sympathy and understanding.

He continued to gaze into her face, ignoring William. "My! My!" he said after a short while, "You certainly have grown up. —You are beautiful!"

Opal was embarrassed. She lowered her head, and then turned to look at William. William did not say a word but colored almost visibly even in the dim light. He took a sip from his glass, and had an intense urge to hit the man. Henry was oblivious to his presence for several minutes. He reached out with one hand to gently raise her face and caress her hair. She looked up and they gazed into each other's eyes. Then Henry withdrew his hand to retrieve his glass and again drain the contents.

"Did you know that my wife left me?" said Henry, at last acknowledging William's presence. "Yes Sir! She left me. But I don't care! You know—I don't care! She was always leaving me—she was always going away—I don't know where." He threw his hand above his head in a wide sweep around. "I don't know where she went or what she did," and after a moments thought, "or who she did it with!" He chuckled at the thought. "I don't give a damn! I just don't give a damn!"

It was getting very embarrassing. William did not want to get into any conversation with the man—the least he said the better—he'd just let the man ramble on by himself. He sipped his drink, exchanged glances with Opal. The band was getting ready to start playing once again.

Henry had been carrying on the conversation by himself, and had drained his empty glass several times. William hoped that thirst would eventually force him to return to the bar. The band started to play again.

"If you ever need anything," Henry said looking at Opal, "you come and see me."

"Yes," thought William, "I know damned well what you've got in mind!" But he kept his thoughts to himself.

"If you're ever in trouble," continued Henry, "just you come and see me. I'll set it all straight." He paused, and was about to repeat his offer when William interrupted.

"We're going to dance, Henry. Excuse us." He held out his hand to Opal and they rose from the table.

"Oh yes," Henry said. "You two just go ahead. I'll just get myself another." He stood up as they went to the dance floor. Once on the floor William guided his partner towards the exit, holding Opal firmly by the hand he pushed open the gate and was out on the street looking for the parked car.

The dawn was breaking when he returned to the estate and parked the car. The next morning he got out of bed in time for a late breakfast. In the afternoon he took out the motorcycle cleaned and polished it, fiddled with it for over an hour before sitting astride the machine and starting the engine. He accelerated the motor several times and rode several times in a slow circle on the driveway in front of the house. Then he rode it back into the garage and turned off the motor.

He was thoroughly bored, and for some strange reason felt depressed. He had thought about the meeting with Thomson and that bothered him; it made him uneasy. He wanted to see Opal but knew that was not possible. He slowly walked past the stables and went inside to pet his horse. On the spur of the moment he decided to put on the saddle and go for a ride. He had no specific place in mind, but when depressed he would often go riding through the property. Soon he was in full gallop along the coast road where he had taken Opal on their first ride.

On the return trip he walked the animal at a more leisurely pace allowing it to rest. As he approached the road leading to Chivers Estate he impulsively decided to go in. He had often gone riding with Bridget, and if she was there she might decide to go again. Slowly he circled the driveway in front of the house and dismounted beside the front steps. He went up the steps to the veranda and was about to knock on the open front door when Constance appeared at the side.

"Good afternoon, Master William."

"Good afternoon, Constance. Is anyone in?"

"No Sur," replied Constance. "Dem all gon' back to Kingston, Sur."

"I thought they were here," said William. "When did they leave?"

"Yesterday sur. De Missus never did tell me she was goin'. She jus' go when she mind teck her." And then she added, "but dem should be back by Friday evenin', Sur."

"Miss Bridget was with her?"

"Yes, Sur, dem all was together, de Missus, an' Miss Bridget."

"Well I called just to visit. I'll see them another time."

He was in no hurry to return home, and walked slowly down the steps, mounted, and for several minutes sat contemplating his move. He took his time to urge the animal into motion down the long winding driveway to the main road. He did not really want to see Bridget, but thought that it might dispel his depression, and in any case it would be a good idea to tell Mother that he had been there. He would have preferred to see Opal, but he knew it would not be pleasant should his mother discover any secrete meetings. The thoughts had him once again giving vent to his feelings, galloping along the road, his white shirt flapping in the wind, and startling people on the road as he sped by.

Harriet was indeed pleased to hear that he had visited Chivers even though there had been no one at home.

"You must go again—soon," she advised. "I am glad you decided to see them again." And then she launched into the details of how helpful Mrs. Barnham had been to them when his father died, and then to what a wonderful girl Bridget was—"Just the right kind of girl for you," she concluded. William left the room, unable to tolerate another word of motherly advice.

The visit to Chivers may have been worth it after all. It seemed to put his mother at ease, and she would be that less watchful. The following morning he was up early, before Harriet. He had gone to bed early and had slept very well, and he felt well. Best of all there was no trace of his headache.

CHAPTER 18

Several uneventful weeks passed. Once again work on the plantation began to intensify, and William found himself fully involved in its affairs. The last year had not ended on a happy note; there had been dissatisfaction amongst the men with their bonus, and there was unrest when they returned to work. The New Year started badly too; William fired two of the men, which would have caused a full-blown strike had it not been for Daniel's intervention. To complicate matters, the shipping agency in Kingston was demanding William's attention, and he was forced to be away for days at a time.

Daniel was doing his best to manage the plantation under difficult circumstances. His sympathies were with the men, but his loyalty was to his employer. Soul-searching moments plagued him from time to time, and he considered "having it out" with Master William, and leaving his job if they could not reach agreement. He remembered the kindness shown him by the Squire, and it was only due to that memory and to the respect that he had for his late employer, that he did not act on his impulses. Nevertheless, he felt that matters might at some time come to a head—he did not know what would precipitate it, but he knew the men were angry enough to face their unyielding employer.

As it happened, Daniel was the catalyst that started it off—and it was a very personal matter. Sapphire, his wife, informed her incredulous husband that their daughter Opal "had been going" with Master William! And a few days later came the news that "they had made a baby!" The prospect of an illegitimate grandchild was not what disturbed him most—it was the fact that his daughter had been "taken" by his employer.

William was in Kingston when Daniel learned of Opal's condition, and his fury could hardly be contained. It angered him further when he found that his wife had given her gossiping habit full range; that she had bragged about it to everyone, and it was common knowledge on the plantation. He did not view it in the same light as his wife; while she was proud of the fact, he was angry and ashamed. They quarreled violently. Even so, he could not tackle William until he returned from Kingston. He would not accept the situation without facing his young employer.

During the day he worried about the consequences of a confrontation, and even if there was anything he could do about it. In the early afternoon he left the field and went to the great house to find William, and if William was not there he would speak to his mother—he would tell her about her son's affair with his daughter. As he neared the front porch, he could see Harriet on the veranda talking to two men. As he got closer, he recognized one to be the local police corporal, a big burly man well known to abuse his power and accept "considerations." The other man he did not know, but from his appearance would have guessed that he too, was a policeman of some kind. He waited some distance away until the men left, and then mounted the steps.

"Afternoon, Mam," he said. "Please could ah 'ave a word wid you, Mam?"

"Yes, Daniel."

"Well, Mam, Master William is away, an' ah would prefer to speak wid 'im, but ah mus' tell you about it, Mam"

"Yes! Yes Daniel. What is it?" She was impatient with the delay in taking her noonday rest. But she seemed to be even more irritated with Daniel.

"It's 'bout Master William an' me daughter Opal, Mam."

"What about Master William?" she demanded sharply. She did not seem surprised that her son's name was linked in the same sentence with that of his daughter!

"Yes Mam. Dem two 'as been togedder, Mam," He wanted to put as delicate a description on the relationship as possible. He did not want to offend Harriet, even though he knew that whatever he said would do nothing less than make her very angry.

"That is quite impossible Daniel." Harriet was decisive in her reply, and even more impatient.

"Yes Mam. I'se tellin' y'u Mam dat dey 'as been togedder. Dey 'as been in friendship, Mam."

"What do you mean, they have been in friendship?"

"Yes Mam, dat is wat ah said." He paused a moment, "Me daughter is to 'ave 'is chile, Mam." He waited for that news to take effect.

"That is quite impossible," Harriet snapped. "Do you expect me to believe that my son has fathered your daughter's baby? That is quite impossible, and I won't hear any more about this."

"Yes Mam, dat is so. Ah only jus' fine out today. An' if ah had known, Mam, it would not be so—"

Harriet interrupted, "Look here, my good man, what you are saying is quite impossible, and I do not want to hear another word about it. Do you understand me?" She was getting very angry, her face was flushed, and she was twisting her fingers together.

"It is de trute, Mam. Everyone here know 'bout it, but if ah had known it would not be so."

"Look here, my good man, you are impertinent to accuse my son of such a thing. If you continue it will be the worse for you. It will mean a lot of trouble for you."

"No, Mam. I doan want to mek trouble fe no one. But Master William an' me daughter was in friendship."

"Look here—I know a crooked thing when I see it. I thought better of you, Daniel. You are trying to get money out of us, and I will not stand for it. If you keep on, I'll call the police and have you charged. In any case, your daughter Opal, is a thief!"

"A tief, Mam? No Mam! Opal is no tief. Why y'u say she tief? She tief sometin' from y'u?"

"Yes! She certainly did. And I tell you that she will not get away with it."

"W'at she tief from y'u Mam?"

"You never mind—you will find out soon enough. And I can tell you that she will not get away with it!"

A sense of panic seized him and without an answer he hurried off in the direction of his house. He opened the gate and entered, and saw that the two men seen earlier were in the house talking to his wife and daughter. He hurried in. Sapphire was engaged in an angry argument with the corporal while the other man was sifting through clothing spread about on the table.

"W'at is goin' on?" he demanded, "W'at is de trouble 'eher?"

The strange man identified himself as a detective from the C. I. D. and told him that they were investigating the theft of clothing from Mrs. Henderson. As part of the investigation they were conducting a search of his house.

Daniel was once again in a state of shock. Things had happened so quickly that he had not had time to work it out. He sat down, held his head in his hands for a few moments.

"No one 'ere is a tief, Sur," he said. "I works fe me money, an' no somebody in dis house is a tief."

The detective picked up the dress given to Opal; he picked up the pair of shoes and several of the silken undergarments. "'Ow did y'u get dese clodes?" he asked, looking sternly at Opal.

"De missus did give dem te me, Sur," she answered, her voice quivering.

"Y'u tellin' me dat y'u missus did give dem te y'u?" he asked sarcastically, and waited for Opal to confirm.

"Yes, Sur. She did give me furst dis one dress. An' den she did give me de shoe and de pantie dem. An' she did say to me I'se not to say to nobody dat she give dem to me."

"Well, I can tell y'u dat dis is de dress, and dis is de shoe, and dis is de pantie dat Mrs. Henderson did tell me dat is stolen. An' me t'ink dat y'u tief dem."

"Y'u go a'x de mistress if she no give dem te me," pleaded Opal. "De missus will tell y'u, Sur."

Sapphire interrupted, almost hysterically, protesting her daughter's innocence. Daniel intervened, relating the evening when he returned from work finding the women excitedly discussing the dress. All the arguments were to no avail.

"Y'u come wid me," said the detective firmly. "We go speak wi'd de Mistress." He gathered up the garments, took Opal by the arm and led her out of the house, followed by the distraught parents.

At the house the detective requested the presence of the mistress. He mounted the stairs to the veranda, and displayed the seized articles. Harriet was seen to be nodding her head in agreement, picking up one item and then another, confirming her ownership. They spoke in low tones and the words not heard by anyone below.

Opal stood in the driveway looking hopefully, incredulously, at her mistress, not believing what she was seeing. She turned to her parents standing beside her, "She did give dem to me. As God is me witness, I never tief dem!"

The detective gathered up the clothes and prepared to leave. Opal was distraught, hysterical, "Please, Mam, tell dem y'u did give me de clothes, Mam," tearfully she pleaded, "Tell dem I'se no tief, Mam!"

Harriet ignored her. She spoke a few more words to the policeman in a low voice. He quickly rolled up the clothes, and descended the steps.

"Y'u is to come wid us," he said curtly to Opal. The poor woman did not know where to turn; she looked pleadingly towards the veranda where her mistress stood. "Please Mam," she sobbed. "Tell dem I'se no tief—tell dem. Oh please Mam! Tell dem!"

Harriet did not react; she stood on the veranda looking down, smiling. Opal turned towards the policeman.

"As God is me witness, Sur, I never tief dem!" And then she broke down completely, falling on her knees, sobbing, hysterically weeping, her head almost on the ground.

Daniel moved to comfort his overcome daughter, but was prevented from reaching her by the corporal. The detective produced handcuffs, and lifting Opal by the hand snapped them on. Harriet stood on the veranda looking triumphantly at the events taking place below. Then she turned and disappeared into the house. The policeman took the young girl's arm and led her out towards the road, her mother followed hysterically pleading with the men to release her daughter and protesting her innocence.

"We will look out fe y'u," Daniel called to her several times. She was led out on to the road for the long walk to the Port Antonio jail. On the road they were soon out of sight. Then he put his arm around his sobbing wife and together they made their way home.

CHAPTER 19

William arrived at the plantation half an hour before midnight. His mother had already retired, and showed no signs of awakening, so he cut two slices of bread and made himself a jam sandwich. The milk in the ice box was warm and on the verge of turning sour, so he had to drink water. Finishing his snack he went to bed right away. He was hardly awake the next morning when his mother walked into his room without knocking.

"William." she began. "What have you and that woman been carrying on?"

"What woman are you talking about?" He sat up in the bed.

"You know very well what I'm talking about—the headman's daughter, Opal."

"Uh?—What are you talking about, Mother?"

"Daniel was over here yesterday to see me. He told me that his daughter is pregnant and that you are the father. What do you have to say about that?"

William did not answer for almost a minute. He sat on the edge of the bed rubbing his head with one hand. "Oh God!" he said to himself. "Not that!"

"I knew it! I just knew it!" ranted his mother. "I knew you were having an affair with that woman, and you lied to me. How could you?"

"I don't know," he answered weakly. "I just don't know."

"What will people say when this gets about? You have done a very foolish thing."

"Well it's my business and none of theirs," he answered trying to find some defense and justification for his affair.

"It is my business, and people will make it their business too. How could you do such a stupid thing? Didn't you think about it? I knew from the start that you were carrying on with that damned little whore."

"Well, it is my business and no body else's."

His mother was angry enough when she entered the room, but now she was unbridled fury. She screamed at her son, accusing him of utter stupidity and disregard for her. She berated him for fully fifteen minutes until he didn't answer back. He sat on the edge of the bed looking disconsolately at the floor.

"Well, you don't have to worry about that woman," she said at last, "I've seen to her, and she will not bother you again. I've seen to that!"

"What do you mean, I don't have to worry?"

"I knew from the very start what was going on—if I had not made plans—anyway, I've got rid of her and she will not bother you again."

"How did you get rid of her?" he asked. He knew his mother was capable of anything, and he was now concerned for his erstwhile lover.

"I had her arrested—yesterday. So she is in jail."

"You can't have her arrest her for that! What was she arrested for?"

"I had her arrested for theft! She's a damned thief!"

"Did she steal anything from you? How could she be in jail?"

"She stole my clothes. A dress, shoes and other things."

"But—she wouldn't steal from you—she liked you—she wouldn't do that."

"She stole my clothes and I had her arrested."

It began to dawn on him what his mother had done. The idea was shocking even though he well knew his mother and what it could mean to anyone that offended her.

"Good God! Mother! You gave her those clothes. I know you gave them to her. How could you have her arrested for stealing them?"

"You were having an affair, so I did something about it. I got rid of her. It will teach her a lesson not to step out of line. The little bitch! And it'll teach you a lesson too!"

William stared at his mother hardly believing what he was hearing. He stood up without saying a word, picked up his towel and went to the bathroom.

That morning Daniel was up very early. He had not slept thinking over the events of the past day. Sapphire had cried for hours before she finally fell asleep. He did not know if William had returned from Kingston during the night, but he wanted to see him right away. As it was light, he wentover to the great house, and looked into the garage for the car. The car was there, so he knew William had returned. He sat on the kitchen steps until the cook appeared to light the stove and make the breakfast. Together they drank tea and ate, discussing the events of the previous day. Soon voices could be heard coming from the house—angry voices in argument—that was something quite unusual. The cook and maid crept to the dining room to listen in and glean the latest developments, and when the shouts ended they quickly returned.

"De mistress and Master William catch fight! It 'bout Opal" they reported. This news confirmed Daniel's belief—that his daughter was indeed pregnant with Master William's child, and furthermore, that his mother had a hand in the arrest. The scandal gave the servants a great deal to talk about, and word spread quickly through the estate.

William and his mother sat down to breakfast almost at the same time. They did not speak one word to one another, and the maid was unable to get any new information. Harriet finished her breakfast and went to her room, and William went as usual to his office. He came out in an hour to make his usual tour about the property. Daniel had been waiting for him to appear. As William made his way to the stables he saw Daniel still sitting on the kitchen steps, but he did not say the usual "Good morning." Daniel did not speak either, but followed him closely along the pathway and into the stables. The horse was already saddled standing idly in its stall.

"'Mornin' Master William," Daniel started off when they entered the stall. "I mus' speak wid y'u."

William did not answer, and he did not turn to look at Daniel. He was sullen and angry. The morning row with his mother did not leave him in a pleasant mood, and it was as though he knew already just what Daniel wanted.

"It's 'bout me daughter, Opal. De police did tek her away las' night."

"Yes. I know about it."

"She is no tief, Master William, an' y'u should know dat. She never tek anyt'ing from y'ur mudder."

"Well, I don't know about that, Daniel. That is not something I know about."

"I t'ink dat y'u knows 'bout it. An I t'ink y'us knows more dan jus' dat." Daniel was beginning to press his case. Up to that point he had resolved to be calm and rational, but his employer's indifferent and off-handed attitude was beginning to anger him. It gave him the courage to speak his mind in much stronger terms.

"What are you saying, man?" asked William. "What do I have to do with your daughter's arrest?"

"Y'u an' me daughter was goin' togedder, Master William. Y'u knows w'at I'se talkin' 'bout Sur."

"Her trouble has nothing to do with me, Daniel."

"Y'u and me daughter was goin' togedder, and now she is to 'ave y'u chile. Y'u mus' tek' care of her now dat she is in trouble."

"You have a damned nerve talking to me like this. My mother told me what you said to her yesterday. I don't know where you got that from, but if you carry on with this I'll have you charged."

"How can y'u talk like dat, Master William? You tek me daughter, an' now y'u say y'u doan't business wid it?"

"I've nothing to do with your daughter's condition. She's in jail because she stole clothes from my mother, and there's nothing I can do about that."

"Yes Sur, y'u mus' tek care of her now. Y'u mus mek it right. Y'u is de farder."

"I'll do no such thing! You are trying to get money out of me! Do you know what they call that? It's called blackmail! It's a criminal offence, and I will have you charged! Your daughter is a thief!"

"Y'u is de damned tief!" Daniel blurted out, no longer able to contain his anger. He shouted, "Y'u is de damned tief—y'u tief de men dem wages—y'u mek baby wid me daughter an' y'u say y'u doan business! Dat is worse dan tief!"

"Get out! Get out of here, you're fired!—Get out!"

Daniel could no longer restrain himself. A volley of abuse and swear words were shouted at the young man. "Y'us goin pay fe dis," he threatened. "Y'u tink dat y'u can treat people like dirt, but y'us goin pay fe dis." He quickly made his way back to his house.

He had not calmed down when he reached his house. Sapphire was surprised to see him opening the gate and entering the house. She had never seen him in such a rage, but they sat and talked for several hours. He wanted to go to Port Antonio to see Opal, and find out what had happened to her, but he did not leave his yard.

In the late afternoon several workers came by. The word had spread very quickly through the estate. The argument with William in the stables had been overheard by several of the workers, and they had passed it on. The fact that he had accused William of 'stealing' from the workers reinforced their loyalty to him. Some who were inclined to view him as an extension of the owners' authority, now saw him as a strong supporter of their cause, and they were now a willing supporter. Furthermore, they wanted to enlist him as their leader for a showdown fight with the owners. They were talking about a work stoppage to force concessions. Daniel would not accept the role of strike leader, even though he was in full support of the action. He was no longer an employee and had nothing to gain by taking part. Besides that, his mind and thoughts were with his accused daughter, and he knew that it would take all of his time and efforts to see her released from jail. Also, it would affect his chances of finding employment on another plantation; he would be branded as a troublemaker.

Whatever the men did would be done with his full support but without his leadership.

The following morning, he borrowed a bicycle and rode to Port Antonio. Before he was on his way, he saw the men gathered in a small crowd near the produce sheds. They had acted out their frustrations and no work was being done on the plantation, and he gained some satisfaction from knowing that. As he rode past the men cheered and began to chant. "Dan is de man! Dan is de man!" He waved but he was far from being cheerful—in fact, he was in a desperate state of depression—so deep he had never experienced before—he could easily have sat down and cried—but he didn't—men did not cry—no matter what!

In Port Antonio, he went to the police station and the jail. The corporal allowed him to see Opal. That morning she had been taken before a Justice of the Peace, who decided that she should remain in jail until the next sitting of the courts, not even expected for at least six weeks, and she would be confined until that time. The news was bad, but little that could be done to change it. He talked to the corporal, gave him money hoping that it would make his daughter's time there a little easier, not that he had great expectations of that. Nevertheless, it should make it easier for him to see her and bring in food and anything else that she needed. Leaving was heartbreak for them both.

Daniel arrived back at the plantation in the mid-afternoon. The workers were gathered in a crowd at the front steps to the great house. William was on the veranda his mother beside him. He was speaking to the men in a vain effort to have them return to work. Daniel dismounted on the fringe of the crowd. There were angry exchanges in progress between workers and employers—rather than getting things settled, matters were getting worse. Soon he was seen and again the chant went up, "Dan is de man! Dan is de man!"

He did not want to get involved and he did not stay long even though he was vitally interested in the outcome, and wanted to take part in protests. His position was precarious enough—William might call the police and have him charged for instigating a riot if matters got out of hand, and given the mood of the men that could easily happen.

Several days passed and the strike continued. The days extended into weeks and still there was no settlement. Productivity for the year was at serious risk and little if any fruit would be shipped out. The strikes had spread to other plantations and many estates across the island had ceased operations. But some workers were facing severe hardships; everyone was affected, and after a month or so without work, some men were talking about returning to the fields. With little work to be found locally, Daniel had been extending his search further and further away from home, and still there was nothing to be found. Soon he realized that if he intended to continue working it would be necessary for him to go away, but that was a contentious issue with his wife, who ignored the real problems, happy for him to spend his days about the house on their property. For his part though, the money owed to Master William was constantly on his mind, and he worried about the action his late employer might take if the debt was not paid. He knew that it had to be repaid and it was important for him to find some kind of work.

CHAPTER 20

Since his daughter's arrest and the onset of the strikes, life had become increasingly difficult—it seemed to be just too much to bear. Daniel and his family were, for the time being, in considerably better circumstances than were most of the other workers, except for the fact that when the strike ended, as it would some day, he would not be going back to work. The family could survive with what they produced from his little piece of land, but ultimately, he must find work somewhere, perhaps away from home—even in another part of the country. Harriet and William Henderson, he knew, would see to it that he was not hired locally, and there was the money to be repaid. The date for his daughter's trial was several weeks away, and he could not be away during that time—both he and his wife wanted to be witnesses, and he was desperately hoping she would be freed. He had to wait for the trial before he left to search for work, and the strain of waiting was taking its toll on the family—he held his wife more than partly responsible for their daughter's predicament, and they quarreled frequently, sometimes violently.

The day of the trial finally arrived. It was an important day in the town, with many cases to be heard, and a large crowd, mostly curious spectators, gathered about the courthouse. Daniel and Sapphire appeared at the courthouse several hours early, hoping to see their daughter before the trial, but they were not allowed to talk to her and so joined the crowd on the front steps to the courthouse. They were not there very long before Harriet and William Henderson arrived in a car driven by their chauffeur. As the car approached a sudden silence fell upon the crowd, and all eyes were on them as they disembarked and entered the courthouse. Many in the crowd were aware of the circumstances surrounding Opal's arrest, and they had already taken sides.

The judge had arrived from Kingston the previous day and had taken rooms at the hotel up on the hill near to the Courthouse. It was expected that he would be there for at least a week until all the local cases had been dealt with. He finally made his appearance descending the steps from the hotel accompanied by the Clerk of the Court and a uniformed policeman. The judge was decked in his red-trimmed black robes and wig, and it cast an air of seriousness over the entire gathering. He was a somewhat gaunt, sinewy, serious looking, middle-aged Englishman, seen as most likely to dispense justice untempered by mercy, and neither was he seen likely to allow any accused the benefit of doubts. He quickly made his way into the courthouse and disappeared inside. The crowd followed filling vacant benches and standing in the isles against the walls. The witnesses were given no preference in seating, and some were forced to stand outside until called.

Major Henry Thomson was among the spectators. He had somehow entered the court room unnoticed, and had not attracted much attention by his presence even though he was known by many in the crowd. William and his mother sat together on a bench near the front row. Some thought it strange that Henry did not sit among the white people or with the owners of the Manor House Estate, and that he sat amongst the mostly black spectators. Harriet spotted him and drew William's attention to the fact.

"Why do you think he is sitting there?" she said in a whisper. "He's mixed up with all those black people," she commented. "He is just a common man—he's no better than they are."

"Yes, Mother."

"He's just a vulgar, dirty man," she continued. "He sleeps with nigger women! That's why his wife left him!"

Since William's return from England Harriet had recovered from her feelings of desperate loneliness, and since she did not need Henry's company her dislike and hatred for him had intensified. She was not about to miss an opportunity to compare her son's affair with his lifestyle, and to show her disgust.

Opal's trial was not the first on the docket, but when called, it was over in less than an hour. The prisoner was charged and Harriet was called to the witness stand. She identified the garments found in Opal's possession as being hers, and asserted that they were stolen. The police gave evidence to the effect that the garments had been seized from the house of the accused. Sapphire took the witness stand to say that the clothes had been given to their daughter on two separate occasions, and that Opal had been told not to tell anyone about the gifts. She asserted that the articles were given, not stolen. The Judge directed the jury to disregard her evidence because she had no direct knowledge of how the garments had been acquired. In the witness box Opal was nervous and constantly on the verge of tears as she related her version of events. In the end she tearfully begged the Judge not to send her to jail. It was a moving scene and many in the courtroom voiced their sympathy, which prompted the clerk to call for silence.

The judge summed up the evidence for the benefit of the jury: "What are the indisputable facts of this case?" he asked rhetorically. "The missing articles of clothing were identified as being those of Mrs. Henderson. That is a fact. The articles were sized from the home of the accused, and that is a fact. The accused states that her employer gave them to her, but her employer denies that to be so. Who should the jury believe? Should they take the word of a well-respected property owner, or should they accept the word of a servant accused of theft and facing the prospect of jail? The answer," he proclaimed, "was pretty obvious—It's a matter of common sense!"

He commented further, that the suggestion of the defense witnesses and from the defendant herself that Mrs. Harriet Henderson had lied on the witness stand was quite inconceivable and could not reasonably be ascribed to a person of Mrs. Henderson's position. He declared that the motives the defense witnesses ascribed for that were utterly beyond belief, and directed that the jury ignore those statements. Finally, he directed the jury to bring in the appropriate verdict, and they dutifully complied.

"Opal Hutchings," the judge's words echoed ominously through the hushed courtroom. "You have been found guilty of stealing from your employer, and you persist in saying that you are not guilty. You have shown no remorse for your dishonest and criminal actions, and I find that reprehensible. Furthermore, you have concocted an incredulous story that is clearly a slander on the reputation of your employer, and I find that particularly reprehensible. You betrayed the trust that your employer placed in you by stealing her property. For your criminal actions you should serve a sentence of five years at hard labor. But, you are a young woman and this is your first offence, and I am inclined to be lenient. You shall serve three years less one day at hard labor. Your time to be served in the Kingston Penitentiary." And then to the bailiff, "Take her away."

The tearful, sobbing woman was taken from the court to the jail cells in the police station.

Immediately on the conclusion of the case, Harriet and William hurriedly left the court and headed for their car. As they left their departure was watched in silence, but when they descended the steps to the street, murmurs quickly became shouts of abuse from an openly hostile crowd. The crowd closed about the car as the door slammed shut and the chauffeur started the motor. Several people milling about in the road delayed their escape as the crowd pressed closer, shouting abuse at the occupants through the windows and rocking the vehicle back and forth. The car leapt forward only to be stopped once again and the rocking resumed. The harassment continued for several minutes with the car inching its way along, until finally the roadway was clear and the vehicle sped off. Harriet sat huddled in the back seat, terrified by the open hostility of the crowd. William too, was fearful that the violence would get out of hand, and he moved towards his mother to sit in the middle of the back seat away from the open window.

Opal's distraught parents waited all day in the rear of the courthouse for a chance to see their daughter, but that was denied them by the corporal acting beyond his required authority, and in spite of the money given to him earlier. The prisoners would not be transferred to Kingston for the next few days at least, and not until all the criminal cases had been concluded. If they wished to see their daughter they would have to return again the next day or the day after. Reluctantly, sadly they decided to return home. At the end of the week they were once again at the police station requesting to see their daughter. The Black Mariah was still parked at the back of the building, a chilling sight to them both, full of foreboding and depressing thoughts,—the uncertainty that faced their eldest daughter. Three other prisoners were brought out from the cells and placed in the vehicle, they were allowed no more than five short minutes to make arrangements to write, and when the baby came along, to care for it until her release. And then it was a few seconds for a tearful goodbye. The last they saw of her for the next seven months were the few moments it took her to climb aboard the vehicle on the long journey to the Kingston Penitentiary.

The day they took their daughter away, Sapphire did not sleep that night through. She lay awake sobbing, and as the morning hours approached, she fell into a restless sleep. By the morning the sobbing gave way to vengeful anger, and she swore to her husband that Harriet Henderson would live to regret her actions. There was no plan, no strategy, and indeed, it would be virtually impossible to extract revenge against the owner of the Estate, yet she swore that she would have justice. Throughout the day she talked of nothing else but revenge, until her husband had heard it once too often. He lost his patience, swore at his wife, and again they quarreled.

In the evening Sapphire cooked saltfish and yam for their supper. They ate in silence without speaking to each other, and their two younger daughters, sensing the trouble between their parents, kept the silence too. Eating quickly the girls left the table leaving the adults to finish their meal.

Finally, Sapphire broke the silence. "A'h knows w'at I'se goine do."

Her husband did not answer. The impatience and frustration that he had felt for his wife had left him; he was weary and almost resigned to the situation. He acknowledged her statement with a curious expression; if she had a plan he might as well know about it.

"I'se goine to bu'n down dem house, a'n dem wi'd de house!"

"Dat is jus' crazy." Daniel did not give this idea any credence—it was beyond being practical, so he dismissed it immediately.

"Well, dat is w'at I'se goine do. I'se goine bu'n dem up in dem bed."

"If y'u do dat dey will put y'u in prison, a'n dey will hang me fe it. Dey will t'ink I do it and dey will hang me. If y'u want te see me go to the gallows, den bun down dem house!"

The truth of that assessment made Sapphire pause, and she did not say anything for quite some time. Then after some deep thought she spoke again.

"I'se goine put obiah on de w'homan. I'se goine to go to de obiah man an' te'k out a curse on de w'homan."

"Dat is fe no use." Daniel said impatiently, once again he began to be angry with his wife, "Dat never do good."

"But w'at we fe do, den? De w'homan is a wicked w'homan, an' wickedness is fe her. I'se goine fine de obiah man, an' pay 'im."

Her statement had a note of finality about it that would have been useless to argue against, and he had no wish to engage his wife at that time, even though he knew in his heart that obiah would not solve their problems. At least this plan would have fewer consequences if ever it was put into effect, and therefore it was the better of the two. And if it made her feel better then he would not stop her. Even so, it also gave him some measure of satisfaction and hope, and above all, hope was what they lacked most of all.

CHAPTER 21

Harriet was very pleased with herself. Pleased that she was rid of the despised servant girl, that the woman was being punished for the affair with her son, and would be out of her sight for at least three years—enough time for people to forget—she hoped. Nevertheless, it was not a battle won without cost. Her scheme had precipitated the costly strikes, and following the trial it was common knowledge that her son was accused of fathering the woman's expected child. As the days of the strike increased in number, she became increasingly nervous at the crowds that sometimes gathered near the estate. She had seen angry crowds before, but she had not been the focus of their anger, and it was especially upsetting to now find herself in that position. Sometimes in the late afternoon she could hear in the distance the shouts of the crowds as they quarreled amongst themselves. There had been violence on other estates in other parts of the island, and she was worried that it might happen here.

On the day of the trial it had taken a great deal of determination to present herself at the courthouse, even though she knew that she had to be there. And it took courage for her to face the crowd that she knew would be there. William too, had found it stressful, especially outside the courthouse. It was all still visible in her mind—the open hostility of the crowd—almost being prevented from leaving—and the rocking of the vehicle had terrified her. By the time she arrived at the Manor House Estates, she had considered more than once that the best thing she could do would be to return to Kingston until the strikes were settled.

In the next few days nothing happened that would have made her put that plan into effect immediately. William carried on as usual, inspecting the property, and seeing to it that the lone gardener tended the animals and that the buildings were secure. He had taken to riding his horse with his rifle resting in his lap, but there had been no need for those precautions. The household servants were not on strike, and they went about their duties in the usual manner. Fortunately, Mrs. Barnham was in Kingston during the weeks before and after the trial, and was unaware of the rumours circulating about her neighbour's son. Harriet and William had thus been spared that degree of embarrassment. As soon as Mrs. Barnham returned, Harriet paid several visits to Chivers Estate to discuss events and future plans. There had been no movement towards a settlement, and they agreed to continue until there was an offer from the workers, however long that would take.

The following Saturday morning, Harriet, not wanting to expose herself so soon after the trial decided that she would not to go to the market. Instead, she sent the cook with the chauffeur, and the shopping was done without event. By the next Saturday she thought that enough time had passed, and it should be safe to go as usual. It was a miscalculation on Harriet's part—she had not been forgotten—the resentment towards her was just as intense, and it only required her presence for people to be reminded. In the market several vendors refused to answer her questions regarding their wares, and they pointedly refused to sell to her. One woman picked up her basket, turned her back and strode away, leaving Harriet embarrassed and standing alone. But she persisted, determined to make some purchases. Soon enough she realized the futility of the effort, and as she tried to leave a small crowd of market women at the entrance blocked her exit. There was no physical contact, but there were shouted insults and abuse hurled at her from all directions. One particularly vocal woman stood directly in front of her, their faces almost touching, the woman shouting all the while. It ended when the woman turned her back and strode triumphantly away, the cheers of the crowd echoing in her ears. The cook was close by but she did not attempt to intervene, and Harriet was once again unnerved. At that point she made up her mind to return to Kingston.

The market expedition had been a dismal failure, and she instructed the chauffeur and the cook to prepare for her return to Kingston early in the week. By mid-day on Sunday, her bags were packed and placed in the car, ready for the early departure the next day.

CHAPTER 22

The Maroon came and went like a ghost in the night. There was never a hint that he was about to appear, and then suddenly, there he was. And when he left, no one seemed to notice that he was gone—he just evaporated, like a puddle of water after a heavy rain. As a result no one knew when he was about to appear or when he left, and the relief that some felt at his leaving, was never evident for a day or two. In the dark of the night the Maroon was often out alone, making sudden appearances in unexpected places. He seemed to be on some kind of mission, but no one knew what his mission might be, and if he knew, he never told. While he was about, a strange quiet seemed to take over as though a spell had been cast. Few would walk out alone at night, and most made certain to be home before it was dark, never straying far from a light or company of some sort. It was widely suspected that he was working 'obiah' and at the very least was consorting with duppies! Little children were kept in order, obedient and polite with the threat "de obiah man—'e is out dere—'e niam bad pickney, an 'e goine come and get y'u!"

Difficulties with the law were not new to him. Little bits about his life had ebbed out over the years, and what was not fact had been invented and garnished with fantastic tales—how one full moon night he was credited with making the moon disappear—turning it into a glowing red spot, high in a cloudless sky! But the facts were that he was a convicted felon. He killed a man in a fight and luckily escaped the gallows to serve only ten years hard labor in the stone quarries at Rock Fort. He had twice been arrested in Port Antonio by the corporal, but his stays in jail had been brief. On those occasions his prison past was introduced as evidence against him in a futile attempt to prejudice the Justice of the Peace.

He was by any standard, an odd looking man; his face was quite round—like a full moon. His nose and mouth were small which made his face and head seem that much larger and rounder. His head was covered with a mass of thick curly, very black hair. His eyes were deep-set, piercing and penetrating; two glowing, glistening spots of light against the jet blackness of his skin. He was not a big man, but very muscular. His neck was short and thick where visible, giving the appearance that his head was directly attached to his stocky chest.

He clothed himself with an array of various garments bequeathed or gathered wherever possible. Even though his dress was unusual it did not attract much attention, he always seemed to be wearing far more clothes than necessary—sometimes two coats over two pairs of trousers, all with numerous little pockets, natural or created, to hold all kinds of small articles—tokens—and morsels of food. Around his neck, mostly hidden from view by his clothing, he wore a necklace made of small dried bones. Every now and again he would remove a bone and grant it to a 'patron' as a keepsake for some favor. His clothing reeked of tobacco smoke from the very strong 'donkey rope' tobacco to which he was addicted and always carried, and the fumes oozed from every crease. Although his odor was decidedly objectionable he never attempted to lessen it; to him it was a distinct enhancement—it repelled not only people, but also the fleas, lice and bed bugs to which he occasionally came in close contact. He carried a thick, club-like walking stick, and a small crocus bag tied around with a long piece of thin rope that dangled over his shoulder.

Where he lived and how he survived no one knew, but he seemed to do very well on the generosity and goodwill of the public, somewhat fearful of his powers, and ever eager to bestow a meal and shelter for the night. As far as anyone knew, he had no close relationships with anyone, and he never showed any interest in developing any. Nevertheless, he had enemies, and at the head of that list was the police corporal stationed in Port Antonio. From time to time, on one pretext or another, the corporal had arrested and jailed him for a night or more, only to have him set free by a Justice of the Peace in the morning. Needless to say, the Maroon did not take kindly to these detentions, and their mutual dislike for one another was well known. The corporal made much of those occasions, making sure that everyone knew he had jailed the Maroon, in spite of his mystical powers, for which he showed the greatest contempt. The corporal hoped that this open disregard for the powers of darkness would enhance his image and standing in the town, and at the same time diminish those of the sorcerer. In point of fact, it did little to lessen the awe and reverence with which the Maroon was regarded.

Several weeks after the trial and conviction of the headman's daughter, the Maroon made an appearance, and as usual, he arrived unexpectedly, on the outskirts of Chivers Estate. He did not venture on to the property until he had been invited—on an earlier occasion he had been driven off by an irate Marjory Thomson who had little patience or liking for the man. Not wishing a repeat of that scene, he had kept his distance. Marjory, of course, was not there, having left the island many months earlier, and soon he received his usual welcome from Constance. She however, kept her distance having a healthy fear of the man, limiting her contacts with him to a distant conversation, but always making sure that he was well fed, and that he knew just who was responsible for the meal he was enjoying.

"Miss Constance send dis fe' y'u," the maid was instructed to say, whenever he was handed a plate.

As the news of his arrival spread, Sapphire sent word and two days later he arrived at the gate very early in the morning. Sapphire was up and about when she noticed the man at the gate. Not recognizing him in the early morning light, she went to investigate and quickly brought him into the yard. As the rest of the family awoke she prepared tea and boiled cornmeal for their morning meal.

The Maroon was not a man given to much conversation, but Sapphire on the other hand was never short of words. In considerable detail she related the history of events leading to her daughter's three-year prison sentence. They were sitting in the back yard under a breadfruit tree when she divulged her reasons for wanting to see him, but he did not show much enthusiasm or interest. He did not explain his reluctance, but evidently the Henderson family was somewhat out of his reach and it would be a difficult curse to place. Sapphire was persistent, and the offer of money was a persuasive argument, and he finally agreed, accepting her proposition.

It would take a few days and in the meantime advance payment must be made. Sapphire returned to her room to fetch the few shillings in loose coins that she had been saving. They were not to be placed in his hand—their hands were not to touch while payment was being made. He pointed to the ground between them and with his stick he drew a circle in the dust. The coins were placed in the circle and covered over with dirt where they remained until the bargain was struck. When the talk was over and agreement reached, he slowly uncovered the coins gathered them up, wrapped them in a soiled piece of cloth and placed them in a pocket. He did not stay there that night. In the early afternoon after again being fed, he picked up his bundle and wandered off.

Harriet remained in Kingston for over a month during which time William made periodic visits to the Estate. Much of the unrest had subsided, and even though the strike was still officially on, the initial enthusiasm had waned. A number of the men had made their individual peace and returned to work, and there was open talk of a full return to work even without an agreement. It was clear that very soon the strike would be over. The estate owners had vanquished the movement without making any concessions whatsoever, but even a token concession would have done much to relieve the bitterness and resentment that lingered long afterwards, and would eventually come back to haunt them. Finally, the men let it be known that they were ready to go back to work, and the news reached Kingston. Shortly thereafter, mother and son were back at the Estate, triumphant in their victory, and ready to ensure strict working conditions.

Sapphire had been patient during their absence, but eager for their return. The weeks went by and there was no sign of a curse—there was nothing to show that the contract had been fulfilled and that the Henderson household was cursed. Sapphire did not see the Maroon again—the man had taken her money and disappeared, and that, she reasoned was not much of a trick! Still she was patient and hopeful, but as the weeks passed with the Hendersons back, she became very impatient indeed. Daniel, of course knew about the agreement even though he had not been party to it—it was the business of his wife alone, and not his concern. Sapphire began to talk to her husband about what she saw to be a broken agreement. The more she talked about it the angrier she became, but Daniel was non-commitment, and he did not remind her that he had told her not to waste their money.

Another man now filled Daniel's former position, and there was no prospect for employment at the Manor House Estate. In his search for work, Daniel went over to Chivers Estate to see Henry Thomson. There had always been a good relationship with Thomson and this had not changed because of the strike and the trouble with William, if anything, it had strengthened. Thomson put the question to Mrs. Barnham, who had more important things on her mind; she was promoting her daughter Bridget and encouraging an engagement with William. She was not about to employ a man that had been fired by her prospective son-in-law, even though she had some admiration for Daniel. If Thomson wanted, he could give him jobs from time to time, and make use of him on a non-permanent basis, as long as the Hendersons did not get to know about it—if they found out that would end it. Thus it was that Daniel was able to find employment and earn some money—not a lot—barely enough to keep the household together, but better the little than nothing.

Several months later Sapphire got a long delayed letter from her imprisoned daughter. The news it brought was not bad considering her condition; she had been transferred to lighter duties to await the birth of her baby in the next few weeks. But why had her mother not answered her first letter sent weeks earlier? She had not received an answer, and, she pointed out, that sending letters cost money, and because she did not have any money, she had to borrow it—and she also had to repay it—so please send three pence when writing. If her mother sent three pence, she explained, she could repay her loan, keep a penny for her next letter, and buy four Paradise Plums. Little did Sapphire know that the first letter, addressed 'Care Of the Manor House Estate,' had been delivered into the hands of Harriet Henderson, and that it had been read and promptly destroyed. Sapphire sat down immediately to write but soon gave up the effort—she was not used to writing and found it tiring. She proposed to have her husband finish the job. The letter remained unfinished on the table, even though every day she read it and made small additions or corrections.

Several days later there was a disturbance at the Estate house. The trouble this time was with the servants, and it began early in the morning. The maid as usual had attempted to enter the pantry, but ascending the steps to the porch she had found a string tied across the two posts at the top baring the way up the stairs. Suspended on the string were two 'hex' dolls impaled with several long, sharp Macker thorns. The maid would not open the door nor enter the house, and neither would anyone else. The word spread quickly, and soon there was a gathering—half-a-dozen or more—talking excitedly, pointing and examining the 'obiah,' but none would cross the line. These were clear signs of a curse upon the occupants of the house!

It was an hour or so later that Harriet was up and about demanding to know why her breakfast was not ready, and why the maids had not appeared. She opened the pantry door from inside, and for a few moments stood motionless and speechless. First she was angry and then very frightened. She was still a 'country girl,' and from early childhood had been told about the power of witchcraft. Even though she professed not to believe in its powers she was not about to tempt fate and remove or even touch anything.

William was soon on the scene examining the evidence carefully. He proposed to remove it, but was prevented from doing so by his agitated mother. They confided together and decided to send Raymond, the yardman on his bicycle to fetch the policeman from Port Antonio. The policeman was some time coming and arrived after mid-day. He collected the evidence and removed the string. He would be investigating the matter, he assured Harriet, and would certainly report back to her. His first suspect was Daniel and his family; they had cause, and he paid them a visit immediately. They all were surprised and very interested in the development. They asked him more questions than he asked of them, so much so, that the policeman decided that they could not be responsible. He ended up empty-handed but still determined to find the culprit. After he left, Sapphire could not contain her elation. She burst into hysterical laughter and for fully fifteen minutes almost could not control herself, ending up with the tears flowing down her cheeks, laughing and crying at the same time. At last, the contract has been filled. It was the greatest day that she had had since her daughter was taken away, and all she had to do now was to wait for the curse to take effect.

CHAPTER 23

A month went by without any sign of a curse, but Sapphire did not give up hope. She imagined that some fatal disaster would befall the Henderson household at any time, and every day she made inquiries of any and all that had daily contact with the Manor House. One morning her attention was diverted by a man at her gate standing astride a bicycle ringing its bell impatiently. It was the postman from Port Antonio with an official looking brown envelope, "On His Majesty's Service," which had to be delivered personally and signed for. He had ridden all the way from Port Antonio to deliver the letter, and he had lost his way several times, he was hot and thirsty, and not in a good mood. Nervously Sapphire took the letter, signed her name and sensing the man's mood offered him something to drink, which he rudely refused, saying that he would rather sip from the spring. Sapphire, impatient to know what the letter was about, retreated to the house. Daniel was at work, but as the letter was addressed to them both, she carefully slit it open. The letter, type written, came from the Kingston Penitentiary to inform them that their daughter had given birth to a healthy baby girl on the 14th. of September, and that both mother and daughter were in good health. The letter further advised them that there were no facilities in the Penitentiary for the care of children born there beyond a period of one month. The said child must be removed by the 15th. of October or it would be placed in the Government Orphanage.

After reading the letter over several times, Sapphire remembered her still unfinished letter, and she immediately set about completing it. There was so much that she wanted to know—how was her daughter surviving? What did the child look like? Was she a big child? And many other questions were racing through her mind. She was energized by the news. Excited! She would go to Kingston as soon as possible, but she must finish the letter first.

When Daniel returned home it was already dark and mosquitoes were everywhere making life miserable. He was also excited, relieved and pleased to know that his daughter was well despite her ordeal. "T'ank God." He breathed a silent prayer of thanks.

It was only the matter of fetching the child from Kingston, and they began to make plans. Sapphire wanted to go immediately, but Daniel felt it was better to leave it until nearer the 15th. of October. After all the child was only little more than ten days old, and he felt that the new mother should be with her child for as long as possible, and even a month was too short a time for them to be together. His wife finally agreed, and they continued to make plans. Later Daniel sat at the table to complete the letter. He would ride into Port Antonio the next day, buy a three-penny money order and mail it with the letter.

Early the next morning he borrowed a bicycle and was back at work shortly after lunchtime. His work at Chivers Estate had been going very well and he had kept out of Mrs. Barnham's sight even though she would not have caused him any trouble—it was just as well, though, not to be seen. William had been to Chivers several times unannounced, but he had not seen Daniel.

When October arrived it brought with it the rainy season and heavy rain that fell incessantly. Sapphire planned to leave for Kingston two days before the deadline in mid-October, pick up the baby and return immediately. A week later they decided to advance the departure because of the weather. Sapphire packed up what clothes she needed, food for the journey, baby clothes, keepsakes and clothes from earlier times, all freshly washed and carefully packed. She found a small baby's rattle, a gift to her last child, now broken but still with its rattle.

On the morning of her expected departure the rain was exceptionally heavy. Nevertheless, they gathered up the bundle prepared for the journey and made their way through the rivulets and puddles out to the road. They covered themselves with pieces of old sailcloth to ward off the downpour, and sheltered under a tree as best they could, keeping a sharp eye out for the bus. The drivers habitually sounded their horns approaching every bend in the road, but with the rain so heavy, they well may not have heard it. An hour passed and still there was no sign of the bus, in fact there had been no traffic whatsoever. The noon hour came and went, and they were hungry, wet through and cold. By early afternoon they concluded that the bus must have broken down, and decided to wait no longer, but try again the next day.

By morning the rain had eased somewhat, and again they waited anxiously for the bus to come into sight. Finally the blaring horn was heard, and the vehicle appeared. Daniel stood in the middle of the road and waved his arms until he was sure the driver had seen him. It slowed to a halt. He paid the fare to Kingston, Sapphire boarded, and was soon lost from sight. In their brief conversation the driver told him there had been washouts on the road, and many roads, he said, were barely passable. The bus to Port Antonio took the long route to Kingston going through Morant Bay along the coastal road. It was a much longer journey, but at least it did not have the mountains to contend with, and was perhaps, considering the weather, the safer route.

The next two days seemed to take forever to pass as Daniel waited impatiently for his wife to return. Still, he was not sure that the road conditions would allow her return as expected, or that the bus would be on time—the bus had a timetable, but seldom kept to it. There would be little gained by standing on the roadside at the expected arrival time, so after having eaten an early supper, he took a lantern and made his way out to the road. When it got dark he lit the lantern and placed it beside him so that it could be seen some distance down the road. He was not concerned that the bus would not stop. Sapphire would have instructed the driver and the Manor House stop was well known.

He sat on a large stone resting against the bank that rose sharply at the side of the road. A cold breeze was picking up strength as it usually did after nightfall, but better a cold wind than the mosquitoes; at least he would be able to rest without having to constantly whisk them away. Some time after nine o'clock he was roused by the blaring sound of the horn. He hurriedly rose, picked up the lantern and held it high above his head. The bus slowed and stopped. It was loaded to overflowing with weary passengers; half-a-dozen passengers had to dismount before Sapphire could reach the door with the child bundled in her arms. Several passengers obligingly passed her small package out to her. Daniel took the child as she reached the doorway, and she retrieved her possessions. They thanked the driver and waived him on his way.

Even with the lantern held close to the child's face Daniel could not see what lay wrapped in the blanket. It was very cool with the strengthening 'norther,' and they hurried home. At home he placed the baby on the table as his younger daughters crowded around to see the newest member of the family. Sapphire took charge and unwrapped the blanket. She picked up the child, cradled in her arms, and showed them the little treasure she brought back. The baby that she revealed left them open-mouthed and speechless—she was the most beautiful little creature they had ever seen—or ever would see for that matter. The child's complexion was almost white, the hue of rich cream! Her face was the image of a little china doll, fine, light curly brown hair, very fine features and a hint of oriental eyes—a most beautiful infant if ever there was one. Sapphire and her daughters could not contain themselves with their astonishment and admiration, and Daniel too, was almost overcome with amazement—he could not find words to express his feelings!

When the initial excitement had passed and the two daughters were rivaling each other for the privilege of cuddling and feeding the child, Sapphire sat at the table to eat her supper. She was very tired and hungry not having eaten since the early morning. The journey from Kingston had been long and exhausting, and now that it was over and she was safely in her home, the effects were being felt. It had been a strenuous three days and she was ready to collapse into bed. Daniel sat opposite and nibbled at some dry bread. Between mouthfuls Sapphire related the events of the last two days. Opal, in spite of her confinement, was managing well in prison, and she was looking forward to getting back home. Their parting had been very sad as the young mother kissed her child goodbye— the baby would be nearly three years old the next time she would lay eyes on her. She would be a big girl and would not know her natural mother.

Daniel had thought a great deal about the child during the previous weeks, and he had very mixed feelings. He did not know how he would react to the child of his previous and much despised employer—even though at the same time she was also his daughter's child. Should he reject the child, being the illegitimate daughter of a man whose mother was as wicked as the Devil himself? Or should he welcome the innocent child, as a grandfather should? All these thoughts had plagued him long before laying eyes on the little infant, but he had not thought about how he would feel after seeing the baby. There was no hiding it though, Sapphire and his daughters were so proud of her. Sapphire was so filled with pride and excitement that it almost removed the tragic events that preceded her birth—to her they almost did not matter any more—having such a beautiful grandchild was more than compensation.

Daniel was trying to sort out those emotions as they sat talking, but he did not raise the subject to his wife—this was something that he would have to adjust to by himself. It was near midnight when the baby had been fed and put to bed and they were able to get to sleep.

For the next few weeks' life settled into a quiet routine. One evening as they sat at the table, Sapphire produced the Birth Certificate that she brought back with her from Kingston. In the excitement of the moment, she had forgotten to show it to her husband, and he examined it curiously. On the line "Name of father:" were the words "William James Henderson." For a few moments the significance of the name did not enter his consciousness. He read it over again slowly, thinking. Then he began to get angry—he would have preferred it to be blank, or "Not known," even if that implied illegitimacy. Again he read it over thinking—everyone knew who the father was, and here it was typed on an official document and registered. He reached for his indelible pencil and moistened the point; he was about to scratch through the words and write in "Not known," but he stopped and thought about it again. Maybe that was something his daughter should decide, and maybe that was the way she wanted it. He decided to leave it as it was. Of one thing he was quite certain, if the registrar had known who the father was, the name would not have been placed there. And he was glad that he had not removed it. "Dat is dat!" he said to himself with some satisfaction. On thinking it over, to some degree it had righted a wrong.

When he came home in the late afternoons he often took the baby in his lap, sat in a chair and played with her. "W'at we goine call dis little t'ing?" he said to his wife, holding up the child to his face, looking into her eyes and shaking her playfully until she smiled back at him. "We 'af to fine a name fe'er."

"Opal mus' name her." Sapphire answered. "It fe'er chile, an' it fe'er to name her."

"Did she tell y'u w'at te name her? She doan't giv' y'u a name?"

"No. She doan't say nuttin'."

"Well we mus' write and get de name. It will be a lang time for her to be wi'd out a name. De time is still two years and six mont's before she come back. Dat is too long to wait. Y'u doan't t'ink so?" And turning again to the child, "Meantime, I will call y'u 'Pretty Precious.'"

Somehow the name stuck. Everyone agreed—the little baby was very pretty and very, very precious—the name was fitting. Without the benefit of a christening, her name became Precious!

CHAPTER 24

For the next few weeks the family went through a process of adjusting to the presence of a new baby in the household. It was an easy adjustment though, as everyone was so anxious to attend to the baby's needs, and she was seldom left alone even for a minute. Soon enough they fell into a daily routine: the two daughters, Jewel and Ruby, would take turns during the day, Sapphire would oversee everything, and Daniel, when he returned from work, would pick up the baby, sit in a chair and play with her for an hour or more until there were more pressing things to be done. As the weeks went by, Sapphire would take the child in her arms and accompanied by one or other of her daughters, set out to walk towards the coastal road, cross to the beaches and sit under a tree. Towards the early afternoon, she would return in time to cook the evening supper. At first she was careful to avoid the pathway leading to the Manor House Estate, and was careful not to trespass onto Estate property.

As time went by and she had not seen either Harriet or William, Sapphire became somewhat careless and occasionally crossed through the property to reach the beach by a shorter route. She did not at that time want to be seen by either Harriet or William, but the baby had grown and was getting prettier every day. She was so very proud of her new grandchild that she wanted to show her off to everyone, especially to her friends and acquaintances. Such a lovely little baby cancelled the negative aspects surrounding her existence, and was more than compensation for their suffering. One morning she decided to run the risk of being seen and decided to take the child into the Manor House Estate itself, and show her off to the servants and workers there.

Towards mid-morning, she packed up her usual bundle, and with Jewel beside her, Precious in arms, they took the pathway to the Manor. It was a fine, cool morning, and along the way they met several of the workers who stopped to talk and look at the new grandchild. When they were seen in the distance, some of the servants rushed out excitedly, anxious to have a look. They were ushered towards the kitchen area with everyone gathered around to hold the baby, ask questions, give their opinions and lots of advice. In their minds, there was no doubt that the father was William Henderson, and indeed that matter could hardly be contested in the light of the living evidence. In the excitement time slipped by unnoticed, and they continued talking and gossiping for the rest of the morning. Suddenly a hush fell upon the gathering, and quickly one by one, the maids slipped away leaving only Sapphire holding the baby, and Jewel standing by. The mistress of the house had suddenly appeared on the scene.

Harriet was as surprised as was Sapphire. Sapphire quickly stood up clutching the child to her and looking straight at the other woman. Jewel stood by, awkwardly and nervously picking at her finger nails not knowing what next to expect. In appearance Jewel could easily be mistaken for her older sister, even though there was over a years difference in their ages and other differences were noticeable too. But Harriet had mistaken Jewel for the baby's mother, who she thought to be still in jail. For several moments no one spoke. Harriet stood still looking at both the women in turn, she took in little breaths as though she was about to say something, but each time she didn't, and no words came out.

"What are you doing here?" she demanded, finally. "What are you doing here?"

Sapphire did not answer—she did not know what to say, and resolved not to answer at all. She hurriedly picked up the baby's sheet that had been placed on a stool, and prepared to leave.

"What are you doing here?—You dirty thieving bitch!" Harriet screamed as anger replaced her initial astonishment. "What are you doing here?—Get off my property!"

The abuse aroused Sapphire. No woman had the right to speak to her like that—not even Harriet Henderson!

"Who y'u call thieving bitch?" she shot back, taking a step closer. "Y'u is dutty thieving bitch!"

This was head-on confrontation, and Harriet was not used to being on the receiving end. The step forward was seen as very threatening, and she took a step backward. Quickly she turned around to make sure that her way was clear for a fast retreat if necessary. Sapphire pressed her advantage.

"Y'u call y'u own flesh an' blood dutty? Look 'pon y'u own flesh an' blood— Look whooman—Look 'pon y'u flesh an' blood!" She held the baby up towards Harriet's face pushing the baby nearer.

Harriet looked at the child for a few moments not speaking, just looking. In the few seconds she adsorbed the full significance of the baby's fair complexion, and the likeness to her son's features registered quickly in her mind.

"Look 'pon y'u gran'chile, whooman. —Look 'pon y'u son baby.... Y'u wan' tek her? Y'u can hold 'er. —Here, tek 'er—she y'u own flesh an' blood!" And Sapphire pushed the baby even closer.

Harriet recoiled, unnerved, but a few moments later she regained some of her composure.

"You get out of here," she ordered. "Get out of here and don't ever come back!" She needed some support and she needed to establish her authority; she turned and shouted for reinforcement.

"Raymond!" she shouted. "Raymond! Come here at once!"

Raymond was the yardman. He had been hiding in the background and he dutifully appeared. "Yes, Mum."

Turning to Jewel, "What are you doing out of jail? When did you get out of jail? You dirty thief! If I ever see you on my property again you will be back in jail!" and turning to the yardman, "Raymond, throw these people off my property. Make sure they don't come back!"

Raymond turned slowly towards Sapphire. He did not relish the task and he moved slowly. Gently he took hold of her arm and helped to hold the baby.

"Please, Miss Sapphire," he began, " y'u better come wid me."

Sapphire did not resist, she turned her back to Harriet and was led off towards the pathway, Raymond on one side, Jewel on the other.

"Miss Sapphire! Indeed!" muttered Harriet incensed by the deference he had shown the woman. Angrily she turned to the other maids, "Don't you ever let that woman in here again. Do you understand me?"

When William came back that evening Harriet was still fuming. She vented much of her anger on him.

"I don't want ever to see or to hear anything about that woman and her family. This is entirely your fault. If you had not been such a fool!"

Sapphire, too, was still very angry when her husband returned home from work that evening. She did not want to tell him everything about the events of the morning. She knew he would get angry with her for being so foolish as to provoke Harriet. But she was so angry that she began to tell him just little bits of what had happened. It was something that she just could not keep to her self.

"Dis marnin' me buck up wid Miss Harriet," she began, as if it had been just a casual meeting and nothing in particular had taken place.

He started to question her and soon had the full story. He was very angry and frustrated—why did his wife do such stupid things? Provoking the Henderson family would only cause trouble for them, and could not his wife see that? He lectured her sternly, and ordered her never again to venture onto the Estate. Finally she agreed, and at that point Daniel was willing to listen to the details of the encounter. He found a certain satisfaction in knowing that Harriet had seen the child, and would no doubt have realized that her son was indeed the father. There was a certain satisfaction too, in knowing that his wife had faced up to the despised Henderson woman, but he did not tell his wife of his feelings. In his bones he felt the incident would lead to more trouble for them.

Several weeks passed and once again Sapphire and her daughters began to take their daily walk down to the beach. Their meeting with Harriet was not forgotten by any means, and Sapphire could easily work herself into a rage by just thinking about it. She did that every so often, and then seemed to forget about it for a few days until she repeated the process once again. As she thought about it and fantasized about what she would do if ever the opportunity came her way again, she began to stroll and loiter by the entrance to the Estate, hoping that Harriet would pass by. A number of times she met people walking along the road and workers entering or leaving the Estate, and they gathered there to talk and gossip. This practice continued off and on for several more weeks before finally Harriet passed by. As she was driven by, Harriet did not notice much more than that there were some people gathered at the gate. On the second occasion though, she made it her business to see who was there, and it was easy enough to spot Sapphire with the baby.

"The nerve of that woman," she thought, and tried to think of some way that she could put a stop to it. Several days later the woman was there again. "She must be stirring up trouble with the workers," she concluded. After the forth and fifth sighting Harriet decided that she must do something about it. When William came in for supper that night it was the only thing on her mind.

"That damned woman has been hanging about the gate with that wretched child," she told him. "I want you to get rid of them. There is no reason for her to be there, and I don't want to see her hanging about there."

William wanted to know if they were trespassing or damaging the property, and his mother could not assure him of that.

"If they are not trespassing, or damaging the property, I don't think we can stop them," he finally said. "They have to be breaking the law in some way before we can do something about it."

"Well, they have no right to be here at all!" his mother answered. "They don't have a right to live here."

"What do you mean?"

"They are even living on our property."

"Yes?"

"Your father gave them that piece of land—the land they live on, and they never paid a penny for it. I never—never agreed to it. I always told him it was the wrong thing to do, and sure enough it has turned out that way."

"That's right!" said William, thoughtfully. "They never paid for it—but they own the land—."

"I want you to get rid of them. You must get rid of them anyway you can. Get rid of them!…. I can't stand the sight of them!"

William recalled the loan registered against the lot as security for the building materials. "They still owe us money for the building…. It is about a hundred and fifty pounds, I think—it was just for the lumber."

"William," said his mother sternly, "I want you to get rid of them once and for all."

"I don't know how it could be done, Mother," he said, "but I'll talk to Mr. Barrow about it. He may be able to foreclose or something, even though they own the land."

Mr. Barrow was the solicitor and barrister living in Port Antonio. As far as anyone knew, Mr. Barrow had lived there all his life, with the exception of the few years it took him to qualify for his profession. He knew literally everyone living on the Northeast end of the island, and equally so, he was known by everyone, rich and poor. He had the most equitable temperament for a lawyer; he seldom became personally or emotionally involved in his cases, and he treated each case with total dispassion. With such a philosophy it was hard to see why he would ever be engaged as an advocate, yet still whenever someone was in need of legal service, he was always the lawyer called. He was very well liked and had a very good practice indeed. He had been a close and personal friend of the Squire and his wife, and had often been a dinner guest at their Estate house, but following the Squire's death the friendship had waned.

True to his word, in a few days William visited the lawyer's office. At the meeting there was no indication, one way or the other if the loan could be foreclosed, but Mr. Barrow advised that after the legal fees and costs of the court action, it would certainly not be worth the trouble. William passed that information on to his mother and would have forgotten about it except that she kept reminding him, and insisting that it be done. For a while, William having better things to do, ignored his mother, but in the end suggested that she should talk to Mr. Barrow herself, and Harriet immediately agreed.

In the course of his business, Mr. Barrow had encountered all kinds of people seeking legal advice and his assistance. Most had clear motives for consulting a lawyer; some were merely common criminals wealthy enough to afford his fees, and looking for ways to avoid the consequences of their criminal action. Some were looking for 'justice,' but most were attempting to benefit financially by putting their case before a judge. He had never had a case motivated purely by a vindictive desire to deprive a family of their possessions and their home, and he had reservations. Generally speaking, he was never concerned with the motives—the rights or wrongs—of his clients, but in this instance he was concerned, that if successful, it would inflict hurt and harm on innocent people—for no other reason than the desire to hurt and harm.

Harriet did not hide her reasons for visiting her solicitor in his office—indeed, her emotional anger became quite evident during the discussion. Mr. Barrow advised her against pursuing. He was disgusted with Harriet's insistence and frequent repetition of her reasons for continuing. In the end Mr. Barrow accepted the case, but decided he would not pursue it with enthusiasm or vigor. Their first-name friendship ended that day; he let her out of his office with a curt "Good Morning Madam!"

In a week Mr. Barrow sent his letter of acceptance and advised that in his opinion they could not be evicted from the property; that Harriet could only press for repayment of the outstanding balance, the amount owed for the building materials. Eventually though, they could force bankruptcy if the money was not paid, and then perhaps the sale or seizure of the lot in lieu of repayment. It would take some time to get that all done, it would cost much more than the land was worth, and it would not be a financial benefit to them.

Harriet read the letter to William. "I want them off our land! I want them off at any cost, and I don't care how much it will cost! You tell Mr. Barrow to go ahead with whatever he needs to do."

Jamaican Lore—De darg sey'im wont work, 'e will sid-down an look, for 'e mus' get a living.

CHAPTER 25

Sapphire and her daughters now made it almost a daily habit to loiter at the gates to the Estate. Over the course of the months she had met a goodly number of people, all inclined to gather there and socialize. Some were on their way to work or returning from work. Some like her were idling away the days without having any particularly compelling work, and many had no work at all. From time to time, some brought along rum, which was often shared, and among those always carrying a bottle was a man by the name of Simpson.

'Mr. Simpson,' as he was known, was a big man, very muscular and good-looking. He always wore a wide smile and a pleasant, jolly expression, but his jovial expression and witty conversation hid the real character beneath. In point of fact, 'Mr. Simpson' was a most unsavory character. Everyone knew about Simpson, how he lived and what he did, but yet still, because he did not so much prey upon his weaker neighbors, but mostly on well-to-do landowners and tourists, he was widely accepted and even admired. Nevertheless, he did have enemies especially among the men whose women he had seduced, or whose wives and daughters he had introduced to sailors, and to prostitution. For his chief source of income, unsteady at the best of times, was procurement of women for the sailors and tourists when the boats came in. At other times he poached from the various estates and plantations, making him the bane of estate managers. He could often be seen striding along the coast road, singing or whistling a tune, with a large bunch of bananas or sticks of sugarcane balanced on his shoulders.

Sapphire was still an attractive woman not yet at middle age, and her two daughters were even more attractive, in fact they were very pretty girls indeed. Simpson immediately recognized the potential, and directed his attention towards the women. Sapphire was at a vulnerable stage in her life; so far there had been serious family problems, and relations with her husband were not cordial. Furthermore, she was bored, unhappy, and looking for some excitement—something to lift her spirits above the daily, unvaried routine. When Simpson first turned his attention towards her, she was not averse to some innocent flirting. She was immensely flattered that he should be paying her so much attention, even though she was well aware of his reputation with women, and typically she thought, she could keep control of any relationship. His constant attention was overwhelming, and within a few weeks she was ready for any adventure.

Sapphire had taken to sitting on a fallen coconut tree just off the road, the child in her lap, and others sitting or standing on the road nearby. The bottle of rum was a very effective assistant to his purpose, and Simpson began to sit beside her as they drank together. He would whisper every now and again in her ear, she would laugh and giggle, hanging her head down laughing.

"Go'wey man!" she would say, jokingly, and push him playfully aside.

One afternoon when the rum had been finished, they sat together on the fallen tree, and Simpson whispered in her ear. Sapphire, who was still holding the child, called out to her daughter. "Jewel, come tek de baby." She stood up, stretched her back and handed the baby over. "Mr. Simpson have som'tin he goine sho' te me"

Together they went towards a wooded section some hundred yards further down the beach. They entered the bushes and were hidden from view. They went in several more yards before Simpson quickly cleared the leaves and rubbish from a patch of fine sand and spread a coconut sack. Quickly, Sapphire undid her under garments and they fell to the ground. Simpson loosened his trousers and they fell to the ground, exposing his large and stiffly erect penis. Sapphire lifted her dress well above her breasts and lay down on the sack, spreading her legs widely, and pulling him down beside her. In less than fifteen minutes they returned to the others, and Sapphire took the child back from her daughter.

It was over a week before Sapphire and Simpson once again wandered off down the beach together. And a few days later they were again off down the beach to the trees, and each time it took longer for them to return. After several weeks it became the accepted thing that they would take a long walk together down the beach to the sheltering trees. Jewel seemed to accept her mother's behavior without questioning her, but privately she was embarrassed and did not like it.

Ruby appeared not to have noticed until one day she naively voiced her thoughts. "Wher' dem goine?" she asked aloud.

There were smiles and titters from those that heard the question, and then a voice from the gathering came back in answer, "Dem goine down to Merriment chile!" Everyone laughed except Jewel and Ruby.

Two young men, little more than boys were interested in the girls, but they had not been able to attract favorable interest. The girls considered them too immature to merit their attention, and found their pranks annoying—they did not like soldier crabs thrown in their hair, or down the front of their dress—but the men persisted.

One day, as Sapphire and Simpson were on the way to their secluded rendezvous, the two boys took off as fast as they could run, along the road in the direction of the sheltering bushes. Crouching low, they stealthily entered the grove, their intention was to spy on the two people hidden amid the trees on the beach. Half an hour later they returned, quietly laughing and whispering to each other. They spoke quietly to several others when they rejoined the group sitting about.

In an hour or so, Sapphire and Simpson returned, and Simpson again turned his attention to the girls. A while later a man from out of the gathering approached Simpson and spoke quietly in his ear, turning around to look in the direction of the two youths. A little later Simpson got up and sauntered slowly, casually, towards the two boys. As he got nearer, one of the boys saw him approaching and sensed the danger. He jumped up and was away as fast as his legs could take him. Simpson tried to grab him, but the boy was out of reach and made good his escape. The other boy was not so fortunate; he had not seen Simpson coming, and when he did, it was too late. He scrambled to his feet but tripped and fell. Then he frantically attempted to roll out of reach and regain his feet, but Simpson was on top of him, holding him in a very secure grip.

Simpson did not waste any time in punishing the lad; he picked up the boy with both hands and dropped him face down to the ground where he remained momentarily stunned. Simpson placed his foot on his back to keep him there and then pulled his trousers down to strip the boy of his pants. He reached over to a small tree growing nearby and broke off a stout branch that he cleared of leaves and twigs, all the while keeping the squirming youth pinned to the ground. Using the thicker end he beat the young man severely about the back and buttocks, wailing him unmercifully. A minute later the branch broke and was useless as an implement of punishment, so he used his hands to beat him about the face, and his knuckles to clout him about the head. The young man at first fought off the blows as best he could, but in a minute he could only submit with cries for mercy and tears of pain. When Simpson had satisfied himself that he had extracted sufficient retribution, he stripped him naked, and left him sitting on the ground, completely nude in the midst of the gathering. The youth sat sobbing for several moments, then slowly he picked himself up, nursing his cuts and bruises, gathered up his clothes that were scattered about, and still sobbing, limped to the sea to wash and treat his injuries.

At first he sat at the waters edge with the waves washing over his legs. He filled his cupped hands and poured the contents over his head, face and back. This brought him some relief, so he lay on the beach with the waves washing over his naked body. He rolled further down into the sea, and was soon standing waist deep, splashing the water over himself. On the beach no one paid attention as he splashed in the water and dipped beneath the surface. But suddenly there was an agonized cry for help, and a scream of terror that seemed to last for ages. It electrified all those on the beach—there was a stunned silence as attention turned to the boy bathing in the sea. Then someone shouted "Shark! A shark tek 'im!" The scent of his fresh blood in the sea had enticed the huge preadator into the shallow water.

He thrashed about with his arms beating in the water, and then he disappeared below the surface. He reappeared again gasping for air and shouting for help. Two men ran to the waters edge, followed there by several others, and in spite of the risk the men entered the sea to rescue the young man. One man grabbed hold of an arm and was able to pull the mangled body onto the beach. Blood was gushing from several wounds, from his arm and from a deep gash on his thigh that seemed to have almost severed his leg. The man picked up the shirt lying on the sand, wet it quickly and placed it over the gaping wound in and effort to stem the bleeding. It had little effect; the sand and the water around was stained crimson, and the blood continued to gush. The young man was moaning and crying softly, but he soon stopped, lying quite still, with his eyes and mouth wide open. It took less than five minutes for him to expire.

Sapphire and the girls were distraught by the sight of the naked body on the sand; Ruby emitted a histerical scream and burst into a flood of tears. They left the beach and were quickly on their way back home. For several days following they did not leave their home, and for several weeks they did not return to the beach. Sapphire was the first to return there, and she went alone. But soon the tragedy was forgotten and once again they were among those gathering on the beach near the gate to the Manor House Estate.

On several occasions Simpson had offered the girls rum to drink, which they had refused, but he had been taking a more and more commanding position. As a result the girls had become scared of the big muscular man, even though he always appeared to be playful, always smiling and joking when he spoke to them. But the girls had met some younger men there, and were developing attachments. The attention from these men rivaling each other was overwhelming at times, but was something of a protective barrier to the persistent Mr. Simpson—there was safety in numbers—even though he never hesitated to chase the young men away whenever he wanted.

Jewel's particular interest was a young fisherman, and she often knew when he would be away at sea. On those days she had no interest in going with her mother, and began to make excuses. She offered instead to look after little Precious at home. The child was now almost two years old and was very active, and someone had to keep a constant watch on her. Sapphire was happy to be relieved of that responsibility for at least part of the day, and on those days Sapphire would then go alone.

At home if Daniel was present, they never talked about what happened during the day at the beach, unless there had been something unusual, and Sapphire did not ever tell her husband much of what took place there. If she told him anything it was in a very casual way avoiding details and particularly any mention of her lover. Daniel had learned that Simpson was sometimes among those gathering at the gate, but he did not know that it was pretty much a daily occurrence. He cautioned Sapphire about the infamous Simpson, not that she did not already know, but even so he trusted his wife, and he could not imagine that she could become involved with another man.

Jamaican Proverb—Better fe ride a jackass dat carry y'u dan a horse dat trow y'u.

CHAPTER 26

For the next year or so there was little change in their lives. Mr. Barrow sent demanding letters, but they had been unable to repay any of the money owed, and after the third letter no one paid any further attention. Daniel's job at Chivers Estate simply did not pay enough in wages, and though he had talked to Henry Thomson about a raise, none was likely to be forthcoming. Thomson was sympathetic to Daniel's situation, but he was not able to help.

William had found it impossible to give the business in Kingston his best attention while he was living on the north coast, and so for the sake of the more profitable enterprise, he was obliged to move back to Kingston and make visits to the Estate whenever necessary. His mother was happy about the move, she had had enough of the problems there, and was constantly irritated by the sight of the Indian woman with the white baby loitering outside her gate—it was a reminder of an unhappy past. Soon after their departure Mrs. Barnham too decided that a similar move was desirable. Bridget had not shown much interest in the estate and had developed no aptitude whatsoever in managing its affairs. Her mother had abandoned efforts to educate her in that regard, and now only wished to see her married to William Henderson. If she remained at Chivers the couple would be separated and there would be scant chance of any engagement.

William's hired headman, Burke, came from a different part of the island. Burke was a well-educated light-skinned middle class Jamaican, about the same age as William. He had gone to a good school in St. James Parish, but he never talked about it to anyone—in fact he never talked about his family or his private life either. He was working on a sugar cane plantation in St. James Parish when William lured him away with the offer of a higher salary and hints of even better things to come—if things worked out right—a house would eventually be his.

In fact, the house was almost a promise made, and Burke intended it to be a promise kept.

Burke did not come alone; shortly after he moved to the Manor House Estate, he hired two rather disreputable characters also from his former employer to be his foremen. One was a swarthy, light-skinned man with thick semi-straight black hair, kept in place and shiny with liberal applications of coconut oil. He had the appearance of a 'Latino' although he was Jamaican bred and born, and to enhance the exotic image of a foreigner, he called himself 'Pedro,' and often spoke with an artificial accent. The other man was a 'Rastafarian,' with the typical appearance and braded dreadlocks common to that sect. He was known as 'Rasta' or Rastaman.

As the months passed the date for Opal's release from prison came ever closer. It had been a long and difficult three years for Daniel and his family, and they were praying for happier times when Opal returned. Another letter from the persistent Mr. Barrow dampened their anticipated celebration—it arrived two days before Opal's expected return and threatened the seizure of all personal property. It depressed Daniel deeply, during which time he found it hard to think clearly. Already he had been put into bankruptcy, and now there was the risk that the bailiffs would move in and seize everything in his house. Also there was the risk that the seizure might be extended to the land and they could be dispossessed of their home. At times the frustration drove him to fits of almost uncontrollable anger and he would rage and swear vengeance against William and his mother. If he were to be driven out of the house that he built for his family, and the land given to him by the Squire taken away, he could not rest quietly. And then at other times when his broken bones were aching, and he was so wearied, he would have quietly surrendered.

Two days later the whole family waited at the bus stop on the coast road to meet Opal. It was late evening when the bus came into view, and they saw her for the first time in the three long years of her imprisonment. She was greeted with hugs and many kisses from everyone. Precious had fallen asleep in her grandfather's arms and had to be awakened so that her mother could see her and hold her. The baby was of course, the first person that Opal wanted to see, and she was literally smothered in her arms, so much so that the child was overcome and started to cry. The party immediately picked up Opal's small bundle and headed towards their home along the mountain pathway. Opal hung on her mother's arm, and Jewel hung on Opal's arm all the way talking, asking questions.

Sapphire had fixed a special meal to celebrate her homecoming. She had made a special trip into Port Antonio to buy flour and sugar to make a cake. She also spent thru'pence for a dozen Paradise Plums, which she had kept hidden, and only brought out later as a surprise treat for everyone to enjoy together. There would be one each for everyone, and the rest would be for Opal, to celebrate her return home. For the evening the greater problems were forgotten and were not mentioned until the next day. Opal was very distraught by the news, but was preoccupied with her daughter and could not leave her alone. When she went to bed that night, she insisted that they sleep together in the same bed, and through the next week they were inseparable.

As the days turned into weeks, Opal was still obsessed with her child and indulged her outrageously—little Precious could do no wrong. After some weeks the other women in the house were tiring of the indulgence, and they undertook to correct the child whenever necessary. Opal saw this as interference in her affairs and quarrels broke out between the girls, and she even quarreled with her mother several times. With the threat of being turned out of their home hanging over them and looming ever closer, there was little room for much contentment.

Daniel had searched without success for a better job. He had sold his most valuable assets months earlier so that they could not be seized, and what little money not spent was carefully hidden away. Since that time he was forced to walk the seven odd miles twice each day to and from his work at Chivers Estate. It was often a long and painful walk that could have been made shorter if he took the path through the Manor House Estate, but he dared not risk that. Henry Thomson was sympathetic and did what he could to help, but there was not really much that he could do to make things better for them. He had been drinking regularly off and on, and most days existed in a state of semi-intoxication, and his drinking had been getting steadily worse. Daniel was becoming worried about the man's health, not that he could do much about it. In the meantime, he took over on the days when Thomson was unable to work.

Sapphire had often thought of ways in which she could get money. She had talked to Simpson, and he of course, had a ready solution at hand, and he had wasted no time in urging her to take it up. He had propositioned her a number of times before and Sapphire had indignantly refused.

"Me no want no dutty man come fingle me!" she told him as she angrily dismissed his suggestion. She was insulted and angry that her lover would offer her to other men, but as time went by she overcame her angry feelings, and the lure of easy money made her think more about it. As the days passed and the ever persuasive Simpson talked about it, he explained that she did not have to become a prostitute to make money, but she just needed to act like a prostitute so as to collect the money.

The scheme, as he explained it, was very simple: he would get payment from the 'customer' for getting her, and once he had the money she could go with the 'customer,' get him drunk if possible and then just disappear. Or, she could do whatever she wanted—make him pay more money and "den' giv' im lit'le sumptin," if she felt like it. It was very easy, he told her, "Me do it all de time!" The opportunities were not there every day, only when the boats came in, so one had to act decisively at the right time. There was little risk he told her, because the same boats never came back for weeks—sometimes never—and by that time the 'customer' would have forgotten all about it, even if he was still with the ship. Finally, Sapphire rejected the idea fearing the reactions of her husband and family if ever they found out.

Two months after she returned home, Opal was very restless. While in prison she had been kept constantly busy, and while it was very pleasant to be free and be able to do as she pleased, she began to be very bored and wanted to find work. She began to take long walks with her little daughter into the countryside to spend the day. She would pack up food and drink for the day and wander off. While on these walks she met many of the men that used to work for her father, and she went to places that she had never been before.

One morning she decided to visit her father working at Chivers, to take him his lunch as she had done in happier times when he was working at the Manor House Estates. She took the long route along the coast road past the Manor House gates and on to Chivers. She knew that Mrs. Barnham was away so there was no fear that they would meet. But she also did not want to be seen by Constance, the housekeeper, or Henry Thomson. Nevertheless, she began the long walk up the driveway to the main house. Halfway there she could see someone in the distance walking towards her leading an animal by the reins. At first she thought it was one of the men, but as she got nearer, she saw that it was Henry Thomson. She had not expected to meet anyone other than her father, some of the workmen and perhaps one of the maids. At first a streak of panic made her think of turning back towards the road, but second thoughts convinced her that running away would not save her, and she might as well face up to the unexpected meeting.

As they drew closer, Opal grasped the hand of her child close by, and unconsciously began to tighten her grip.

"Marnin' Sur," she said. She looked into his face for a moment while he was preoccupied with the mule. She recognized the same lost expression that she had noticed over three years ago in the 'Paradise Bar.' Somehow the feelings of sympathy that she had experienced then returned to her—he must be very lonesome and unhappy, she thought.

For a few moments Thomson did not answer. The mule began to shake its head, and he grabbed the rein with both hands. When the animal settled down he turned to look at her as though he was searching his memory to recognize her.

"Morning," he finally said. "And who have we got here?" with his gaze turning towards the little girl. Bending over he spoke to Precious, "And who is this little girl?"

"She me daughter, Sur." Opal replied, unconsciously tightening her grasp even more.

"Mamma! Mamma! Y'u hu't me han'!" and she struggled to break free.

"She is your child?" Henry asked showing some surprise. As he asked the question, he looked intensely at Opal, and then he understood the significance of the differences in their complexions.

"Ah!" he said, nodding his head knowingly. "Well, isn't she just a picture! She's a very pretty little girl," he complimented her. He squatted down so that he was only a little higher than the child, and he reached out, took her hand and held it gently. At that point the mule bared its teeth and aimed to bite him on the back. Somehow he might have been expecting it because he quickly jumped out of the way, and would have fallen over had he not held tightly on the reins. The mule continued its aggressive attack rearing its head and getting closer. Henry yanked on the reins and struck the animal sharply across its face with his riding crop. It reared but backed off and Henry again yanked hard on the reins, waving the riding crop threateningly so that the mule could see it. In a few minutes he settled the animal.

"Goddam mule," he said, when it was quiet again. "It's a savage beast," he said to Opal. "The damned animal bites!" He turned his attention again to the little girl, "And what is your name?" he asked.

"Preci'us. I'se Preci'us, Sur." She stood on one foot and shyly twisted her little body about.

Opal stood quietly by, surprised at the interest and evident kindness that the man was showing her daughter. She felt proud, but not comfortable and did not know just how to reply.

"Well let me see if I have something for little Precious," he said standing up and searching in his trouser pocket. He took out a pocket knife and several coins and finally took out an old shilling worn almost smooth on both sides with age and use. He held it up for the little girl to see. Squatting down again, "See, I do have something for you!" And he held the coin out towards her. "Here is a little present for you." He put the coin in the palm of her hand and closed her fingers over.

The little girl looked at the man and then at her mother, evidently not knowing if she should accept it.

"Tell de gentleman t'ank y'u Sur," coaxed Opal.

"T'ank y'u, Sur," and she opened her hand, looked at it for a few moments, then turned to look up at her mother.

"Look, Mamma. Look Mamma!"

Opal took the shilling. It was a long time since she had held one in her hand, in fact she could not have remembered the last time even if her life depended on it. She turned to Henry,

"T'ank y'u Sur," she said. "T'ank y'u Sur." and then after a long pause, "But we can't t'ek it Sur," and tempting as it was, she held it out to return it.

He looked at the woman in surprise. No one had ever refused to take money from him before, so why would she?

"Why not?" he demanded, a little annoyed. "Why can't you take it?"

"It not right, Sur."

"Not right! How could it not be right?"

"No Sur. It not right."

Opal had suddenly remembered the last time she had been given a gift—the gifts she received from Harriet Henderson—and that led to three years in prison. Gifts like that could just be a trap. But Henry did not take back the coin.

"It's a present," he said. "It's just a present for your little girl. Why can't you take it?"

"Presents, Sur, can bring trouble, Sur."

"What kind of trouble?" he demanded, once again impatiently, sensing that the woman must think he was propositioning her, and that irritated him. He never propositioned women! He had never had the need!

"Look," he said, softening his tone, "It is just something for your little girl. I think that you could use it, so you take it for her."

Opal began to feel very uncomfortable, and again found it difficult to reply. Should she trust him? She knew that her father liked him, and as far as she knew, thought well of him in spite of his drinking. But she did not wish to offend him either. For a few embarrassing moments she fidgeted nervously with the coin and no words were spoken, and then she finally answered.

"Well, y'u says so, Sur. Den t'ank y'u again Sur. I will keep it fe 'er."

Henry continued the conversation, asking her why she was there. Opal explained that she had only come just to visit her father. They walked together up the driveway towards the house. On the way Opal glanced every now and again at his face. She noticed that he looked so tired and pale, and seemed to be struggling along as though it took a great effort. When they reached the house, Henry told her where to find her father, and he led the mule off in the direction of the stables. She followed his directions and soon found her father in a back segment. They had been suckering bananas all morning and were hot and tired. The men were glad for the interruption caused by Opal's appearance, and they stopped work one by one and gathered around to talk and play with the little girl. It was close enough to lunch time to break off for the morning, so they sat around and ate. In an hour or so the men went back to work. Precious had fallen asleep on some dried banana leaves, and she was not needing any special attention. Opal lay down beside her, closed her eyes but did not go to sleep. By mid-afternoon the sun disappeared behind some low clouds and the cool of the night was just beginning to be felt in the light breeze.

Opal prepared to leave and return home. She would leave an hour or so before her father and expected that he would overtake her on the way. Opal took the little girl by the hand and took the pathway to the estate out buildings. They were approaching the stables when Opal saw some object to the side of the pathway. It was too far away for her to see what it was, but it arroused her curiosity and she quickened her step. As she got closer she could see three of the Estate dogs, two were sniffing at some object on the ground. Twenty yards nearer she could see that it was a body stretched on the ground, and soon recognized the person to be Henry Thomson. He had evidently collapsed and lay huddled on the ground his head resting on one arm, his face in the dirt. She tried to turn him over but he was too heavy just to be moved that way. She took hold of his arm and pulled him up, and as she did so saw a large bleeding wound just below the shoulder, and the front of his shirt was covered in blood. Struggling she managed to turn him onto his back. His face was covered in dirt, in and about his mouth. She wiped his face clearing the dirt from his mouth and eyes as best she could. He moaned and slowly opened his eyes. He did not seem to recognize her or to know where he was.

"W'a happen te y'u Sur?" she asked.

"What happened?" he asked. "What happened?"

"Y'u mus' be fall down, Sur." And after a few moments, "How y'u feelin' now, Sur?"

He did not answer, but tried to sit up. He wasn't able to even with her help, and she let him lie down again. He rested on the ground for several minutes before he again tried to get up. The effort was too much and he again lapsed into near unconsciousness.

"Mr. Thomson, Sur, y'u is hurt Sur. Y'u rest here Sur, I go and get help." Turning to Precious, she said, "Y'u stay here. Y'u hear me—y'u stay wi'd de gentleman. Stay!"

She ran towards the main buildings hoping to see someone—anyone. It was getting late and there was no sign of anyone being about. There was no one in the kitchen when she looked, and one of the dogs nearly tripped her as she went to the servants' rooms and knocked hard on the first door. The cook was half asleep, but got up quickly when told what had happened. She knew where Constance was and went off to find her, fixing her clothes as she went. The yardman, also enjoying a late afternoon siesta, came out of his room combing his hair. Opal told him to hurry out to the stables, and he took off immediately. Constance and the cook were soon back to get the details of what had happened. Together with Opal leading the way they were soon standing around the man on the ground. The yardman was already there looking at the prostrate man, asking questions but getting no answers.

"Him is sick," he told Constance.

"No. He mus' be fall down," said Constance looking at the bloodied shirt. "Him mus' be fall down"

"We mus' tek 'im to 'im house," the yardman said. "Come giv' me little help, Tek 'im arm. Mek 'im stan' up."

Opal was holding his head in her lap, still trying to get the dirt off his face. He opened his eyes, and with a dazed expression looked at the people about. They made him sit up, but when the yardman took hold of his arm, he let out a cry of pain, and they let him lie back again.

Constance bent over to look into his face, "Mr. Thomson, Sur, W'a happen te y'u, Sur?"

"The damned mule," he said feebly, "The damned mule!"

The yardman had been examining the bloodied arm and the wound. "It de mule, Miss Constance. Look 'pon it—de mule mus' be bite 'im."

"Come," said Constance. "We mus' tek 'im to 'im house."

The yardman took one arm and helped him to stand up. Constance put her arm around his waist and held his injured arm to his chest, and with the others following they managed to get him to the steps of his house. He was too heavy to carry up the steps to the veranda, so they put him to lie back down again. More help would be needed to get him into the house. There was no one else at the main house, so Opal told them where the men were working, and that her father would be on his way back home very soon. The yardman was dispatched to find Daniel and bring him back as quickly as possible. While they waited, the cook found a cushion to put under his head, and they made him as comfortable as possible. Constance arrived with a glass of water, and Opal raised his head. He was shaking and very pale, but consciousness had returned, and he told them what happened. The mule suddenly bit him on the arm, knocking him to the ground, and then it trampled him. How he managed to get away, he did not know.

It took half-an-hour for the yardman to return with Daniel. They carried him up the stairs into the dining room. There was a couch in the drawing room, and they laid him out picking up his feet and taking off his shoes. Opal had been following closely and she stood at his head to loosen his shirt collar. Daniel and Constance discussed the situation; Henry had been without a housemaid and cook for several weeks, Constance told him. How he had been managing on his own, she did not know, because he had been sick off and on. Perhaps he had not been eating properly—substituting whisky for solid food. They should get him to bed, and cook should fix him something to eat. Daniel and the yardman again helped Henry to get up and get to his bedroom, where Daniel removed his clothes and got him into the bed. Constance and the cook returned to the main house to fix his meal.

By that time it was quite dark. Daniel found the lamps and lit them taking one into the bedroom. Henry seemed to be sleeping—he lay in the bed with his eyes closed.

"How y'u feel now, Sur?" Daniel whispered.

Henry did not answer right away. "Not good. Not so good."

"Miss Constance soon bring sum'tin fe y'u to eat. An' den y'u will feel better."

The yardman, Opal and Precious, were in the pantry waiting for Constance, and she brought the food within the hour. She took a spoon from a draw and handed it with the plate of food to Opal.

"Y'u tek it in to him," she ordered. "Y'u mus' mek 'im eat."

Opal took the plate into the bedroom where her father was sitting with the sick man. They propped him up, and Opal gave him several spoonfuls before he said he had had enough and lay back to closed his eyes again. Opal returned to the pantry and told Constance that he did not want any more.

"But he not take any," she said looking at the almost untouched plate. "Here give it to me. I will show y'u how to mek 'im eat." And she took the plate and went to the bedroom.

"Mister Henry, y'u mus' eat sum'tin, Sur."

She pushed a spoonful towards his mouth, and tried to get him to open his mouth. He turned his head away, still with eyes closed. Constance looked at him wondering what should be done next. She put down the plate and put her hand on his forehead. After a second or two, she drew it back in astonishment.

"'E is very sick, Mr. Dan. 'Im 'as a fever"

Daniel came over and placed his hand on his forehead. Indeed, the man was running a high fever. He looked over at Constance.

"Sombady mus' stay wi'd 'im. He can't stay alone fe de ni'te."

Opal brought in a glass of water and placed it on a table near the bed. She put her hand on his forehead to gauge his temperature—someone would have to stay with him until the fever went down. Constance immediately excused herself, saying that she had her responsibilities elsewhere, and could not be available. Opal would have to be the person she said firmly, and because her father had been working all day he would need to get his rest. They discussed the situation and agreed that Opal should be the one. Constance would be near at hand and if he got any worse she could fetch help. Daniel took a bed from the maid's room and put it in the dining room so that Opal and Precious could sleep close by, and Constance would send the cook over with supper for Opal and Precious.

CHAPTER 27

It was late in the evening when Daniel finally left to return home. Opal had settled in with Precious, who went to sleep as soon as she had eaten. With everything now quiet in the house, Opal went in to see how her patient was. He was asleep but even in the dim light from the oil lamp, she could see that his face was very flushed. His fever must be high, and she considered getting Constance. There should be some medicines in the house she thought, and went to the bathroom to search through the cupboard shelves. There were no medicines there, but she found a small enameled basin, which she partly filled with water. She found a small face cloth, rinsed it out and put it in the basin. Returning to his bedside, she wrung out the cloth and placed it on his forehead. Several times she wet it, wrung it out, and replaced it without wakening him.

After a while she left the cloth in place on his forehead and went to look at her daughter. Precious was fast asleep in the bed, so she took the lamp, raised the wick and began to explore the rest of the house. There were two more bedrooms off a hallway. She entered the first and began to look around. There was nothing unusual about it, nothing in the room that she had not seen in rooms at the Manor House Estate. The wardrobe was empty, as were the drawers of the dresser.

The second room was evidently the bedroom used by the Major's wife, Marjory. Sheets were still on the bed but obviously not used for a long time. In the wardrobe several dresses and under garments were on hooks and hangers, and there were several pairs of shoes scattered on the floor. The dressing table had a broken nail file, a brush, comb, and a hand mirror with a split in the wooden back, all part of a set. She opened the drawers and began looking through the contents. In one she found a hairclip and a headband. She tried it on and looked at herself in the mirror. In the dim light from the oil lamp she thought it suited her, and she would have liked to keep it, but in a few minutes she put it back and opened the other drawer. It contained a number of drug store bottles and ointment containers, a large, half-empty bottle of Vicks, and a bottle of Bayer Aspirins. Just the thing she needed, she thought taking out the bottle. She closed the draw and began to explore the last one. It did not have very much of interest except for two almost empty perfume bottles. She picked up one and smelt the contents and then replaced the stopper. The perfume in the other bottle was very strong and sweet. She put a finger over the opening and tipped the bottle to get some on her finger. The liquid seemed to pour out all over her fingers and ran down onto her hand before she could wipe it off on her dress. Suddenly the perfume filled the air with its strong sweet aroma. She tried to wipe it off her hand but the smell was there to stay. The concentrated liquid had got under her fingernails and penetrated into her skin. She quickly replaced the stopper, picked up the bottle of aspirins and returned to the pantry.

For several minutes she tried unsuccessfully to wash the perfume off. The odor was still on her hand and on her dress where she had wiped her hand. It would fade away, she hoped and not be so noticeable in the morning. She picked up the bottle of aspirins and tried to remove the cap, but it was very tightly closed and it took her several minutes to get it open. Finally opened, she went into Henry's room and took out two tablets. Holding them in her fingers she tried to arouse him by shaking him lightly. It took three or four shakes to get him just to open his eyes, but then he closed them just as quickly. She shook him again and again and he was finally awake.

"Mr. 'enry, Sur,' she said, "y'u mus' t'ek dis medsin' Sur."

He turned and was about to fall asleep once again, but she kept shaking him.

"Please Sur, t'ek dis medsin," and she pushed one tablet into his mouth through closed lips. She lifted his head for him to drink. He took the other tablet in the same manner, and lay back down. His eyes were now open and he turned to look at his nurse. His fever was still raging. Opal wet the cloth, squeezed it dry and wiped his head.

"You smell sweet," he murmured.

He turned towards her, but his eyes were not focused, and he did not recognize her in his feverish state, but the smell of the perfume seemed to have jogged his memory in some strange way.

"I must be dreaming!—Where am I?" He turned away again and was quiet for several minutes. Opal pulled up the sheets to cover his chest and placed her hand on his head again. The fever was raging and he was very hot to her touch. She wet the cloth again and wiped his forehead and temples. Several more times she repeated her efforts to reduce the temperature, but it did not seem to be working very well. He was becoming restless, turning his head from side to side and mumbling deliriously. She fetched a chair from against the wall and placed it beside the bed. It was easier for her to sit next to the bed and wipe his head. For over an hour she kept up the effort to cool the fever, and she was getting tired. With her arm stretched out holding the cloth on his head, she rested her head on her outstretched arm and closed her eyes. In a few minutes she again wet the cloth and replaced it. She rested her head on her arm again, closed her eyes and fell asleep. Several times during the night she awoke to cool the fever, until finally, she fell into a deep asleep.

Opal awoke with a start—someone else was in the room. Constance was standing over her looking at her with a most disapproving expression.

"W'at is dis?—W'at is dis?"

"Miss Constance!—Mornin' Miss Constance." Opal sat up unsteadily, wiping her face with one hand, and then standing up. "Mr. Henry—him very sick in de nite." She bent over and took the cloth from his forehead.

Constance looked closer at the still sleeping man and placed her hand on his head. His temperature had cooled somewhat, but he was still feverish.

"I wonder w'at do 'im," she said thoughtfully.

Opal picked up the basin of water and went to the pantry. She needed to use the toilet and went outside. At the cistern she filled the washbasin jug, and finding a small piece of soap, she tried again to wash the perfume from her hands. She could smell it on her hands and it was very noticeable on her dress. Taking the jug of water into the pantry she again washed her hands. She thought that she had succeeded, but in reality, she had only got more used to the smell, and to her it did not seem to be so strong, but the odor was still all through the room. In the kitchen she lit the fire and put the kettle on to boil. Precious was now awake and she went to attend to her. After the little girl was up and dressed, she returned to the pantry to toast some bread over the stove fire. She made a pot of tea and placed it on the stove to keep warm. In a few minutes Constance was in the room.

"How him do las' nite?" she inquired. And then she started to smell the perfumed air.

"W'at dis smell?" she demanded, looking at Opal accusingly, approaching her and sniffing the air as she went, finally grabbing her skirt to lift it towards her face. "W'at is dis?"

Opal had already worked out her excuses. "I'se lookin' fe medsine," she explained. "Mr. Henry, 'im was very, very sick in de nite. I doant know w'a fe do. I go to look fe medsin, an' I fine Aspirin," she picked up the bottle. "An' I mek 'im tek it fe de fever."

Constance glared, "W'at y'u tek me for? Y'u mu's be tek me for a fool!"

"No! No Miss Constance! Me no tek y'u fe fool——."

"Y'u in 'a Mrs. Thomson t'ings. So don't y'u lie te me! Y'u lookin' fe sumpt'in dat doant belong to y'u. Y'u lookin' to tief!"

"No! No, Miss Constance, I'se look for medsin to give Mr Henry." Again she held up the aspirins, "Him was very sick in de nite, an' I t'ink I mus' fine sumptin fe 'im. I fine de aspirin in de draw, an' when I tek it up, de perfume—it did spill out on me han'. It in a' de same draw an' me no see it in de dark. De bottle tu'n over on me han'."

Constance weighed the almost credible explanation—it wouldn't be so easy to challenge. Her suspicions about the woman's intentions lingered, and she would have to keep a closer watch. But in the light of more urgent matters she decided to let the questions rest for the time being.

Together they fixed his breakfast and took it into the bedroom. The sun was up now and light was streaming through the open window. During the night his injured arm had bled and the sheet was stained with dried blood. Constance took a closer look. The mule had inflicted a pretty nasty bite, as bad a wound she had ever seen, and it was now showing signs of infection. It would have to be washed and dressed. She ordered Opal to boil up a large pot of water while she went to find some towels and cloth that could be used for a bandage. Daniel arrived before the dressing was completed, and he looked in to see how his employer was. He helped to make him more comfortable in the bed, and urged him to eat. The fever was beginning to return and he had eaten very little, lying back in the bed with eyes half closed. Opal entered with the bottle of aspirins and a glass of fresh water.

"W'at dat y'u have dere?" Daniel demanded.

"It medsin fe 'im fever."

Daniel took the bottle to examine it and the contents. "Where y'u get dis from?"

"It was in 'a draw. Me fine it las' nite. It good for fever," she explained.

"Where y'u get dat from?" demanded her father. "Where y'u fine out w'at good for fever?

"When I was in Kingston. Dat is w'at dey give me for fever when I was in Kingston. It very good."

He opened the bottle, examined the tablets, and closing it again to read the label. After a few moments he decided that at worst it couldn't do any harm, and might even bring good results. Aspirins were unheard of in that part of the world, and there was reluctance to using anything other than the tried and true remedies known so well in the countryside.

"Him mus tek some bush tea," suggested Constance. "I will mek it."

"Y'u mek up de tea," said Daniel. "Meantime he can tek dis medsin."

CHAPTER 28

In ten days Henry was able to sit on the veranda in a large wicker chair, a blanket wrapped around him and his feet propped on a stool. He had lost a lot of weight and was very weak and gaunt. During the time of his illness Opal had not returned home but had stayed at Chivers living in the cottage to be near him, but now he was feeling a lot better. Opal and Precious had lost much of their initial shyness and reserve during that time, and treated him, not with familiarity, but with much less deference. Henry in turn, began to regard Opal more as a friend rather than as a servant, and the little girl was a delightful distraction. She sat on the floor and played little games by herself, every now and again, running to his side to ask some question, or make some childish observation, and as he began to feel better he told her stories.

At the end of two weeks both adults were used to one another and conversed comfortably and freely together. One morning he asked her if she would like to stay and work for him as his housekeeper. Opal had thought about the possibility, almost wishing that it would happen, but when the offer was made, she hesitated, and wanted time to think it over. She would have to ask her father, she told him, and would need his permission. She would ask her father in the morning when he stopped by on his way to work.

The following morning Daniel did not appear. Opal was frustrated that she could not yet give her agreement even though she had already made up her mind to accept regardless of what her father said. Again the following morning, Daniel did not appear, and Opal was becoming concerned that he was sick, or had had an accident. In the morning she made the breakfast and did the necessary chores before speaking to Henry about her father's absence.

" Im mus' be sick, Sur," she told him. "Im never do dat before, an' ah would like little time to go 'ome and see."

"Good. I have been wondering what has happened to him. He has not been here for several days. You go and find him."

When she was about to leave, Opal went into the bedroom. "I'se goine, now Sur."

"When do you think you will be back?"

"After noon."

"That's good. I will need you, you know."

"Yes Sur. I will come back Sur."

"Very good then. Take care now." And as she was going out of the room, he called out to her again. "Before you leave, look in my drawer over there by the table," and he pointed. "Open the drawer. There is a bag in there. Pass it to me."

She passed him the bag, and he took out a ten-shilling note. "Here," he said, handing it to her. "I owe you this, so you might as well have it now."

"Tank y'u Sur," she said. "Tank y'u." She took the note and quickly left the room.

Henry had been managing to get about by himself, but he had not left the house as yet, and he hoped that it would only be a few more days. He could keep Precious with him while her mother was away.

It was not quite mid-morning when Opal arrived at her home, and opened the gate to walk towards the house. Sapphire and her two sisters were sitting outside around the cooking stones. She could see her father moving about inside the house.

"W'at happen to Pappa?" she called out to her mother as she approached. "Im no go to work?"

"Lawd 'ave mercy 'pon us!" Sapphire called back. "Y'u doan kno' w'at a trouble we 'ave chile!"

The three women went to her side all talking at the same time. "De bailiff man come yesterday an' tek out everyt'ing from out a' de house!"

"Everyt'ing is garn. De men dem tek everyt'ing!" and she started to weep, wiping her face on her skirts. "Come chile, I tell y'u 'bout it. How dey come and tek poor people t'ings! Lawd 'ave mercy!" and the tears began to flow freely.

In a few moments everyone was sobbing over their loss. Daniel, hearing the voices outside, joined the group unnoticed, but he gathered his family around him without speaking, and just held them together. They remained there for some time until the sobbing eased and then they sat down by the cooking stones.

"Dat who'man, Mrs. Henderson, she is wicked—a wicked, wicked who'man. Ah wa' we fe do now? We 'ave no bed to sleep on, an' we 'ave no table to eat on! We doan't even 'ave candle stick fe light. De who'man mek us live like darg—sleep on de ground, an' eat off de ground like darg!"

"W'at we is to do now," Daniel said, "is to mek up bed. We mus' get banana leaf—plenty, plenty. An' we mus' mek up mattress to sleep on. It better dan de ground. An' w'en we done dat," he continued, "we mus' look bamboo an' bullrush an' mek a table." There was a long pause as their minds turned to the more immediate problems and to how best to handle them. "When y'u tek up de banana leaf, mek sure y'u shake dem out good an' shake out de spider dem," he added.

In a few hours he had directed his family's energy towards making the best of their situation, and everyone was busy gathering the primitive materials with which to refurnish the house. In the early afternoon, Opal told her parents about the offer of employment from Henry Thomson, and she took out the ten-shilling note to show them. It pleased them that she would have a job—it was the only good thing that had happened for some time. Furthermore, it would be two less family members to worry about, as she would be living away from home with her daughter, and would be able to make some small contribution towards their needs. In the meantime, she would have to hurry back to Chivers Estate to prepare Henry's dinner, and look after her daughter.

"Here, Pappa, tek de money," Opal said just before leaving, handing him her weeks wages. "Tek it, y'u needs it."

He took her hand and held it for several minutes, just holding and shaking her hand but not speaking. He was reaching the limits of what he could endure, and he was too emotional to reply. He was an honest man, he had told himself, and he had worked hard all his life, and he had done no wrong, and it was just too painful. Why should he be treated so harshly? What had he done to deserve such treatment?

Opal arrived back at Chivers Estate in the late afternoon to find that Henry had been drinking again. While she was away he found a bottle of rum and one drink had led to another. Fortunately no harm had come to her daughter, and Opal was able to get her employer into bed, where he quickly fell asleep.

From time to time over the next months, Henry would buy a bottle and imbibe heavily. On those occasions he was quite fearless with his invitations to her to share his bed, but when he sobered up in the morning he would apologize, promising not to repeat the offence. But Henry was a man with numerous broken promises, and for a while that too was a broken promise. In his younger years breaking his word about drinking or carousing with women was not an issue. It had never bothered him so much either before his marriage or after, that he had ever resolved to stop. For some unknown reason it bothered him now. Perhaps it was the fear that he would fatally offend his housekeeper, she would tire of his persistence and leave, and above all, that was something that he did not wish to happen.

Opal and her daughter were a cheerful distraction to the endless routine of managing the plantation. The little girl in particular, had struck a tender cord, and he looked forward to getting home in the afternoons when he could play with her, and there seemed to be some purpose to his life now that they were living in his house. Often he took her in his lap to read or to show her pictures and tell stories. Some days, the little girl would take his hand and they would walk about the garden or down to the stables to see the mule that had bitten and trampled him so badly.

Despite these distractions though, Henry was from time to time driven to his drinking. When the urge became unbearable, he would go to the roadside shop and buy a few bottles of rum, enough for a three-day binge. The stash was smuggled into the house when his housekeeper wasn't looking, to be hidden away for opportunity in the evening. Usually, though he could not hold off before supper, and he would take a quick snort as he concealed the bottles. After a while the signs became clear to Opal. In the afternoon he would show little interest in playing with the child, and when he did not eat much at the table, Opal began an immediate search for the hidden stash.

It became an exercise in deception; she had to find and remove the bottles without letting him know what she was up to; she was on a mission of find and remove, and all this had to be done while he was otherwise occupied at the table. After several failed attempts, she became expert at knowing where the bottles were hidden. He was not very imaginative in finding new places to hide his treasure, and it would take only a few minutes for Opal to find them. Secretly she enjoyed his expressions of confusion when he could not find his elixir. He would curse and swear under his breath, but he never told her what he was looking for, and dared not ask her help. Through it all Opal remained aloof and straight-faced, as though in ignorance of what the fuss was all about, but quietly enjoying every moment.

Opal like her father, was a very practical and intelligent person, although she was uneducated and unschooled. Being in the house during the days with time on her hands, she began to look at the books and magazines that Marjory had accumulated over the years and were scattered about. Her curiosity and imagination was stimulated. In the evenings, after they had eaten, she began to ask Henry questions; she wanted to learn to read well enough to understand the books. Henry was happy to explain and to give the lessons, and after a while, the lessons were extended to other subjects besides words and meanings—it began to include numbers and calculations. Very soon she became quite adept.

Through all this the two people were becoming genuinely fond of each other; they seemed to have a deep concern for the welfare of one another. When he came home in the evening, hot and exhausted, she saw to it that he was comfortable on the veranda with a cool drink of lemonade or freshly squeezed orange juice. Often his tired expressions of fatigue—almost of hopelessness, affected her deeply, and she wanted to comfort him if she could, but dared not.

It had been a natural characteristic of his throughout his life, that he quite unconsciously engendered in women a desire to help him—nay, to save him! And that urge, many a time, had led to their undoing. Had they known better they would have seen that he could not be saved! Opal was not immune to those feelings of empathy, regardless of the fact that she was only a servant in his house, and that his problems were mostly of his own making. So far there had been no intimacy between them, but that was soon to end. Within a few months Opal had in fact, become his lover. There was a difference in their ages, but that was never a problem. Henry was a natural romantic lover; aging had refined his art, and he knew how to please women. For his part too, he was prepared to accept all the responsibility that it entailed, and was even happy to claim the little girl as his own daughter. When he thought about it—if he thought about it at all—it mattered little to him what people would think or say, but he knew that people would talk and say unkind things. Life for him, he thought, was getting short. What mattered to him most was that he had a beautiful woman to be his companion and his lover, that he made her happy, that he was happy too, and that the relationship brought out the best qualities in both of them. Society would condemn them both, but he had never paid much attention to society.

Jamaican Proverb—A man build de house but a wooman mek de home.

CHAPTER 29

During this time things had not gone well for Daniel and his family. Mr. Barrow, being pressured by Harriet Henderson had sued for nonpayment of the loan. Mr. Barrow, for his part, was in sympathy with the defendants, and quite uncharacteristically, had attempted to dissuade Harriet from pressing the case.

"There is no profit forthcoming from this action," he explained. "There will be a net cost to you. The court costs exceed the value of the land." And he added, "It is similar to the seizure of the personal possessions, which if you recall cost you forty-five pounds, ten shillings, and—four pence," he said, looking over the account. "The sale of the furniture returned just over six pounds!"

"I am not interested in what it will cost me," snapped Harriet. "I want those people off my land!"

"Very well, Madam. If that is what you want—it shall be done."

In due course, Mr Barrow obtained an order for possessions of the land if the loan was not paid by a certain date. That date had come and gone, but the family continued to live in the house, every day expecting to find the bailiff at the door with a writ of possession. The strain had been almost unbearable, and the family was on the brink of disintegration. In his heart, Daniel felt that his wife was to blame for their problems—if only she had not pressed Opal into going to work at the Manor House all of this would not have happened. If only she had not provoked Harriet Henderson by taking the baby over to the Manor House and confronting her. They quarreled almost every day. Their daughters Jewel and Ruby were caught between and could not understand how a family that just a few years before had been so happy and secure together, and now, so quickly had crumbled beyond recovery. One morning Jewel packed up her clothing and left. She went off to find her young fisherman lover, but Ruby remained at home with her parents.

Daniel was confused and plagued by indecision. He had no plan worked out should the fatal day arrive and they be turned out of their house—the home he had worked so hard to build for himself and his family. He agonized every minute of the day, and questioned himself—why? Why should he be treated in such a shameless manner—what had he done to deserve such a fate? He would survive, of that he was quite sure, but what of his wife Sapphire? They were not 'living' together any longer, but he still had feelings for her; he did not wish to see her hurt in any way, and he still had a lingering hope that one day things would be all right again. He decided that the best he could do for her would be to send her back to Swift River to live with his aging uncle, now a widower. But he did not discuss this idea with Sapphire, hoping to get a calm moment when tempers were cooled enough for reasonable discussion. In the meantime he continued to work at Chivers Estate, thanking God, that at least he still had his job.

He returned from work unusually early one Saturday morning to find a man in the house with his wife. It was the notorious Mr. Simpson, and the sight of the man whose reputation was legendary made him seethe with anger. As he came in he paused to watch, and he could see that the man was conversing on very familiar terms with his wife and young daughter, and it did not take much to deduce just what the man was doing there.

"W'at de hell is dis man doin' in me house?" he demanded from Sapphire.

"Im come te see me!"

"Get to hell from out'a me house!" he shouted at Simpson.

Daniel was by no means a strong man, and certainly was no match for Simpson. The injuries he sustained as a boy when he fell from the coconut tree were very painful from time to time and limited his physical ability, but at that point he was angry enough to have courted suicide by attacking the man.

Simpson slowly picked himself up and sauntered towards the doorway. Turning to Sapphire he said, "Now 'member w'at I tell y'u. —Y'u 'member now?" he pointed his forefinger at Sapphire and gave her a knowing look the significance of which did not pass unnoticed by Daniel.

Daniel watched him leave and go out onto the road. Angrily he turned to his wife, "W'at y'u 'ave to do wid dat man?"

"He is a fren'," Sapphire answered.

"W'at kind of man y'u keep as fren'? Dat man is a whoremonger. So how y'u keeping fren' w'id 'im?"

"Me keep me fren' as me like," answered his wife.

It was the occasion for another violent quarrel. He swore and cursed her, and accused her of being unfaithful—being nothing better than a whore! In the heat of the argument Sapphire admitted that she had 'been with Simpson,' and that she had no regrets about it! Her life for the past year had been miserable, she was sick and tired of living like that, and it was all his fault!

"Y'u is to get out'a dis house! Y'u is to get out now! Likes of y'u doant belong in dis house!"

He went to their room snatching up pieces of her clothes and other articles belonging to her, and quickly collecting a handful. Sapphire watched him for a few moments and then suddenly realized what he was about. She grabbed a trailing piece, tugging to get it away, but he held on tightly and the garment ripped. With Sapphire trailing behind holding on and crying to him to stop, he went to the fence and threw the clothes out on to the road. Without stopping to look, he went back to get another armful, and in less than a minute the second armful followed the first. And a third quickly followed that. Sapphire was frantically picking up the scattered garments, crying hysterically and shouting to him to stop. With a few final pieces in his arms, Sapphire stood in the doorway blocking his exit and pleading with him to stop.

"Get to hell out'a me way who'man," he shouted in her face. She stood firm. With his free arm he shoved her violently backwards so that she fell against the wall. He threw the last pieces over the fence, and she followed them out on to the road, gathering them up as fast as she could. He shut the gate behind her, jamming it from the inside so she could not re-enter. From over the gate she hysterically pleaded with him and begged him to let her return. He was not listening and went back into the house, swearing, cursing, and mumbling to himself.

In an hour or so Sapphire had stopped her pleading and was sitting on the ground leaning against the gate sobbing. In a little while, Ruby quietly got up and went outside to talk to her mother through the fence. Throughout the quarrel she had remained quiet and fearful that it might become fatally violent, and she had huddled in a corner of the room. Now she was worried about her mother—where would she stay during the night? Ruby sat down against the fence as they talked in hushed voices for the rest of the day. Towards midnight both women were exhausted and still they had not decided what should be done. Inside the house was dark and quiet, and they assumed that Daniel had fallen asleep. Ruby removed the lock and let her mother into the yard. Together they quietly went back into the house. As they entered they heard Daniel stirring, but he did not wake, and they lay down together in Ruby's bed and went to sleep. Sapphire was awake very early the following morning. She gathered her scattered garments into a tight bundle, all that she could carry, and started down the road to search for and find Mr. Simpson.

CHAPTER 30

The day Sapphire left was the last time Daniel saw his wife—they never met again. When he got up that Sunday morning he it was as though he was recovering from a long sickness—he felt ill. Later in the morning after he had eaten, he did not feel much better. Ruby watched him nervously as he made some tea and ate, but they did not speak much to each other, and not about the events of the day before.

"Ah soon come back," he said wearily as he left the house and wandered out onto the Estate property.

He did not pay particular attention to where he was going. The countryside was all familiar to him; he had been through the entire property so many times while employed there. He did not want to meet anyone, particularly William Henderson or his Headman, Burke, and he did not want to meet any of the plantation workers either, even though he knew them well and considered them to be his friends. He was just too depressed to talk to anyone, even close friends, so he chose to wander in the areas that were not used for any purpose, the wilder, uncleared parts that had never been cultivated and never used.

Many years before when the plantation had been worked by slaves, a certain area had been set aside as a place to bury the slaves that died. No one ever went there any more, night or day, for fear of the "duppies"—the restless spirits—that were known to rise from their graves. For a certainty it was known that the unhappy spirits wandered about, and could do one harm. Those that had been wronged and badly used in their lifetime were unable to rest in their graves, and often sought revenge in their afterlife. Their revenge, like rain, fell on good or bad with equal force, except of course, that the consequences were much worse than just a dousing rain. It was not a place that he would have gone to under normal circumstances, but he was so despondent that he was not afraid to meet the spirits, and would even have welcomed an encounter with someone from another world. They could not hurt him more than he was already hurt.

Few of the graves were marked with headstones or marking stones. Those buried after emancipation, by virtue of their conversion to Christianity received Christian burial rites, ironically though, not in consecrated ground. Many of the more recent graves had been marked with stone and wooden crosses, but few were now standing or even existing. He found the burial ground, stood at the edge looking at the low mounds, toppled crosses, and depressions where the earth had sunk into shallow hollows. The place had been completely neglected for years and was overgrown with huge trees, bush, hanging vines and mosses, imparting a truly supernatural and ghostly atmosphere. He slowly walked through the cemetery before finally sitting down on a pile of stones that marked a grave. There was some lettering carved into the mildewed, moss covered limestone, but the inscription could not be read.

"Ah!—A'h come to sit wid y'u!" he mumbled to himself and to the moldered body in the grave. "Y'u is lucky lucky man. —Y'u langtime dead man!"

He closed his eyes, hung his head and silently spoke to the body below and prayed. He felt that henceforth his life would never be the same. He knew he had lost everything that he had worked for all his life—his work, his house and home, his wife, and his daughters too, all would soon be gone. He wondered if he should not just die—perhaps kill himself. He felt very close to the bodies in the graves below. He was among those wronged in life, but he reasoned, he did not wish to wander the earth as a spirit seeking revenge, and therefore it was not a good time to die. When one dies there should be no hate in a man's heart—there must be no hate towards any man—the spirit must be contented and happy!

The day was more than half gone when at last he began to feel as though some strength had returned to him—almost as though he could again face the world and the trouble that he knew would be coming. When at last he opened his eyes a mist had descended and enveloped the entire place. It swirled about obscuring his view, clearing and then again obscuring his view. It had become a ghostly place indeed! For several minutes he could not understand what seemed to be a sudden change—it had been a clear bright day when he started out, and now there was this heavy fog usually seen only in the mountains. He tried to get a clear view, and then in the distance he could see some movement at the far side of the graveyard. Startled, he looked again and was certain there were people moving about at the edge of the cemetary. Their presence shocked him—scared him, and for several moments he was no longer depressed—he was frozen where he sat unable to move. Yes! There were people at the edge of the cemetery!

In disbelief he wiped his eyes again to see through the mist, still swirling around. They were there—he could see them! Apparently they had not seen him, or if they had, they did not pay him any attention. They seemed to be occupied— he watched—they were putting a body into the ground—it was a funeral party! He tried to listen if they were talking, but there was only the wind in the trees and silence—there was nothing to hear. As he watched they were obscured from view, and then as the mist cleared they reappeared. Finally they began to fade and then they were gone. He sat unable to move, straining his eyes to see if they were still there. When at last they did not reappear, he began to wonder if he had not been imagining it all, and the more he thought about it the more curious he became. He wanted to find out; he got up and went towards the place where he had seen the men. There was no sign of a new grave when he got there—he searched about and still there was none. He must have been dreaming!

Then he suddenly realized that the day was almost over and that he was hungry. He should be getting back home and talk to Ruby about where she should go when they were finally evicted. He returned home quickly the way he had come. The gate was open wide when he got there, and there was no sign of Ruby in the house. The house seemed to be emptier than ever, only his clothes, a few cooking tins, half of a coconut shell used as a bowl and a few discarded garments remained scattered about. For several minutes he was almost panic struck—he wondered if something had happened to Ruby. Outside the house he looked up and down the road, in the back of the house and in the latrine. He called out her name several times but there was no answer. Then he began to reason—he looked about for her clothes—there were none to be found—Ruby had taken her clothes, so she must have left knowing where she was going. This set his mind at ease for a bit, but he was still worried and could only hope that she would be safe.

He searched the house and in the garden to find food for his supper; there was hardly anything left, and as he lay down to rest he was still very hungry. He would have to go to the shop in the morning and get food. He decided to leave early, and as planned he left before the sun was up.

He arrived at the shop just as the Chinese man was opening the doors. They knew each other well and exchanged greetings. Daniel told him what had happened the day before, and the man listened impassively without much comment. He had not seen or heard any news of his wife or daughters, and there was nothing to report. Packing his groceries in a sack he started off to return home. It was just passed mid-morning when he arrived back home, and as he entered the gate he saw that a man was in the house searching through what was left. Quietly he closed the gate behind him and went to the side of the house to look through a window. The man inside was Burke. Quietly he mounted the steps and was in the room when Burke turned and saw him. He was visibly startled and took a step backwards before opening his mouth to speak. But Daniel spoke first.

"W'at y'u doin' in me house?" he demanded. "Wat y'u doin' in me house Mr. Burke?"

"It is no longer your house," Burke replied. "This house belongs to Mr. Henderson now."

"Well Sur," Daniel continued. "W'en I tells y'u dis is my house it is my house, an' y'u is to fine' y'uself outside. An' if y'u is not outside by time I count t'ree, I'se goin' t'row y'u out!"

"Alright Daniel," Burke conceded. "Alright. I don't want any trouble with you, but you will see when I come back." He moved quickly towards the doorway out on to the steps and turned to Daniel once again. "Mr. Henderson has told me to make sure the house is empty, and that means you will have to get out."

"Get outa me house," Daniel shouted, and at the same time moved towards him in a threatening manner.

Burke did not stop to argue the point. He was quickly out of the gate, standing in the roadway. He turned to Daniel again, still at the top of the steps. For a few moments it seemed as though Burke was about to say something, and then he must have thought better of it. He turned and walked on a few paces, and as the distance between them grew, it gave him courage to redress his unceremonious eviction. With the distance between them, he felt safe and was ready to argue the point; he stood his ground. He shouted back, "You're a damned thieving lot, and when I come back, you had better be gone."

Daniel was seething with anger, and frustration. It was as though there was nothing he could do to help himself—he had been overwhelmed by circumstances quite beyond his control, and there was little he could do about it—nothing to fight against. Suddenly, uncontrollable fury overtook him and he lost all capacity for reasoning and self-control. For several minutes he went insane; he did not know what he was doing and had no power to stop himself. He dashed out of the house following the man that had just left. As he raced towards him he searched the ground for stones and found two. With all his might he hurled a large stone at the now hastily departing figure. It went head-high missing its target by inches, but the second one that quickly followed, struck the man on his shoulder as he turned and it knocked him to the ground. Fortunately it did not strike his head, as it would surely have killed him, but even so, he had been hurt. Burke sat in the middle of the path looking at his assailant in fear and surprise. Daniel was searching for more stones, and Burke seeing this, had no doubt that he would be killed if he stayed there longer. He got up holding his injured shoulder, and hunched over he ran down the pathway for several minutes before stopping to turn around again, look for his assailant and nurse his injury.

Daniel found several more stones but when he looked again there was no one in sight, the man had fled. Angrily he threw the stones away and returned to his house. As he entered anguish replaced his temper, and in a few moments he broke down completely, and he began to weep. The emotional outburst lasted only a few minutes before he was able to control himself.

"O God!" he thought, "What have I done? What have I done?"

His violent reactions had been quite uncharacteristic—so much so that he did not understand himself. Everything had happened as though in a dream. How could he have done such a thing? What if he had killed Burke? Even now he deeply regretted what he had done, and would have given anything for it not to have happened. He sat outside until it began to get dark in the evening. He was emotionally exhausted and did not eat before going to sleep. He awoke very early the following morning to find that depression had left him, and he felt better. He must have been exhausted because he had slept very soundly, and felt so much better for it. His head had cleared and he could think.

Burke's two hired men were strangers in the community and kept mostly their own company, not mixing to any extent with the local people. They took their orders directly from Burke, and had positions of favour and authority. The workmen who had been there for years, resented the newcommers, but not only that, Burke's men were feared because of their brutish manners, especially the Rastafarian, who always carried a very sharp cutlass. Furthermore, from time to time they 'skimmed' the wages of the workers to ensure their continued employment, and they bullied the weaker workers.

Daniel knew he could be arrested and charged for attacking Burke, but on thinking it over concluded that Burke would not take that route—he would more likely bring his men with him to extract his revenge. He was sorry for what he had done, not so much because of the possible consequences, but because it was a savage thing to have done, and it was not his way of doing things. But he couldn't undo it. Maybe, with the passage of time the anger would subside, and if he could avoid Burke and his henchmen for a while they may give up looking for him. But Burke would probably soon be on his way back bringing his men with him; he should make plans and be on his way.

About a year earlier he had buried money in the back garden for emergencies. Along with the money was the deed to the property, his birth certificate and the agreement he and the Squire had signed. These had all been wrapped tightly in brown paper tied with string and put into a small biscuit can with a tightly fitting lid. He dug up the tin, put the money in his pocket, and the can was put in the sack along with other personal possessions. He collected all the groceries and stuffed them into the sack, and some yams that he dug from the garden. What remained in the house he did not want to leave, but if he was to live as a fugitive they would have to be left. Hurriedly he hid the sack in the bush some distance from the house where he hoped it would not be found.

He locked the gate before leaving, and took off to Chivers. He had not been to work for several days, and although he did not think that would be a problem, he wanted to explain his absence, and he wanted to see Opal, to tell her what had happened between him and her mother. At Chivers he found her in the kitchen. They were so involved talking that they forgot about Henry. He appeared unexpectedly at the kitchen door with the little girl asking for her lunch.

He told Henry about the trouble with Sapphire, and then ate with Opal in the kitchen before leaving to go to work. Among the workers in the back segment were several men he regarded as good friends. He told them what had happened between him and his wife, and about the incident with Burke; that he would probably loose his house, and that Burke's men might be looking for him. They all agreed to tell him if anyone came looking or asking for him, and even to help hide or defend him if necessary. Although he had been part of management he was fortunate that he had many good friends amongst the workers who regarded him as one of them, and they were quite ready to help him if they could.

Opal was very anxious to know about her mother, where she was and what she was doing. She was also anxious about her sisters, but her immediate worry was for her father, if he could be arrested, and where he would live when he lost the house. On the estate there were vacant rooms at the back of the stables that were used as living quarters for workers who could not return home at night. At present they were empty and Opal suggested that he could stay there. He had a good supper before leaving to return to his house.

It was just getting dark when he left—a half-moon was rising over the eastern mountains; it would not be one of those very dark nights, when it would be so difficult to make ones way even on a familiar path. Nearing the house, he cautiously approached from the back before deciding to go inside. There just might be someone in the house waiting for him. He had almost reached the back fence when he heard a low growl, then snarling, and then a chorus of growling and barking erupted from a pack of wild dogs. He jumped back as the dogs rushed the fence where he stood. He knew the fence was strong enough to keep dogs inside, but he was not sure the gate was closed, and that the dogs had not been left free to roam. He quickly backed off and hid in the bush, crouching down. Someone might be in the house, and they could release the dogs if the gate was closed. He remained quiet until the dogs stopped barking; no one appeared or called to the dogs. There was no light coming from the house and he guessed that there was no one there—that the dogs were only put there to keep him out. He searched in the bushes and found a stout branch, which he broke off and stripped of smaller branches. He needed a weapon if the dogs were free.

Again he approached the fence and again the dogs were aroused, jumping up at the fence, barking and snarling viciously at him. As he walked slowly around towards the gate the pack followed him on the other side becoming more and more agitated as he moved. Two of the animals started to dig under the fence in a futile attempt to break out. As he got to the gate he could see that it was closed, but was it locked? Cautiously he approached and poked it gently with the stick. It held firm. He went closer and tested it. It was locked and did not yield. He could not see into the house, but he was now certain that no one was inside. The pack continued their barking, growling and snarling with ever increasing ferocity, and he knew as a certainty, he would never get into the house. In the dim light he saw a white object stuck to the middle of the gate. He put out his hand and removed a sheet of paper pinned to the gate. There was writing on the paper and he examined it closely, but it was impossible to read, so he folded it and put it in his pocket. He had to decide what he was going to do for the night—he would need a place to sleep.

It was getting very late and he was tired; he needed to rest. Without access to his house rest would not be possible staying where he was. He decided to recover his sack, return to Chivers, and sleep in the stables where he knew he would be safe and comfortable. He retreated from the gate to look for his sack. He looked in the bushes behind the tree where he thought he had hidden it; it was not there. Perhaps it was another tree or another bush? He searched around without success. The dim light from the moon was not bright under the trees and in the bushes, and it gave the place quite a different and confusing appearance. After searching about he was not even sure that he was looking in the right places. Again he searched where he thought it might be, still without success, and then he began to think that someone must have found the sack and taken it away. With that depressing thought in mind, he returned to Chivers and spent the rest of the night in the stables.

It was just getting light when he awoke in the morning. For a while he lay where he was and tried to think. Then he remembered the paper he had taken from the gate the night before, and dug it from his pocket. It was a legal notice of eviction from Mr. Barrow. It informed him that the property had been seized in lieu of unpaid debt and would no longer belong to him, that he could contest the seizure by appearing in court; that he would be trespassing if he chose to remain there, and that he would be prosecuted if he did so. Furthermore it required him to surrender the deed to the Court House land registry. Upsetting as the notice was, it was something he had expected, although he did not fully understand all the consequences of the notification. He assumed that Burke had put the dogs on his property to keep him and anyone else out. He did not have much choice in the matter; he knew nothing about the law and did not have the money to get legal advice, but he would talk to Henry Thomson.

He got up and dressed, went to the house and waited outside the kitchen for Opal. Soon he heard sounds of movement and voices coming from her room, and she appeared with her daughter. As they had breakfast he told her what had happened during the night. Daniel met Henry as he left the house. They walked together to the stables as Daniel told him what had happened. He produced the eviction notice and Henry read it over without comment, and then he read it again still thinking.

"This is a difficult thing for you, Daniel," he said at last. "To do anything about this you need a lawyer, and you know, lawyers cost money. Sometimes a lot of money. But I don't think this is legal anyway. I don't think that what they are trying to do here is legal, but the trouble is you need a lawyer to fight it in court." Henry paused, and then continued, "As I understand it you have full title to the land and the money you owed was not for the land, so I don't see how they can take the land back. If the money owed was for taxes, then the property could be seized, and only the government can do that. And then it would belong to the government. It would not belong to William Henderson."

Daniel was beginning to understand.

"If you have the deed keep it. Don't ever give it to them. You keep it safe, because that deed says the land belongs to you even if someone else is living there. Whatever you do, make sure you keep it. You had better go and search for it now."

Daniel was soon on his way back to his house, anxious to find the bag with the deed and all that remained of his worldly possessions. Over and over he thought about it trying to remember exactly where he had hidden the sack.

Nearing the house he went into the bushes at the side of the roadway and again approached the house from the back. There was no sign of anyone there, but he was sure that the dogs would still be there. He did not want to arouse them, so he skirted the house to the place where he was sure he had hidden the bag. He did not see it and looked in another place. Still he did not find it, and he began to panic, searching wildly about in the bushes. Not finding it he stopped to rest against a large tree, looking about, and then, as if by inspiration, he suddenly recognized the hiding place. Slowly, breathlessly, he approached, and then, thankfully, he retrieved the sack still with all his belongings. In all the excitement of the search, he had not paid much attention to the house, and he was looking through the contents when suddenly there was a shout and voices coming from the direction of his house. The dogs started to bark excitedly. He turned to look and saw two men by the gate, one was pointing in his direction. Both men had seen him. One opened the gate and let the dogs out, while the other made his way quickly through the bush in his direction. He closed the sack and took off as fast as he could into the bush.

The pathways through the bush were familiar to him and he made the best use of the cover crouching low as he ran. Some distance further, he stopped to see how near his pursuer might be. No one was in sight, but he could hear the dogs barking. He stood to get a better view. He could not see the man who had started after him even though he might have been quite close, hidden from view in the bush. He could see the Rastafarian still outside the gate with the dogs. Three of the dogs were running about in an aimless state of excitement, while the other two had started to fight and were embroiled in a ferocious dogfight. The man was vainly trying to separate the dogs without getting bitten in the process.

He was about to resume his escape when he saw movement in the bushes not far away, and then a shout, and then the man was whistling and calling the dogs. He took off again as fast as he could, still keeping low to the ground, heading into higher ground. In the lower hills the land had been partially cleared for bananas, but there were only waist-high plants growing which provided little cover from view. He would be seen if he crossed over into the denser bush further up the hillside, but he did not hesitate—he knew that if the dogs took up the chase there would be no escape. The prospect of being torn apart by a pack of wild dogs did much to spur him on.

He started across the clearing, darting from side to side to avoid tripping on the small plants and piles of rotting banana trees cut down after the last harvest. Halfway across his pursuer saw him and shouted again for the dogs. The man was still in hot pursuit, but the dogs were not following. He reached the edge of the bush and turned again to look. The man was almost halfway across the clearing with several dogs following, but they had not seen him or picked up his scent, and were not showing much interest in the chase. He had lost ground, and at that rate would soon be overtaken—and if the dogs saw him they would be on top of him within minutes. Breathlessly he resumed his flight, looking for places that would offer some refuge, hoping that he might run into a work party on the plantation—but he knew that was unlikely. Then he thought about the cemetery—the abandoned graveyard—people did not like to go there, and the men—they were strangers, certainly they would not know about it. He made a sharp left turn, zigzagging through the bush, every once in a while turning to see if his pursuer had gained further on him.

About five minutes later and out of breath, he reached the edge of the cemetery. He looked about for a place to hide. He was exhausted from running up the hillside, and he needed to catch his breath. There was no obvious place, but perhaps an obvious place was not the best—it would be the first place they would look—he should find an unlikely place. Some of the graves, instead of mounds were shallow sunken holes, overgrown with creeping bushes and vines. Looking about for a better place he could hear the dogs getting nearer—he did not have much time—he would have to make a decision. He found a hole by accident, almost stumbling into it as he went past. It did not look like a hole until he tripped and nearly fell into it. The bush had grown up around and over the grave, and it had the appearance of a mounded grave. Quickly he lifted the bush and slid down under, pulling the bushes back over the place he entered. He lay still and heard footsteps approaching.

The man was walking slowly, evidently examining the strange place. He could also hear the dogs moving about. He took a deep breath as the footsteps got closer, and then he held his breath as they went past. He lay very still, not daring to even breathe for minutes, until he could hold his breath no longer. And then he could hear voices. The other man had arrived to join the hunt.

"W'at kind of place is dis?" one asked in a low voice.

"Me no know!"

"Me mebber see any place like dis!"

Then silence, only movement through the graveyard. The men were searching for him, sure that he was hiding there, somewhere. Then one man whistled and called to the dogs. He could not hear a whispered conversation. Then one man spoke in a low voice.

"Me no like dis place, man. —it is a graveyard, man. —duppy place!"

"Come, man let us go. 'Im mus' be garn long time."

"No! No! 'im a' hide here! Mek de dags fine 'im out!"

Minutes went by as the men encouraged the dogs by poking in the bushes here and there. The dogs were not helpful and showed no interest whatsoever. With the excitement generated by the men in trying to activate a search, the dogs started to fight again. A few minutes later they had separated the animals and resumed the search.

"Come man, 'im garn long time."

"Little time more. Me t'ink 'im is here."

And then the men were talking again but he could not hear. A few minutes later there was the sound of footsteps departing. He breathed a deep sigh of relief.

"T'ank God!" He closed his eyes, and breathed freely again.

The dogs had not picked up his scent, but he knew if they had seen him, he would have been torn apart in minutes. He rested another ten minutes, lying quietly in the hollow before cautiously removing the bush and crawling out. He brushed off the dirt and rotting leaves, retrieved his sack, and slowly made his way out of the cemetery into the bush beyond. He had his sack and did not need to go back to his house; he would make his way back to Chivers going through the Manor House lands until he got there. He could have gone down to the road where the walk would have been easier, but there was the risk of meeting the men. Going through the bush would take at least twice as long, and he would not get to Chivers until the evening, but it was safer.

He arrived at the back road leading down to the Manor House in the late afternoon. On the way he stopped at the stables and left his sack under the bed in one of the out rooms, and then he made his way to the back of the house at the kitchen. Opal was in the kitchen preparing the evening meal.

"Where y'u been?" she asked breathlessly. "Ah did t'ink y'u come back long time. Me did fret fe y'u Pappa!" Her voice was anxious and her face showed her concern.

"Ah did 'ave some trouble,—" he began to explain, but she interrupted.

"Two men was here lookin' fe y'u all day. Me nebber see man so bad! One a Rasta! Dem was swearing an' cussin'! De bad word jus' fly outa' dem mout'! Ah 'fraid so—Ah can't tell y'u! An' dey was lookin' fe y'u!"

"Me buck up wid dem, and dey try to run me down. Dey sick de dags 'pon me."

"Lawd! Pappa!" Opal gasped.

"Luck was wid me, chile," he continued. "Ah give dem de slip in de graveyard, an' de dags doant help dem."

"An' den w'a happen?

"Me drop down in one a' de graves, and cover up me self wid bush. Dey pass by an' no fine me—de Lawd was wid me, chile!"

He sat on a small bench at the kitchen table, resting his head in his hands. He was exhausted both physically and mentally, and still he could not relax. They continued to talk, discussing what should be done next. Opal gave Henry his dinner and returned to eat in the kitchen with her father and daughter. For the night, it was decided that he should sleep in her room with Precious, and that he should not risk staying in the stable rooms. It might be safe in a few days to sleep there, but for the time being they should all stay together at night.

The following morning Daniel returned to work as usual in the far section. Towards mid-morning Henry appeared on a horse—he had given up on the mule. The work on the plantation was almost completed for the time being, and would not resume for at least a month. There would only be work for a few of the men for one or two days every week, and the rest would not be needed until it was time to pick the fruit. Daniel knew that the job would not last through the year; he had managed the workforce so many years as headman at the Manor House Estate. Henry was there to tell the workmen that the work would be over at the end of that week. Daniel was not included, even though there would be little for him to do.

That evening Daniel went to the stable out-room. For a while he rested on one of the beds, and then decided to have a bath. Under the standpipe the water was very cold, but it felt good to be clean once again. Dressed again, he went to the kitchen at the back of the house to see Opal. She was not there, so he went to the front of the house where he found her sitting on the veranda playing with her daughter. Henry was there too, joining in every now and again. They did not stop the play when he appeared, so he joined them sitting on the lower step. Precious soon noticed him sitting alone and went over to him throwing her arms around his neck from behind, hanging there for a few minutes before climbing into his lap. She picked up his hand and began playing, separating his fingers to count them. After a few minutes, Opal went off to prepare the supper, and Henry left his chair to sit on the steps beside Daniel.

"Some bad news for you, Daniel," he began. "William Henderson was here this afternoon asking me about you, if you were working here."

Daniel continued to let the little girl count his fingers. That Henry and William had a mutual dislike for one another he was well aware; he had seen them disagree many times in the past. Henry was now living with Opal, and that would lead to further trouble with William if he found out. It could make things very difficult for everyone, especially for Opal and her daughter. He wrapped his arms about his grand daughter and hugged her as though to protect her, and waited for Henry to continue.

"He said you had assaulted his headman Burke, and that he was going to lay charges. I told him you were in your rights to throw the man out—that Burke was trespassing in your house and you had every right to throw him out. Anyhow, I don't think he will do that, but the worst thing is he expects to take charge of Chivers Estate."

They continued to discuss these events and the more they talked about it the more Daniel realized that he could not remain at Chivers—he would have to move on. He was an irritant to Harriet and her son—more so to Harriet—and they would stop at nothing to be rid of him and his family—he had already seen what Harriet was capable of. Even the goodwill of the Major and Mrs. Barnham might not save him, and Burke's men might eventually catch up with him—he could not avoid them forever, and he did not like the idea of having to live constantly fearful and watching for those men. He worried about his daughter and grandchild; he would not be able to protect them. Also Henry too, might be forced to leave. All in all, the best thing he could do for them and himself would be to go away. He had reached that conclusion when Opal called Henry to the table.

Daniel ate his supper with Opal in the kitchen, and told her of his decision.

"But w'ere y'u go, Pappa?" she wanted to know. "All y'u life y'u live 'ere, an' now dey mek y'u leave?"

"Never mine. Me will mek out. Ah will fine work fe do. Y'u will see."

Later that night, Opal told Henry and begged him to help her father, and persuade him not to leave—to help him and keep him there.

"Well, I can help him only so much. If William takes over Chivers then there's very little I can do to help him. I might have to leave too!"

That was a very sobering thought that kept her restless most of the night.

Daniel knew that at the end of the week he would not have any real work to do. Furthermore, if he stayed at Chivers, he would have to live with the constant threat that Burke's men would find him. He could not live comfortably with that threat hanging over him. He did not have much choice—he would have to leave and find work in some other part of the island, where he was not known, and where William could not damage his reputation. There was nothing to be gained by putting it off, so he wanted to leave as soon as possible—the very next morning if possible. He told Henry of his plans in the morning. At first Henry tried to disuade him, but seeing that he was quite determined, Henry went to his wardrobe to find him some better clothes. Later in the morning he gave him money, enough for a week or two until he could find a job. In the morning he said his goodbyes, and gave Opal the deed and his birth certificate for safekeeping. Just before noon, with a bundle under his arm, he walked to the coastal road to await the bus to Port Maria.

CHAPTER 31

When the Henderson family again took up permanent residence in Kingston, William was the only member to return to Manor House Estate regularly, at least once, and usually twice every month. He was unsure about Burke, but not for any special reason. He did not like the two men Burke had employed to work on the estate; they were rough, surely men, and one was a Rastafarian with dirty, long braided hair, and they were too close to their employer for his liking. He never had anything to do with them, but for all that, he was prepared to tolerate them as long as there were no problems. William therefore made regular visits to review matters with Burke, and to make sure that there were no urgent problems requiring his attention.

Harriet never visited the estate at all during that time, not that she had lost interest in what was going on there, but because she found the day-long drive quite tiring. When William came home he was required to make a full report to his mother, even though she now had little meaningful input to what took place there. William had developed something of a 'deaf ear' to his mother's instructions, and usually followed his own instincts. Sometimes she asked about Daniel, if he had as yet been evicted, but William, in spite of his mother's constant nagging, had never seen that as a matter for immediate attention. He had pangs of guilt at times and felt that he should leave things as they were if there was no real reason to change. He even had a wistful longing for his erstwhile lover, and that stopped him from making their lives more difficult if it could be helped. Burke though, had been a bit of a pest; he was living in one of the rooms off the servants' quarters, which he found quite unbecoming to his position of headman, and he complained at every opportunity.

The time in Kingston though, had been quite eventful for the young businessman. Although he was not enthusiastic about the proposition, he had been pressured into an engagement to Bridget Barnham. It happened that year at the Barnham's New Year's party with a large number of guests present. He had just come off the dance floor with Bridget and they joined his mother, Mrs. Barnham and a number of guests standing about with drinks in hand.

"Here come the happy couple," said one in the group half seriously, but loud enough to be heard by everyone near by. "When are you going to announce the happy day William?"

The question caught him off guard. What happy day? He was embarrassed, and at a loss for a quick reply. He had not shown any particular interest in getting engaged; he had only casually dated Bridget, and had never given her any reason to think that it was his intention to propose marriage, even though for some it was the unspoken expectation. His mother had constantly asked the same question; he had ignored it and had never committed himself in any way. He liked Bridget, but he was not 'in love' with her, and he did not feel passionate about her, and certainly not in the same way that he had felt about the headman's daughter, Opal, who was often on his mind.

Before he could catch his breath another member of the group joined in, "You are such a lucky young man," she piped up. "Bridget is such a delightful girl! You will make a lovely couple!"

Bridget blushed noticeably. William looked at her still groping for words.

Another member of the gathering, assuming their engagement was being kept a little secret, joined in with "congratulations and best wishes for all the happiness in the world!" Contradictions or protestations at that point were out of the question. William was so off guard that he could only politely mumble his thanks. Mrs. Barnham took a step closer to him, impulsively threw her arms around his neck and kissed him, while his mother beamed with delight. He had not wanted it nor had he sought it, but he was now trapped, engaged to Bridget Barnham. The word spread quickly through the partygoers, many offering their congratulations and best wishes, and there was no turning back.

Six months later, in the middle of June, it was a grand wedding; Bridget Barnham became Mrs. William Henderson. It was quite the social event of the month, if not of the year.

Following the honeymoon there was some discussion about where the newly weds should live. As both families had large spacious homes on the outskirts of Kingston, there was no need for them to either buy or rent their own home, which is what they would have preferred. Harriet, even before the wedding, was very insistent that they share her house. Living with his mother, married or single was not a big change for William, and it affected him little one way or the other, but it was a different matter for his new wife. Bridget, very much like her mother when she was young, was easily persuaded to do things that she really did not wish to do. She was not the kind of person to insist that her preferences be considered by others, and she agreed to live in her mother-in-law's house, but she was not happy with the arrangement.

A year after marriage Bridget had not adjusted very well. Mrs. Barnham had left the couple to work things out on their own, but Harriet, living in the same house, was constantly involved in the young couple's affairs, so much so, that Bridget was restless and very unhappy. Both mother-in-laws yearned for grandchildren, but a year after the wedding they were still disappointed, and there was no indication that things would change very soon. As the months went by, Harriet, with growing impatience, nagged her son constantly, and at times she directed her acrid comments towards her daughter-in-law. Mrs. Barnham, although no less anxious, spoke quietly to her daughter 'about the problems' and concluded that a change in their living conditions was what was needed.

Bridget wanted to return and live in her mother's house, but her husband strongly opposed the suggestion, knowing that it would unsettle his mother, and goodness knows where that would end. If they were to move into the Barnham house, there would have to be a good reason to do so, so as not to offend his mother. For a while the problem simmered without solution until Mrs. Barnham found the key; if she were to move out of her house and leave it vacant, it would be there, available for the couple. She could return to Chivers and live there— after all, she reasoned, her daughter was now married and she had accomplished her mission by moving to Kingston, so there was no longer any real need for her to remain there. A month later she had once again transferred her residence to Chivers, and her daughter had moved into her house in Kingston. And eight months later she was rewarded with the happy news that her daughter was pregnant, and the baby expected before Christmas.

The Henderson Trading Company was prospering as William found new opportunities for profit and expansion, and took advantage of them. Part of the expanding business came from the export of produce collected from various north coast plantations. A number of these estates were either too small, unwilling or unable to profitably handle the shipment of their own produce, so, by combining the shipping of produce under one organization, William was able to realize significant efficiencies—and profits. As there were much larger quantities to be collected and shipped it was necessary to obtain additional storage and shipping facilities on the north coast, and William found exactly what he needed. Just outside the town of Annotto Bay there was a disused warehouse wharf and pier that had fallen into disrepair. These were purchased and the buildings quickly renovated.

Labor management had never been William's strong point, and being pressed for time he put Burke in charge of the project. Burke could manage the day to day operations with direction and instructions from him, and he would continue to let Burke hire the workers, arrange the necessary transport and storage of the collected produce. He knew Burke hired men that he deemed unsavory, and although he was hesitant, he allowed Burke the freedom to hire as he pleased, just as long as the jobs got done.

From time to time William and his wife came down from Kingston to stay at the Manor House Estate, and Bridget would use the opportunity to stay with her mother at Chivers, often for several days. William was occasionally in contact with Henry Thomson to co-ordinate shipping arrangements and other matters, but the meetings were short, businesslike and not friendly.

Their respective responsibilities did not overlap or conflict, which was fortunate in light of their mutual dislike for one another. Nevertheless, William was uneasy and resentful of the fact that Henry worked happily for his mother-in-law, and that she was evidently quite satisfied to keep him there. Henry's continued employment was unnecessary, he thought, as Burke could manage both the Estates, and if Henry were let go there would be less costs and greater profits. For several months he was reluctant to voice this opinion to Mrs. Barnham, but he was only waiting for the right time and was on the lookout for an opportunity.

With his child expected in a few months, he felt that the opportunity was close at hand, and in a moment of bravado he told Henry that he expected to take over Chivers Estate. That news unsettled Thomson, as intended, and William hoped that it would result in his leaving Chivers.

Several months after Daniel's departure there had been no new developments at either estate. Henry had become very fond of Opal's daughter and treated her as if she were his child. The little girl displayed the brightness and intelligence of her grandfather. Henry was constantly astounded by her curiosity, by her desire to learn, and he dedicated himself to teaching her at every opportunity. It would be such a pity if the little girl was denied the chance to learn, and it worried him that he was hardly in a position to change that. He talked to Opal many times as he tried to find some way in which he could get the child into a good school and keep her there. At one point he even considered approaching William—after all, he was her father and certainly bore some responsibility for her education. Opal, on the other hand, would not hear of it, and she refused to give it even a second thought. Henry finally agreed when he realized that William would almost certainly refuse.

After Mrs. Barnham's return to Chivers, Opal was careful to keep her daughter out of sight, and to avoid meeting Mrs. Barnham. The child's complexion would lead Mrs. Barnham to believe that Precious was Henry's child—but under the circumstances, it was preferable by far, not to arouse the woman's curiosity. She did not wish Mrs. Barnham to know that Precious was her daughter and that she was in fact living with Henry. Precious was almost five years old, and could be easily kept out of sight at that age, but as she grew older, it became far more difficult. A year later, Precious often wandered freely about the grounds, and had already been seen a number of times by the curious and interested Mrs. Barnham.

On Sunday afternoons Mrs. Barnham usually went for a drive in the country, and was therefore not often about the house or garden. In her absence Henry and Opal would sometimes go for a walk together, holding hands with Precious in between. On one such Sunday afternoon Mrs. Barnham did not go on her usual excursion. A visit to friends in Port Antonio had been abruptly cancelled, and she found herself without any planned diversion, and was a little depressed. Instead she went for a stroll about the garden. It was a sudden and unexpected meeting when she came face to face with Henry, Opal and Precious. Everyone was surprised, and for several moments no one spoke, and when they did, it was exactly at the same instance. Everyone was saying "good afternoon" at the same time, and then everyone was a little embarrassed, and realizing that they started to laugh at their own discomfort.

Mrs. Barnham was quite delighted to meet them even if for only a few minutes. As Opal had expected, Mrs. Barnham was most interested in Precious—she knew that Henry's children were very much older, and she wanted to know whose child she was, her age, and just about everything else. When she learned that Opal was the child's mother, she was quite unable to conceal her astonishment—she wanted to know more. It would not have surprised her if Henry was her father, and her curiosity might have ended there, but hearing that Opal was her mother raised the natural question, who then was the child's father? Was it Henry? Mrs. Barnham was tactful enough that she did not ask, but it was clear that it was foremost in her mind. She must find out!

The conversation having reached that far concluded with casual pleasantries, but not before Mrs. Barnham issued an invitation to Precious to visit her one afternoon in the following week.

"You must come and visit me. Soon," she said. "Come and have tea with me on Tuesday. I have some English biscuits—I know you'll like them!"

Tuesday afternoon came and went to the complete satisfaction of Mrs. Barnham, and to Opal it brought relief. For the few days prior, Opal had been worried and anxious—she did not really understand just why she was so anxious—the worst embarrassment had already happened when they suddenly met Mrs. Barnham in the garden, so not much more could happen. Precious did not know who her father was and she probably never wondered, but she knew that Henry was not, so no secrets could be betrayed. But Opal did not like the idea that Mrs. Barnham might know they were living together.

A few days later in the morning, Mrs. Barnham appeared at the front door to Henry's cottage. Precious was at the dining table with books spread untidily before her and Opal was in the pantry. Both responded immediately to Mrs. Barnham's knocking, but Precious got there first, and took Mrs. Barnham by the hand to lead her into the dining room. Her daughter's cordial greeting and her eagerness to see Mrs. Barnham surprised Opal, but she returned to the pantry when Mrs. Barnham became engrossed with the little girl and her storybooks. Opal returned half an hour later with lemonade to find them still deeply adsorbed. Mrs. Barnham stayed for over an hour, and as she left to return home for lunch, she insisted that Precious be allowed to visit her soon again.

Mrs. Barnham's curiosity and interest in the child had peaked and she was determined to find out who her parents were. This was not entirely idle curiosity on her part, she was genuinely interested in the pretty, bright, little girl, who reminded her so much of Bridget when she was little, and it reminded her of the happiest days of her life. She asked Constance about Precious, but Constance was hesitant to say anything more than what she knew to be the facts; that Opal was her mother and that Henry was not her father. Because William was married to Bridget, Constance would not have dared repeat the gossip about her son-in-law—that she would not do—it would be far too upsetting for her mistress to learn the truth, and if she ever did, it would not be from her. But this did not in any way satisfy Mrs. Barnham—Constance could be wrong, and Henry could still be the child's father—she would have to get to the bottom of it.

CHAPTER 32

A month or more passed and Mrs. Barnham was none the wiser, but she had not lost her determination find out. William visited her a number of times, but it had not occurred to her that he could be the child's father—it was not a possibility that she would have entertained, even for a second. By asking him, she would be accusing him—accusing him of having an affair with a servant girl! Furthermore, her curiosity was more a woman's thing than a man's, and at the first opportunity she would ask Harriet.

During that time she had not seen Bridget for almost two months, and Mrs. Barnham was a little annoyed by her daughter's neglect. She therefore issued an invitation to her daughter—more in the nature of a command—to visit her the following weekend, and to bring Harriet as well. There were a few minor items of business for them to discuss and get cleared away, but more than that, it would be nice to see them all again. Harriet could stay at the Manor House if she preferred, and visit her for tea and dinner on Saturday night. The invitation was accepted, and Mrs. Barnham immediately alerted Constance to expect guests for the weekend.

By the Saturday morning everything was ready; the sandwiches prepared, Joseph was churning ice cream, and a large cake was baked, beautifully decorated with bright sparklers and red cherries. When Mrs. Barnham made her inspection just after lunch, everything looked so lavish—so nice—it would be a pity if only Harriet, William and Bridget were there to enjoy it all. On the spur of the moment she decided to invite Opal's little girl—she had become quite fond of her, she was very entertaining and had fine manners; there would be no harm in having her there. In fact it would be good for her too, to meet other people besides those just living on the estate. Constance was dispatched with the invitation for Pre to appear at the Great House at four o'clock.

The invitation was not unusual—there had been a number before, and a pattern had already developed. Precious was bathed early in the afternoon. She had a new frock that Opal had just sewn using the cloth from one of Marjorie's abandoned dresses. With her hair brushed and lightly curled, and her new frock, she made a very pretty picture indeed.

Being a Saturday afternoon, Henry was home for lunch and for the rest of the day. He offered to walk over to the Great House with Precious at four o'clock. It was nearly ten minutes after the hour when they left, so they hurriedly made their way over. They mounted the front steps and were immediately seen by Mrs. Barnham who was expecting them. On the veranda she thanked Henry for bringing her, and he left to return home, saying that he would call again at six o'clock to see her home. Mrs. Barnham bent over to admire the new dress, saying how pretty it looked, and then taking Precious by the hand she led her into the drawing room where every one was assembled.

"I would like you meet my new ward," she announced. "Her name is Precious."

All eyes were turned towards the little girl. Bridget was sitting in a chair with William standing nearby, and she smiled a greeting. Harriet had been examining the ornaments on a shelf against the far wall, and she turned around as Mrs. Barnham entered. Her gaze was fixed upon the child, staring, and then her mouth opened slightly as she gasped. For several seconds she just stared, and then clouds began to gather before her eyes obscuring objects in the room. In the child's face she saw the face of her son, William. It was as though she were looking at his photograph through a heavy mist. It was the kind of recognition that only a mother or grandmother could see in a near relative, and it shocked her beyond belief. The clouds grew thicker, the room began to tilt one way, then another, she swooned and fainted, collapsing on the floor before anyone could reach her. Everyone's attention had been on the child, and when they turned about it was to see Harriet lying crumpled on the floor.

Bridget gasped as William rushed to his mother's side. In a moment everyone was bending over her, fanning her face and raising her head to place a cushion. Mrs. Barnham rushed to the bedroom for her smelling salts, and Constance poured a glass of water. In a few minutes Harriet opened her eyes—it was like a dream and nothing seemed real. It had been a shock but she recovered quickly. William produced a small brandy and soon his mother was seated in a chair, once again completely recovered. No one asked her what had happened, or why. But it was just a fainting spell, she explained.

The visit was something less of the success that Mrs. Barnham had hoped for. Harriet recovered quickly, but remained very quiet and subdued for the rest of the afternoon. Bridget was obliged to return to the Manor House with her that evening, thus depriving Mrs. Barnham the opportunity to talk privately with her daughter or to question Harriet.

As soon as Harriet was alone with her son it all came streaming out, "Do you know who that little girl is?" she asked him with heated emotion. "She is your daughter!"

He sat passively without answering, staring vacantly about the bedroom. How would his mother know that? He wondered. He would not have noticed any likeness to his features, and he was sure that no one else had. But in his heart he knew that she was indeed his daughter.

"How did she get here?" Harriet continued. "Why is she here?"

"I really don't know, Mother. What makes you think she is my daughter?"

"I could see it in her face. There is no doubt—she is your daughter—the child you bred with that dirty little whore you were fooling around with. How you could have done such a stupid thing I don't know."

"How can you be so sure? I thought that the woman was in prison, and you said that would be the last of her."

"That child is your daughter—I know that for certain. You will have to get rid of her or she will be after you for money. Think of the scandal if your wife and her mother ever find out. It will mean the end of everything. Oh! William! What have you done!" She covered her face with both hands.

Impulsively, without thinking, he asked, "Is that why you fainted?"

The question caught Harriet by surprise, and it was acutely embarrassing for her, and for several seconds she groped for an answer. "It was a terrible shock," she said at last.

"Alright, Mother," he said weakly, trying to set her mind at ease, "I will find out." At that moment Bridget entered the room and the conversation ended. William approached his mother, "Good night, Mother," he said, and kissed her on the cheek.

Mrs. Barnham was not particularly suspicious about Harriet's sudden fainting spell; she did not see any connection between Precious and Harriet's sudden collapse. Harriet may just not have been feeling very well at the time she thought. Constance on the other hand read a great deal into the incident, and soon it was common knowledge on both estates, garnished with all kinds of rumor and gossip.

"She eye catch de chile an' she drop down same time!"

174

"Dat is fate!"

"She wickedness ketch up wid her!"

When Precious got home she instantly conveyed the news to Opal and Henry. From her description of the event—the woman's penetrating stare, fixed on her face, and then her collapse, there was no doubt in their minds that Harriet had recognized the child.

"Why did she look at me like that?" Precious was upset and wanted to know.

For Opal, it was Harriet's sins overtaking her, but she did not derive any particular satisfaction from the event. Henry was certain that Harriet had recognized Precious, and he was not amused—he knew the woman and he worried about it. However, as the days turned into weeks and nothing unusual occurred, he became much less concerned, and gradually they did not think of it at all.

It was now almost a daily occurrence that Precious spent the morning with Mrs. Barnham reading stories or being taught to read and write, and with the increased tutoring, she was making excellent progress. Henry had been concentrating on language, insisting on correct words and pronunciation. Although he was Jamaican born and bred, from an early age he went to a public school in England and had a somewhat 'refined' English accent. It was not a matter of snobbery, it was just what he had grown up with and he never lost the accent. He insisted that Precious at least learn to read, write and speak properly. Good language and pronunciation, he felt was very important.

Some weeks later Henry called in to see Mrs. Barnham about estate matters, and having done that was about to leave when Mrs. Barnham stopped him.

"I want to talk to you about little 'Pre,'" she began. Mrs. Barnham had given up on 'Precious' and had nicknamed her 'Pre. ' "She is a very clever little girl."

"Yes she is," Henry agreed. "She surprises me every day!"

"You know, I have been teaching her, and she is getting quite beyond me. I can't seem to find anything else to teach her. I think she should be sent to school."

Henry had thought about it many times, and it worried him that he did not have the means. He blamed himself that he did not have the money—that he had never saved any money in all his life, and that he had wasted a small fortune in his younger days. But he was embarrassed to confess his faults to Mrs. Barnham—they were pretty obvious.

"I have been thinking about that for some time," he said, "but it would be difficult for me."

"Well I think I could help," Mrs. Barnham said. "In a few years she should be going to a proper school. She is very bright and she learns very quickly. She would do very well."

Henry was wondering just what was coming next, and he did not answer.

"What would you say if I undertake to see that she gets an education?"

"That would be wonderful," he said, "and I would be most grateful." And then he added, "But she is not my daughter, you know. I would have to ask her mother."

"Well, please do that, and then you can let me know? There's lots of time, but it would be good to make these plans now."

"Thank you so much. It's really most kind of you." He thanked her again and hurried home to tell Opal.

Mrs. Barnham sat by herself on the veranda thinking, "If he is not her father, then who is?"

CHAPTER 33

Following their weekend visit, William departed for Kingston early on the Monday morning, Bridget sitting beside him and his mother in the rear seat. They did not return to Chivers or see Mrs. Barnham again that weekend. As soon as they were on the road he started to think and remained deep in thought for the entire journey, hardly noticing the road. There had been no opportunity for him to find out anything more about the little girl introduced to them as Mrs. Barnham's 'ward.' Nevertheless, in his mind he knew that his mother was right— the little girl must be his daughter. It worried him more that his wife and her mother would eventually discover the truth. Still, he pondered his mother's assertion—was the child really his? Was his mother just being dramatic because it was possible, and she had thought about it a lot?

The thoughts whirled through his mind; if the little girl was Opal's daughter then Opal must be living at Chivers. If not, then where would she be living? And then it came to him—she could be living with Henry! He remembered how Henry had reacted to Opal when they met in the Paradise Bar—over five years ago—he remembered every little moment—the look on Opal's face too, as he gazed into her face. A surge of rage and jealousy made his head pound and he nearly lost control of the car. His mother shouted at him as he regained control, and she continued to lecture him about his careless driving for the rest of the journey home.

He had not intended returning to the north coast for at least three or four weeks, depending on the necessity of making the trip, but that would have to change now. He wanted to find out where Opal was staying and wanted to get there much sooner. In the years that had passed he had often thought about Opal—she was far from forgotten, and he wished that things had been different. He even dreamed about her, and fantasized that he could keep her as his secret lover and his mistress. But all this was wishful thinking on his part—his marriage to Bridget was his reality—at least for the time being.

A week later he had arranged to be back at the Manor House Estate, but one thing after another interrupted those plans and it was three weeks before he returned. One of the interruptions was his wife's condition—there was a minor problem with the pregnancy and he had been unable to leave, but everything was fine now, and he was on his way back to the Manor House. On the way he stopped in Port Maria, and then detoured to Annotto Bay to complete some business there. He did not arrive at the estate until well after dark. The next morning after lunch he met Burke on horseback, and then rode over to Chivers.

He had nothing in particular to do at Chivers other than to satisfy his curiosity and find out if Opal was living there. Mrs. Barnham always rested for at least an hour or more after her lunch, so he did not expect to see her, and he could always find some excuse for being there if he happened to meet Henry. He kept thinking about Opal, and his mother's words ringing in his ears, "You will have to get rid of her!" But what could he do about the child? There wasn't really anything that he could do.

He rode through the bush along the pathway connecting the two properties in the rear, and so did not pass by the great house. At the produce shed he dismounted and led the horse by the reins to the stables. He saw no one on the way over—the place was deserted, but that was not unusual at that time of the day. He tethered the horse in the stables and made his way down the path to the Busha's cottage. The house as usual, was wide open, but he did not see or hear anyone, and he went around to the kitchen. In the pantry through the open door he saw Opal. Her back was turned and she did not see him. Quietly he mounted the steps and was almost in the room when she turned and saw him. She froze for a moment, but she did not scream, and she did not speak. Slowly she began to back away from him towards the open door leading into the house.

He watched her without speaking and made no motion towards her. Then he asked, "How have you been?" Now he saw her again for the first time in six years, and he felt a rush of blood as his pulse increased. She looked the same, as pretty as ever, only more grownup, not so girl-like.

Opal did not answer. She glared angrily at him and backed away, startled and frightened.

"I have been wanting to see you for a long time," he continued, and held out his hand towards her. She backed further away and still did not answer. He started towards her and she made a dash for the door. She misjudged the opening and bounced into the wall, and he caught up to her, grabbing hold of her arm and holding it tightly. In panic she fought to get away striking at his face with her free hand.

"I only want to talk to you," he said. "I just want to talk to you."

"No! No!" and she continued to flail at his face with her free her arm and he was forced to hold her other hand to fend off the blows. And then she screamed out "No! No Master William!"

Precious had been sitting quietly in the dining room and she rushed in to see what the screaming was about. Without hesitation she ran at the man holding her mother and attacked him as best she could.

"Leave my Mamma alone," she screamed. "Leave her alone!"

William had not intended any confrontation with Opal. He had hoped to quietly talk to her and even perhaps regain her friendship, but this was getting out of control. He let go her arms and backed away. He was not going to get anywhere if the struggle kept up and he backed further away through the open door where he had entered.

"I only wanted to talk to you," he said again, quietly. "Only to talk to you."

Opal turned around taking Precious by the arm they ran into the bedroom and slammed the door shut.

For several minutes William waited. He was hoping that she would calm down and return when she understood that he only wanted to talk to her. But she did not reappear, and it made him feel helpless and angry. Slowly he turned and went back to the stables. He did not mount the animal but walked it down the pathway on his return to the Manor House Estate. He had not gone far when he saw Henry on his horse coming towards him from the opposite direction.

Henry was not about to show him any courtesies. What the devil does he want now, he was thinking?

"Yes?' he asked curtly.

The tone irritated William. What with Opal fighting him off, he was not in a pleasant mood.

"I came to see you," he began. There was no use beating around the bush he thought. "I want to know what is happening with your housekeeper and her daughter."

"That is none of your business."

"Are you living with her?"

"I told you, that's none of your business."

William fumed—the blood was surging through his head. He had always disliked the man, and now he hated him—enough to kill him, and he was mad enough at that moment to commit murder.

"I have a right to know."

"You don't have any rights in the matter," Henry answered. "You had your chance and you messed it up. You sent an innocent woman to prison. It doesn't concern you any more."

"What can you do for them?" William asked trying to find the weakest part of Henry's argument. And then in an exaggerated, sarcastic tone, "Are you going to marry her?"

"I will marry her if I choose—and I will adopt her child if I choose. You will not be able to interfere."

The answer rang true—it seemed to William that it was his honest intention. All the wishes, hopes and dreams of ever having the woman again vanished in the moment. The answer struck him like a blow to the stomach, it seemed to take the wind out of his lungs and leave him feeling weak and helpless. He took a deep breath, then another, and then he lunged towards Henry, sitting on the horse. He would settle the matter by killing the man—that now was his only option. Henry saw him coming and reacted quickly, backing the horse away, and raising his riding crop as if to strike.

"Don't think of it, William!" he shouted. "Don't even think of it!"

Henry and his horse were now out of reach, but William had not given up yet. He made another attempt to grab at the reins and bring Henry down. Again Henry was ready and drove the horse straight at him, hitting him with the animal's side and knocking him to the ground with a kick from his boot and stirrup. The horse made a complete about turn to face him again, but Henry did not let the horse trample him, as he very easily could have done. He stood the animal over him in a threatening position.

For a while William remained on the ground, looking up at the animal standing over him. Then slowly he picked himself up and dusted off his clothes.

"I'm going to get you fired! I am going to fire you. Think about that!"

William held his horse steady and mounted. "Think about that, Major!" He said as he turned and rode on.

As he neared the Manor House, his anger had not subsided, "I'm going to kill him. —I'm going to kill the bastard!"

That night his anger and frustration had not abated. He went to the stables and saddled his horse again. He mounted and turned the animal's head towards the open pathways. In the dim light of a half-moon, he was barely visible as horse and rider galloped through the night like a ghost in flight.

William had not lost his anger when he got up the next morning—in fact, he had simmered all through the night. His prime objective now was to get rid of

Henry Thomson. It made a great deal of sense to let him go—Chivers Estate could manage without him if Burke was given the additional responsibility. The problem was to get his mother-in-law to agree, and that would not be easy. The commonsense argument—one of saving money—was the best reason that he could put forward, but that alone would not persuade her. He knew that Mrs. Barnham was very comfortable having Henry there. If he could put himself in a very favorable light, then he might persuade her that it was a reasonable thing to do. Also, he might mention without stressing the matter that he and Henry did not always get along, and he could say that Henry was uncooperative at times and thus hindered the work.

By the time he had eaten his breakfast, he had worked out a plan. He would introduce his plan in a manner that would be sure to put Mrs. Barnham in a good mood—he would talk to her about the expected baby, and he would do that right away, before returning to Kingston. If this did not succeed he would have to fall back on a more drastic solution, but one way or another, he would see the last of Henry Thomson.

He packed the car in preparation for his return to Kingston, and towards the mid-morning drove over to Chivers. He parked the car by the front entrance, and entered the house from the veranda without knocking or calling out. Mrs. Barnham was sitting at the dining table with Precious, where they were looking at pictures and reading a story together. His entry did not surprise Mrs. Barnham, because she heard the car drive in and expected to see someone, but Precious was startled and seemed very afraid when he entered the room. The memory of the man struggling with her mother in their house the day before was fresh in her mind, and here he was again. She jumped up from her chair and stood behind Mrs. Barnham, evidently scared and looking for some safe retreat. "It's alright, dear," Mrs. Barnham said soothingly. "It is only Mr. Henderson. He's come to see me." And then to William, "Hello William. I didn't know you were here."

Precious did not seem convinced—she stayed close to Mrs. Barnham and as far away from William as possible. Mrs. Barnham was surprised by her nervous reactions but pretended not to notice; in fact it alarmed her too and aroused her curiosity. She took Pre by the hand and led her to the edge of the veranda.

"Pre, why don't you run home now, and then come back tomorrow? Mr. Henderson and I have some business to discuss, and I'll see you again tomorrow. Bye now."

Precious did not need urging, she ran down the steps quickly, and all the way home. Mrs. Barnham watched her turn the corner towards the cottage, and then

181

returned to the dining room, "What brings you here?" she asked. "How is your mother?"

"Fine, thank you. She's fine, and she sends her love."

"And Bridget?"

"Oh, she's very well too. There was a bit of a problem last week, but she's fine now. And the baby is fine too."

They were sitting on the veranda when Constance brought lemonade.

"Will it be a boy or a girl?" Mrs. Barnham mused. "If it's a boy what will you name him?"

"If it is a boy, Bridget wants to call him James—after Father. Mother doesn't like that—she wants us to name him William."

"Bridget was very fond of your father, you know. He was such a dear man."

"I had thought of Charles—after your father," said William, thinking that this would please his mother-in-law, and perhaps put her in a more pliable frame of mind.

"Oh, I don't think so," said Mrs. Barnham. "He died a long time ago, and I hardly got to know him very well. Although—I think he was a good man—I hardly remember him. If it's a girl, what will you name her?"

"I like Alice," said William smiling, shamelessly trying to build her goodwill.

Mrs. Barnham said nothing. She just smiled and looked at him—he had overplayed his hand—she knew he was trying to get on her good side. In spite of that she was a little flattered.

In a while the subject changed to matters of the estates, William saying that he was working to reduce the costs. He outlined several steps that he had already taken and said that more were necessary, and then be broached the subject that was foremost on his mind.

"A fair saving could be had if Henry Thomson were let go," he said as he explained the details.

Mrs. Barnham was quiet and thoughtful, and she did not interrupt—he may have said enough for the moment. So that was what it was all about, she thought. "I'll have to think about it," she said at last.

That was very noncommittal, William thought. He would have to strengthen his argument.

"There is another problem," he began. "You may know that Henry and I often do not see eye to eye about the way things should be done." He let that take effect too, and then he added, "He can be very uncooperative at times, and it's difficult to get things done."

"Oh," said Mrs. Barnham, "I wasn't aware of that. I always found him to be most helpful. Always."

William pressed his argument, "I really think it would be so much better if he were not in charge, and there would be some real savings too."

Mrs. Barnham was not happy with the suggestion; Chivers was her property, and she could run it the way she wanted and with the manager she wanted. Nevertheless, she was not going to lecture her son-in-law about minding his own business. In all probability he would acquire the estate in several years when she was no longer alive. Reducing costs was worth thinking about.

"I'll think about it William," was all she would say.

CHAPTER 34

Mrs. Barnham was quite excited by the news that she would be a grandmother before the end of the year, and she thought about it often. A day later though her attention returned to Pre and her morning visits. The child's reaction to William puzzled her when she thought about it, and then she thought about Harriet's fainting spell. That was strange too, because it happened when Harriet was looking so intensely at the little girl's face. Could there be some connection, she wondered? She decided to ask Pre if she knew William or Harriet. The little girl had always been so honest and open in talking to her; she was absolutely above guile, and she would tell the truth if asked. Mrs. Barnham decided not to leave it too long.

Two days later, in the middle of the daily lessons and without a prior hint, Mrs. Barnham asked, "Why are you so afraid of Mr. Henderson?"

Pre looked up, surprised by the question and unable to find an answer. She sat fidgeting with her pencil, her eyes fixed on her teacher. Mrs. Barnham knew immediately that there was something hidden in the child's mind and it would need a little urging to bring it out.

"It's alright, Pre," she said reassuringly, putting her hand on the child's arm and patting her gently. "I know that you're afraid of him, and I only wanted to know why."

For several seconds, Pre still could not find words, but she was trying, searching for some way to explain. "Well— " she said, and then stopped. "I— I"—and then stopped again. The words would just not come out.

"It's alright, Pre," Mrs. Barnham said again. "I won't let him hurt you." And then she added, "not while I'm around. Now why does he frighten you?"

The little girl took a deep breath, "He was in our house."

"He was in your house?"

"Yes, he was in our house, and was hurting Mamma!"

"How was he hurting your mother?"

"He was holding her like this," and she grabbed her arm with one hand. "And Mamma was screaming, and fighting him. I was screaming and fighting him."

Mrs. Barnham was shocked. This was far more than she had expected, and she wanted to know more. "And then what happened?"

"We ran into the bedroom and locked the door."

"And what happened then?"

"Well, he just went away."

"Why was he fighting with your mother?"

"I don't know. He just said that he wanted to talk to her."

"And what did your mother say?"

"She was shouting 'No! No!' And I was shouting leave my Mamma alone!"

"I see," said Mrs. Barnham. "I see." Then she added, "Well, he is not going to frighten you again. And he is not going to fight with your mother again. I will see to that."

A large part of the puzzle had been put into place, but it was not yet complete. Mrs. Barnham now had her suspicions, but they would have to be confirmed. It seemed that William was indeed the child's father, and that could explain a great deal. But the idea was very upsetting, and very disturbing, and she wondered how Bridget would take the news if and when she found out. But she would not learn it from her mother, even though that might be the best way. She only hoped that she was wrong—totally wrong—but what other explanation could there be? It would be a difficult family problem to resolve—already she was harboring disturbing thoughts about her son-in-law.

There were several choices open to her; she could ignore the whole thing, hoping that it would fade away and be forever forgotten. Or, she could bring it all out into the open, and hope that that would clear the air without doing too much harm. She had committed herself to helping Pre and to putting her through school—she could not turn her back on that promise for the sake of saving William some embarrassment. The delicate condition of her pregnant daughter worried her—it would not be wise to let her know of her husband's past at this time. And then there was the question of William's continued involvement with Opal; just how involved was he? Perhaps that was why he wanted to fire Henry—maybe it was to get rid of Opal and her daughter too? Or maybe it was just to get rid of Henry to allow him to continue an affair with Opal? Whatever it was it would have to stop immediately. For the next eight weeks though, and at least until the grandchild was born, she would have to keep her thoughts to herself.

Several uneventful weeks passed during which William did not appear at Chivers Estate, and Mrs. Barnham continued her meetings with Pre. A month later as the time approached, Mrs. Barnham traveled to Kingston to welcome the arrival of her daughter's baby boy. She did not stay there long—Harriet was not particularly friendly, and resented her presence in Kingston, so a week later she was back at Chivers.

After the New Year William visited her again, partly on business, and partly to bring her up to date on his new family. Bridget was still unable to travel long distances by car due to her carsickness, and would not be back on the north coast until she was feeling better. Mrs. Barnham would have to travel to Kingston if she wanted to see her daughter and her grandchild at any time. He again took the opportunity to ask her if she had given any further thought to discharging Henry. For a while it had looked like the problem was going away, but William's inquiry reawakened Mrs. Barnham to the fact that it was still very much alive, and it annoyed her.

"I told you already, William," she chided him, "I'll think about it and when I decide, I will let you know." At that point she had already decided; under no circumstances would she let Henry go. If she did, it would allow William—and his henchman Burke—access to her property, and she had no intention of allowing that—not while she was alive.

The following morning Mrs. Barnham settled Pre in with her books and then called Constance to sit with her for a while—she wanted to go over to the cottage for a few minutes and see Opal. She surprised Opal who was busy in the pantry.

"Opal," she called to her. "There is something I must talk to you about. Do you have a few minutes?"

"Yes mum."

"Can we sit somewhere and talk?"

"Yes mum. On the veranda," and she led the way.

"You know I'm very fond of your daughter," she began, "and I would like her to be happy. I don't want to see her hurt."

"Yes, mum?"

"But there's something that worries me very much, and I do not want it to become a big problem for us all. I hope you won't think I'm prying into your personal affairs, because I'm not. It is because the problem concerns me and my family as well."

"Yes, mum. What is it?"

"Precious is afraid of Master William. I know this because when he came over to see me she was very afraid of him. I sent her home for the day—you remember? The day she came home early? She must have told you why."

Opal thought for a few moments, then she said, "Yes mum, she did."

"Pre told me later that you were fighting with Master William, and you were afraid of him too. I want to know why. Why is he troubling you?"

Opal could not look Mrs. Barnham in the face. She sat uncomfortably in the chair fidgeting with her apron, and twisting her fingers together.

"It's alright, Opal," Mrs. Barnham continued. "I think I already know, but I want to be sure."

"I don't rightly know why, mam."

"Well, you must have some idea. Is Pre his daughter?"

For several minutes Opal could not answer—it was becoming too embarrassing and too painful for her to find words. Her eyes were brimming with tears running down her cheeks. Then she buried her face in her apron. In a minute, through the tears and sobs she answered, "Yes Mam. Yes he is."

For several moments Mrs. Barnham sat pitying the distraught woman, and then she left her chair to sit beside her. She put her arm around her shoulders and held her head close against her shoulder.

"There, there," she soothed. "It's alright—It's alright—it's all over now"

The sobbing soon eased and Opal was drying her tears. "It was very hard for me, Mrs. Barnham," she explained. "He is her father and he let her be born in prison. That was a terrible thing for him to do."

"She was born in prison?" Mrs. Barnham was astounded, "You were in prison?"

"Yes, Mam—for three years. They sent me to prison because of it."

Five years ago Mrs. Barnham had not been abreast of the rumor and gossip of the day. Indeed, she had been living in Kingston during the time of Opal's arrest and trial, and heard nothing of the scandal. She urged Opal on to tell the complete story. It was over an hour later that a thoroughly upset Mrs. Barnham returned to her house. She could scarcely believe what she had been told, but nevertheless, doubted not a single word. There has been a terrible injustice done, she thought, and it must be righted. And she would see to it.

Harriet was a strange woman, Mrs. Barnham thought; it was so cunning and vindictive to have planned it all. And poor Opal, innocent and naive, easily fell into the trap. But there was no excusing what Harriet had done—she had tricked the girl and lied in court—that was a criminal act—she could have been sent to jail. But Mrs. Barnham had no intention of doing that. Nevertheless, she was determined to see that Harriet did not get away with it. For several weeks she thought about it without finding some way to 'bring it home' to Harriet—that she knew—that everyone knew what she had done—and let her suffer the disgrace.

A month went by during which Mrs. Barnham did not change her behavior towards Harriet. They only met twice during that time; she remained as friendly as ever although she was constantly looking for an opportunity to bring it out into the open, and find some reason to talk about it. She was determined that it should be a lesson to Harriet, but when that happened Mrs. Barnham knew that Harriet would no longer be a friend. They would still be sisters-in-law, but they certainly would not be friends, and she would have no regrets about that.

Several days later Constance reminded her that it was her birthday in three weeks, and wanted to know what celebrations were planned—Constance always made a cake for Mrs. Barnham's birthday.

Mrs. Barnham usually acknowledged her birthdays with a small family gathering—and Constance's birthday cake—but this was her sixtieth birthday, something of a milestone in one's life, and perhaps there should be more than just a family gathering. As she thought about it that night, it occurred to her that this might just be the chance she was waiting for. She recalled how Harriet had fainted when she first saw Pre—now she knew why—obviously it was the shock of recognizing her son's illegitimate daughter. Perhaps it was also the fact that Pre, despite the color of her mother's skin was white, and was a charming little girl— one who would make any parent very proud. Little did Mrs. Barnham know that Harriet had seen the little white baby many times before, in the arms of a black woman, standing outside her gate, and recognition had been very easy.

"She made a mess," Mrs. Barnham thought, "and I'm going to rub her nose in it before I'm through."

The following morning Mrs. Barnham told Constance she had thought it over, and she had decided that, as it was her sixtieth birthday, she would have a big party and invite all her friends. Preparations started right away; the guest lists were made up and the invitations were written. There would also be houseguests and friends coming from other parts of the island, so all the spare bedrooms had to be cleaned, tidied and the beds made. The meals were planned and extra help was decided upon; two maids from the house in Kingston would be brought over for a week to help out in the kitchen and with the household duties. When Harriet was told about the party, she offered to help too, and offered to open the Manor House for overnight guests. Her offer was gladly accepted.

The party was to be an all-day affair; beginning in mid-afternoon. The guests, upon arrival would be offered tea or drink, sandwiches and cake. In the evening there would be a ball, dinner would be served, and then dancing into the night until the sun came up the following day, if there were guests still willing and able. An orchestra of eight was to be hired and brought from Montego Bay for the night.

Mrs. Barnham had ample and efficient help for things to be arranged; Bridget arrived from Kingston with her baby and the maids. But there were some plans that Mrs. Barnham kept to herself; she intended to invite Henry and Opal as guests. Because Opal's presence at such a gathering would be very disturbing to some people, and especially to Harriet, it had to be kept a secret. Above all Harriet must not know.

Early the next morning Mrs. Barnham went over to Henry's cottage and delivered the invitations. It was to be a formal party, black tie and evening dress, she told them. Henry was asked about his dinner suit, if it still fitted, and apparently it did; he had not outgrown it in over twenty years. Mrs. Barnham insisted that he wear his military medals—all five. There was nothing more splendid at a dinner party, she said, than to see the ribbons against a black serge jacket. Henry smiled and accepted; he was looking forward to the event; it had been such a long time since he had worn his evening dress.

But Opal was flabbergasted and immediately refused, excusing herself because she did not have a dress to wear. But the real reason for refusing of course, was that she had never been to such a party before, and was not used to mingling with white society—she would not know how to behave, she would feel out of place and would be embarrassed. It did not seem to make a difference that Mrs. Barnham literally begged her to accept; she steadfastly refused.

"You must be there—I will be offended if you do not come." But still she shook her head.

That night Henry tried to persuade her again. "I will teach you between now and then," he said. "If there is something you don't know ask me—I'll show you, and we can practice. It will be lots of fun. We can practice dancing too."

Henry understood exactly how Opal would feel, and he knew that he would have to build up her confidence, and he thought that it would be a good chance for them to be seen together. It would have to happen some time, he said, when they got married. But Opal had her mind made up and she would not change.

Mrs. Barnham had not given up—the whole point of having the party was getting Opal to be there, and not letting Harriet know. If Opal did not come or Harriet found out who was invited it would be for nothing and Harriet would have escaped. Opal had to be there, and Harriet must not know. At breakfast Mrs. Barnham brought up her plan and talked to Bridget about her intention of inviting Opal and Henry to the party.

Bridget was amazed at the idea and not very receptive. "Why? Why on earth would you do that?" she asked incredulously.

"It is something I have to do," explained her mother, not intending to divulge her real reasons.

"But why? Why would you ask a black woman to your party? It's going to be so-o-o-embarrassing."

"It goes a long way back," said Mrs. Barnham, "and it is something I should have done long ago."

"But Opal is only going to be embarrassed, and she won't have a good time. So why would you want to put her through that? That's cruel!"

Mrs. Barnham could not reveal the real reason for wanting Opal there. To do so she would have to tell Bridget the whole sordid tail about William's affair, and what Harriet had done to Opal. She wanted to spare her daughter the truth about her husband and his mother—at least for the time being—but at the same time she did have other reasons that she knew were meaningful too.

"You know your great-great grandfather owned a lot of slaves, and he was not a very kind man. Slavery was an awful thing, and it is something we should have made right a long time ago."

"What on earth does slavery have to do with Opal coming to your party?"

"Well we can't make it right for the slaves that suffered—there is nothing we can do for them now, and it's too late to say 'sorry,' and what good does 'sorry' do? But we can make it right for those living today, and at least we can show that we are sorry—that at least we are not like our ancestors—that we think differently—that we are different."

"O God! Mother!" Bridget said in utter exasperation. "How are you going to do that?"

"It's my way of showing that I know our ancestors were in some ways not good people, and that I am sorry for what they did. We have to show some respect now, and that is what I want to do."

"But only some of Opal's people were slaves—most came here freely from India."

"Yes, I know that, but she is a symbol—she is a black woman and represents black people who were slaves. I don't know anyone more deserving, or who would be a better symbol."

"No one will know why you are doing that, so why do it?"

190

Mrs. Barnham was disappointed at Bridget's reaction; she did not seem able to fully explain or persuade her daughter. She was crestfallen and showed her disappointment. "I do have other reasons as well, Bridge," she said, somewhat subdued. "They are good reasons believe me, and I want you to help me. You must help me. Some day you will understand."

Bridget sensed her mother's feelings, and was quiet for several minutes. "Alright Mom," she said. "It's your party and I'll do whatever you want." She leant over towards her mother, put her arm around her shoulder and kissed her on the cheek. Mrs. Barnham smiled as Bridget sat down again to finish her breakfast.

"What I want you to do," she began, "is to go over to see Opal this morning. Tell her you want her to go into town with you to get a dress for the party. Joseph can drive you. When you get there, you pick out the best dress you can find for her. Get everything that she needs—shoes, purse, a broach, bracelet, gloves—everything. Make a list so you don't forget anything. She must try on the clothes when you are in the shop—she will be too embarrassed to refuse in front of the owner, and make sure everything fits. If it doesn't, have the dressmaker alter it."

Bridget listened quietly—thinking. Then she said, "It will be fun! I don't think she has ever done anything like that in all her life! It will be lots of fun!" Full of enthusiasm, she hurriedly finished her meal and went over to see Opal.

Mrs. Barnham's scheme succeeded—the chance to have an evening gown was too much for Opal to resist, and by the evening, much to Mrs. Barnham's relief, Opal had accepted her invitation. That evening Henry started giving her lessons in dancing, manners and etiquette that lasted late into the night.

For several days the excitement of having a beautiful white silk evening gown had Opal forgetting her initial objections and reservations about attending. She put on the dress several times and looked at herself in the mirror, enjoying every moment. Henry was entranced—to him she had never looked more beautiful. He watched quietly sitting on the bed, and then he went towards her, and with both hands cupped her face, drew her closer to him and kissed her gently. She put her arms around him, they held each other closely for several moments, and then he helped her to undress.

Within a week though, her doubts and nervousness returned and she was again voicing objections. Bridget had visited her several times during that time to talk about the coming event, and sensed Opal's increasing anxiety. Henry too, began to notice, and privately talked to Bridget.

"She's having doubts," he told Bridget. "She lacks confidence and needs reassurance. I'm doing the best I can, but it's not helping. If you talk to her and show her how to do things I think it would help a lot."

Bridget agreed that she could help a bit, but was not entirely convinced; she did have other things that she wanted to do. Nevertheless, she mentioned it to her mother by way of conversation.

Mrs. Barnham reacted immediately and with alarm. "We must make certain that she comes," she almost shouted at her daughter. "You must help her—I want you to help her—whatever you can do."

"Alright, Mother," Bridget replied quietly, not wanting to upset her mother any further. "I'll visit her every day between now and then. Whatever you want me to do."

Bridget was as good as her word and spent every morning at the cottage with Opal. They talked mostly about the party, what was expected of guests, how the guests should behave, and they acted out the parts. Opal, in spite of her unschooled upbringing, was an intelligent person with a desire to learn and she had a keen sense of humor. They laughed at their mistakes and began to enjoy the daily contacts. Like her mother, Bridget enjoyed teaching, and Opal was a good student. But not only that, a real friendship was developing between them; Bridget began to think of her and to treat her almost like a sister. As the days passed, she thought about her mother's words and the reasons given for the invitation. The more she thought about it, the more she liked the idea and agreed that it was the right thing to do even though she had no hint of the real reason. Beneath the unpolished manners and unrefined speech was a fine, intelligent and sensitive person, and she began to relish the prospect of defending her if necessary before a prejudiced society.

At the breakfast table and at other times, Bridget talked with her mother about the party and how well Opal was progressing. Constance was often in the dining room during these times, or listening quietly to their conversation from the pantry, and she very soon became aware of the fact that Henry and Opal had been invited to the lavish party. At first she was just curious, but very soon she became infuriated and indignant. Envy and jealousy raged within her. There could be no good reason for Opal's elevation into high society! If a black woman was to attend—if any such person was to be invited—then she, Constance, was as good as any, and should have been chosen. Constance was very, very angry; she sulked and muttered to herself throughout the day. Back in the kitchen she told everyone—she talked and complained to everyone in loud argumentative tones hoping that her employer would overhear and indeed she did.

While Mrs. Barnham had been thinking only about rectifying some wrongs, she had not considered the effect on her employees. They would not understand and would not see Opal as a symbol designed in part to correct the deep injustices suffered by their ancestor's in bondage; they soon began to share Constance's envy, jealousy, and outrage. It took Mrs. Barnham a few days to sense the bad tempers prevailing throughout the household, and it puzzled her. Fortunately she did not dismiss it as being the result of the extra work required of everyone, and she continued to look for the real cause of the discontent. She was not entirely a stranger to Constance's moods and bad temper; every now and again Constance would show her dissatisfaction with the state of affairs, and would mumble and grumble for several days until the mood passed. Previously, Mrs. Barnham would ignore it as long as it did not affect her or get out of hand, and in time it had passed. On this occasion the muttering could not be ignored; there was too much at stake, and she asked questions. Constance vented her feelings and was not short with her answers; Mrs. Barnham was very quickly fully informed.

It had been her intention all along to extend the party in some measure to the servants and the working staff, but there had been little if any plans made to do this. Discussing it where Constance could overhear, she decreed that all the servants and household help should also partake in the birthday celebrations and that they should have a party of their own after the work was done. Mrs. Barnham ordered the extra food, drink, and gifts, enough to satisfy everyone. The news of these plans spread quickly and energized everyone. They quickly forgot their objections and eagerly went about their work. Constance was only partially satisfied, and she continued to grumble, but everyone else was indeed very happy with the arrangement, and they looked forward to the event.

The day before the party William returned from Kingston bringing with him two houseguests. Bridget had planned to leave Chivers that night and return with him to the Manor House, where she would stay until their return to Kingston in a few days. As she collected her clothes in preparation for his arrival, Mrs. Barnham entered the room and began to help. After a few minutes the conversation changed to the matter that she had in mind.

"I just want to remind you, Brige, not to tell William that Opal will be at the party. If he finds out he will tell his mother."

"Oh yes, I know," Bridget replied somewhat impatiently. "You've told me before."

"Yes, but I just want to make sure that you remembered. Now promise me. Will you promise?"

"Yes, I promise."

As arranged William appeared in the late afternoon, and he did not stay at Chivers for any length of time. Bridget was waiting for him, and they left almost immediately.

The following day began quite early for the staff as they hurried to complete the final arrangements. For Mrs. Barnham the day began as usual, with a light breakfast of tea and toast. At the table was a small decoratively wrapped parcel, a gift from Bridget placed there by Constance. Mrs. Barnham opened it to reveal an exquisite porcelain figurine. Her delight was clearly evident as she showed it to Constance. In the meantime the maids at Chivers were still rushing about in anticipation of the guests arrival in the afternoon.

In mid-afternoon guests began to arrive and were greeted by Mrs. Barnham. Many brought presents that were gratefully accepted and displayed on a table at the far side of the veranda. Tea, sandwiches and cake were served, and drinks for anyone wishing to get an early start on festivities. They gathered on the veranda and in the decorated garden, and soon there was a sizeable crowd chatting as they greeted friends, and wandered through the garden. The house and garden had been decorated with lanterns, candles, streamers, chairs and benches had been placed outside. The real party would not begin for several hours when champagne would be served, and the festivities would then continue with the dinner, dancing, a toast to the hostess, and on into the night and morning hours. The orchestra from Montego Bay arrived and soon began to tune their instruments. There was to be a brief intermission after tea in the late afternoon, to allow the guests a short rest and time to dress. At eight o'clock, when everyone was present, the festivities were scheduled to begin.

Henry and Opal did not attend the tea party; both were nervously checking their clothes to make sure that everything was as it should be. They could hear the voices coming from the main house, and it increased their sense of nervousness and anticipation. As it began to darken, the voices subsided and a strange quiet descended over the place. One of the boys began to light the lamps in the garden. Opal decided to take her bath and start dressing. Henry sat on the veranda playing with Pre until it was time for her supper, and at that time he also went to bathe and dress. He did not hurry—he did not want to arrive early— it would be better if everyone was already there when they entered. He expected that their appearance might cause a sensation, and he was mentally preparing himself for that time. He was more concerned about Opal, wondering how she would feel and how she would react—it was bound to be a test for them both, and he was hoping that it would end well. Before he was dressed the orchestra started to play, and he knew that the party had started, and that it was time for them to be there.

Before leaving he decided to have a quick drink. To his surprise Opal accepted his offer to have one too. She had very seldom taken a drink before, but he filled the glasses, and standing together, they toasted each other, and were on their way. As they left the room he took her hand reassuringly and looped it through his arm in the way that he had shown her.

About the estate the word had circulated that Opal would be attending the party, and that she would be wearing a very fine dress. By some this news had been greeted with a great deal of excitement, and by others with disbelief and skepticism, but their curiosity demanded that they be present to see for themselves. A small crowd had gathered near the Busha's cottage in anticipation of their departure, and as the couple left the house a shout was heard, "Dem is on de way!" and the numbers grew. The crowd pressed around lining the pathway to the great house. There were many greetings, "Evenin' Sur," and "Good nite' Sur." and many "Oos" and "Ahs" as they moved along, like Royalty attending a function with crowds of admiring citizens, both Henry and Opal acknowledging the greetings with bows and smiles.

When they reached the steps, he paused to check her appearance and to straighten his medals. The band was still playing as they mounted the steps and entered the large drawing room filled with the elegant guests. They paused in the doorway for a moment, searching the crowd for their hostess.

It took hardly a few seconds for conversations to be cut off in mid-sentence and all eyes turned towards them. Mrs. Barnham had been anxiously waiting for that moment; she had only just whispered to Bridget to expect them at any time. Immediately she deposited her glass on a nearby table and went over to welcome them. Taking Opal by the hand, she kissed her on the cheek, and led her into the center of the room. It was a spectacle never before seen in that part of the world—it could have been a scene from some fanciful adventure tail in some exotic place—a native princess and her consort greeted by a queen! And the guests were stunned!

In the middle of a sentence Bridget left the group she was with and followed her mother over to their side. William was not with her and he watched incredulously from another part of the room—he could not believe what he was seeing as Bridget took hold of Opal's hand to lead her into the room. Harriet was transfixed—unable to speak—she too, could not understand what she was seeing as conflicting thoughts passed through her mind. Together Mrs. Barnham and Bridget led the couple around the room to introduce them to the other guests, but in the initial confusion a waiter serving drinks collided with some guests and almost toppled the contents of his tray. That event caused a mild distraction and some relief from the penetrating stares.

The orchestra played on, but the room was hushed as many guests were exchanging questioning looks, wondering 'who on earth is this couple?' Slowly the conversations resumed, but every so often heads turned and curious glances were cast in their direction. The gathering was quite subdued, and for some time the room was hushed and restrained. Apart from the fact that the woman was black, it was not surprising that their entry created a sensation. Henry was impressive in his formal dress, tall and handsome, a bright red cummerbund about the middle and the medals glistening on his jacket. Opal was no less so; her evening dress of light cream-colored silk did not hide the shapely body beneath, her dark lightly curled hair was kept in place by a sparkling tiara that gave emphasis to her features and the curve of her face.

William made his way over to his mother's side. As he got there they exchanged guarded looks and he whispered quietly in her ear. Opal remained close to Henry's side who became involved in an animated conversation with a government official, the Director of Public Works. Bridget returned to her friends and was quickly bombarded with numerous questions.

"Who is that couple?" they asked, and incredulously, "are they *your* friends?"

Bridget answered casually and briefly, declining to give much detail. Some of her old school friends refused to be satisfied.

"Who is that handsome man with all those medals?" one asked, and again Bridget was evasive with her answers, as they remained the object of intense curiosity.

Among the guests there were a number of prominent businessmen and government officials including the Aide-de-Camp to the Governor, a Captain Parker, and the Chief Inspector, Inspector Higgins, ex-Scotland Yard, London. Their curiosity drew them over towards Henry and soon they were chatting together.

Henry had not experienced such an occasion since he left England many years ago; it reminded him of his years spent in the army and evenings in the Officers' Mess, and somehow that excited him, and in that frame of mind his old wit and humor returned. In the Mess he had often been at the center of conversation and activity; if anything was going to happen it would surely happen around Henry Thomson, and most of his fellow officers wanted to be there when it did. Soon there were gales of laughter and the numbers around him grew. He had once again been socially accepted, and with Opal by his side, the acceptance extended to her as well. The gentlemen had few qualms about being near and chatting to such an attractive woman, even though much of this acceptance may well have been due to the quantities of alcohol they had consumed. The following morning though, they may have heard complaining words from their wives, and they may have had some sober second thoughts. But for the moment at least, there were few signs that the matter of skin color would in any way prevent them from flirting with a very attractive woman, and having a jolly good time.

As the evening drew on the portly Captain Parker initiated the dancing; from across the dance floor he approached Mrs. Barnham with a jaunty swagger, taking her hand and bowing low, he invited her to join him in a lilting Strauss waltz. Quickly other guests joined in, including William and Bridget, Henry and Opal. On the dance floor they passed several times but ignored one another. The orchestra played three more pieces before breaking. There was one more trios of dance music from the orchestra, and then Captain Parker, who had been designated the Master of Ceremonies, announced that the dinner was being served, and guests could partake at their pleasure, and he escorted Mrs. Barnham into the dining room. After dinner he proposed the toast to their hostess and led the guests in a rousing rendition of "Happy Birthday!" Half an hour later the orchestra resumed playing and the dancing continued well into the early morning hours.

William sulked throughout the evening. He was angry and jealous, and desperately wanted to dance with Opal—to have a chance to talk to her again—she looked more beautiful to him than ever before. But under his mother's watchful eye, he dared not approach her. He was angry with his mother too; she had destroyed his relationship with Opal, and pressured him into marrying a woman he did not really love. And if Henry could be seen with Opal and be accepted, then why on earth couldn't he have done the same?

Harriet was very angry; she knew why Opal was there—she understood the reason and knew it was intended as a slap in the face. She hated her sister-in-law now, and she would tell her so, and then she vowed she would never to speak to her again. Their friendship, such as it was, was over. Just before midnight Harriet could stand it no longer and she called William to take her home. She ordered him to bring his wife too. Harriet left without saying good night to her hostess or thanking her for the evening's entertainment, but Bridget said 'good night' to her mother and some guests, and excused Harriet's behavior. The following day Harriet angrily insisted that they return to Kingston immediately. She left her houseguests to fend for themselves wondering what had happened and if they had been the cause.

Jamaican Lore—If y'u see ole' woman runnin', doant stop te ax "w'at is de matter?"—run too!

CHAPTER 35

On the coast road, Daniel did not have very long to wait for the bus. Soon the grossly overloaded vehicle made its appearance, and he waved it to a stop. He paid his fare and took a place outside the bus clinging to the rungs of the roof ladder, there being no space inside for another person. In Annotto Bay passengers dismounted and new ones were taken on, and Daniel used the opportunity to get a place inside the bus. He remained seated for over an hour while the driver refreshed himself and refueled the bus for the next segment of its trip. In the time he made himself comfortable, closed his eyes and dosed off.

When the journey resumed it was late afternoon and rain was threatening. The bus took off with all the speed of which it was capable, swaying wildly from side to side, less fortunate passengers clinging to bus and possessions for the sake of dear life. It was hardly out of the town when it started to rain, and before long everyone was more than a little wet. Many of the windows did not close and some were missing entirely. Those sitting next to the windows tried desperately to shelter themselves with newspapers, parcels or clothing, and those sitting beside or behind them paid equally the price of their failed attempts.

The heavy rains slowed the journey and added to the hazards of night driving, not that it seemed to hinder the driver in any way. He kept his foot pressed hard down on the pedal—he had an appointment with a lady that he did not wish to miss, and like many a sailor, he had a ladyfriend in every port—he well knew the bosom on which he would rest his head that night. Nevertheless, it was past midnight when they arrived in Port Maria. The driver parked his vehicle, announced that the journey to Kingston would resume at seven o'clock in the morning, and with that he picked up his little bundle of personal belongings, and left the bus and passengers to their own devices.

Daniel, along with several fellow passengers had no place to go, so they made themselves as comfortable as possible in the bus and tried to sleep. Daniel was awake before dawn and left the bus in the dim morning light. It had stopped raining but water was still dripping from trees and rooftops. There was no one about and he went in search of an open shop. He had not eaten since early the previous afternoon, and was hungry. There were several stores at the intersection in the roads, but none had yet opened their doors, so he selected one with a bench, and waited for the shopkeeper to open up for business. When it did he bought cheese, bread, and dark brown sugar, which he mixed with water in his tin cup.

At the shop he made inquiries—there was little work if any to be found in or about the town—maybe in the foothills, at a coffee estate still operating. He decided to explore the possibilities, even though he had not been encouraged, and he knew his chances were poor, but at least it would be closer to home than going on to Ocho Rios or St. Ann's Bay. He would need food for the search, so he bought more cheese, bread and brown sugar, and a piece of salt fish. Getting directions he set off immediately.

The road lead directly towards the mountains but it was not a steep rise for several miles. The day would be very hot and he was glad to have started out in the early morning. By mid-morning the sun was shining from a cloudless, blue sky, and he was feeling the rise in temperature. The road wound around the side of the mountain rising towards the gap between the peaks, six thousand feet over to the other side. Along the way the ferns grew thick and green, and every once in a while, little springs flowed from the steep banks to cross the road on their way to the river in the valley below. Several times he stopped, filled his tin can and drank the fresh cool water. At mid-day he stopped again beside a small spring, searched in his bag for the bread and cheese, broke off small pieces and ate slowly. At the side of the road someone had been clearing a small plot of land. The bush and branches had been piled at the side of the road, but there was no one about from whom he could ask directions. From the side of the road he surveyed the clearing, and then looking at the pile of branches, he selected a straight, stout branch to use as a walking stick.

Towards mid-afternoon he tried to quicken his pace; as yet he had not seen any signs that he was nearing his destination, and he wanted to be there before nightfall. A mile or two further on the road divided, one road went to the right and the other to the left. In the town there had been no mention of the fork in the road. Which road should he take? He hadn't the least idea, and there was no one about to ask. Looking up towards the mountain he could see several huts scattered about, perched on the mountain sides, half hidden by trees, but he didn't know how to reach even the nearest one. He simply had to make a choice—right or left? He chose to keep to the left, a path that would take him into the Blue Mountains of Portland. The road wound endlessly up, following alongside the river some distance in the valley below—it seemed to have no end—and still there was no sign of any plantation. Rounding a bend, at last, there was a little hut not far off the road and he decided to get directions. A narrow pathway branched off the road leading to the hut, and he followed it to a small clearing in front of the small dwelling.

There was no one in sight, but there were clear signs that someone lived there. He shouted, "somebady here?"

There was no answer so he called again, and still there was no answer. He looked around behind the house and saw no one. Once more, he cupped his hands about his mouth and shouted, "Somebady here?" No one appeared and he decided to continue on his journey. As he turned to go he peered into the darkness of the hut and saw movement.

"Somebady is here!" he said speaking to the figure hiding in the hut. He waited, and still there was no sign of anyone about to appear. That was strange, he thought—unusual. Then suddenly a little girl appeared running away from him down the pathway towards the road.

"Come, chile. Me doan't hu't y'u," he called after her. "Me lookin' fe direction."

She disappeared into the bushes at the side of the path. She was frightened of him for some reason, and he decided it was best to leave and get directions elsewhere. He had almost reached the road when a man appeared approaching him, the little girl following, clinging to the back of his trousers. The man was walking purposely up the pathway towards him, a half-full coconut sack slung over his shoulder, and a cutlass swinging in his hand. Aggressively he strode towards Daniel—menacingly.

"W'at y'u doin' 'ere?" he demanded.

Daniel was taken aback and took a step away. "I'se lookin' fe direction."

The man looked at him curiously, doubtfully, and made no reply.

"I'se lookin' fe de coffee plantation, man. —Y'u little pick'ny frighten', but me doant hurt y'u chile."

"Y'u is a coolie man!" The man accused him, shouting. "Y'u go in'a me house?"

The man approached. His manner was aggressive and threatening, and Daniel backed away. The man's eyes were flaming red, bloodshot, glaring angrily at the stranger.

"Y'u is a coolie man, an' y'u go in'a me house!" the man shouted again. "Y'u go in'a me house!" he repeated. —"I'se goin chop y'u!"

The man dropped the sack raised the cutlass above his head as he rushed towards Daniel. Daniel reacted quickly; he raised his stick to counter the attack. The stick being much longer than the cutlass was an effective defensive weapon. As the man swung the cutlass Daniel deflected the blow. He swung the cutlass again with the same effect. Daniel pointed his stick at the man's head, threatening to club him if he attempted another attack.

"No need fe dat, man!" Daniel shouted, and held the stick pointed at the man's head, "No need fe dat!"

The stick held the man at bay and Daniel edged his way passed holding his bundled possessions at the ready to shield himself as he backed away. The man did not attack and as he reached the road, a volley of abuse and curses followed. He did not respond and breathed a sigh of relief as he quickly continued on his way.

He was shaken by the incident and kept thinking about it—he could not get it out of his mind—it had upset him, and he wanted to get away from the place as quickly as possible. He quickened his pace although the road was much steeper now that he was in the mountains. Several miles further on the sun had gone down behind the peaks and the skies were darkening. He passed several small houses by the roadside, but did not stop. He would be a great deal more cautious when approaching strangers in the future, and it would be dark in little more than an hour. At the next roadside spring he stopped again to rest and eat.

The road was now much closer to the river, and it would not be difficult to cross to the other side of the valley, but the road on the other side was not visible and he had not even glimpsed it—he may not find it in the dark. He finished eating and started off again. A mile or so further on the evening was drawing on. He started to search for a place to spend the night, and as it seemed he would spend the night on the road, he searched for an overhanging rock that would provide some shelter. Earlier he had passed several good places where he could have sheltered against the steep bank under an overhanging rock, and he hoped to find another. As the light faded he could see small twinkling lights of the settlers' huts appearing about the mountainside. He had not found any sheltering overhang, but looking into the valley he could see a small isolated hut some distance above the river—not a safe place, he thought, if the river was in flood. He decided to investigate the possibility of staying there for the night.

The pathway to the hut could be partly seen as it descended from the road, but it was some distance away, much further up the road than he expected, and it took longer to get there. In the gathering dusk he carefully descended the narrow pathway; he did not want to stumble on loose stones and possibly fall, and he kept his eyes fixed on the path. Also, the path was much steeper than it appeared from the road. Occasionally, he looked up to assess his position, when suddenly, he was transfixed—he was looking at a ghost! There was a ghostly white apparition in the middle of the pathway not more than a few feet away!

He froze in step, unable to move or speak. For a moment he did not believe his eyes. He looked again—it was still there, moving towards him. He turned prepared to beat a hasty retreat up to the road, when the approaching image became more distinct—it seemed to define the thin figure of a woman, clothed in a white, wispy shroud, and it took on a more human form.

Momentarily he held his retreat as the figure advanced. It was now in distinct view, but the initial conception of a ghost was not dispelled—in his mind the figure was supernatural, and he was ready for immediate flight. And then it spoke.

"Ah, Misterman! Y'u come at last!" And then triumphantly, "Y'u Come! Y'u come!"

The woman was now clearly in view, and Daniel's panic began to subside—but what did it mean—"Y'u come?" The woman was a short step away.

"Coolieman come! Coolieman come!" she sang, dancing in rhythm to her chant. "Coolieman come! Coolieman come!"

He stood still as the woman, dancing, circled him, and then moving first to one side and then to the other. She looked closely into his face with a penetrating hypnotic gaze that held him transfixed.

"Me did know y'u was comin'—Me did know y'u was comin'. Me was lookin' fe y'u—me did know y'u was comin'!"

CHAPTER 36

To the people living in that part of the country, she was known as Maddy, but no one would ever call her that to her face. The local people, denoting the respect or the fear, or possibly even affection, with which she was regarded, always addressed her as 'Miss Maddy.' Of course 'Maddy' was not her real name; her real name was Salome Williams. Maddy had moved away from her family home and lived alone for many years, and the family connections had long been lost. She had out-lived most of her near relatives and there was little chance of past relationships ever being renewed.

Maddy was by far a more suitable name—many considered her to be more than a little crazy, but sometimes 'crazy' in the 'right' kind of way. Spirits sometimes possessed her, and everyone was certain that she had magical powers, mystical insight, and could certainly 'work obeah!' Her reputation had grown over the years, and with the years came 'de wisdom' and 'de power!' Many sought her council and cures, and she was seldom known to have given bad advice, although scientific evidence and careful attention to the facts, could certainly dispute that opinion.

The 'house' in which Maddy lived was a one-roomed hut, put together with small light branches, woven basket fashion between the larger upright branches. The roof was a thatch of dried coconut and banana leaves, thick enough to keep out all but the heaviest rain. The hut had a door and one window opening with a shutter, and so arranged that the openings could be closed at night and in the rainy season. The hut was strong and well built, and although Maddy never did any of the repairs herself, there were always willing helpers to do the necessary work in exchange for various favors. The hut was in an isolated part of the valley, not far above the river, but just high enough above it that there should be no danger from the flooding that occurred every now and again in the rainy season.

Surrounding the hut was a small yard in which grew a few trees—a breadfruit tree, a pear tree, and an orange tree—and in which were planted a few vegetables. The hut and surrounding yard were always neat and tidy, and although it seldom needed the constant attention, the yard was swept with a bramble broom every day.

The nearest neighbor was up the steep mountainside, over a mile away; the distance between them suited both Maddy and her neighbors, each appreciating the privacy and the distance that separated them. The distance between them however, was not great enough when the moon was full, because it was on those nights that Maddy would engage in her rituals. At those times no one dared approach or go near. Some might watch from a safe distance up the mountain high above, but safety was in the distance between them, and that was always maintained. On those nights the strange voice, the chanting, and the beating of a drum were heard, even above the constant rushing sound of the river flowing through the valley. From the rise of the full moon, Maddy could be seen in the distance, like a ghost in her white flowing gown, white turban bound about her head, a wind-blown veil, arms uplifted, dancing, kneeling, rising and falling, until the set of the moon, when all would again fall silent, except for the constant rushing sound of the river flowing through the valley.

Later the next morning, Maddy would rise up from a hypnotic sleep, weak and exhausted, brew some tea, and return again to her bed. The following day the white gown, turban and veil would all be washed clean, bleached white in the sun, hung out to dry, and then carefully packed away in readiness for the next full moon. It would be several days before she would recover, and during that time visitors were welcomed if they came to minister to her needs, cook a meal, bring some little gift of fruit or fish, or bring news, sit and engage in idle gossip.

CHAPTER 37

"Come wid me." The words were spoken in a whisper, their faces almost touching. And then Maddy turned, leading him down the pathway to the little hut. She entered the hut but Daniel hesitated at the doorway for several moments considering whether to follow. She returned, took his arm and pulled him into the room.

A small lantern cast its faint light about the sparsely furnished room. She pointed to a woven mat in the corner. "Dere y'u bed," she said pointing. "I mek it fe y'u. Y'u to rest dere."

Daniel was curious, and puzzled by this strange behavior—the woman must be crazy. But he was also a little fearful of this strange woman who seemed to have such power over him—fearful that she might be completely deranged and might harm him, even though she did not appear to be violent. He looked about the room, hesitating, considering. He needed a place to stay for the night, and here was the shelter he needed—given to him by some strange twist of fate. The woman was certainly a little crazy he concluded—he would not harm her, but he was not sure that she would not harm him—that she was not seeking a human sacrifice! If his fears were unfounded he would find some way to repay her when he left in the morning. He placed his bundle on the mat, and turned towards her, at last finding words.

"Well, ah t'anks y'u, Mam."

"Come, Mister Coolieman, tek de pan an' fetch water. Go fetch water." She handed him a large tin can, and without answer, he went to the river, filled it and made his way back to the hut. When he got back, the cooking fire was blazing and flames were leaping up between three large stones. She took the pan and placed it on the stones to boil. She sat on a low stool and peeled a large yam and a piece of breadfruit. They sat beside the fire watching the licking flames, occasionally stoking it with a dried branch that kept it blazing. Soon the water was boiling vigorously and Maddy poured out half and brewed some tea. She dropped the peeled vegetables into the boiling water, and soon they were eating. They did not talk much; her name was 'Miss Maddy," she informed him, but she did not ask for his—she had already named him 'Coolieman.'

"How y'u did know I was comin'?"

"De voices tell me!"

"De voices?"

Yes, de words of de spirits! Dey tell me! Dey tell me everything!"

"How dey tell y'u?"

"De spirits speak to me many time—an' dey tell me. Ah hear de voices in de nite, an' dey say de 'coolieman comin'."

He would have to take that as an answer, and would not question further—he would have to accept her answer as incontestable fact.

They finished eating and Maddy gave him a cup of her tea. It was too hot to drink, so he blew on the surface to cool it before taking a sip. It was not a 'tea' that he had ever tasted before, but it was not unpleasant to the taste, and as he was thirsty he drank it all. As the time passed they finished eating and it was quite dark, Daniel rose to wash the utensils and prepare for bed, but as he stood he was overcome by a dizzy spell, almost falling over. He quickly sat down again holding his spinning head in his hands. For some strange reason he could not think—he was beginning to loose his senses. In a minute or two he regained his balance and stood up again.

"Ah!" he sighed, "I'se tired. I'se ready fe me bed."

Maddy stood up too but made no move to steady him. "Go to y'u bed. Go tek y'u rest."

He needed no further urging. He staggered off into the hut, and threw himself on the mat. He lay there a few moments, eyes wide open looking at the thatched roof without comprehension. The whole world was spinning wildly in a circle above him. He felt sick—a minute later he closed his eyes and fell into a deep sleep.

Sunlight was streaming into the hut when he opened his eyes. He lay still looking up at the roof, through the open door and through the window at the blue sky above. None of this he recognized and memory did not return to him—he did not know where he was and could not remember how he got there. He lay quietly trying to remember, but after five minutes or more still could not recall, and he sat up. As he did so a dizzy spell engulfed him and he rested his head on his knees. As it cleared he got up unsteadily, made his way to the door, leaning against the frame to steady himself as he looked about. There was no one in sight, and gradually he began to remember events of the day before. He made his way out of the hut to sit on the tree stump near the cooking stones. His head seemed to be separated from his body; he could think now, but he had no control over his body, and lacked the strength and will to take control.

Maddy appeared struggling up the pathway from the river carrying a pan of water. He watched her, unable to assist. As she got closer, she placed the pan on the stones, and turned to face him.

"Ah! Mister Coolieman! Y'use up."

He nodded, and after a few moments, "Mornin'," was all he could manage. He rested his head again on his arms folded over his knees, and drifted off to a dream world, widely differing thoughts racing through his head without any seemingly logical connection.

"Ah will fix y'u little sumptin' te eat," she said at last. "Y'u mus' eat little food now."

He remained motionless while she prepared the meal. In an hour they had both eaten and Daniel was beginning to feel better. But he was still unable to take control of his mind and body, and moved about as if in a trance. He desperately wanted to wake up, but he could not make that happen. He passed the rest of the day dazed and in a dream-like state.

In the early evening, Maddy again prepared the meal without his assistance. It was as though she did not expect any help, and cheerfully sang to herself as she slowly went about her activities. Throughout the day, besides her singing, she carried on animated conversations with unseen spirits. They seemed to ask incomprehensible questions, to which she provided lengthy and equally incomprehensible answers. And sometimes the voices made her angry and a heated argument would break out. Her behaviour would normally have aroused his curiosity, but Daniel was beyond the point at which he could question anyone's behaviour. Again she provided his food and a cup of her potent tea, which she gently urged him to drink and watched him as he swallowed it all without objection. Within an hour he collapsed on the mat in his place in the hut, and was quickly in a deep sleep.

The following morning he awoke only an hour or so later than his normal waking hour. The sun was already up, and so was Maddy. He felt better than the day before, but still he moved in a dream-like world, unable to master his body and mind. He went down to the river and bathed his head in the cold water. It made him feel better, but it did not clear his head, and he returned to the yard again to sit on the tree stump near the cooking stones. The following day passed in similar fashion.

In the morning Maddy cooked cornmeal for their breakfast, all the while singing and conversing with herself.

"Y'us to pick river reed fe me te day," she announced when he had eaten.

"Yes, Miss Maddy," he answered. He gave it no further thought—she wanted reeds—he would collect reeds.

She took his arm leading him down to the riverbank and pointed down the valley where the river flowed out of sight. "G' down de river little piece," she directed him. "Y'u fine' reeds at de bankside. Pick de dry reed an' bring dem fe me."

"Yes, Miss Maddy." And he set off immediately. By mid-morning he had collected a large bundle of the reeds and made his way back to the yard. He deposited his load just outside the hut where Maddy was sitting.

"Now we'se goine mek' basket!" she announced.

"Me never mek basket, Miss Maddy."

"Y'use to watch me den," she instructed.

He spent the rest of the day weaving baskets under Maddy's supervision. By early afternoon all the reeds had been used, and he returned to the river to fetch another bundle. The next two days were spent in similar fashion until there were a dozen or more baskets.

As the days passed he began to feel better, but he was not in command of his mind or his actions—Maddy was his mistress, and he did her bidding unable to fight against it. He understood, but could not resist.

Several days later he wanted to shave. His treasured razor, a gift from the Squire many years ago, had been in his bag along with his other possessions, and he went to get it. He had given little thought to his bag over the past few days but now that he wanted it, it was not to be found. He searched the hut without success.

"Miss Maddy. Wher' me t'ings?" he asked. "Me mus' trim me beard."

"Y'use not to do dat. Y'use to let it grow!"

What he heard annoyed him. He wanted to shave, but Maddy said "No!" The fact that Maddy said he was to let his beard grow did not lessen his desire to shave, and he wanted the bag with his things. But again he could not disobey. For a few moments he stood looking at his mistress, searching for words that would not come. "Yes, Miss Maddy," he said finally, and sat again on the tree stump.

Later Maddy appeared to fix the evening meal. "Tomorrow y'use to go to de market and sell we basket," she informed him. "An' den y'use to buy t'ings."

He just nodded his agreement. This was an interesting change in his routine. He wondered if she would be accompanying him on the trip, and then he did not know where the market was, unless it was the market in Port Maria, miles away.

"Y'use to tek de money and buy kersine oil. An' salt," she added, as she went about her preparations. By the time the meal was cooked and they were eating, the list had grown to almost two dozen items of need. How could he remember all of them? But he said nothing.

The next morning began with preparations for the journey to market. The baskets were tied together in two large bundles with a piece of thin rope and arranged so that they could be slung over his shoulders. Maddy gave him his lunch and fixed food for him to take. She gave him a small handful of loose coins, no more than a few shillings with which to buy the items of need in the event that he did not sell all the baskets. Shortly after she gave him directions, helped to load the baskets on his back and sent him on his way. He would walk through the night to get to Port Maria in time for market the next day, and still in a dazed state it never occurred to him that he might not accomplish the task. As he set out it was a strange sight—completely hidden by the baskets. It looked as though they were alive—moving unaided, along the road.

He struggled up the steep pathway to the road above, and turned in the direction of the town some twenty-five miles or more away. The baskets were not heavy, but they were cumbersome, and the sheer volume was difficult to manage. Nevertheless, he shifted the load several times until he found a comfortable position, and then he quickened his pace. The strange narcotic brew that stupefied him, seemed to numb his mind and dull any physical discomfort from his boyhood injury and the load that he was carrying. In his mind there was only one objective, and that was to get to Port Maria by the morning in time for market day.

On the road there were women traveling, some in groups, all on their way to the town, with head-baskets, and hampers on the occasional ass, all loaded to overflowing. They were strong women carrying heavy loads, and they walked at a brisk pace overtaking him and passing without a word. During the night he stopped only once, for a brief rest to eat, and to drink from a roadside spring. He arrived within sight of the town as the early light was breaking, and made his way to the market. He deposited his load in a clearing near the entrance where he would be visible to anyone entering. He found a wooden bench by the fence that enclosed the market place, stretched out and closed his eyes.

As the daylight broke market women began to arrive and to set out their wares. For a while he remained stretched out on the bench, but soon two women were angrily squabbling over a preferred place in the market. One claimed it as being traditionally hers, while the other claimed it as being the first to arrive there that day. He sat up and watched the confrontation from a distance. The woman in possession stood her ground, and appeals by the other to her supporting friends failed to move her. Finally, she wandered off, still grumbling, to find another place for herself.

Daniel set up his baskets in the place he had selected, but before he had untied the second bundle he had already sold two. Within the hour he sold three more, and it looked as though he would sell them all, and it would be a good day. By early afternoon he sold the last one, and it was time for him to buy the things Maddy needed. He found the small Chinese shop near the bus stop and gave the shopkeeper his list from memory. He bought a coconut sack and put the groceries in it as they were handed to him. There were still things on the list that were needed, but the sack was already half full and quite heavy. He would not be able to carry them all, besides, it had taken all his money with the exception of a few coins. He bought some food to take with him and to eat before setting off on the return journey. Failing to find a place to sit and eat, he returned to the market.

The market women were packing up their baskets and rolling up their sacks in preparation for their return home. It was an opportunity for them to engage in frivolous socialization—telling stories, jokes, exchanging gossip and news from other parts of the country. The hard work for the week was almost over, and this was a brief interlude before setting out on the often strenuous journey home. Boy friends met girl friends, held hands, exchanged gifts, promises, and kisses, and then separated. Some left without delay, loading their double baskets, one on top of another, skillfully balanced on their heads, thankful that they were some hundred pounds lighter than when they set out two days earlier. Others awaited the arrival of a mule dray or cart on which they would load their possessions and their exhausted bodies for the bumpy, bruising ride home. By the time Daniel had finished eating, the market place was fast being deserted.

He nibbled at some dry salt fish as he set out on the return journey, the sack slung over his shoulder. As he trudged up the road towards the mountains weariness began to overtake him. He felt very tired after walking for less than an hour and he rested by the roadside. He would have liked to stretch out and go to sleep, but he knew that wasn't possible, and he started off again. He used each little roadside spring as an opportunity to stop, rest and drink before moving on. He met only a few people on the road, and none were market women returning home, they would be along later. In his state of mind, he did not much want company—the effects of the narcotic tea were still lingering, and he was too tired to talk to anyone. He struggled on through the night, until at last he felt he could not go on without a rest.

In the darkness he found a place to lie down. Using the sack and its contents as a headrest, he stretched out, folded his arms over his chest, closed his eyes and dozed off. In the night several groups of market women passed by without noticing him, and those that did paid him no attention. It was just getting light when still weary and unrested, he got up. He was chilled to the bone and his clothes were wet with the night dew, but he wasted little time before starting off again. The mountain road seemed to be all the more steeper than when he first passed by, and every step was a concerted effort. His progress was slow, his injury was painful and hunger made him weak. It was passed mid-afternoon when he rounded a bend in the road and saw Maddy's hut down in the valley just above the river. It lifted his spirits and he quickened his pace. Soon he was standing in the yard before the hut handing over the supplies. Immediately after he was resting on his mat in the shelter of the hut.

Maddy soon came in with a mug of tea. His head had cleared somewhat during the past day that he had not drunk her brew, and even though he was exhausted, he almost had sufficient willpower to refuse the drink. He sat up and took the mug from her hand but he did not drink. She watched him keenly, every now and again gesturing with her hand, urging him to sip, but he did not. After a few minutes, she gently took his hand raising the mug to his lips and tilted it towards his mouth. Her expression was intense, her eyes fixed firmly on his. He looked into her eyes; helpless now to refuse he began to sip the warm, sweet, strange tasting liquid. He found it satisfying, relieving his hunger and exhaustion, but he knew that his mind and body would not be his when he awoke the next morning.

CHAPTER 38

Daniel was once again under her spell, under her control and unable to exercise his will, and she made certain that he remained in that state by nightly doses of her potent, narcotic tea. There was no need to force it upon him, it was only necessary for her to prepare the brew and put it before him and he would drink, even though he knew it clouded his thinking and befuddled his mind. In another way, it was a strangely satisfying and blissful state; he was free of anxiety and fear of any kind, and he could work effortlessly, throughout the day without tiring.

Several days later, while they had breakfast, a small bright yellow bird alighted in a tree near by. It attracted their attention as it flew past, and Maddy followed its flight keenly, watching its every movement as it perched in her orange tree.

"Ah!" she said in a low voice, as she again engaged herself in conversation. "Ah! It time te ketch little song bird." And then she repeated it to herself several times. When the bird again flew off out of sight she turned to him, "Y'u mus' get river reed te day," and when they had eaten she sent him down the valley to collect reeds once again.

He soon returned with a bundle, which he deposited in a pile near to the tree stumps. She picked up two reeds, tested their strength and flexibility. Placing them in a cross she began to weave the bottom of a cage, instructing Daniel to follow her directions as she progressed. He had seen these cages before, but their construction had never intrigued him, and he had never wanted to make one, but by the evening they had almost completed two cages. Maddy placed them side by side in the yard to await completion the next day.

"Now is time to put bu'd in de cage," she announced, and she fetched her knife from the hut, and then she went to the Breadfruit tree. In the main trunk she made several deep slanting cuts until the white milk-like sap was oozing freely down the side of the tree. The next morning the sap had coagulated into a thick, sticky resinous mass, which she scraped together, removing small pieces of dislodged bark and unwanted contaminants. In all, there was a small lump of the sticky resin, which she placed on a clean stone to cure in the sun. A few days later it was again scraped into a lump and washed clean in the river, and worked well with her fingers. When satisfied that it was clean, she popped it into her mouth and chewed it for several hours between the few teeth remaining in her mouth, making it soft and flexible.

When all this preparation was completed, she fetched her long, picking stick and hooked down the highest branch of the orange tree that she could reach from the ground. On several of its branches, she spread a layer of the sticky breadfruit gum, muttering to herself all the while.

The orange tree had been selected in preference to any of the other trees or bushes around. She knew that the yellow 'canaries' often perched in those trees, and it would be the best place to set her traps. The following morning there were no birds caught, and neither the morning after, even though several canaries had been seen during the day. It was almost a week before an unfortunate bird was to settle on the sticky gum and become stuck. In the mean time Maddy had been preparing for its arrival; the cages had been completed and strengthened, and a loop placed at the top so that it could be hung from the branch of a tree.

"Ah! Me ketch y'u now!" she gloated as she saw the trapped bird still struggling to be free.

Carefully and slowly she pulled the branch down and grasped the struggling bird, and then slowly she dislodged its tiny feet from the sticky gum. Holding it firmly, she removed the traces of gum from the feet and placed it in the cage, where it was kept for several days until it became accustomed to its prison. Every morning she fed the bird, and throughout the day she would pick up the cage and talk to the frightened creature, sometimes whistling and twittering at it urging it to sing. But the bird did not respond.

A week later the little bird still had not uttered a peep, and Maddy was becoming impatient. She took the cage into her lap and for several hours coaxed the bird without success. She was impatient and shook the cage violently several times. The bird fluttered wildly in its cage, and when it had settled again on its perch, it still would not sing.

"Y'use goin te sing fe me," she threatened. "I'se goine mek y'u sing, little b'ud!"

Maddy went into the hut and searched for several minutes. When she reappeared she held the stump of a small candle in her hand, and a needle in her mouth with the thread hanging down. She lit the candle from the embers of the cooking fire and placed it on the stump. She took her handkerchief from about her head and carefully put it into the cage to cover the terrified, fluttering bird, and holding the bird in the cloth, withdrew it from the cage. The ends of the handkerchief were tied together to form a bag from which the bird's head protruded. She sat on her tree stump and held the bird in her lap, crouching over, the bird held securely with one hand, the fingers clasping its head so that the head could be manipulated—the eyelids held open between thumb and forefinger. Once this position had been obtained, she took the needle from her mouth and put it into the candle flame, holding it there until the tip glowed red.

"Ah!" she muttered to herself, "now's de time. Now's de time fe y'u, lit'le bird. I'se goine blind y'u yeye!"

Holding the unfortunate bird steady on her knees, its eyelid held open, she quickly placed the heated needle on the eyeball, scorching the tender surface. There was hardly a wisp of smoke or the smell of burning flesh. The bird squeaked its agony, and struggled vainly to escape, but was held secure. The procedure was repeated on the other eye, and the unfortunate creature returned to its cage. For a few minutes it stumbled blindly about the cage, finally coming to rest against the side huddled and quivering, head bowed, suffering unspeakable agony.

Daniel watched the gruesome proceedings thankful that he had not been ordered to assist. His head swam, and he heard voices—one telling him what he should do, and the other voice telling him that he could not. It was as though his mind and his body were split in two, and he was watching himself from above, from some distant place. The distant body was telling him that he should leave, but his real body was a prisoner to the strange woman, and he could only do her bidding.

The following morning the bird was still huddled against the side of the cage—it had not moved during the night. To Daniel it appeared to be on the verge of death, but Maddy, if she thought so did not show it. She placed a small handful of rice grains in her mouth, and then retrieved the limp creature with both hands to place it in her lap. Holding its head she opened its mouth with one finger, and taking the rice from her mouth forced several grains down its throat, every so often flushing them with water dripping from her fingers. Finally, she felt the little crop to assure herself that the rice grains were where they should be, and then she returned the bird to the cage. Early in the afternoon, the bird was no longer leaning against the sides, but was standing on its own, still in miserable condition. Maddy repeated the forced feeding twice each day during the days that followed, and the bird recovered its strength, but sadly, not its sight—it hopped blindly about the cage stumbling into the sides.

One morning Maddy had neglected to feed the bird, and at mid-day the bird still had not been fed. When she remembered and went to the cage, the bird was walking about the cage blindly pecking at the ground, as though it was feeding, even though there was nothing there for it to eat. She spread a small quantity of rice before it, and to her delight, the bird picked up and swallowed several grains, and when more was spread, the bird was able to feed itself. Some water placed in the cage was similarly found and drunk without assistance. It was no longer necessary for her to force rice grains down its throat or give it water to drink; the bird had survived, but the objective of having a captive song bird had not been reached—the bird did not utter a sound in spite of the constant coaxing.

The singing lessons continued for several days, and Maddy began to show her impatience with her stubborn pupil. During the day the cage was hung on a branch of the orange tree, and each time Maddy passed she would stop to whistle or twit at the bird and encourage it to sing, and still it did not respond. Then one morning as they finished the morning meal, Maddy took down the cage.

"Y'u not sing f'e me?" She spoke seriously to the bird. "Y'u will neber sing f'e me." She turned to Daniel, "it a' she bu'd," she told him. "She bu'd neber sing sweet bu'd-song."

She opened the cage, grasped the bird and withdrew it. Then with her other hand she quickly grabbed the head and wrung its neck. It hardly fluttered as she held the limp body, swinging from her hand. With the fingers of both hands she felt the tiny body through the feathers, "Y'u doant good to fry up," she said, speaking to herself again and looking at the tiny carcass. She threw the body into the glowing embers of the cooking fire, and immediately the air was filled with the putrid smell of burning flesh and feathers.

CHAPTER 39

During this time Daniel spent his days in a constant dream-like state, doing his mistress's bidding, fetching water and firewood, and aimlessly wandering. He often went down to the river and sat on a large rock where the current swirled around. Looking down into the clear water he could see small fish swimming against the flow, and where the water was still, little black tadpoles of various shapes and sizes sheltered.

One morning he went further up the valley, removed his shoes and waded into the river up to his knees. Looking down into the water he could see several Cray fish moving about, back and forth under a rock. He decided to try and catch them, but when he put his hands into the water they darted under the rocks or backed away, always facing the hand nearest. He reached around behind the rock with his other hand and felt the Cray fish in his hand as it darted under the rock. He tried to grab it, but it escaped. Using the same approach he finally managed to capture one, but in seizing it he cut his thumb on the sharp spikes over its head. With a lot of determination he was able to catch five Cray fish, which he triumphantly brought back to show Maddy, and to cook for their supper that night.

In the days that followed, whenever he could, he went fishing for the Cray fish, but never with the same success. Although there were numerous Cray fish in the river they were difficult to catch and most days there were none to be had, at other times only one or two. The lone catches were kept alive in a can of water until there were at least four, enough for an evening meal.

From time to time several people had visited Maddy. Sometimes they brought little gifts, but mostly they came quietly, spoke softly to Maddy, cast curious looks in the direction of the bearded coolie man, but they never spoke to him, and when they had concluded their business, they disappeared as quickly as they had come. Early one afternoon Maddy had a visitor—a young mother with colicky baby. The child, not more than a few months old, would not stop crying, and the mother was at her wits end. In her desperation she paid a visit to the woman with strange powers and magical cures. From the moment the woman appeared the child had not ceased it's crying, but the crying did not disturb Maddy and she took the infant in her arms.

"Y'u come back te nite," she instructed the mother. The woman hesitated, apparently reluctant to leave the child. "Y'u go now," Maddy said firmly. "Y'u lef baby wid me now," and she pushed the woman towards the pathway, urging her onwards.

As soon as the woman was out of sight, she turned to Daniel. "Mister Coolieman. Quick now. Go down de river little piece. Cross over to de odder side an' go up de bankside. Look about pon de place an' fine cow-itch. It is plenty about, but mine it doant ketch y'u. Bring back one big seed. Go now, quick quick!" And she urged him towards the river.

Daniel went down to the river and crossed over to the other side as he had been instructed. He climbed the steep bank and looked about for the cow-itch plants but did not see any. The bush and weeds were thick and he searched the area for over an hour without success. Reluctantly he decided to return and admit his failure, and again he went towards the river, but as he reached the bank he saw what he had been searching for. Sure enough, it was as she had said, there was cow-itch growing on the bank. He found a large pod with the dark brown velvety hairs covering it, and carefully plucked it.

"Good! Good!" She exclaimed when he gave it to her. The child had been put to lie under a tree on a small mat platted from coconut palm leaves. It had not ceased its wailing, gasping for breath at every pause. Maddy went to the child, picked it up and removed it's clothing so she held it naked in her arms. She turned it over to expose its back, and then she picked up the cow-itch pod.

"Now," she instructed herself. "Jus' brush de bottom," and she touched the child's bottom with the pod, drawing it down across the tender skin. The reaction was instantaneous. The child immediately stopped its crying. As she turned it over again, the eyes were tightly shut, the little hands were outstretched, rigid, fists tightly clenched, the mouth wide open, and not a sound was uttered. For several long moments, the small body remained tensed and rigid, not inhaling, not exhaling—not even breathing! Daniel, even in his stupefied state of mind, was alarmed—the child was surely dying! And then the entire body turned crimson red—he had never seen a black body turn red, and still not a sound was heard.

As Maddy replaced the clothing the child drew a breath, but it did not cry. She put it to lie on the mat under the tree where it fell into a quiet and restful sleep. In the late afternoon the mother returned and the child was still soundly sleeping. She handed Maddy something hidden in her clasped hand, and it was quickly placed in a pocket without examination.

CHAPTER 40

It was now three weeks and a few days past the last full moon, and almost two months since Maddy had performed her rituals under its glowing light. Three weeks ago for several nights, rain and dark heavy clouds had obscured the moon, and the influence on the lunatic woman was minimal, and although she was restless, the spirits did not move her to action. Now, the days and nights were clear, and as the moon grew larger and brighter, its mysterious powers began to affect the woman and draw her under its spell. During the few nights as the moon waxed, Maddy stayed up as long as the moon was visible in the sky. It affected her from the early evening, and ended when the moon disappeared behind the mountain peaks in the west. During the days she began to show the effects of her restlessness and lack of sleep. She often fell asleep, and as she became obsessed with the phase of the moon, she lost interest in every thing else—she hardly ate and she ignored Daniel, even neglecting to cook his food and prepare the narcotic tea. By the time the moon was full, Daniel had not taken the drug for several days, and his mind had almost returned to normal. His balance had returned and he remembered why and how he had arrived at that place. He must get away, he thought, now that the woman's hypnotic spell was broken he had the chance to escape.

On the night of the full moon, quite oblivious to his presence, Maddy prepared herself for ritual. Her white shroud was laid out and by the early evening she was already robed, aromatic herbs were smoldering on the dying fire, and her candles were lit before some sacred altar. Daniel cooked and ate his supper before there was even a hint of darkness. The food he prepared for Maddy had gone untouched, so he put it in the hut, intending to take it with him when he left.

As darkness fell the moon had not yet appeared over the mountain ridge, and Daniel went into the hut as if preparing for bed. Maddy stood before her altar, occasionally stretching out her arms towards the east imploring the rise of the moon. As it came over the mountain the ritual suddenly commenced with a loud cry of ecstasy. It startled him momentarily but he remained quietly in the hut, not even venturing to the doorway to watch. In an hour or so, the place was brilliant in the moonlight, and he could even see objects within the shadow of the hut. The ritualistic dancing and chanting had not yet reached a climax as he searched the hut for his bag and his possessions. Some had been removed from his bag and were scattered about the hut, but he retrieved as much as he could find, including his precious razor. He also found some money and pocketed a few coins. Standing in the shadows, he watched, waiting for his chance to leave. Some minutes later that chance came and he slipped out the door to get behind the hut. In the shadows he made his way down to the river and crossed over to the other side. He struggled up the bank through the bushes looking for the pathway that was supposed to be there—that he had never found—the one that would take him to the road on the other side of the mountain. He made his way up the steep valley without finding the path, but found the road. From above the valley, above the faint sound of the river, he could still hear Maddy singing and chanting, but he did not stop to listen. He started towards the mountain gap not knowing how far, or how long it would take to reach it.

As the hours passed and the moonlight faded he stumbled several times; it was difficult to make his way safely, and he lay down against the bank side, deciding to rest until the morning. Soon, before he knew, he had fallen asleep, and when he awoke it was with some surprise that he had slept so soundly. In spite of an uncomfortable bed and the night dew he felt well rested. He found the food he had cooked for Maddy the day before, and ate most of it. At the roadside spring he washed his face, and with a small piece of soap he shaved off his overgrown beard. It was a difficult and painful experience; the beard was thick, the blade dull, and the skin beneath was tender and soft, and without the benefit of a mirror he cut himself several times. He doctored the wounds and set out once again.

Towards mid-morning he could hear the grinding sound of a motor vehicle in low gear, evidently struggling slowly up the mountain road. The sound echoed through the valley, and it was difficult to tell just where the vehicle was—even if it was on another road. As the sound grew neared he knew the vehicle was behind him and would soon pass by. Finally it rounded a bend and began to overtake him. He stood to the side and watched a lorry filled with large limestone rocks slowly pass. There were two men in the cab, and one sitting on the rock pile in the back. They did not acknowledge his presence as they passed and soon disappeared from view around the next bend in the road. He continued on his way, but the sound of the lorry did not seem to diminish. He had not gone much further when he turned to see another lorry approaching and soon to overtake him. Again he stood to the side of the road and watched it pass. There was only the driver in the vehicle—no one sitting on the load of limestone rocks. Impulsively, the thought entered his mind—he could hop on to the lorry from the back. As it passed he ran the few steps to catch up, threw his bag onto the rocks, and climbed aboard without being seen.

The lorry continued to struggle up the steep grade making slow progress for the next hour or so. Finally, they rounded a bend in the road, and Daniel saw that the first lorry had stopped and the men had dismounted. Quickly, he gathered his bag and slid off the back. He waited as the last lorry joined the first. The driver dismounted and approached the men in the leading vehicle. The men were talking but he could not hear what was being said. He sat on the bank to let them complete their business. Five minutes later, still in conversation, the men were unloading the rocks by hand, one at a time to the side of the road. It took them the better part of an hour to discharge the loads, and when completed, they boarded their respective vehicles and took off round the next bend in the road, out of sight. At that point Daniel resumed his journey.

About a mile further along the road he came upon more piles of limestone rocks dumped by the side of the road—the unmistakable signs that roads were being repaired or new ones being built, and there was a good possibility of getting work. Moments later he heard the vehicles returning down the road towards him. Without the steep grade and their loads, the trucks were traveling considerably faster than before—recklessly. He kept well to the side as they came into view and quickly passed.

As he rounded the next bend in the road, he could see two women in the distance, each sitting atop a limestone pile, each hammering away at the brittle, white stones, breaking them into smaller pieces. The first woman stopped swinging her hammer as he approached.

"Mawning, Sur," she said, taking a brief rest.

He stopped in front of her to wipe the sweat from around his neck and face. "Afternoon," he replied. And then added "It afternoon now, Miss."

The woman smiled and nodded, and for several moments they both rested without speaking. Then he said, "It too hot to bruck rockstone?"

"Never mine it hot or cold, Sur," she answered, "We mus' bruck rockstone every day like we tek tea."

"Den who do de work 'ere?" he inquired.

"De government man, Mr. Pursey. Dem mek de road fe' de land settlement at John Crow Gap."

"Y'u knows wher' 'im deh—dis Mr. Pursey?"

"'Im was 'ere dis marnin' but now 'im garn up de road fe 'im lunchtime."

"T'ank y'u miss. T'ank y'u," and replacing his handkerchief he started off once again. Some distance ahead, another pile of limestone rocks heaped high on the bank at the side of the road. A young, attractive black woman sitting astride, rested her sledge and watched him keenly as he passed below. He nodded towards her as he passed, intent on continuing.

"Hey!—Hey!—Pretty Man!" The woman called after him as he passed. The shout was unexpected. He stopped several yards ahead and turned to look up at her.

"Pretty man, where y'u goine?"

He took a step towards her. "Me go look fe work miss. Fe de bossman."

A moments pause, "me knows wher' 'im deh."

His interest was aroused. If she knew where the bossman was, the woman could save him time and effort.

"Ah knows wher' him deh," she repeated. "Y'u wan' te know where 'im is?"

"Yes, miss." He took out his cloth and wiped the perspiration from his face, waiting for her to speak. He took another step closer, folded his handkerchief and stuffed it into his pocket. He waited for her to answer, but the woman only looked him over without speaking, and then she started to laugh quietly to herself. He watched her curiously for a moment or two; he was being made fun of and he did not have time for that. He smiled at her, waved in her direction and started off again.

"Come 'ere, Pretty man." The woman called to him again.

Again he stopped and turned towards her.

"A'h 'ave sumptin' fe y'u," she said.

She bent down searching through the stone chips that surrounded her bare, dust covered feet. She picked up a large sparkling crystal of quartz that in the sunlight reflected bright prismic colors. She wiped it between her fingers, blowing off the dust as he approached. He was now curious and interested in the flirtatious young woman—she was an attractive woman, but it could be helpful to have a friend, and a little patience might be rewarded, he thought. As he got nearer, her skirt spread wide over her bare legs suggestested nakedness beneath. She threw the crystal towards him and it fell at his feet. He stooped to pick it up and slowly stood to look up at her, sitting high on the pile of stones, her skirt still spread wide over her bare legs. With slow deliberation, her gaze fixed intensely on his face, she pushed the skirt down between her legs, denying him little more than a glimpse of all beneath.

He held the crystal in his hand for several moments looking at her before examining it, and then returning to look at the woman again. She was playing flirtatious games with him, and he started to smile, almost laughing but not quite. Her expression had been solemn and serious but slowly it changed—she returned his smile, and quietly they laughed together.

"It pretty, eh?" she asked.

"Yes, miss, very pretty," he twisted it in his fingers to catch the light.

"Y'u keep it, den" she said. "It will bring y'u good luck."

"T'ank y'u, miss." He examined it again before putting it in his pocket. "Ah keeps it to 'member y'u." And after a few moments, "tell me wher' de bossman deh."

"Im is not so far, up de road a little piece. He 'ave 'im tent pitch in de bush, up de hillside by de river. W'en y'u come to de river, y'u cross over an' go up de hillside. 'Im is dere in de bush."

"T'ank y'u miss. An' good afternoon to y'u."

She picked up her sledge and resumed crushing the limestone rocks. He continued on his way, but the pitched tent was much further than "up de road a little piece."

CHAPTER 41

It so happened that Edward Pursey, an affable Englishman and experienced civil engineer, had been looking for an assistant—someone, who could read, write, and calculate. Daniel fitted in perfectly, and immediately found himself on trial for the job—and the pay was good too. The days of trial passed quickly resulting in a steady job at the end of a week.

Daniel had no place to live and 'camped out' near by under a crude shelter that he built from bush and brambles. A week or so later, rain during the night produced a miserable assistant the following morning, and Pursey insisted that he move into the tent with him. After another week went by they were getting along very well—they worked, cooked meals, ate together, and slept under the same canvas. The tent was not luxurious accommodation, but for Daniel it was a far cry from sleeping on the ground, under the open sky with only bush to ward off the rain and damp. Every fortnight or so Pursey returned to his home in Kingston, leaving Daniel in charge of the camp and the surveying instruments— to see that they were not stolen.

With nothing to spend his wages on, Daniel soon saved a fair sum of money. It was becoming something of a problem to keep, and a month later he asked Pursey to look after the money for him. Pursey took it to Kingston and opened an account at the Post Office in Daniel's name. Every so often a lodgment was made and Pursey returned the bankbook showing the amount on deposit. Soon Daniel began to think of himself as a wealthy man—he had never had that much saved in all his life, in fact he had never had a bank account before.

By Jamaican standards the road construction was going well, but in reality it was very slow indeed. There were four gangs of six men each whose job it was to swing their picks and hack a road out of the mountainside. The gangs rotated in turn, but still it was exhausting work. The surveying was completed much in advance of the construction itself, and although Daniel was now the unofficial foreman on the job, at times he found that he did not have much to do other than to see that the men were kept working.

He often thought about the woman he met on the road, sitting on the pile of limestone rocks. He would take the crystal out of his pocket and look at it thoughtfully, sometimes for several minutes. She had certainly brought him good luck, and if for nothing else, he would like to thank her! As Pursey's assistant he was required to visit different sites during the day where the work was being done, and on several occasions had wandered off looking for her. He had not seen her, even though he had been past piles of rocks where she would have been working. He did not know her name, but even if he had, he hesitated to ask anyone about her.

As the weeks passed the work was due for an inspection by the Chief Engineer from Kingston. The inspection would take three or four days, and Daniel was told that he would have to vacate his place in the tent, give up his cot, to make room for the visitor. The shelter he had built earlier was still there, but it was woefully inadequate, so Pursey supplied rubber ground sheets to reinforce the shelter and make it rainproof.

Pursey left for Kingston early on a Saturday morning, and Daniel prepared to move his things out of the tent early on the Monday morning. By noon the work had stopped for the day, and there was not much to do about the camp after the workers left. It was getting very hot and humid, and he was bored with no one around. He sat about the campsite for a while idly picking at the bark of a branch in the fire, thinking about the woman he met on the road, and wondering where she lived—he was hopeful they would meet again.

After eating his lunch he decided to go down to the river, find a secluded spot, take a bath, and cool off in the river. He usually bathed at night in the privacy afforded by darkness, but at night it was quite cold and not very pleasant. On such a hot day the cool water would be very refreshing. He collected a piece of soap and a towel and went down to the river.

Even though he had been there over three months, he had not explored very much of the river in either direction, so he wandered up the stream. There was no possibility that he could loose his way or get lost, so he picked his way around the huge boulders that inhabited the river valley, and he did not pay much attention to what lay further ahead, only stopping occasionally to look about, and note his whereabouts. Some distance further upstream, as he paused he thought there was some movement at the edge of a huge boulder lying almost in the middle of the riverbed. He looked again but did not see anyone, and he continued on. Further along when he looked again someone was there—he might have to put off his plans for a bath, he thought, but he would still be glad to meet someone. Later on he could explore the river in the opposite direction if indeed someone was there and taking a bath was not possible.

The huge boulder must have been there for centuries; it was bleached clean and white like some ancient fossil from the depths of the earth. Perhaps at some time in the distant past it was dislodged from the mountain above and had rolled down the valley to rest mid-stream. Or maybe it was expelled from the bowels of the earth by some prehistoric volcanic eruption. But the years and the weather had washed it clean and white.

He approached where the way was easier, and as he rounded a smaller boulder still some distance away, he saw a figure in clear view—there was a woman, completely naked, her black body silhouetted in the sunshine against the white bleached boulder. He was transfixed—startled and for the moment, confused. This was completely unexpected—he did not know if he should advance, or tactfully retreat, so he hesitated and watched. The woman did not move, her eyes were closed, her face turned up towards the sun, basking in its warmth. It was a beautiful sight! The woman had a lovely, beautiful body—a vision seen only in his dreams! And he took it all in. She had not heard nor seen him. Then, it was as though she awoke. She opened her eyes and was dazzled by the brilliant sunlight; she could not see the man watching her. She squinted about as her eyes became accustomed to the light, and suddenly she saw him. Instinctively she raised her arms to cover her breasts, but she remained motionless, looking at him. Then, slowly, he recognized the woman—it was the woman who gave him a sparkling crystal for good luck. And she recognized him—the man she had given a sparkling crystal.

Silence, and then, "Pretty man!—Y'u fine' me!"

He could not find words to reply—he remained motionless and speechless, just looking, and then slowly he approached. He held out a hand towards her, and she did not back away. As he got closer he saw the same expression he had seen before when they first met, when he stooped to pick up the crystal. Slowly she uncovered her breasts and with both hands cupped them towards him swaying suggestively from side to side. The seductive, taunting gesture transfixed him motionless. Then she turned slowly and strode away, swinging hips from side to side as she walked towards the rear of the boulder. He reached out towards her, but she anticipated his reaction and darted out of reach. He quickly followed. Behind the boulder she let him catch her.

They lay naked, resting on the soft, sandy strip behind the boulder, "W'at y'u name?" he asked.

"Pearl."

"Pearl," he repeated softly to himself. "It a pretty name." He reached for his trousers and retrieved the sparkling crystal. Holding it up to the light he turned it between his fingers, "It did bring me good luck."

She smiled as he turned towards her and kissed her again—on her neck—again and again, all over her body. She wriggled and twitched in an avalanche of his caresses.

In the late afternoon he returned to the campsite alone. He was famished, not having eaten since the noon. He made his supper and went to sleep almost before it was dark. The next morning he was up early and moved his possessions out of the tent. He cleaned up the tent and the camp in anticipation of Pursey's return the next day. He was in a hurry to meet Pearl as they had agreed to spend the day together beside the river. He collected some food and hurried off towards their rendezvous, the large white boulder in the middle of the river valley.

Pearl was already there when he arrived. She was again lying naked on the narrow strip of soft sand, basking in the sun. On the way there she had picked a large quantity of silver ferns from the plants that grew in the mountain country. A feature of these leaves is that bright, silvery spores transfer an exact imprint of the leaf when placed on a surface and patted or firmly pressed to the surface. While waiting she had covered herself—her arms, legs, stomach, forehead, face and cheeks—as much as possible—with the silvery imprints. From a short distance, she appeared as a nymph, wearing some skintight silvery fabric over her entire body.

"W'at y'u do?" he asked surprised by the unusual sight.

"Put some 'pon me back," she instructed him. He obliged until her whole body was completely covered, from head to foot. Satisfied, she stepped away onto the sandy beach, and started to dance. For the next fifteen minutes she held him spellbound, dancing, and singing to keep time with her movements. Finally, tiring, she flung herself on the beach beside him. He put his arms around her and held her close as she regained her breath.

Later, they went to the work camp. While he cooked supper he told her that he would be sleeping in the bramble shelter, and he suggested she join him there. Pearl had a better idea—that he move in with her. She shared a one-roomed hut with a couple and another woman some distance away, but there was room for him, and she was sure that the others would not mind, especially if he paid some rent. He thought it over for a second or two and then agreed.

Pursey returned to the camp just before noon, accompanied by the chief engineer. Daniel was overseeing the roadwork when the two men arrived and was not in the camp to meet them, but they fixed 'Bully Beef' sandwiches for their lunch and began looking over the surveys, and later they went off to inspect the work.

When the work stopped for the day, Daniel returned to the camp to start preparing the evening meal, and when the engineers returned the supper was ready. Before they ate the chief searched in his knapsack and produced a bottle of whisky. He poured large portions for himself and Pursey, and had taken a sip or two when he remembered Daniel. He poured another glass and invited Daniel to join them. They had finished their meal when Pursey noticed a woman standing some distance away at the edge of the campsite. It was Pearl, but Daniel had not seen her. She stood watching without approaching. He called to Daniel, " there's someone there, Daniel. Have they come to see you?" he asked.

"Ah. Yes sur." He put down his dish and went over to her for a few moments. "Ah soon come," he said. "Wait fe me. When dem finish I will come."

CHAPTER 42

The rising sun never reached the valley settlement until well into the morning. The people living in the dozen or so huts were used to it, and did not seem to mind getting up when it was sunless and the air quite damp and cold. By about nine o'clock, the sun, hot and strong, came blazing its way over the mountain ridges to disperse the mists and fog, and every hint of the nighttime chill.

Daniel and his newfound lover Pearl, moved into the small valley settlement ten days after their passionate encounter by the river. Daniel rented a small one-roomed hut from the enterprising landlord who had built the houses in the clearing, and who visited the place once a week, without fail to collect his rents. Collecting the rents from a few tenants might not have appeared to be a difficult task, but the inevitable excuses, arguments over what was owed and what could be paid, usually took a full day to settle. For the number of houses there, the settlement was grossly over populated, as each hut was occupied by far more people than would have been thought possible or healthy, but for all the congestion, they appeared to be comfortable and happy, and to thrive.

As soon as they moved there Pearl took up housekeeping duties in exchange for the wretched work of crushing limestone rocks. She was now a member of a privileged group, the 'wife' of a gainfully employed man and she could spend her days—most of the day, at any rate—in leisurely activities and idle gossip. They had been there almost a year and life had been good to them; both were happy and contented with their situation. Daniel, for his part, enjoyed his work as assistant to the road engineer, and he had saved a fair sum of money. Some of this he kept with him, hidden in the hut, some had been deposited in the Government Savings Bank, and some he had "loaned" to other tenants to forestall their eviction, not ever expecting it to be repaid.. Comparatively speaking, he was a wealthy man though it did not appear so, and he looked forward to returning some day to Chivers Estate to see his daughter and his grandchild, but he had no definite plans in mind.

In essence, Pearl was a lazy woman, narcissistic and self-indulgent. Her ultimate pleasure would have been to deck herself in lavish dresses, bright sparkling gems and precious stones. But such pleasures could only be enjoyed in her imagination and in her daydreams. In spite of these preoccupations, she was cheerful, good-humored and constantly entertaining, and as a result was adored by her lover.

When they moved into the settlement, she brought with her little more than the clothes she was wearing, and her most precious possession—a piece from a broken mirror—her 'glass.' The glass was indispensable to her wellbeing, and she kept it with her at all times. It was used to fix her hair, and frequently to examine her face and body. Daniel was aware of this preoccupation, but he was bemused, and even at times joined in to indulge her whims and fancies.

The piece of 'glass' had come into her possession some years earlier through the misadventure to a Mrs. Robinson's wardrobe. While the said wardrobe was being moved into Mrs. Robinson's new home it was inadvertently dropped from the cart, and the mirror did not survive the accident. The half-dozen curious and interested spectators who were gathered about to watch the transfer of Mrs. Robinson's furniture, were gleeful at the catastrophe; one and all, they pounced upon the pieces of the broken mirror scattered about. In a matter of seconds there was not a piece to be seen, except for some fine splinters and a few jagged pieces still remaining in the frame. These were slowly and cautiously being removed by the cart man responsible for the accident. He silently bowed his head, submitting to the shouts and curses from an enraged Mrs. Robinson. Pearl was one of the beneficiaries of the incident, and to ensure her ownership, scratched her 'mark' on the back with a sharp pin.

Evelyn and her man, long-time residents of the settlement, occupied the hut across the dusty pathway that separated the two abodes. By right of being there first, Evelyn claimed privileges in items of common usage in the settlement. Rivalries had quickly developed, and there had been incidents of pushing and shoving, accompanied by insults and derisive comments. Each woman could go about their leisurely activities during the day without much contact, and that was a good thing, but towards evening both women would settle down to prepare the evening meal, and it was during that time when disagreements arose between them. There had been heated arguments over possession of the cooking fire, and blows were almost struck when Evelyn spitefully doused the fire, leaving only a wet smoldering pile of ashes and charred wood for Pearl to rekindle.

For the most part though, there was much in common between the two couples; essentially their interests were similar, and they spent their days in similar fashion. They rose in the mornings at about the same hour, and the women passed their days idly in gossip and talk with the other women in the community. And yet they were bitter rivals, filled with jealousies and hate.

Pearl who did not have to get up early, like those who had to go to work, or those who had morning teas to brew, stood by her window basking in the sunshine. Leaning against the window side was her prized possession, the piece of the broken mirror. She passed the time examining every small blemish on her face, occasionally finding a blackhead, which she exorcised between forefingers.

Evelyn, from across the pathway, peered occasionally from the window or the doorway of her hut, but tiring of watching her rival, she finally pulled a dress over her naked body, and finding a brightly colored band tied it around her waist as a belt. Barefooted, she stepped out of the hut to the path. She neither looked at nor spoke to Pearl as she passed along, ignoring her as though she did not exist. She soon disappeared amid the scattered huts and trees. Pearl would have done the same thing had she the opportunity, but now that her enemy was out of sight, she could relax, and think of other things. She pulled on her dress, tied a band on her head, and sauntered out, down the pathway in the opposite direction, towards the river flowing some hundred yards further down in the valley. The departure of her rival had set her at ease—she was relieved—she did not feel inclined to squabble that morning, but inadvertently she had also lowered her guard. Normally she would have pocketed her precious glass, or at least hidden it somewhere in the hut, but this morning she forgot it leaning on the window ledge, within easy grasp of anyone passing by.

Over an hour went by before Pearl remembered about her glass—that she did not have it with her, and that she had left it on the window. Hurriedly she returned; the glass was nowhere to be found—it had disappeared. Frantically she searched, first inside the hut, and then the ground outside by the window. She cast suspicious glances in the direction of the hut across the pathway; there was movement within—Evelyn was there, she knew, she could sense her presence, hiding in the shadows. Suspicion and anger rose within her, but she searched once again for the missing glass without success. Now she was certain—the mirror had been taken, and the only person who could have taken it was Evelyn. Rage flamed within her—she was going to get it back.

"Y'u tek me glass," she said walking towards Eleven's hut. "Y'u tek me glass," she repeated in a loud voice, even though no one was yet visible in the hut.

A few moments went by and Evelyn appeared in the doorway. "Me no see y'u glass."

The accusations were repeated—shouted!

"A' w'at me want wid y'u glass, gal?—Me no see y'u glass."

Several people appeared, a few half-clothed children came running. They gathered in the pathway to watch developments.

"Y'u tek me glass—me lef it deh on de window, an' y'u tek it up." And turning to the gathering crowd, "De gal tek me glass. Me lef it on de ledge an' when me come back it garn." And then turning again towards Evelyn, pointing an accusing finger, "Y'u dam well tek me glass, an if y'u no tek it where it deh?"

A crowd gathered as if out of nowhere. "S'mady tek Pear glass." Someone transmitted the news to new arrivals.

"Me no see de glass," said Evelyn, speaking mostly to the gathered spectators. "A'h w'at me goin' do wid y'u glass?" The denial was weak in the light of vehement accusations, and, as if everyone did not know what she would do with a piece of broken mirror!

"Y'u gimme back me glass," demanded Pearl. "Y'u dam tief. Gimme back me glass!" There was a murmur from the crowd. Here was an accusation that had to be strongly denied.

"Y'u call me tief!—Y'u call me tief!"

Evelyn was the larger stronger woman, and if need be, intended to use her size and strength to win her case. Threateningly she approached the other woman, "Y'u call me tief!—Y'u call me tief!"

For the moment Pearl was disarmed as the prospect of physical conflict loomed. Frustration and anger swelled within her. She turned away from her opponent, now within arms reach. The tears gathered, and turning towards the crowd, "De gal tief me glass," she told them, almost sobbing, looking down and away from her opponent, wringing her hands in her thin dress. "De gal tief me glass!"

Evelyn sensed victory was at hand, and pressing her advantage she pushed the other woman in the back, throwing her violently forward. "Y'u dam liar! Y'u dam liar y'u. Y'u loose y'u glass, an' y'u call me tief!"

The shove was unexpected, and realizing the loss of her precious glass, Pearl threw reason and caution aside; blind rage filled every part of her being. Like a wild cat she sprang at the other woman, teeth and talons bared for combat. The flared claws came down across the face and closed on the loose dress around the neck. The tearing fabric was not heard above the shrieks from both women as they closed for the fight.

A cheer went up from the crowd now not only interested, but also committed spectators. A little boy went running through the settlement, shouting as he ran, "De gal dem fight! De gal dem fight!" He announced it like a town crier.

The announcement was hardly necessary; the shouts and cheers from the small crowd were sufficient to attract everyone's attention and they all came running. Within minutes a sizable crowd had gathered, the new arrivals pushing from the rear for a better view, and those in front pushing back to give the combatants space. The two women fought on unconcerned by the attention. Biting, punching, hitting and clawing, the fortunes moved back and forth from one to the other. For a few moments Pearl seemed to have the upper hand, only a few seconds later to have the situation reversed. Soon their dresses were nothing more than rags still around the arm, neck or waist. They would never again have the need for modesty; every part of their anatomies had been fully revealed to the watching crowd. Dust and dirt covered their bodies, giving them a strange appearance, especially about the mouth, eyes, and bleeding bruises, where the dirt caked into a mudpack. A woman in the front line grabbed two little open-mouthed boys from between her feet, clouted their heads as she admonished them for viewing such a spectacle, quite unfit for young eyes to see. They withdrew to nurse their bruises.

As the fight took a pause there appeared, suddenly, in the dust, the piece of the broken mirror. A gasp went up from the crowd, and some pointed, "Look!! De glass! See de glass!" As the fight resumed, the glass disappeared in the dust beneath the combatants, and again it reappeared. "Look! See de glass!

The exertion of the encounter was beginning to take effect; the women were tiring, and both paused to take breath. Evelyn loosed her hold on Pearl's hair to deliver a punch on the side of the face. Pearl retaliated with a head-buck to the nose, quickly followed by another, and grabbing a forearm held it long enough to inflict a bite. The brawl continued; the two women, dust covered, naked, bruised and bleeding, rolled and tumbled, cursed and screamed as each found some moment of victory or suffered some defeat. An elderly woman in the crowd was appalled by the savagery, "Oh Lawd!—Oh Lawd!" she moaned. "Lawd 'a'v mercy!"

Size and strength however, began to have the upper hand; Evelyn was astride and on top of the smaller woman whose arms she held pinned to the ground. They paused for a moment to recover their breath. This, if anything was a victory for Evelyn; she was no less bruised and battered than was her opponent, but even so there was no indication that the fight was yet over; it would likely resume, and perhaps conclude with a different outcome.

From the back of the crowd came a shout, "W'at 'appening' here?" it demanded. The voice came from Daniel. "W'at de hell goin' on 'ere?" he pushed his way to the front. He shoved Evelyn to the ground, and stooped to lift Pearl. "W'at de hell goin' on?"

"Evelyn—tief—me—glass," sobbed Pearl, brokenly, in explanation. He put his arm around her, and with her head buried on his shoulder, he led her quickly to the refuge of their hut. Someone in the crowd searched in the dust, found the glass, and returned to its owner as she entered the hut.

Evelyn sat in the dust for a few moments, "Me never tek de glass. Me never did tek de glass," she sobbed. With her dress in rags and her arms around her breasts, she stood up and ran to her hut followed there by two women from the crowd, who went along to console her.

It was a few weeks later that Evelyn and her man left the settlement. Their departure was unnoticed and without event. They packed their few belongings in two coconut sacks, and made their way to parts unknown.

Jamaican Lore—De darg sey "no matter how cloth is cheap, 'e nar buy none."

CHAPTER 43

A week later Pearl was not suffering much physical discomfort from her fight with Evelyn. Most of the cuts and bruises were healing well, with the exception of a nasty cut on the side of her face and cheek. She examined it constantly, but for all the attention it was not getting better, and a month later the scar was still very obvious across her cheek. All kinds of remedies had been applied, but the injury had removed the skin, leaving a much lighter, pinkish area, that was quite disfiguring. She talked of nothing else, constantly asking Daniel how she looked and what did he think she should do about it. He gave her money to buy ointment, but a fortnight later it had not worked its magic, and she was as depressed as ever.

The women from the settlement suggested various treatments to heal or hide the scar, and some treatments, unfortunately, made it worse. Its visibility was having a very depressing effect on her mood and temperament. Her friends tried in vain to cheer her up, but the fight had changed her. It was the humiliation that she never talked about that worked constantly in her mind and eroded her temperament, and the scar was a constant reminder for everyone to see. She was no longer the cheerful, humorous, carefree person that she had once been. Daniel tried, without success to cheer her up and make her feel better, but she was deeply depressed, and for all his efforts, she continued to sulk throughout the day, and the departure of her enemy several weeks later did little to improve matters.

From time to time the settlement was visited by a few traveling salesmen—merchant peddlers—offering a wide variety of goods; pins and needles, threads, buttons, broadcloths, beads and trinkets, ointments, balms, and cures for whatever ailed you! The most successful of these peddlers came with a cart drawn by a small, much abused, long-suffering donkey. But the most fascinating peddler rode a bicycle—or rather pushed a bicycle—with two heavily loaded hampers and two baskets, one at the front attached to the handle bars, and one at the rear, attached to the sadle seat of his machine. He was a crafty, sly character sporting a goatee beard, who given half the chance short-changed his customers. Daniel took an immediate dislike to the man, and warned Pearl to be careful in dealing with him.

"He a 'scuffler,'" he told her. "He lookin' to pick up t'ings he doant put down."

Pearl had always been a steady customer for his trinkets and bracelets, and she had spent a fair sum with all of them. Even so, it would still be difficult to see how any of them could have earned a living from the farthings and ha'-pennies they gained from each sale. But with the highly visible scar on her cheek, Pearl was no longer buying earrings or bracelets; her paramount concern was on finding a cure for the disfiguring scar. Noting the loss of his sales, the 'scuffler' was anxious to find replacement, and sensing Pearl's interest, claimed to have a cure; one that would remove the scar entirely. Pearl wanted nothing less, and offered whatever it would take.

The cure, he told her, was a secret ritual and very private, and they should not be disturbed while it was being worked. Within a short time Pearl was convinced, and quite prepared to undergo his treatment. The next time he came she must be ready, he said, and that would be in two weeks or so. But Pearl was impatient—that was much too long to wait—it would have to be sooner, she insisted.

If it was to be sooner, the man said, she would have to pay in advance; a shilling would be enough, and Pearl was obliged to pay. She took the money from the hiding-place in the hut, and a week later the bearded pedler returned.

In the privacy of her hut the 'scuffler' produced a long piece of cloth, insisting it was necessary to bandage the scar, her head and entire face. After some persuasion Pearl agreed, and he wrapped the cloth around her head, over her eyes, nose and mouth, but loose enough to allow her to breath freely.

"Dis is goin' to tek time," he told her. "Y'u mus' lie back on de bed," and Pearl lay down. He began to rub his hands over her head and face mumbling incantations as he worked his 'cure.' The ritual continued for more than a few minutes, and then from his bag he produced a bottle of over-proof white rum. Pouring a small amount on his hands he wiped them dry on the bandage, allowing his 'patient' to inhale the vapours. As the alcohol evaporated it was supplimented by additions from the bottle, and after a while Pearl was in a state of semi-intoxication. He probed her several times to be certain that she was unconscious, and then he began to caress her breasts. He ignored her mumbled objection, and after more applications of the rum, she did not react. At this point he lifted her dress and removed the underwear which Pearl had started to wear. He dropped his trousers, spread her legs, and raped the unconscious woman. Shortly after, he was completely satisfied. In a few minutes he removed the cloth from around her face.

Half-an-hour later Pearl was recovering from her stupor, not aware of what had taken place or what had happened to her. The man was still in the room.

"How de mark?" she asked as her senses were returning and she searched for her glass.

"It not garn yet," he told her. "It a bad mark an' it goin tek more treatment. But giv' it li'kle time."

He helped her to get up and steadied her sitting on the bed. "It will need more treatment."

"W'ere me glass?" Pearl wanted to know. "Pass me glass," she said as she rubbed her hands over the scar, feeling the swelling, which had been irritated and inflamed by the strong alcohol; the scar was much larger and more noticable.

He did not produce the mirror and Pearl was becoming aggitated; she kept rubbing her fingers over the scar, noticed the increased swelling, and wanted to look at it. "Pass me me glass," she ordered.

He looked about as though searching, and pretending not to have found it he got up. "Me doant see y'u glass," he said. "Ah mus' go now."

Hastily he prepared to leave, quickly he gathered the bandage and bag, and was out of the hut within a few seconds, leaving Pearl to find her glass and recover on her own.

It took Pearl an hour to more or less to regain her full senses, and when she did she was more aggitated and angrier than ever. The scar was now greatly inflamed and swollen, and was far more noticable—and then she began to wonder about her missing underware. What happened while she was drugged? "Where me panties?" she asked herself, and as her head cleared it dawned on her what had taken place. In the privacy of her hut she broke down, and sobbed bitterly. Daniel was never told.

The money they kept hidden in the hut was there for use in paying the rent and purchasing food, and whatever household items they needed. It was a far larger sum than would ever have been normally used, but Daniel did not have any other place to keep it should some money be required at short notice. He checked it whenever more was added or some was taken out, but it was not a preoccupation with him, and he relied on Pearl to use it carefully and see to its safekeeping. Over the weeks it had grown considerably, and one Saturday afternoon, when adding his weeks pay he told Pearl he would deposit it in his saving account. On the Monday morning though, he forgot to pick up the money and take it with him to work for Pursey to deposit.

He returned home late in the afternoon to find the hut deserted and there was no sign of Pearl. There was no supper cooked and all her personal items were missing. For several minutes he looked about the room, wondering what had happened. Then he went to make inquiries; if anyone had seen his Pearl. Finally he found someone that had seen her leave that morning with a bundle under her arm, but that person had not spoken to her, and did not know where she was going. Other than that he learned nothing, and after an hour or so, he returned to his hut, hungry and depressed, hoping to find something to eat. As he entered the hut, suddenly he thought about the money and anxiously went to the hiding place. The money was gone—not a penny remained—the entire amount had been taken. He sat on the floor, dazed, his head reeling, confused.

"Why had she deserted him? They had not quarreled. They were still lovers, and he still loved her. Later in the evening he found something to eat and spent a miserable night quite unable to reconcile events.

The following morning he began a more detailed questioning of Pearl's friends and the people that knew her. He visited the hut that they had shared when they first met and questioned the women still living there. They were equally confused and curious, and none could shed any light on the reason for her departure. During the time she had lived with them Pearl had not told them much about herself, or where she came from, and they did not know where she would have gone. No one seemed to know what part of the country she came from, and Daniel, when he thought about it, had never found out either—not for certain, anyway. He knew of places where she had been but he did not know where she came from. He wanted to search for her, but did not know where to begin. If he did that, he reasoned, it would take days and he would loose his job. He would continue to make inquiries, stay where he was, hoping that she would return.

A week later he was still searching and hoping, but as the weeks passed and there was no sign of her, he was very depressed indeed. The change did not escape Pursey's notice. In the past they had often talked about personal matters, so Daniel was not hesitant to tell him the sad story. Pursey had sympathy and consoling words to offer, but also said that he should face the prospect that she would never return.

A few months later the road had reached a point where it would have to cross the river. There was indecision about how it would continue. Should there be a bridge over the river or just a ford? Pursey wanted to start the construction of a bridge as he judged it to be the most desirable. At some time in the future it was expected that the road would go through the mountains to connect the city of Kingston to the North Coast—a much shorter way than the torturous route presently available. However, a bridge would cost too much, and the Department decided that it would have to stop the work for at least a year until the money became available. The decision to halt the work was not made public until the last moment. When the workers were told it came as a bitter shock and there was considerable anger. Everyone would be out of work.

Daniel was as angry as the men—it was unfair not to give them notice, but he kept his temper. He knew that Pursey was not to blame, and he would need a reference from him to get another job. Also, Pursey had deposited his money in the Government Saving Bank in Kingston; that evening they talked about how he could get the money. Pursey expected to return the following week with a truck to close down the camp, and he could bring the money back with him. It was agreed that Daniel would stay on for that week and assist in closing down the camp.

On the Friday afternoon the workers were to receive their final pay, and the cash was, as usual, to be brought up by car from Annotto Bay. After mid-day all work ceased, and the men, in sombre mood, were impatiently awaiting the arrival of the car. Anger was evident amongst the men as they threw their tools into wooden crates to be shipped back to Kingston. It was several hours later that a truck arrived instead of the car. The truck had been sent because the Head Office had decided to close the camp down that weekend, and not leave it until the following week. The men were paid off and one by one they wandered away, still angry and grumbling.

The sudden change in plans worried Daniel; if Pursey was not returning the following week, how would he get his money? The truck driver was there to load the truck and Daniel's help was not needed, but as soon as he had a chance, he spoke to Pursey. Pursey had not thought about it—indeed, getting Daniel's money back to him was not his major concern at the time, but he promised to work something out.

Daniel did not go back to his hut in the settlement that night, instead he stayed the night and slept in the tent as he had done before. Early the next morning he helped load the lorry, and by mid-day everything was on board. There was a lot of food; cans of 'Bully Beef,' condensed milk, dried beans, oatmeal, sugar, salt, and a few utensils that were not being taken back, and Pursey gave it all to Daniel. He wrote a glowing letter of reference and gave it to Daniel. As Pursey was about to board the lorry Daniel asked him again about the transfer of the money, and how he intended to send it. Pursey said he would have it transferred to the Post Office Saving Bank in Annotto Bay; he would need his bankbook and identification to withdraw it. If there was a problem he should write to him, and he gave him the address.

They shook hands and said good-bye. Daniel stood at the side of the road as the vehicle slowly drove past. Pursey waved from the driver's side, and then was out of sight. He turned towards the campsite—it was strangely quiet and deserted, lifeless and very lonely. He walked through examining the deserted camping site; where the tent had been pitched was dry and dusty, the fireplace was cold and filled with wood ash, there were scraps of litter and garbage still scattered about. A feeling of loneliness and depression came over him, so he sat down on a large stone, just thinking.

In a while he turned his attention to the food and items Pursey had given him. He packed them into a wooded box and a sack, hid them in a thick bush away from the campsite covered over with some waterproof sheeting. He was glad to have got the food because he only had his last weeks pay, and having the food meant that he would not have to buy much for a while.

He was worried though; he had not paid his rent for three weeks and his pay would not be enough for that. For the last three weeks, every Saturday afternoon he had been away looking for Pearl and had missed the weekly visits of the landlord collecting his rents. There was no chance that he could get more money until he went to Annotto Bay, and that was a long distance away—besides, why would he want to return to the settlement? He had almost reconciled himself to the prospect that Pearl had taken his money and would not come back to him, so why would he want to stay there? It was not the loss of the money that bothered him though—it was just the manner in which it was done that made him feel so sad—they had always been so happy together.

The unpaid rent bothered him and he wondered what he could do about it. He took the money from his pocket and counted it even though he knew exactly how much he had. There was not enough to pay the three weeks rent; certainly not enough for his needs, and for how long he did not know. The rent was due that very day; Mr. Johnston the landlord, would be there all day and would certainly demand payment if they met; the man was very persistent; he would have to avoid meeting him. Then he thought about the loans he had made to the other tenants - he was owed much more than what he owed - but still the unpaid rent bothered him. His things were still in the hut; he could not leave without them. He hoped that Johnston had not taken them to ensure payment, so the sooner he went back there and collected them the better. He decided to go back that night, just as soon as it was dark, but he would have to repair his old shelter and sleep there that night.

He repaired the shelter and ate before it began to get dark. As he waited for the darkness he made plans; he would not stay there in the hope of finding Pearl; he would just have to forget about her and move on. The unpaid rent bothered him; he did not feel it was right not to pay, but he couldn't do much about that; the rent would have to be owed—at least for the time being.

As soon as it began to get dark he set out for the settlement. It would take an hour to get there so it would be quite dark by then. Quietly he walked up the pathway leading to the scattered huts. He could see some of the people moving about in their huts, and a few moved from one hut to another. He could hear voices and conversation and occasionally a burst of laughter, but he did not meet anyone. He kept to the darker areas as he approached his hut, and as he got nearer he could see a light inside—there was someone in there. He moved in closer to see better, leaned against a tree to be hidden in the shadows, and waited. After a while a figure appeared in the hut, but he could not see who it was, and then all was still again. He kept watch and waited. It was almost two hours later that the person began to move about again. The light was being moved, and then the door opened and a man stepped out. It was Mr. Johnston. It seemed that he was staying in the hut, perhaps awaiting the return of its missing tenant.

The man picked his way down the pathway towards the latrines, some distance away. Daniel watched him enter and close the door. That was the chance he was waiting for. Quickly he entered the hut, and in the darkness he fumbled for a match. He had left a candle on the table and it was still there. He lit it and looked around. Most of his things were still where he had left them, and it did not look as though they had been disturbed. He bundled them up and stuffed them in his sack. He took another quick look around holding the candle to see into the corners. He left a few pots, a tin plate and a few utensils—he had replacements given him by Pursey and would not need the ones he left. He blew out the candle, replaced it on the table and looked out the open door. Outside there was no sign of anyone. Keeping to the shadows he again made his way down the path leading to the road and back to the campsite.

CHAPTER 44

A day after recovering his belongings from the settlement, Daniel was on the road to Annotto Bay. He spent the day before packing up in preparation for the journey; he knew it would be a long and tiring trip, and decided to take as much of the food as possible, and with his other things, he had two heavy bundles to carry. He set out early in the morning, and by afternoon, from the mountain elevation, he could see the town, the bay and a ship anchored off shore. It seemed to be so near—just a few minutes walk, but it was deceptively far away, and by the late afternoon he was still in the mountains. He had hoped to reach the narrow coastal plane before it got dark, but was still far out of the town. He stopped to rest and eat, and then was on his way again.

The night came on quickly with a speed and darkness frequently known in that part of the world, but he kept up his pace. For the most part the road followed the valley and the river flowing below. On the side of the river the bank went over a steep incline with almost a sheer decent to the river. To wander off the road or to stumble in the darkness could mean a bad fall, perhaps serious injury, so he kept to the side of the road nearest to the mountain. He passed roadside dwelling places, small thatched make-do huts, stuck to the hillside, off the road, dimly lit with oil lamps, and occasionally guarded by packs of half-starved, barking, snarling, dogs. An hour or so later the road left the river and became less steep, and an hour after that the coast was clearly visible where it met the sea, even in the darkness of the night. The sky was lit by millions of stars, quite overwhelming by their numbers and brilliance. He passed a small church and it gave him a surge of energy; he knew that he had reached the coastal plane and would soon be in the town.

But it was after midnight when he arrived. The town was completely deserted and all the shops tightly closed. He was exhausted and desperate to find some place to lie down and shelter; along the coast it frequently rained in the early morning hours. He wandered down the main road through the center of the town and then followed a road towards the beach a few hundred yards away. Through the scattered coconut palms he could see a dim light; there must be a building at the end of the road. As he neared, the outline of a large shed-like building appeared. It was a large warehouse, and a pier that extended into the sea. A lantern hanging on a post gave out dim light near the doors to the building. If there was a light there, then there must be a watchman.

"Hoi! Hoi!" he called out as he approached. He did not want to venture too close; many an innocent party had met an untimely end by suddenly waking a sleeping night watchman. But there was no answer.

"Hoi! Hoi!" he shouted again, and waited for a reply. None came, and he called out again, and still there was no reply. The man was evidently away, a very sound sleeper—drunk—or dead!

He walked along the side of the warehouse out onto the wharf. There was another lantern at the rear of the building near to the half open door of a lean-to shed. He called out again and got no reply. He went to the door and poked his head inside.

"Hay man," he called out. "You in dere?" Inside the room a lamp was dimly burning on a small, low table, but he could not see anything in the room. In a moment or so he made out the shape of a man sleeping on a low cot in a corner. He pushed his way through the doorway. The man was breathing deeply sound asleep. He entered the room; he just wanted to lie down. He looked for a comfortable place, and using his bundled clothes as a pillow, lay down on the floor and closed his eyes.

Towards early morning it started to rain heavily and Daniel awoke. The rain did not last long, but he did not go back to sleep, he lay, eyes closed, listening to the restful sounds of the waves lapping against the wharf and the water dripping off the roof. In a while the man stirred and sat up with a groan. The lamp now hardly gave out any light—the shade was smoked and it seemed to be out of oil. The man attempted to revive it by raising the wick, but it responded for only a few moments and then went out. He mumbled a curse and replaced it on the table. He picked up a stick lying beside the cot and without noticing the extra body lying on the floor, stumbled from the room.

Daniel remained quiet for the next ten or fifteen minutes before getting up to look outside. There was no one in sight; the day was just beginning, and in the half-light he felt cold, even though there was no wind. He went to the end of the pier and washed his face. By the time he returned he could just make out the shape of a man coming towards the wharf. He waited until the man was nearer.

"Mawnin' Watchie," he called out as the man approached still some distance away. The man stopped in his tracks; slowly approached, peering at the stranger. They both stood silently looking at one another for a moment or two, and then Daniel recognized the man—it was the Maroon! The man that Sapphire called upon five years ago to put a curse on the Henderson family. They had not met nor seen each other since, nor had the Maroon seen Sapphire, which was a good thing, because she would certainly have demanded the return of her money. The obiah had not worked—William and his mother were both thriving, they were as well as ever without the hint of a curse.

Daniel was surprised to see the man, especially working as a night watchman—he would have considered him unsuitable for that position, having such a bad reputation. But soon he found out that Burke, the overseer working for William Henderson, had hired him, and that the warehouse and warf belonged to William Henderson. That was not good news; Daniel did not want to meet William or Burke, or any of Burke's men; they would not have forgotten about him, even though it was several years since the incident with Burke.

The Maroon was equally surprised to see Daniel, and while they brewed tea and cooked breakfast they exchanged their news. Daniel told him of his troubles with Burke, explaining that he did not want Burke to find him there. The watchman agreed to help him if need be; even though he was employed by Burke, the Maroon disliked both his employer and the foremen men that worked for him. He would not do anything to help them against a friend. When they had eaten they sat at the end of the pier. Watchie made a cigarette with the tobacco taken from his pouch, and after a while he produced a fishing line, bated the hook and threw it into the water.

"Time te ketch fish," he said, and then added, " every day a man can fish, not every day 'im will ketch fish!"

Daniel did not know the man well—they had only met a few times before, but he was getting to know him better. The Maroon had a primitive sense of justice and fairness, even though he would not have hesitated to take advantage of anyone, including friends, should the opportunity arise. The man had not changed his ways; he was still a mysterious, puzzling character, and still intimidating.

The fish were not biting that morning, and the bait was replaced several times without success. After a while the man stood up, stretched and looked out to sea.

"De fisherman comin' in," he observed, looking out over the wide expanse of sea. "We can buy fish."

By any standards it was a magnificent day; the wind was freshening, blowing inland from off a sparkling blue and purple sea. White caps were forming from as far out as anyone could see only to crumble gently when they reached the shore. The incredible beauty and tranquility of nature's designs are often wasted—lost and ignored when there is so much glory to experience, and seldom is it paid due honor.

Daniel stood and looked but he did not see any signs of boats or sails. Several minutes later there were still no signs and he sat down again. About ten minutes later he looked out to sea again and sure enough there were two sails on the horizon. He stood again and watched the sail rigged canoes bearing towards the shore with a steady breeze. People were gathering on the beach beside the wharf, but none joined them on the wharf or at the end of the pier. First two women came with shallow pans, and then three children, and soon there was a crowd gathered near to the pier and on the fisherman's beach beside the wharf. Everyone was waiting for the fishermen and their catch, urging on their particular favorite, and chatting excitedly in anticipation of their arrival.

The boats were tacking parallel to the coastline, first in one direction, and then in the other, bows rising high in the sea, one boat leading by what seemed to be only a few yards. They bobbed up and down as they overtook waves and the spray went high over the bows. As they neared the crowd became more interested and excited in the contest, and some shouted their encouragement. The boats were still some distance from the shore and within a few minutes would pass in front of the pier. Abruptly the trailing boat made a sharp tack and headed directly towards the beach, taking the leader by surprise and gaining the lead. The other boat made the same tack, and then both boats were racing towards the land catching all the wind possible, still overtaking the waves and driving up the spray. The race was on to the finish and excitement filled the spectators. Most seemed to know the names of the fishermen, and bets were being made on who would be first.

" Joshua de bess' man," said one, and several others agreed.

"Him loose two time las' week," said another

"Joshua! Joshua! Joshua!" the children chanted.

The two boats, viewed from the end of the pier appeared to be neck and neck, still racing with the wind. The boats would beach in the shallow sheltered area beside the wharf, but the first one in gained the esteem of the crowd and the privileged position nearest the wharf. It was clear now that one boat was indeed ahead of its competitor. They crossed paths and as they did so the leader faltered, the wind taken from his sails. Now barely two hundred yards from shore, the second boat overtook the temporally slower leader, crossing its path again, and sideswiping it as it sped onwards. The collision did not damage either craft, but it confirmed the outcome of the race. The shout from the crews were carried in by the wind and echoed by the crowd. Within a minute the leader beached his boat in the coveted place beside the wharf.

"Jushua win! Joshua win!" the children shouted.

There were three men in the boat; Jushua, at the helm, a big man, well built, bearded, in the prime of life. His mate, a smaller man that in looks could have been a brother. The third man, riding in the bow, wore little clothes—a flower-bag shirt with holes cut for head and arms, extending no further than his hips. As the boat entered the shallows he jumped out of the bow to steady the boat and guide it to a gentle birth. He made no effort to preserve his modesty—in fact some pride was evident at his naturally endowed physical features, and he appeared quite eager to display them! As the boat beached he stood in the water less than thigh deep with the waves gently lapping between his legs, in full view of all and sundry. The crowd had been there before, and they paid little attention. They gathered around to inspect the catch and make their purchases.

The looser drew in on the outside. Angrily he shouted at Jushua, "Y'u cut me man. Y'u cut me bad."

Joshua ignored the accusation sheepishly, knowing full well that it was a justifiable and truthful complaint.

"Y'u damn fool man! Y'u cut me—y'u want fe bruck up de boat dem?"

And again Joshua ignored the accusation, sorting and unloading the catch onto the wharf.

The bottom of each boat was thick with fish of varying sizes and species. There were three large Bonitos, which Joshua lifted high to show the crowd as he placed them on the wharf. The buying and selling started immediately and went on at a quick pace. The looser and his crew displayed their catch on the beach, but as he moved back and forth, he deliberately bumped into Joshua as they passed.

"Hay, man, y'u cut me." There was anger in his tone and he seemed unwilling to let the matter rest. "Y'u play damn fool wid we life, man." Joshua continued to ignore the man, although the anger and rivalry could have easily caused a fight. The man turned to the crowd still complaining, and then was distracted by a woman trying to make a purchase, and he soon found compensation in the bounty of his catch.

The bowman of the second boat was similarly attired to the bowman in Joshua's crew, and also showed little concern for his nakedness, but in a few minutes both men withdrew to the higher beach, and clothed themselves in the privacy of some sheltering coconut trees.

Two more boats arrived, and then another, all with good and interesting catches. No one produced any fish as large as Joshua's Bonito, and some wanted to know how they had been caught.

"We see dem run, man," Joshua explained. "Dem come after de Mullet. So rite den, man, ah say, 'mek up de sail,' an ah trow out de troll line. As soon as we mek speed—Wham! 'im strike! An ah tek 'im in. Lickle later ah tek in anodder."

The various hauls were placed on coconut leaf mats spread on the beach in rows. The crews had first pick of anything they caught which they could either sell or keep for their own use. It might have seemed that the entire town at some time visited the fish market that morning. Some taking fish without paying, in exchange for some favor or service granted in the past or to be granted in the future. Joshua did not sell the largest Bonito; he cut it in half and gave one piece to a little boy who appeared from out of the crowd. By the early afternoon, all the fish were sold, the boats hauled up on the beach, the sails and coconut mats tucked beneath, and everything put away.

Daniel joined the crowd on the beach and bought two fish that he took to the end of the pier. Both were well sized, with large silvery scales that flicked up in every direction as they were scraped off. Some landed on his arms and quickly dried in the hot sun, curling and embedding themselves into his skin. Watchie placed the fish in his pan and covered them over, ready to cook later.

In the afternoon they cooked the fish with several large green bananas. The fish were salted and fried in coconut oil with peppers, crisp and brown. Watchie ate the two fish heads picking off bits of flesh with his fingers, and sucking off every little bony piece. With relish he gouged out the eyes, little glazed white balls that he chewed and sucked and then swallowed, assuring Daniel that fish heads were the best parts of any fish. And to eat the brains made a man 'slick' and wise!

It was a good meal, the most satisfying that Daniel had had in the last few days, and with a full stomach, it made him sleepy. With nothing better to do, he collected some empty sacks from the warehouse, shook out the insects, lay down and went to asleep. Watchie flopped into his cot and he too was quickly fast asleep.

In the late afternoon Daniel awoke, feeling much the worse for having slept. He sat up unsteadily waiting for the drowsiness to leave him. Behind the warehouse at the end of the pier he stripped off his clothes and swam a few feet beyond. As soon as he was in the water his head cleared, but he did not stay in the water more than a few minutes. He rinsed off with fresh water taken from a steel drum at the edge of the warehouse roof set there to catch rainwater. He dressed, and returned to the room.

Watchie was awake and he seemed to be full of energy, his eyes were piercing and bright; they had regained their hypnotic quality. He moved excitedly as he prepared himself for some evening activity. It aroused Daniel's curiosity, but he did not question him. He sat on a box in the room as the man groomed himself—he must have a woman somewhere, Daniel thought, and will likely be out most of the night.

"A'h have likle bisnis in town te nite," he said at last.

"Uh huh." Daniel grunted. And then, "Doan't y'u watch de warehouse nite time?" he asked.

"Me no have te watch," the man answered.

"How y'u mean, y'u doan't have to watch?"

"No s'mady come up here—dem is too, too 'fraid."

Daniel took in his meaning—people were afraid of him—perhaps his mystical powers would do them harm, even when he was not there.

"Obiah fraid dem," the Maroon confirmed. And after a while, "Y'u tek de bed te nite. Ah 'ave te see a man in town." He sat on the cot and without bending down to look, he probed under the bed with his stick. He retrieved a battered old biscuit tin and searched through the contents, took out several items that he wrapped in a small piece of cloth and tucked them into his pocket.

"Y'u tek de bed te nite," he said again as he went out the door and off towards the town. Daniel was not inclined to sleep on the cot—he just might not be sleeping alone, and he did not wish to become a host to parasites.

Once alone Daniel left the darkness of the room and walked out onto the pier. It would soon be time to eat something and prepare for the night. He would not have to cook but did not want to eat after dark. He was making plans—he hoped to get his bankbook from the post office, but he would have to wait until it got there, and that might take more than a week. When he got it, he decided, he would withdraw some money and return to Chivers Estate, to see Opal and his grand daughter. And he was anxiously looking forward to that.

He closed the door to the room and ate outside. Not having anything in particular to do he wandered down towards the road, and was undecided in which direction to go. He should get to know his way about the town; at least find the Post Office where he hoped his bankbook would arrive in a few days. And then he would be off and on his way back to Chivers. He found the post office in a government building just off the main road that also served as the police station and the jail. The building was locked shut with no one around. A house at the back of the building appeared to be inhabited, and he knocked on the half open door.

A voice called out, "Yeah? De Carpie not 'ere. W'at y'u want?"

He waited without answering. In a moment a woman appeared at the door.

"Yes, sur?" She looked him over curiously, disapprovingly, wiping her hands in a soiled apron tied about her middle, and then she stepped out of the entrance and sat on the doorstep. It seemed that she was just resting from whatever she had been doing inside the house, and was glad for the chance to stop.

"De Crpie garn 'bout him business, and 'im not come back te day," she told him.

"It de postmaster me's lookin' for," Daniel explained.

"He garn up town little bit, but de office is close up."

"T'ank y'u mam," Daniel answered. "A'h will come back again."

She remained seated on the steps watching him as he wandered off towards the center of the town and out of sight.

At the corner shop there was a small group milling about, passing the time and generally socializing. Two men were playing checkers, moving the pieces briskly, with the spectators cheering every capture. Four more were playing dominoes, slamming the pieces down hard on a thin board at every move. Others were watching these activities, making bets, occasionally offering advice to the players and cheering on the victors. Daniel joined them, and watched for a while, and was soon engrossed in a heated debate over the right moves to be made during the play. Activities ended when the shopkeeper closed his doors at ten o'clock, and Daniel returned to the room on the wharf.

In the morning Watchie had not returned, and there was no sign of him the next day either. Again he found himself without much to do other, than to see to his own personal needs. He fished off the end of the pier for several hours, catching several small fish.

Between the coast road and the sea, the sandy beach varied in its depth, and was perhaps a hundred yards at the widest point. It curved along the bay extending about a mile in both directions from the warehouse. There were many mature coconut trees, the occasional sea grape and mangrove that provided a good degree of shade and privacy when needed. Later in the afternoon he wandered along the beach exploring it to the end, a protrusion of sharp black volcanic rocks. As it got dark he returned to the room and went to bed.

The next two days were spent in the same way—fishing, cooking, and exploring the area, and just anxiously waiting for the post office to open and his bankbook to arrive.

Jamaican Lore—Bud doant need no pocket watch to know when time 'e pickney mus' nyam.

CHAPTER 45

On the Friday morning Daniel went to the Post Office to inquire about the transfer of his bankbook and the money deposited. The post office clerk was reading a ragged strip of newspaper, and it was nearly five minutes before he condescended to give him any attention. At last he folded the paper and approached the window.

"Yes mon?" he asked curtly.

Daniel asked if his bankbook had been transferred from Kingston. The man did not answer, but turned around and shuffled through some loose papers on his table. He picked them up one at a time, and read each one. Fully ten minutes later he returned to the window.

"An' who is y'u?" he asked.

Daniel produced the letter of recommendation that Pursey had given him, and offered it as identification. The clerk picked it up as though it might soil his fingers and examined it with an expression of weary skepticism.

"So who y'u say write dis letter?" he inquired when he had read it over at least twice.

Daniel explained again. The man read the letter again slowly, rubbed a sweaty thumb finger over the signature smudging it before handing it back, so much the worse for the examination.

"An who is dis Mister Pursey?"

Patiently Daniel went through the explanation again.

"An 'ow much money y'u say he holding fe y'u?"

That was none of his business, thought Daniel, but he did not want to antagonize the man—he preferred to have co-operation if at all possible, even though that seemed very unlikely.

"Me doant rightly know how much it is. Mr. Pursey 'ave de bankbook an 'im is de man dat mek me deposit each time. It 'bout thirty-six pound an' twelve shillings."

For almost a minute the clerk looked him over in obvious disbelief, and then at last, "Y'u doant look to me like y'u is a man dat ever see thirty-six pound an' twelve shillin'!"

That was an observation that had not occurred to Daniel. True enough his clothes were on the verge of becoming rags, and he certainly did not appear to be a man that well off. For a moment or two he looked at himself trying to imagine how others would see him. The man was not far off the mark, but it would take too long to explain the circumstances of his appearance, and in any case it was none of the man's business.

"True, Sur," he said with a wan smile, not wanting to irritate. "Den no book is transfer?" he asked again.

"No book is transfer." The man left him standing at the window.

"Ah will come back den," he called as the man went back to his newspaper.

The weekend passed without event, but when Monday morning came, Daniel was up early. He had less than a shilling in his pocket and if the money did not arrive in a day or two he would be unable to buy food. He could survive for a while by picking up fallen coconuts and catching fish, which was easy enough, but that could not go on too long. He would be a wealthy man if the transfer were completed. He waited at the post office for the window to open and the clerk to appear. The news was disappointing—the clerk informed him there had been no transfers from Kingston. The next day he made his inquiry in the late afternoon rather than in the morning. The news was the same, and he was beginning to loose patience—the change in his pockets had dwindled further. He left the post office deep in thought with little attention paid to his surroundings, and he did not see the woman standing in the doorway at the rear of the buiding. As he passed she called after him.

"Hey! Babboo!" It was the woman he had spoken to several days before.

'Babboo' was not exactly a complimentary term—usually used in a derogatory sense to address Hindus of lower status. For the moment he was angered, but resolved not to take offence.

"Y'u ave sometin' waitin' fe y'u?" she called out to him in a somewhat teasing and provocative manner, as though she knew something, but wasn't about to say. She must have seen him go to the post office a number of times, and was probably curious to know why. He just nodded as he went on his way.

"It is dere," she called after him in a low voice, looking in the direction of the post office and as though she did not wish to be overheard. "It come dis marnin'."

He stopped in his tracks. "It come dis marnin'?"

"It come dis marnin'," she confirmed, as he came closer. She placed her forefinger over her lips to indicate the confidential nature of their conversation, and glanced in the direction of the post office once again.

"How y'u kno' dat?" Daniel questioned.

"Me was dere w'en it come, an' me hear 'im talk to de driverman 'bout it. He did say dat it was big money fe y'u. Y'u 'ave big money?"

"Den why he doant give it te me?" Daniel asked, ignoring her question.

She shrugged, "Me doant kno'. He put it in'a 'im lockup box."

"Den why he doant give it te me?" Daniel questioned again, speaking more to him self than to the woman. "He is a tief? He goine tief me money?"

"Me doant kno'," she answered in almost a whisper. "Y'u come back tomorro'—axe 'im one more time—see w'at 'im sey."

"T'ank y'u missus. Dat is w'at ah will do. T'ank y'u." He took the woman's hand held it for a few moments, but as he let go her hand she held on to his tightly.

"Tank y'u again mam," he said, once again shaking her hand and releasing hers, and again she did not let go of his. He recognized her intentions—possibly her desires—but he was preoccupied and concerned about his deposit. He did not want to reject her or offend her—after all, she might have helped him, and through her he knew his bank book had arrived.

"A'h mus' go dis time, mam," he said softly. "I'se so sorry mam. Ah mus' go, but ah will come again to see y'u."

She did not answer as she slowly released his hand. She looked sad and lonely he thought, and then he was really sorry that he did not stay. He made his way back to the warehouse. Why would the man be holding his deposit, he wondered? What could the man possibly gain by doing that? And why would the woman want him to sleep with her?—Was she after his money? Was she in league with the post office clerk? Did they intend to rob him? He would have to be careful, he told himself. But stealing the money would be very difficult—impossible if not withdraw from the account. Thinking it over he decided that all he really needed was the bankbook—the money was safe if left where it was, in the bank.

It was late afternoon when the Watchie reappeared. Daniel had just climbed out of the water at the end of the pier, and was drying himself. As soon as he was dressed they started to fix their supper. The Maroon had brought back food with him and they sat down to eat. Watchie did not have much of interest to say, but Daniel listened politely to his chatter, and later told him about the postal clerk and the deposit held.

"'Im is a tief," Watchie said. "Me kno' tief when ah look in dem yeye! An' a'h can tell y'u dat man is tief!"

This did not make Daniel feel better—it was not what he wanted to hear, but it reinforced his feeling that the clerk had designs on his money. "How ah goine get me money?" Daniel wondered aloud, and then silently they pondered the situation.

"Ah goine axe 'im again tomorro'," Daniel decided. "Ah goine give 'im a chance—. One more time."

"Me 'ave little money, Watchie said, after a while. "We'se good fe now. Y'u doant need fret 'bout money fe now."

Daniel gave him a questioning look—he had money?

"Pay time is dis week," Watchie said. "It's me pay time come Saturday."

That at least was good news and something to be hopeful about. But just the same, Daniel thought, he would have to find some way to get his bankbook.

The following day, in the morning the two men went to the post office. Watchie remained behind as Daniel approached the window and called to the clerk. After a few minutes the man appeared, and before Daniel could again ask, the man was shaking his head denying the arrival of his bankbook. Daniel had been getting angrier by the second and reason seemed to be deserting him. The man's attitude was superior, condescending and provocative, and by the time he reached the window, Daniel was filled with blind rage, determined to have the man produce the book. With both hands he grabbed the man's shirt and jerked him almost through the window so that he was sprawled across the small window counter.

"Y'u gi'e me me book!" he demanded, shouting in the man's face. "Ah knows dat it is 'ere. Ah knows dat it come in!"

He held the man tightly in his grip glaring into the terrified man's face, shaking him violently. The suddenness of the attack had unnerved the man completely, he was unable to speak, and he made no effort to resist or break free. Watchie was now standing beside Daniel, and the sudden violence of Daniel's attack had surprised him too. He was jubilant. He danced up and down shouting all the while, "lick 'im Dan! Lick 'im!"

"Y'u get me book now?" Daniel told the man, shaking him with every word, but the man was helpless and made no sign that he was about to comply. Daniel tightened his grip and yanked him further through the window, as though he would soon have him through the window and on the ground at his mercy.

Watchie was dancing all the more, "lick 'im Dan! Ah tell y'u, lick 'im!"

"A'right. A'right," the man finally said. "Ah go—look—see if it come."

"If y'u doant do dat I'se comin' to get y'u," Daniel threatened before letting the man loose with a final jerk.

"It might be come now," the clerk said weakly as he straightened himself out. He opened a draw and took out a small metal deposit box. He placed it on the table and with a key from a bundle on his belt he opened the lock. There were several government envelopes in the box that he quickly sorted, and selecting one he approached the window.

His hands were visibly shaking as he handed over the envelope. Daniel snatched it without a word, turned his back to examine the envelope and its contents. It was his bank passbook with a record of the deposits and an account of the balance. He put it in his pocket and without a word to the clerk, beckoned to Watchie who followed him back to the warehouse.

Daniel was still angry and fuming when they arrived. He sat at the end of the pier by himself for over an hour until he calmed down. Again he had surprised himself at his behavior—suddenly loosing his temper and the rough treatment delivered to the clerk, even though the man deserved it. It reminded him of the incident with Burke. The clerk might talk to his friends so he should be careful. He did not have his money in hand and that was just as well—it would be too risky to keep it in his pocket, and it was quite safe where it was for the time being. He decided not to return to the post office again, not even to withdraw some much-needed money. It could put him at risk if the man had friends and wanted to rob him. In the meantime he could borrow money from Watchie for food and for his bus fare back to Chivers Estate.

Watchie was in high spirits—Daniel had retrieved his bankbook, and payday was only two days away. Everything was fine, and he was going to celebrate! Daniel, on the other hand was only relieved, and was thinking only about returning to Chivers. Also, he was uneasy. What if the clerk had friends in the town? He might seek revenge for his rough treatment, so Daniel decided to stay quietly at the warehouse until he left the town in the next few days—he did not want another confrontation, and he declined Watchie's invitation to join him for a night on the town. That decision did not dampen Watchie's spirits, or his decision to go by himself and celebrate the coming of his payday.

Having eaten, Watchie took off and was soon out of sight. Later on Daniel wandered off the wharf a short distance along the beach. He sat on a fallen log resting against a coconut tree. The town was quiet, and he could see several fishermen on the beach getting ready for a night of fishing. An hour or so later several boats were ready, and the men were gathered in a group, waiting to shove off. If the wind did not pick up they would have to row the boats out several miles and await the offshore winds to take them to the fishing grounds.

It was not quite dark when Daniel saw a figure running towards the wharf carrying a small bundle under his arms. Every few seconds the man would slow his run to a fast walk seemingly to catch his breath, and then he would start to run again. As the man got nearer he was surprised to see that it was Watchie and he went to meet him at the warehouse. He was breathless and could hardly speak.

"W'at happenin'?" Daniel asked. The watchman was too breathless to explain and he hurried out to the end of the pier. The sack appeared to move about as he held it tightly and placed it on the ground. Carefully he opened it sticking his hand deep inside, as the sack fluttered about. Then he withdrew a large white gamecock that squawked in protest as he held it up by its legs.

"Me fine 'im pon de road." Watchie explained, holding the bird with both hands. "Quick. Pass me knife."

"Where y'u sey y'u fine it?" Daniel asked. He could hardly have just found it on the road, and he made no move to get the knife.

Watchie was not about to argue the point. Changing his grip he held the protesting rooster tightly by the wings and reached for his fishing knife resting at the edge of the pier. He placed the struggling bird on the ground and put a foot on its back to keep it there. With one hand he grabbed its head, and with the knife in his other hand he severed the head completley in one clean cut. The blood squirted wildly about in all directions as the bird vainly struggled, wings beating wildly. He held the head for a few moments examining it carefully before putting it to one side, and then he removed his foot letting the headless bird run loose. It still had life in its body and struggled to stand, the wound on the neck spurting blood in a wide circle. He was splattered with blood as the headless rooster ran about in its dying moments. Watchie was laughing, gleeful at the spectacle—excited—until the bleeding subsided and the bird lay twitching on the pier. He pushed it several times with his foot urging it to run once again, and then obviously disappointed, stood quietly a few moments watching its final death throws.

"'Im dead now," he said a trace of disappointment in his voice.

Everything happened so quickly Daniel did not have time to react. He was sure the rooster had been stolen, and if so he thought, it was not a good idea to have killed it. What if the owner appeared to claim his property?

"Wher' y'u get de rooster?" he questioned again.

"Me fine 'im 'pon de road. 'Im was runnin' 'pon de road, and me catch 'im."

Daniel did not believe it for a second—the man had obviously stolen the rooster, but if he was going to deny it, there would be no point to argue and accuse him of lying as well. He was disgusted—the evident pleasure the man derived from killing the rooster. He moved away, deciding to leave him to his own devices and to take no further part in it. Somehow he felt betrayed—for the short time they had lived together they seemed to have had something in common. Now he thought the Maroon was just a common thief, and he feared that their close connection would implicate him in the crime.

Watchie picked up the head and examined it carefully. "It a good head," he said looking over to Daniel. "It a sweet piece!"

He placed the head to one side and immediately started to pluck the feathers from the dead bird, throwing the loose feathers into the sea. Having done that he cut it open and removed the entrails, saving some parts in a cooking pot. Then he cut off the legs and wings, and carved the rest into smaller pieces, all of which he placed in his cooking pot. All the while, as he went about this business, he was humming and muttering to himself.

Daniel avoided the man for the rest of the night and went to sleep without speaking to him again. In the morning he decided to let the matter pass—it was not his affair if the Maroon stole chickens, but he did not want to get involved. All he wanted to do now was to wait for Saturday when Watchie was paid, borrow enough money for his bus fare to Port Antonio and get out of town.

They ate their breakfast together as usual, and Daniel went to fish off the pier for a while. Watchie impaled the cocks's head on a stick sharpened to a point, and he placed his trophy at the entrance to the warehouse, where he stood admiring it for a long while. Several hours later Daniel saw some people on the road coming towards the warehouse. They were walking hurriedly and he could hear their voices as they approached. A woman was waving her arms about in an agitated state. Watchie was in the room and was unaware of their presence until he heard their voices and he poked his head through the open doorway. They were almost on the wharf when they stopped to look at the rooster's head. The woman was shouting and could be clearly heard above the others. She was very angry and agitated.

Watchie ducked back into his room. In a split second he reappeared with his cooking pot in which he had placed the carved up rooster. Without hesitation, he dumped the contents over the side of the pier, where they sank in swirl of ravenous little fish. Almost immediately a long dark shadow darted out from

under the pier through the swarms of tiny fish and disappeared into the depths—
the Barracuda was on the hunt! There were still many feathers easily visible stuck
to the planks of the pier, but the blood that had splattered about was not obvious
on the black tar soaked planks. The splattered blood was more easily seen on
Watchie's clothes if one cared to look closely. The group approached and
Watchie went to meet them.

"Dat is 'im!" the woman shouted, pointing. "Dat is de man!"

"W'at happinin'?" Watchie asked.

One of the men was the local policeman; they had met before. The other man
was his special constable who usually accompanied him as reinforcement on
difficult missions.

"Dis lady sey y'u tek 'er rooster las' nite?" The policeman questioned.

"She loose she rooster?" Watchie asked innocently.

"No sur!" shouted the woman. "Ah see y'u w'en y'u come in and tek it! Y'us
a tief! Y'u ti-ef me fowl las' nite—me see y'u," and she stamped her foot to
emphasize her words.

"Well, w'at y'u 'ave to say?" asked the policeman.

"Maybe she loose she fowl. If she fowl get loose, den she jus' loose de fowl,"
Watchie countered.

"Me doant loose me fowl. Me see y'u come in'a me yard an' tek it." She
stamped her foot again, pointing and jabbing her finger at Watchie.

"Well if ah fine a fowl 'pon de road, me nar' goin' leave it deh. Me no mus'
tek it up?" Watchie reasoned. "Dat is not tief."

The policeman went over to Daniel standing some distance away, and
questioned him.

"Wat y'u name, sur?" he asked.

Daniel complied.

"Y'u live 'ere wid dis man?"

"Jus' til Sunday, officer."

"Y'u was 'ere las' nite?"

"Yes sur. All nite."

"Was dat man wid y'u?"

"Me t'ink 'e was 'ere sur," Daniel lied. "Me neber see 'im leave. Yes sur, me
t'ink 'e was'ere all de nite."

"W'at y'u sey y'u name?"

Daniel repeated his answer. "Me tek down y'u name now," the policeman
said, "fe witness." He produced a short stump of a pencil and a small notebook.
Holding the notebook close to his face, he licked the end of the pencil several

times, slowly spelling the words as he laboriously wrote, "D-a-n-i-e-l H-u-t-c-h-i-n-g-s."

There were more questions and more denials. The policeman was not satisfied. He searched the room, collected a small handful of feathers, and returned to question Daniel. He cautioned him, that as a witness he must not leave town. The woman identified the rooster's head as being that of her stolen bird, and kept up a barrage of curses and loud accusations. The special constable removed the 'trophy' and wrapped it in a piece of newspaper.

During this time, a small crowd had gathered on the road, and they were watching developments with interest. Watchie was protesting loudly, and the people on the beach drew closer. From a short distance away, Daniel saw the special constable take hold of his arms and the policeman place handcuffs on his wrists. He took hold of Watchie's other arm and together they led him towards the road and on to the police station. As Watchie passed the crowd he mumbled curses under his breath and glared defiantly at them.

"'Im is obiah man," one man said.

"Dey mus' put 'im in prison!" said another.

"Dey fine obiah on de wharf. De policeman tek it down."

"'Im mek obiah!"

"De policeman, dem search 'im room."

"W'at dem look for?"

"Mus' be ganga!"

"De Watchie tek ganga?

"No man, chichi in a' 'im head!"

It was safe to belittle the man—to taunt him while he was handcuffed and on the way to jail, but it would be different had he been free. The watchman was feared by most, and strangely enough that was the very reason Burke had hired him—because he was feared, and most people not wanting to risk harm, would keep away. Some in the crowd followed the prisoner to the police station, while others just drifted away.

Even though he knew Watchie to be guilty, Daniel was reluctant to abandon him, and felt that he should help him if he could. Watchie had given him shelter and a place to sleep when he needed it, and he would do what he could for him. In the late afternoon he went to the police station to see how the prisoner was doing, and if there was something he needed. The station door was closed and he knocked hard several times on the solid pine door before there was a bellow of acknowledgement from within. The policeman peered through a crack in the window before opening the door. He was pulling up his trousers and tucking in his shirt, "Yes?"

"I'se come about me fren'—de nite watchie."

"He in de lockup," said the policeman, turning about and walking back into the station still fixing his clothes.

Daniel followed, "I'se jus' come to see how 'im mek out," He explained. "W"at goin' happen to 'im now?"

"W"en de corporal come, he will mek out de summons."

"De corporal? Where 'im comin' from?"

"'Im station is Port Antonio. But 'im go down to Port Maria Thursday, and 'im is to come tomorrow marnin'."

That was news—the corporal was from Port Antonio? Daniel wondered if he was the same burly corporal that years ago had arrested his daughter. Further questioning confirmed that it was indeed the same man, and he did not like him. Intervening on behalf of his friend would probably not be very successful—the corporal had arrested Watchie several times in the past, and they were sworn enemies. If the corporal had anything to do with it, there was not much hope that his friend would be released any time soon.

Daniel sat down on a wooden bench against the wall as they talked. The policeman was pleasant enough despite his officiousness, and they seemed to get along—at least the man did not regard him as a criminal or seem to think that he was involved in the theft.

"An' den w'at happen w'en he mek de arrest?"

"De J. P is to mek a decision at dat time if he is to stay in jail fe de trial."

"W"en time he to do dat?"

"He come Monday marnin' early." And then he added, "Dat man—dat man is a wicked, wicked man. How such a man is y'u fren'?"

Daniel explained the circumstances under which they had met years ago when he was headman at Manor House Estate, and that recently the night watchman had given him a place to sleep. He did not elaborate on the details, but said he planned to return to see his daughter and his grandchild as soon as possible. As far as the policeman was concerned, he had no objections to Daniel visiting the prisoner and bringing anything he needed—as long as he examined it first. He was allowed to see Watchie and talk for a short while through the closed cell door, then Daniel thanked the policeman and left.

That night sitting at the end of the pier, Daniel was alerted by the headlights of a car that drove down the road towards the warehouse. The vehicle was left running with its lights blazing a pathway towards the wharf. In the light from the car Daniel recognized Burke—he was still some distance away, and Daniel was sure that he had not been seen. Burke mounted the wharf and advanced towards the warehouse as Daniel searched desperately for some place to hide. For a moment or two he contemplated sliding off the end of the pier into the sea. However, he had seen the Barracuda several times, and he immediately cancelled the thought. The room was the only available hiding place, and he slipped in without being seen. For several minutes he waited, and then he heard footsteps on the pier approaching.

"Watchman!" Burke poked his head into the room.

Daniel lay down on the floor and covered himself in a corner of the room. He had not yet lit the lantern and inside the room was dark. He was hoping that Burke would not see him as long as he remained there quietly and did not move. Burke called out again, and Daniel kept silent. Sure enough, as he hoped, Burke left, and was soon away in the car.

The close encounter had Daniel up very early the next morning. He would have to find some other place to stay as long as Burke was going to be about the town. There was a crude bamboo hut some distance along the beach on the other side of the warehouse, and he would have to make use of it for the time being. It was not on the part of the beach used by the fishermen, and there did not seem to be any reason for the hut to be there. Having eaten what food he had, he collected his belongings, and took everything over to the hut. The hut itself was in need of some repairs, and he set about effecting them. He collected fallen branches of coconut trees and reinforced the roof and walls. There was already a place to cook, and he collected enough driftwood from along the beach to keep a good fire blazing. Having done all this by mid-afternoon he collected a small bundle of Watchie's things and went into the town to the jail.

The station door was again locked and no one answered his knocking. He went around to the back of the building where the woman he had met two days before was sitting outside in the yard. She hailed him loudly when she saw him.

"Hay! Babbou!"

"Afternoon, Missus."

"Y'u lookin' good te day," she said. "Y'u mus' be get y'u letter? W'at ah did tell y'u?"

"Y'u is me savor!" Daniel confessed. "Ah mus' tank y'u."

She smiled. "W'at y'u lookin' now? Sumptin' more y'u lookin'?"

He ignored the proposition, "Wher' de policeman deh? 'Im is 'ere?"

"De Carpie come in dis marnin' an dem garn to Buff Bay. Dey nar come back teday."

Daniel took in the news—the burley corporal from Port Antonio—Watchie's sworn enemy had arrived—there would be little chance of an early release. But there was more news to follow.

"De busha-man, Mr. Burke was here dis marnin' lookin' fe 'im night watchie," the woman continued, "but dem was garne by dat time, an he nebber catch dem up."

"Busha Burke was 'ere?" questioned Daniel. "W'at 'im lookin' for?"

"'Im look in te see de watchie in de lockup—he did 'ave sumtin' fe 'im, but me no kno' w'at, an' me nebber did see."

So Burke and the corporal were both in town. Burke could help Watchie get out of jail—the corporal would want to keep him there. They would have to work that out between them.

"Well," he continued, "ah bring t'ings fe de watchie." He showed her the bundle he had collected. "Y'u, give 'im 'is t'ings fe me?"

She took the bundle, but their conversation was interrupted by the sound of a car coming along the coast road. They both watched silently as it slowed, and a few seconds later it turned off the road and was on its way towards them and to the station. Daniel did not hesitate; he hastily bid the woman good night and left, taking a path behind the building away from the station towards the road to the warehouse. The car stopped in front of the station; he did not see the driver although he turned and looked several times. It was probably Burke, he thought, looking for the corporal, but whoever it was, he would keep out of sight.

The next day he did not venture far from the hut. He kept a keen watch towards the road leading to the warehouse. No one appeared, but still he kept away from the warehouse and pier. He was sure that Burke would be visiting the warehouse soon again, and he did not want a chance meeting. He would have liked to fish from the pier, but he simply could not risk Burke finding him there. He had only two pennies left in his pocket—not enough to buy anything solid that would sustain him for any length of time; he was saving them in case of desperate need. There was nothing left, having the day before drained the last tin of Pursey's condensed milk. He went to bed very hungry, and spent a restless night.

He was up early while it was just getting light. He scoured the beaches to pick up fallen coconuts and small beach almonds that were scattered about. The almonds were small and sweet, but he could not eat too many; on an empty stomach they would make him sick. There were no good coconuts to be found. In searching around for the nuts he came upon a huge crab, the largest blue crab he had ever seen. It was hiding under rotting leaves when he disturbed it, and it scurried away with its huge claws raised in defense. He quickly found a stick to push it into his sack, but it defended itself with amazing skill, raising its claws and warding off his best efforts. For fully ten minutes he chased the crab, finally getting it into the sack. When he returned to his shelter he filled his pot with seawater and set it to boil. In an hour the crab was cooked and eaten, but it was hardly enough to stave off his hunger.

That night the mosquitoes were everywhere, and several hours later he was still hungry and awake. Even though it was very late, he got up, revived the fire, and went off the beach towards the coast road. The banks along the side of the road were covered in weeds. Among the weeds growing there he had noticed 'Devil's Horsewhip,' a weed much despised because of its long, sharp barbed burrs. However, it had one good use, and that was to use in a smudge. When thrown into the fire it produced a pungent smoke that was a very good mosquito repellant. In the darkness he searched the bank, and was able to reap handfuls, easily found in the darkness because of its strong smell. After collecting a large bundle he returned to the hut, stirred the fire again, and threw small handfuls into the blaze. Soon there was a thick smoke billowing up that he wafted into the hut and about the area. Then he lay down to sleep, free from the ravenous hordes, but still very hungry.

It was now the middle of the week, and although he had not seen Burke again, he was sure that Burke had been there and visited the jail. He got up feeling very weak—he had eaten the crab and only a few almonds the day before; hunger would force him to go into the town to get food. He felt for the coins in his pocket that he knew should be there. To his dismay he could not find them. Again he searched his clothes and where he rested during the night, but they were not to be found. Finally he concluded that they must have dropped from his pocket while chasing the crab—or when he picked the weeds during the night. A feeling of desperation made him break out in a heavy sweat; he had to get some food from somewhere. For several hours he sat or lay, resting in the shade of the hut thinking of where and how he could get food. There was no choice in the matter; he would have to go to the post office and withdraw money.

It was early in the afternoon when he wearily got up and went towards the town. Again he was passing the house at the back of the police station when the woman appeared and called to him.

"Wher' y'u goin' dis time?"

"To de post office, missus."

"Te day is Wednesday. It close up noontime." She looked at him curiously. "Y'u doant know dat government office close at noontime on Wednesday?"

"Oh Lawd!" He was really quite desperate. "Ah forget!"

He sat down on the lower step leading to the house and rested his head in his hands. The woman descended the steps and sat beside him, but did not speak for several minutes. At last she asked, "w'at do y'u man?"

He lifted his head from his hands to face her, "ah lookin' sumptin' te eat, mam." There was a pause before he continued, "ah doant eat fe two days now, mam."

"Why y'u doant eat?"

"Ah doant have food, an' me loose me money. Ah was lookin' to tek some money from de post office."

The woman appeared interested. "Ah can fix y'u up. Y'u stay dere. Ah soon come back." She got up immediately, resting her hand on his shoulder as she rose. "Rest y'u self little bit."

She soon returned with a small bowl filled with boiled cornmeal, some ackeys and saltfish. She handed it to him with a small spoon. He gratefully accepted, and while he ate she watched. When finished she took the bowl and went back into the house, and immediately returned with a large mug of sweetened tea.

"Y'u better now?" she asked as he drank.

"Yes mam. Ah tink I will live a lik'le longer!"

"Y'u stay wid me te nite? She asked.

CHAPTER 46

Burke appeared at the police station early the next morning. He quickly realized that the corporal had nothing in common with the Maroon, and that it would take more than simple persuasion to get the watchman freed. His appeals had no effect; the corporal was unyielding; the prisoner would have to go before a Justice of the Peace, and the hearing was scheduled for the following day.

The morning of the hearing Burke again arrived early at the police station, and was met by the half-clothed policeman, Johnstone. He seated himself on the bench along the wall while the policeman continued to dress himself. The woman that Daniel knew appeared with the policeman's breakfast, which she placed on the table without speaking to anyone. She was in a very unkept state; her hair not combed, her dress hardly on straight, and she left quickly. The officer seated himself at the table and started to devour his meal, dipping the crusts of bread into a mug of tea. Burke watched in disgust as bits of food fell from his mouth to the table and on to his shirt.

A short while later the woman reappeared. "De carpie comin'," she announced, and quickly disappeared again.

The policeman jumped up brushing the crumbs from the table and his shirt. He picked up the utensils and stuffed them on a shelf out of sight. As the corporal's footsteps could be heard, he straightened his clothes to meet the approval of the senior officer, and as the corporal entered the door, he snapped to attention, "Marnin' Corporal."

"Marnin'. Marnin'," said the corporal, touching his cap with a swagger stick. Without hesitation he took the seat at the table just vacated by the junior officer.

"Well, now, Johnstone, how are t'ings here?" he asked as if he did not already know. "W'at is happin in' here?"

"Ah lays a charge of theft against one," the constable began, "an ah lays a charge of the practice of witchcraft against de same one. Sir." He produced some papers that were handed to the corporal.

"Ah tek de names of witness, and ah collect h'evidence of de crime. 'Im is in de lockup now." He went to a shelf and withdrew the cock's head. He placed it on the table before the corporal.

The corporal eyed the 'h'evidence' nervously. "A'rite man! A'rite! Tek it away. Tek it away, man." In disgust he waved it away. "How y'u goine keep it fe de judge to see?"

"I'se goine put it down in salt. Dat will keep it fe de judge, an' de salt will tek up de pisen."

The corporal appeared satisfied. "A'rite, bring out de man, den, an ah will mek out de summons."

The policeman found a bunch of keys in the draw of the table and left to fetch his prisoner. As soon as the man was out of the room, Burke took a ten-shilling note from his pocket and placed it on the table in front of the corporal. He smoothed it out and then turned away, not looking at the man or the bank note lying on the table. When he looked up again the note was gone.

"He's the night watchman working for Mr. Henderson, and we need him to work when the ship comes in. You will give him a break?" Burke asked.

The corporal ignored the question and continued to examine some papers on the table; he did not answer. Then the policeman appeared urging Watchie before him with his hands in handcuffs before him.

The corporal looked the prisoner up and down for several long moments, and then he launched into a tirade. "Y'u is charged with theft of a fowl—to whit—a white rooster. An' y'u is charged with the practice of witchcraft—to whit—casting evil spells."

The corporal and the watchman had met under similar circumstances in the past, and each time the Maroon had escaped the full weight of the law. This time the corporal had 'h'evidence,' and an excellent chance of success. He launched into a recitation of the law, word for word—verbatim—as written in the Act. It lasted several minutes—quite an accomplishment! And when he finished he looked around at Burke and the patient policeman as though expecting applause. The constable nodded approvingly, and Burke did his best to show some appreciation.

The corporal turned to the prisoner again, "Y'u is a wicked, bad man, y'u is. An' y'u is goine to prison dis time. Why una people doan stay in Maroon Town an' keep y'u badness from good people?"

At this point Burke intervened again. "This man is working for me, officer, and I am in need of his services. If there is a fine, I will pay it so that he can be released."

"Dat is fe de J. P. to say, sur," replied the corporal. "An 'im is to be 'ere dis marnin'."

Mr. Coumbs, the Justice of the Peace arrived within an hour, and surprisingly, the corporal agreed to Watchie's release, provided that the fines and the costs of the stolen property were paid. The charge of witchcraft would remain and the trial would take place at a later date. Burke paid the fines and Watchie and Burke left the police station together.

Burke had spent almost two days getting him out of jail; he was angry about the delay and was anxious now to get back to work, but for the next ten minutes or so he berated Watchie for causing the delay. The ship was due to arrive in two days to pick up coffee and pimento, and there was a lot of work still to be done. The lorries would be bringing in the produce over the next two days, and it had to be placed in the warehouse. The ship was on a tight schedule and would be there only for a few hours, so additional workers would be needed. Burke told Watchie to get the additional workers ready to work through the night. Dispensing that information, Burke got in his car and took off at high speed towards Port Maria.

Although he was out of jail the watchman was in an angry mood. He had quietly submitted to a stern lecture from the corporal, his sworn enemy, and Burke had taken money from his earnings to pay the fine and have him released. Following that Burke had continued to lecture him. At the warehouse he complained to Daniel.

"I'se goine fix dem business," he said, and then he repeated himself several times, "I'se goine fix dem business!"

"Never mine dat," Daniel consoled him. "Y'u is out of jail now. Y'u 'ave y'u freedom now man, so w'at do y'u?"

"De carpie tek me piece fe h'evidence, an ah needs me piece," he explained, referring to the cock's head being held as 'h'evidence' in the police station.

There wasn't much Daniel could say to change his mood. Watchie went into his room sulking, and did not reappear for hours. Daniel in the meantime caught several small fish that he scaled and cleaned, ready to fry, and then went to look for the watchman, still in the darkened room.

"Go buy bread fe eat, man," he told him. "I'se hungry, man."

He was answered by a groan, but after some urging Watchie got up and went off to buy the much-needed food. When he returned he was in an improved state of mind.

"Ah knows w'at I'es goin' do," he announced. "I'se goin' fix dem business!"

Daniel was more interested in eating than in discussing the watchman's plans, and he signified his attention with an occasional nod. When they had eaten he was a little more attentive. He hoped to borrow money from his friend for the bus fare to Port Antonio.

"Y'u get y'u pay?" he asked.

"Mr. Burke cut it fe pay de fine," Watchie told him. "Ah can spring y'u a shilling," he said, taking the money out of his pocket and counting it. "Nex' week ah gets paid again, an' y'u get w'at y'u want," he promised, as he handed over the coins.

One shilling was not sufficient even for food so the bus fare would have to wait. If there was more to come by the end of another week, he would have to be patient.

Watchie returned to the subject of the 'h'evidence.' "De carpie keep me piece," he complained again. "Me nebber go widout me piece." And after a long pause, "except one time me put it down an a John Crow tek it up. It jus' drop down an' was garn wid it! Zuip!" He made a swooping motion with his hand to emphasize the flight of the vulture as it flew off with his trophy.

The watchman was obsessed with the loss of his 'piece,' and he talked of nothing else. "I'se goin' fix dem business!" He continued, "ah knows w'at I'es goine do," he said with some satisfaction and a glint in his eye. "I'se goin' fix dem business! Ah knows w'at I'es goine do!"

The next morning a loaded lorry drove in and parked beside the warehouse. The two men that arrived with it cleared out the warehouse and stacked the sacks. By the time they had done that it was after noon, and they left immediately. According to Burke there would be perhaps five or six more loads to come. Two more fully loaded lorries arrived, with the men tired and complaining. They had been up from early that morning and had worked all day without a rest—not even to eat. The lorries had collected produce from five or six small plantations located in the mountains, and there was no one to help them put the hundred-pound sacks onto the lorries. Burke had been about and was urging the men to speed up the work. The ship was expected by noon the next day, and would leave by the early evening, and there were still a number of plantations to visit.

Burke drove in again just after the lorries left, and made a quick inspection of the warehouse; he left immediately. The next day the lorries returned, unloaded produce and had just left when the ship was sighted on the horizon steaming towards the harbor. It would anchor in deep water some distance from the pier. Burke, with his two men, Rasta and Pedro, drove up to the warehouse just as a small boat was leaving the ship. The occupants disembarked at the end of the pier and were met by Burke. The loading operation had to be done by hand as there was no crane on the pier. Small boats from the ship were to be hand-loaded from the wharf, and rowed out to the ship, where a loading crane would take the goods on board.

Even at that time it did not seem possible that the loading could be completed by the time the ship had to leave, and Burke was anxious to get the work started as soon as possible. The ship's crew evidently did not share his sense of urgency, and they were taking their time to sort things out. When the loading started it went slowly; the workers on shore were tired and disgruntled, and there were too few for the job in hand. Burke's men were keeping account, and at the same time driving the men to keep up the pace.

The watchman had completely forgotten about Burke's request, and the extra workers he had been asked to find. He lied without the flicker of an eyelid when he said that no extra workers were available, and he had not been able to get any. Burke was not convinced and was on the verge of firing him when a car entered the road leading to the warehouse.

Daniel had kept out of sight and out of the way, taking up a position on the fishermen's beach where he could see and hear much of what was taking place on the wharf. It was just beginning to get dark when the car appeared, and a man, impeccably dressed in white long-sleeved silk shirt and white linen trousers, wearing a white Panama hat stepped out. A woman was sitting in the back seat holding a small child in her arms, and he spoke briefly to her. As the man approached, Daniel recognized William, and assumed that the woman in the car was his wife. William walked purposefully towards the warehouse to be met there by Burke. He was in one of his moods, angry at the slow progress being made, and he held Burke responsible.

"Where are the extra men?" He demanded. "You had lots of time to arrange for more men."

Burke explained what had happened, that as he had been organizing the loading and pick-up at the plantations, and he had not been able to personally handle the extra help needed. Also, there was no help at the various pick-up sites, as there should have been, and it took much longer to get the lorries loaded. William was not satisfied.

"There will be Hell to pay if we don't make this shipment," he warned. "You were told about it weeks ago, and you had lots of time. If this shipment is not on board by the time the ship leaves—" He did not finish the sentence, but the meaning was clear. "I am going on board to see the Captain."

He joined one of the small boats going back and forth to the ship, and climbed aboard the vessel. When he returned he again spoke to Burke.

"We have until midnight to get everything loaded. We've got an extension of four hours, and you had better get it all done by then."

"The pimento is coming from St. Ann's Bay," Burke told him. "It should have been here by now. If it is not here in an hour it can't be loaded by midnight."

William ignored the warning. "I'm going to take my wife back to her mother's house," he said. "I will be back in a few hours. You better make sure everything gets done." His tone was threatening, and Burke did not reply, but he knew he had been set an impossible task. William left and drove away.

For the next hour or so the loading continued slowly but without incident. Then the men wanted time off to eat and rest. Burke would not allow the break, and although they grumbled and complained, they continued to work. Some minutes later, though, one of the men announced that he had done enough and he was going to take a break, with or without the foreman's permission. With that he walked off to sit and eat leaning against the warehouse wall. Burke ordered him back to work but was ignored, and then Burke fired the man, ordering him off the wharf. The man argued for a while, and when Burke called one of his men to eject the dissident, a volley of abuse greeted him. Several other workers joined in, and soon everyone was involved in a very heated row. Pedro joined the fray, and knocked the man down, and a brawl ensued. When it ended, the men had stopped work and left the wharf to sit on the beach nearby. Burke now had a full-blown work stoppage on his hands, and time was getting short.

Several hours later William returned, still in his white shirt and white trousers. It was a very hot and humid evening and he had rolled up his sleeves, but the shirt was damp with perspiration, sticking to parts of his back. When he drove in he directed the lights of his car on to the wharf to better see what was being done. He was beside himself with rage as he mounted the wharf to meet Burke.

No explanation was good enough for him. "You're fired," he informed Burke. There was protestation as Burke argued the injustice of that decision. Abuse came from William, and Burke continued his protests. At some point

William caught sight of the night watchman, an interested spectator standing near by.

"What the hell is that man doing here?" he asked, but not expecting an answer he turned again to Burke, "what's he doing here? Did you hire that man?"

"He's the watchman. He's the man I told to get the extra workers."

William exploded, "You goddam fool! Don't you know what he is? He's a damned thief. Don't you have any sense at all? You hired a thief to watch the warehouse!" Turning to the watchman he shouted, "Get to hell off this wharf. You goddam dirty nigger!"

"Y'u is dirty nigger!" Watchie shot back. He was enraged—angry enough to kill! "Y'u is a dead man," he shouted advancing towards William, pointing a finger almost in his face. "Ah tells y'u—y'u is a dead man!"

"Get to hell off this wharf," William repeated as Watchie continued to advance.

The men had gathered to watch and some were openly enjoying the exchange, but one of the men standing nearby took hold of Watchie's arm and pulled him away off the wharf, whispering in his ear. In a few minutes Watchie joined Daniel on the beach, still angry, and cursing.

"Rich people is damn tief," Watchie told him. "How y'u t'ink dey get rich?" He answered his own question, "Dey tief from us poor people." Sitting beside Daniel he continued to grumble. "Dey doan' like fe we people," he said. "We's too neager fe neager! We'se too dam' neager fe neager!" He paused and then continued as angry as ever, "but I'se goin' get dem! Dat man is a dead man, ah tells y'u. Dey is out fe get me, man. Dat is why me mek obiah. Dat is why ah needs me piece—I'se goin tek it back!"

He already had some kind of a plan in mind, and he continued muttering and grumbling to himself to which Daniel paid little attention. Watchie's previous encounters with the law and the courts had taught him something about the manner in which those institutions function.

"If de h'evidence gone, den dey doant have h'evidence fe de judge. Den dey can't sey me mek obiah." The prospect of the corporal giving evidence in court, swearing to speak the truth—nothing but the truth—and then being unable to produce any material evidence would embarrass the corporal to Watchie's everlasting delight. The next minute he was chuckling to himself.

He turned to Daniel, "I'se goine tek back me piece," he whispered. "W'en ah was in de lockup ah hear de policeman talking to de w'homan deh, an' he tell her dat he goine away Sat'day nite, so de police station will close down. De w'homan nar stay dere by she self, but de station door at de back will be open fe let her in when time she get back. Ah see w'ere de policeman put down me piece. Ah will jus' go dere an tek it up. I'se goine put one rockstone in fe de cock's head." He mulled the plan over again. "Yes sur, dat is w'at I'se goine do!"

Daniel looked doubtfully at him, not in the least convinced that he would succeed. "Y'u watch y'u self now," he advised.

"Me 'af te go now," Watchie said, and without further explanation he got up and left. Daniel watched him go certain that he was about to get himself into more trouble.

He was gone about an hour. "Me fine me 'piece,'" he announced triumphantly as he produced his trophy, still on the spiked stick with the head wrapped in a piece of paper. He unwrapped his package to display the rotting cock's head—his 'piece.'

"When de trial to come up," he gloated, "dey will 'ave no h'evidence! Dey will kno' ah's obiah man!" he added with evident pride.

"Y'u better not let dem ketch y'u wid it," Daniel cautioned, but his friend was not listening.

Burke had called his men off the job, and they left the wharf together, muttering and swearing at William as they left. They joined the group of idle workers sitting on the beach, from where they could watch activities on the wharf.

William waited for tempers to cool, and then he went to the workers sitting on the beach. What he would do, he said, would give a bonus if the work was completed. And to get them up and keep them going, they would each get half a bottle of rum right away. There were some murmurs of rejection and some of acceptance and then a few minutes later all were back at work.

Calling to one of the men, William handed him a small bundle of crushed notes and sent him off to the shop in town to buy the rum. Burke's two men, Rasta and Pedro, were sitting on the beach; they assumed that they had been fired along with Burke. They whispered together as the man left, and a few minutes later they got up and followed him into the darkness. In half-an-hour the man returned. He was agitated and angry, and he did not bring the rum. He had been waylaid on the way back; he had been knocked to the ground, and before he could call for help the two robbers had disappeared into the night with the entire purchase of rum.

William had little money left, so to keep his part of the bargain, he was obliged to drive to the shop and sign a note in exchange for all the rum left in the shop, which was short a few bottles of the amount promised. This caused another brief work stoppage that only ended when the men were satisfied that the rum had indeed been stolen, and they would still get their bonus and a share of the promised liquor. An hour later the work was going well, but midnight would come and go and produce would remain in the warehouse. Near to the hour a fully loaded lorry from St. Ann's Bay drove in, but there were not enough men to unload it and keep the boats loaded too. It was parked beside the warehouse, where it remained untouched. The driver and his assistant joined the other men loading, but their efforts did little to have all the produce on board.

As midnight approached the ship's officer came ashore with the bills of lading for William, and then he returned to the ship with the last load. At midnight the ship's whistle blew hard three times. From the shore no one could see the anchor being hauled up, or the ship slowly turning about. With another long blast of the whistle it set out to sea.

Rasta and Pedro were now quite drunk; they had rejoined the group sitting on the beach. They were celebrating the fact that William's efforts had not succeeded, and they were drunk at his expense. The Rastafarian was doing his own particular kind of celebrating—he was also smoking his ganga.

As the ship departed, William tallied up the account for each man. It had not been a profitable venture—about a third of the produce had been left behind, and the costs of labor and transport would be high too. There was also the troubling episode with Burke that meant he would be looking for an overseer for the Manor House Estate.

It was amazing how quickly activities on the pier ceased and the men drifted away. The men were tired and quickly everything in the night was quiet. A smudge was wafting its smoke along the beach, where Daniel, Watchie, and a few of the men were reclining half asleep. Daniel was just hoping that William would pack up for the night and go home, then he could get into the room and go to sleep. Burke and his men were nowhere to be seen. Watchie roused himself, saying that he had to relieve himself, and he wandered off into the darkness.

Hot and irritable William left his car and in the darkness strode onto the wharf. He wanted to cool off in the light breeze blowing out to sea. He stood at the end of the pier, opened his shirt, and pulled it slightly from his trousers. He placed his hands on his hips to let the wind blow around him, and breathed in the fresh mountain air.

Suddenly there were two people at the end of the pier, and suddenly they were embroiled in a desperate struggle. The man in the white silk shirt grasped at his attacker and opened his mouth to shout for help. The shout he uttered emerged as a gurgle as a cutlass sliced across his throat and his mouth filled with blood. Again he tried to shout for help, and again the shout emerged as a frothing gurgle, lost in the sounds of the lapping waves. The cutlass rose and sliced across the head, and then across the back, and again across the shoulders. The man in the white shirt fell and rolled to the edge of the pier. The attacker kicked the body and it splashed into the water floating slowly away, face down, followed by millions of tiny fish, out towards the open sea. The shadow-like figure, unseen by any one, disappeared into the darkness from where it came.

CHAPTER 47

The departing ship appeared like a star on the horizon when the men sleeping in the lorry roused themselves. William's car was still parked near the warehouse, but there was no sign of anyone about. The whole place was deathly quiet except for the waves lapping against the pier and the wind rustling the leaves of the coconut trees. The driver wanted to find a more comfortable place to rest for the night, but he had to see William, or Burke to be relieved of his responsibility for the loaded lorry. He went to look for William. In the car and on the pier he could see no one. He began to search other places, a short distance along the beach. He shouted several times and there was no answer, and he was becoming anxious. His shouts aroused several of the men who had fallen asleep on the beach, and they joined him in the search.

"Im 'cuar still dyah," it was pointed out, "so 'im nar gon' far."

Half an hour later several more men had been roused and they joined the search. It was getting more desperate and intense—something could be seriously wrong—someone on the beach lighted a bush torch, and began to search along the beach and warehouse. Someone went into the town to find the policeman; he was not there, but they awakened others in town, and curious to know what the shouting was about they joined the search. Then someone searching at the end of the pier found blood and signs of the struggle. A small boat, launched with a lantern in the bow began to look under the pier and further out to sea. Suddenly the light reflected off the white shirt as the body was lightly tossed on a wave, and there was a shout from the boat. A curious crowd was gathering on the wharf as the body was retrieved and brought in to shore. It was stretched out on two planks taken from the lorry and quickly surrounded.

"S'mady go fetch Mr. Coumbs," ordered one of the men from the crowd.

"Me will go," an answer came back. "Me will go now. Me 'ave a bicycle." And with that he took a running mount of his bicycle, and was immediately lost in the darkness.

"O Lawd!" exclaimed one of the women who had appeared on the scene.

"Lawd 'a mercy!" exclaimed another, "Look pon 'im t'roat!"

"Which man do such a t'ing?" questioned another.

The horror and the shock rippled through the crowd and it heightened the curiosity. One woman, just awakened and eager to see, came running. She was held back by a friend sickened by the sight of a corpse with the head almost severed.

"Doan look!—Doan look!" she said, grabbing at the woman's arm as she passed. "It a terrible t'ing!"

"Ah must see," said the newcomer, wrenching herself free with an impatient jerk. Within a second she was in the circle around the body, and a fraction later she had rejoined her friend, her hand to her mouth, unable to speak.

Daniel had fallen asleep on the beach, but like the others, was awakened by shouts from the lorry driver, and he too had cautiously joined in the search. Suddenly Watchie whose absence had gone unnoticed joined him. He was noticeably quiet and avoided the searchers. Both viewed the corpse when it was brought to shore, but soon retired to the place where they had been lying on the beach. Watchie was nervous and frightened.

"Dey will t'ink ah kill 'im," he whispered to Daniel.

"No man," Daniel said. "Den why dey goine t'ink dat?"

"Ah did tell 'im he was a dead man! An' dey will t'ink ah kill 'im."

Certainly there were grounds for the watchman's concerns. The argument with William had been seen and heard by everyone. But they had been mostly together on the beach through the night. "Ah's y'u witness, man," Daniel told him. "Y'u was wid me all de time."

The watchman was not convinced. "Dey goin sey ah do it." There was a long pause, and then he added, "Dey goin' sey ah put de obiah 'pon 'im and ah kill 'im!"

A short time later, he quietly got up from the beach and went to his room at the end of the pier. Daniel watched him leave the beach, but could not see him enter the room or leave the wharf, all his possessions wrapped in a tight little bundle.

Burke and his two men had taken part in the search, and following the discovery, sat for a while on the wharf. An hour later Mr. Coumbs arrived and took charge of affairs. He ordered the body be wrapped in a sheet and taken to the police station out of public view. Burke met him and they talked about the murder, and what should be done next. Coumbs had to contact the C. I. D. in Kingston, and almost immediately drove off to Buff Bay to send a telegram.

Burke decided that he would go on to Chivers Estate with his men, convey the news, and then go on to the Manor House Estate. He did not tell Coumbs that William had fired him and that strictly speaking, he was no longer employed by the Manor House Estate. Only the men working on the wharf knew; if he did not tell anyone he reasoned, no one of any importance would know. In the excitement of events that night it might be forgotten or ignored and he was willing to take that chance. During the drive back to Chivers he was quiet, deep in his thoughts. William's murder had been a most fortunate occurrence; now there was no one to oversee the estate except him—soon he would be the Busha there!

The two men with him were very much under the influence of their nights drinking, and they still had a bottle of rum they were sharing. There was little conversation between them until one man asked the other, "W'at y'u do wid de cutlass?

The question jolted Burke like a high voltage electric shock—he felt the goose pimples bristle on his back. "What cutlass?" he asked. There was no immediate answer; both men chuckled and smirked knowingly together.

"What cutlass?" Burke demanded again.

"Fe me cutlass," Rasta said at last. "Jus' fe me cutlass. Me t'row it in de back."

Burke had no further questions he wanted to ask—he was sure he already knew the answers. He drove the rest of the way in silence. The men were sound asleep when the car arrived at Chivers Estate and turned up the long driveway, towards the great house, looming dark and silent in the early morning light.

CHAPTER 48

Daylight was just breaking when Burke arrived at Chivers and stopped his car in front of the main house. Quietly he wakened the two men in the back seat, told them to get out and to go home, and not to talk to anyone. They were still intoxicated and slowly roused themselves to stagger of into the morning darkness. No one was yet up or about, and Burke did not want to alarm the household by knocking on the front door. He decided to go to Henry Thomson's cottage—it would be more tactful, he thought, and much less of a shock to Henry than it would be to Mrs. Barnham.

Henry and Opal were easily wakened; both were appalled at the news, and Henry dressed quickly. Within minutes Henry had aroused Constance, and shortly after both were in the house, where Constance went upstairs to wake Mrs. Barnham.

In the meantime Burke took his leave, explaining that he was very tired and needed to rest. He drove away to park the car in the Manor House garage. In the darkness he lit a match to search for the cutlass in the back of the car. Finding it he carefully picked it up, and holding it with a piece of newspaper wrapped it up in a larger piece. As he went to his room he hid it under the veranda to the servants quarters where he could retrieve it later and examine it at his convenience.

Constance had been given the news and told not to tell Mrs. Barnham, only to say that Henry was waiting downstairs to see her urgently. When Mrs. Barnham appeared, he told her that William had evidently been killed during the night—murdered! She took the news calmly, although she was deeply shocked and upset. She questioned Henry about the details, much of which he did not know, and which he was also anxious to find out. The task of telling Bridget was left to Mrs. Barnham, how and when she thought proper.

Henry decided to go to Annotto Bay right away. He ate some breakfast quickly, and was soon speeding along the coast road in an almost reckless manner. In Annotto Bay the town was in a state of excitement. Coumbs was not there when he arrived having returned to his house to have his breakfast, to shave and dress. Henry went to the police station and viewed the body. He emerged quite shaken by what he saw, and sat in his car to recover. He had no liking for William, but seeing the mutilated body was a horrible shock. When Coumbs returned he had nothing to add to what Henry already knew.

Johnstone, the absent policeman, returned in the late mid-morning hour to face an angry Justice of the Peace—being away at such a critical time. Coumbs gave him a proper dressing down for what he saw to be neglect of his duty, and ordered the man to collect the names of everyone that had been on the beach and on the wharf that night. Many of the workers had left as soon the work was over, and they did not know of the murder, but Coumbs set himself up in the station to interview and question as many people as he could. Many were forthcoming and willing, but they had little to offer that was different—everyone told the same story.

Henry drove his car over to the warehouse and parked beside the loaded lorry. The driver and his assistant were still there still waiting for instructions. He questioned them for a long while, but learned little more. Then he told them to put the produce in the warehouse and wait for the police to question them before leaving. He went on to the wharf and out to the pier, where he examined the murder site. The night watchman's room at the end of the pier was bare except for the cot and table. He wondered what had happened to the watchman, considering that there was produce in the warehouse that should be watched. Then he wandered out to the fisherman's beach, back again to the warehouse, and sat in the car.

In early afternoon Chief Inspector Higgins arrived from Kingston with an entourage of six policemen and detectives from C. I. D. William was a well-known businessman on the island, and his murder demanded investigation by the leading detective. As the car drove into town and parked beside the police station, a crowd of curious spectators gathered around. The Inspector was a pale, tall, mustachioed Englishman, straight from the ranks of the London C. I. D. He had an authoritative and commanding air about him; he was distinctly fond of giving orders in a very brisk manner, and having everyone jump smartly to obey. He wasted no time in issuing orders to his men, who snapped to their assignments without delay. One poor officer, evidently misunderstood his instructions, asked a fellow officer for clarification, and received a public reprimand in the presents of the gathered spectators.

From his place on the beach Henry saw the car drive into town, and shortly after he drove over to the station. He had met the inspector at Mrs. Barnham's birthday party, and he had sized him up in a matter of seconds. In the army he had met many such types; he knew the importance of rank, and how to deal with them. He introduced himself again as 'Major Thomson' and offered his assistance. The inspector had all the help he needed or wanted; 'help' from an outsider was regarded as interference and diluted his authority, and he wanted no part of it. Henry was asked to convey sympathy to the family at Chivers Estate when he returned.

The victim's mother was living in Kingston, Henry explained, and was not aware of her son's death. It would be best that she be told as soon as possible, and then they discussed moving the body to Kingston. A motor hearse had been dispatched from Kingston, the inspector said, but would not arrive until later, possibly during the night. The Inspector would be returning to Kingston that night and he agreed to visit Harriet.

Henry did not wait around while the police went about their preliminary investigations. Not having had lunch and not having brought any food with him, he stopped at the grocer's shop and bought bread and cheese—something to carry him over until he got back home in the evening. It was strange to think that William would no longer be around, but he had not yet grasped the full impact—he was still dealing with the horror of the brutal murder. The possibility that William would suddenly be killed was something he had never thought about, and it gave him a strange feeling to think about it—how quickly life can change; how quickly can one die!

During the drive to Annotto Bay that morning, he had been too preoccupied to think about the murder very much, but now as he slowly nibbled on the bread and cheese, he had the time, and wondered why someone would have committed such an awful murder. It seemed to him to be an act of vengeance or impulsive anger, or perhaps instigated by bitter hatred, and only a certain kind of person would commit such a murder. He did not think that it was just a matter of being in the wrong place at the wrong time—whoever did it wanted to kill William. William was disliked, he knew, and he did not think that William had a close friend in all his short life. But who could have hated him to that extent? Most of the plantation workers that he knew did not like William, but they were decent enough people, and he did not know of anyone capable of such a murder. Even though he thoroughly disliked William, he wanted the murderer caught and punished.

He drove his car over to the fishermen's beach once more, deciding to look around the murder site once again before leaving. As he sat in the car eating, he could see several people about the warehouse and on the beach, but a man approaching the warehouse from the far side of the beach looked familiar, and attracted his attention. He watched as Daniel got closer, still not recognizing him. But his curiosity was aroused and he wanted to know who the man was—if he did know him. As Daniel walked on to the wharf, he left the car and followed. The man's back was turned towards him, and he had not seen his face. The man went to the watchman's room, looked inside for a few moments, came out again, and then they were face to face, looking at each other, both surprised and speechless.

It would be hard to say who was most surprised or most relieved at this meeting. They shook hands for several long minutes asking questions of each other and giving quick short answers. Still in conversation, they walked to the end of the pier where the murder had taken place not yet a day before. The blood on the planks was hard dried and darkening in the blazing sun, but still quite visible. For a few moments they stood silently, contemplating and envisioning what had taken place the night before. Then they went back and sat in the car, shaded from the noon sun by tall palm trees. Henry had not finished eating, and he shared what food was left with Daniel.

"You will come back with me?" The question was more in the nature of a command, and Henry was quite certain of the answer. He started the engine for the long drive back.

"Opal will be so surprised—and happy to see you. How long is it now since you went away?" And answering his own question, " it must be nearly four years. You will not recognize your grandchild. She has grown so much."

CHAPTER 49

The inspector arrived in Kingston shortly before nine o'clock. Harriet had finished her dinner and was sitting in the drawing room. She was expecting William and Bridget to call in on their way back from the north coast, and she did not get up when she heard the car drive in—it must be them, she thought. Higgins had met Harriet before, and under the circumstances he did not wait to be announced; he entered the drawing room quickly and was standing before her when she looked up surprised to see him. She stared at him for a few seconds and then panic seized her; she did not get out of the chair. Instinctively she knew that he was not the bearer of good news, and she knew that it must concern William. She waited for him to speak. Her mind was racing, imagining what kind of disaster could have befallen her son. "O God!" She said to herself, "He's had an accident. O God! Don't say he's dead!"

"Good evening, Mrs. Henderson," he began. "Please remain seated," and then he paused, taking a deep breath.

Harriet did not reply.

"Is someone staying with you?" he asked. "I can arrange for someone to come in and stay with you tonight." Harriet shook her head, and he paused, searching for words before continuing. "I have some very bad news for you. It concerns your son William." He let that information take effect too. Harriet's face blanched visibly. Again she said to herself, "O God! O God don't say he's dead!"

"I must inform you that he has been killed."

Harriet's mind went blank—she swooned and collapsed in the chair to be supported by the inspector. The maid went to the dining room when she heard the car, and hearing the strange voice she poked her head into the drawing room. When Harriet fainted, Higgins called and she was quickly by his side. With a bottle of smelling salts and some brandy she was soon revived. Higgins helped her to recline on the sofa, he raised her feet on a cushion, while the maid fanned her with the magazine she had been reading.

The news of her son's death was a bad enough shock, and Higgins did not want to make it any worse; he would not describe the manner in which he had died.

"How? How did it happen?" Harriet asked feebly, "How was he killed?"

"It must have been an accident," the inspector replied. "I'm not sure of the details so we are investigating."

The information did not make much difference to Harriet; he was dead and that is all that mattered. For several minutes she remained on the sofa, moaning softly, and then she was helped to her bedroom. After seeing that she was settled in the inspector left, promising to return in the morning. Harriet was still in bed when he came, and he left without seeing her. She did not reappear until the afternoon of the following day, when friends visited her to convey their condolences.

If in the past it could be said of Harriet that she did not engage in much conversation, then it could be said of her now that she rarely spoke at all. As the weeks passed life for Harriet was like living in a living dream—nothing seemed real, and she expected that one morning she would wake up to find that, indeed, it was all just a bad dream, and William was there. For the months following she became quite reclusive, keeping her sorrow and her thoughts to herself, and avoiding most company. Twelve years ago when her husband suddenly died it affected her very little. William's death was quite different; it affected her greatly.

Harriet was not a religious person, but she had occasionally prayed in the past. Her prayers such as they were, were for superficial and material things: "O God, make William marry Bridget; let them have a baby; let the baby be a boy." Now she frequently prayed quietly to herself, "O God, bring him back to me." Her prayers now were only for William's return, and she convinced herself that if she prayed hard enough God would bring him back.

The day after the murder Mrs. Barnham and Bridget returned to Kingston. Harriet was in a state of complete shock, and Mrs. Barnham took charge of funeral arrangements. Bridget had taken the news without much show of emotion; she remained for the most part dry-eyed, very quiet and solemn. But she kept her young child close to her during the weeks following, and seemed to be consoling him for a loss that he could not yet understand. Some weeks later she confessed to her mother, that she had never 'been in love' with William— she thought their marriage had been 'arranged'—was one of convenience— something that was expected of them, and they did not want to disappoint anyone. Her feelings for him were not affected after learning of his affair with a servant who was now her friend. Her feelings for William were not very strong from the beginning, and the fact that the affair happened years before they were married helped her to erase it from her mind. Even so, she could not help but miss him, and she grieved quietly.

The funeral, several days later, was an impressive affair, with huge crowds lining the road to the church. Four plumed dapple-gray horses drew the hearse driven by a coachman in top hat, funeral bunting and tails. As the coffin left the house three carloads of flowers and a motorcade of well over a hundred cars followed it to the Parish Church in Half-Way-Tree. The hearse itself had glass windows draped with black curtains drawn back to allow full view of a large ornate coffin. Large black ostridge feather plumes atop the hearse at each corner made it a very somber and stately sight indeed. Following the service, the coffin was returned to the house before being transported across the island to the Manor House Estate and placed beside his father in the family vault. For many weeks following, the murder was an endless topic of conversation and speculation.

A month later there had been no arrest, although the police were seeking a suspect—the night watchman—who could not be found. At the Manor House Estate, Burke ignored the fact that William had fired him, and calmly resumed his position as though no such thing had happened. Daniel's house remained empty, and Burke had his mind set on moving in. With William gone he expected that it would not be long.

For weeks Harriet seemed to loose whatever interest she had in management of the Trading Company and the plantation, but after a while she began to attend directors' meetings. She did not contribute much, and seldom offered any comments or opinions. As yet she had not returned to the Manor House, and it looked as though she never would, even though she had been made trustee of the estate.

Although William had never made a will of his own, his father's will had bequeathed to him and his heirs, the entire Manor House Estate, with the Trading Company going to his mother. Without a will it became necessary for the lawyers and the Registrar to clarify ownership of the Estate. In accordance with the Squire's will, ownership was registered in the name of William's infant son, Charles James Henderson, and therefore a trustee of the estate had to be appointed. It became a contentious issue when Harriet was appointed the trustee until the child reached the age of twenty-one. Bridget, being the child's mother, felt that she should be the trustee for her son, and she made her objections known to the Registrar, but without success. However, as the two estates were operated jointly with one another, Bridget was persuaded by Harriet's lawyer not to contest the decision, and because of the tragic circumstances of her husband's death Bridget agreed not to pursue the matter further.

Henry's responsibilities once again included the Manor House Estate, and he was obliged to carry on where William had left off. This meant supervising and arranging for the collection, warehousing, and shipping of produce from the other smaller estates in the association, and he often had to be away for several days at a time. Henry had always distrusted Burke and certainly distrusted his foremen; their meetings were short and to the point. It was obvious too, that Burke did not like him either, and was resentful about taking instructions from him. Henry would have liked to dispense with Burke and his foremen and put Daniel there in his place—after all Daniel had been the headman there for years, and he knew the place better than anyone else. In the meantime Daniel assumed the position of headman at Chivers.

Bridget and Mrs. Barnham were in agreement that Daniel should be appointed Busha of the two estates, and that Burke should be let go, but they were reluctant to make those changes on their own without consulting Harriet— she was the trustee. But Harriet they knew would certainly never agree to Daniel's reinstatement at Manor House, much less being appointed the Busha; for no real reason she had despised him for years, and her son had fired him several years ago. Furthermore, he was the father of the wretched servant girl she sent to prison for 'seducing' her son.

For some time after the murder Bridget was the only person to have any meaningful contact with Harriet, and that was only because of her grandchild. For years Harriet's only desire had been that her son and his wife have a child, and she still had an interest in her grandson. Her son's death only intensified her feelings towards the child, and Bridget often used this as an excuse to visit. But Harriet had not shown any desire to get involved with anything or anyone. She was not involved in plantation affairs, and Bridget did not expect that she would object to Burke's dismissal. However, putting Daniel there in his place was a different matter. Foresight would have told them to make those changes quickly while Harriet was not involved, but that could not be foreseen at the time.

A month after the murder the inquest was called, but there had been little progress in solving the case. Six months later the public had not forgotten about the murder and was again asking questions, expecting some answers. When the inquest was called it was more an exercise to satisfy public curiosity rather than to shed light on the murder. In Kingston, where the inquest was held, only a few of the people present at the time of the murder were called as witnesses; they were some of the people who had given statements to the police, and had very little to add to what was already known. Burke, Rasta and Pedro were not among those interviewed by the police the day after the murder—they had left early in the morning to return to Chivers, and they were not called as witnesses. And the fact that William had fired Burke was never mentioned, and never came to light.

As a matter of interest Henry attended the inquest, and talked to several of the workers who had been on the wharf that night. Although Daniel told him that William fired Burke that night, he wanted some confirmation. When Burke arrived at Chivers the night of the murder, he did not go into details and never mentioned his quarrel with William. If Burke and William had quarreled that night, his dismissal could well be a motive for murder. But he soon dismissed the thought; even though he did not like Burke and distrusted him, he found it hard to believe that he could have committed the crime or even been involved. He did not think the man was capable of murder. On the other hand, either one of his foremen were. Nevertheless, William had angered so many people in the past any one of them might have wanted to take revenge and had simply seized the opportunity.

The finding of the coroner was a foregone conclusion—that the death was the result of foul play—a vicious and brutal murder, perpetrated by a person or persons unknown. It was recommended that the Criminal Investigation Department intensify their investigation, and urged that the perpetrator be brought to justice as soon as possible. Henry spoke with the inspector briefly after the inquest.

"We have a suspect in mind," the inspector told him. "The watchman was fired just before Mr. Henderson was killed. The man threatened to kill Mr. Henderson, and we think that he's our man."

"My headman at Chivers Daniel Hutchings, was there that night," Henry told him, "and evidently the watchman was with him during the night. Hutchings is a man I have known for years—he is very reliable, I trust him completely. They were together during that night, and Daniel says the watchman couldn't have done it." And then he thought to himself—unless they did it together!

"Well we will soon know," the inspector continued, "as soon as we find the man—and we expect to get him—we will know soon enough. I'm sure he's the man we want."

Henry returned to Chivers convinced the inspector was on the wrong track—if Daniel said the watchman did not do it, then someone else did.

CHAPTER 50

Several months passed without any further developments in the case, but it was a great surprise to everyone when one afternoon Harriet arrived at the Manor House. There had been no sign from her that she would ever return, but there she was, back in the Great House, and showing considerable interest in activities there. The morning after she arrived she sent for Burke, and they had a lengthy, and as it turned out, very friendly meeting.

Burke was an unusual person, and somehow at this time he and Harriet 'connected.' Much of this was due to a conscious effort on his part, and they got along well. During the weeks following they met frequently and even began to socialize, to play a card game together. But she had wide swings in her moods; one day she would be quiet and somber; the next she would be angry with everyone; and the next she would be lighthearted and cheerful—at least to Burke. Burke for the most part sensed her daily moods and indulged them, using the opportunity to get her permission to occupy Daniel's vacant cottage. After a while the relationship inspired him to be more presumptuous in his management of the estate. Without her permission he made use of anything on the property that fancied him. William's motorcycle was occasionally taken out and ridden into Port Antonio, and William's horse became his horse, to be used as he pleased in getting about the plantation, or occasionally ridden at full gallop down the front pastures for exercise. Later on he began keeping the animal at his house as he found it more convenient to stable it there.

Harriet was still very angry with her sister-in-law Mrs. Barnham, and when she returned to the Manor House she pointedly did not visit. It gave her the opportunity to show her displeasure, but Mrs. Barnham expected it and was not upset; she ignored the snub as if nothing had happened, and she did not visit either.

Several days later Henry had to see Burke on business matters. Burke was off-handed in his response and raised a number of objections. Henry settled the matter by ordering Burke to carry out his instructions. It was not the job that Burke disliked; he just did not like taking orders from a Jamaican like himself. Burke took up the matter with Harriet. She had not forgotten nor forgiven Henry for rejecting her advances years before, and she told Burke that he could ignore him. It was an attempt to cause friction between them, knowing that it would anger Henry. Henry was not told, and when he discovered that his instructions had not been carried out he went to sort it out with Burke.

After a few minutes of heated discussion, Henry lost his temper and blasted Burke in no uncertain terms. He repeated his order threatening dire consequences if not carried out. In the heat of the moment Henry said that he knew William had fired him, and if he was not careful he could still loose his job. Suddenly Burke was silent; he said nothing, and from that moment he was very obliging.

Burke's reaction was unexpected and it even surprised Henry; suddenly the man had nothing to say for himself. Now he was convinced beyond any doubt that William had indeed fired him and probably the foremen as well. On his way back to Chivers he thought about it; the question of a motive, and the identity of the murderer again presented itself.

The following week Henry was in Kingston and again visited the Inspector. Once again he offered assistance, but again the inspector reacted with disinterest. The Inspector was an opinionated man and did not like the outside assistance, which he regarded as interference. In the meantime he had been searching the countryside for the Maroon. The meeting was about to end on that note, when Henry, determined to spark some interest, told him that his headman, Daniel Hutchings, was at the wharf the night William was murdered.

"Well,"—hummed the inspector, "that's different. I don't think the police questioned him—I don't recall the name. I'll have to get a statement from him. What about Hutchings? Tell me what you know about him"

It was over an hour before Henry had satisfied the inspector's curiosity with a history of Daniel and his relationship with the Henderson family. Some of what he had to say cast suspicion on Daniel too, as the inspector was eager to point out. The fact that years ago Daniel had been dismissed by William and evicted from his house could well be sufficient motive for the crime. He would have to question Daniel, but weeks later the inspector had not appeared, no one had taken a statement from Daniel, and there were no signs of an ongoing police investigation.

CHAPTER 51

Following his long absence Daniel came back to a very comfortable situation, far different to the one he left. He had a job, good pay, the use of a mule to get about the estate, and the people working for him were friendly and co-operative. For the first few days of his return he lived in Henry's cottage with Opal and her daughter, but a week later he was feeling like an intruder, and moved into the servant's room.

Precious had for some time been enrolled in a girl's school in Port Antonio and was proving herself to be a brilliant student. It was all due to Mrs. Barnham's efforts, who had taken it upon herself to visit the headmistress and introduce her ward. Pre did so well in the entrance examination that she was awarded a full scholarship, and at the start of the new term she became a weekly boarder. On Friday afternoons Joseph would take the car and fetch Pre home for the weekend; that was the time they all looked forward to as she always had some interesting stories to tell.

In Annotto Bay when the Maroon failed to appear for his trial on the charges of witchcraft, it reawakened the corporal's antagonism towards the man; he now had good reason to pursue and arrest him. When the watchman did not appear for his trial, the judge issued a warrant for the arrest not knowing that one had already been issued by the Chief Inspector. And for the corporal, it became his prime objective. He recalled events in Annotto Bay that Burke had bribed him to get the watchman's release from jail—just two days before the murder. As Burke seemed to know the man, having employed him, he might know where he could be found. Armed with the arrest warrant and a lot of enthusiasm, the corporal was anxious to make the arrest by himself. The court clerk in the meantime sent a report to C. I. D. notifying them of the judge's order, and that report ended up on the Inspector's desk. As far as the inspector was concerned, the missing watchman was the prime suspect in his investigation, must be found and arrested.

The corporal returned to Port Antonio and wasted no time before interviewing Burke on his own, but he did not get much help. Burke regarded the interview as officious, and all but ignored him, using it as an opportunity to redress the somewhat disrespectful treatment he had received at the corporal's hands in Annotto Bay, all of which, in addition, had cost him the ten shilling bribe. Rasta and Pedro followed Burke's example and also ignored the policeman, and the corporal left in a very angry mood. He sensed that they were being evasive—if not lying, and that they knew more than they were saying. They denied knowing anything about the watchman or where he was, or having seen him since the fateful night, but the corporal did not believe them. The result was that he switched his attention from the Maroon to Burke and the two foremen, regarding them as the prime suspects for the murder.

A few days later the corporal was back at Manor House Estate privately questioning several of the men working there. He did not obtain any important information but was not discouraged, and made several more unofficial visits to question other workers. All the men expressed their dislike for the foremen and for Burke too; some complained about Rasta and Pedro, who skimmed their wages as a condition of continued employment. But there was not enough evidence for the corporal to act upon; most of what he learned was not substantive evidence and could never be used in a trial or even to make an arrest. Just not liking someone was not information that he could use.

A few days later Harriet had a surprise visit from the inspector and three plain-clothed C. I. D. officers. They had left Kingston very early that morning, and were obliged to wait until Harriet dressed and came downstairs for breakfast. The Inspector sat with Harriet on the veranda to talk while she ate, and he had a cup of coffee. The inspector told her that they had some new leads in their investigations, and needed to question Burke. He soon appeared in the distance accompanied by one of the officers, and the Inspector left the veranda to meet them in the shade of a large tree.

The interview very quickly turned to serious matters. The corporal's visit days before had alerted Burke to the possibility of being questioned, and he had carefully prepared his story. He knew a lot more than he could divulge; if he told all that he knew at this time, even if it was the truth, it would connect him to the crime in a way that would be difficult to explain, and he would be asked why he had not come forward sooner. He had to be careful about what he said and he was nervous. Nevertheless he was straightforward in his replies, confirming that he was there; that he hired the watchman about a year before; that William fired the watchman. In the confusion of the night, he reasoned that his version of events was as believable as anyone else's.

"Where were you during the time?" asked the inspector.

This was a crucial question, his answer was important, and he had thought about it. He would say that he was on the beach with his foremen; that the ship had been loaded and had set out to sea. He was not going to admit to the quarrel with William, or that he had been fired, only if questioned directly. If he lied, he reasoned, he could be found out and that would make the situation much worse.

"The men had stopped working and Mr. Henderson was very angry about the delays," he explained. "Everyone had stopped working. After a while Mr. Henderson bought rum to get the men back to work. He needed the help; it was too much work for just a few men."

There were more questions but the inspector seemed to be satisfied, and he did not comment. He had not questioned anyone else about Burke's activities, so there were no contradictions revealed. Still in his mind the missing watchman was the suspect; he wanted to know about the watchman, and he continued asking questions. What kind of a man was he? Why had he been hired? Who were his friends?

Burke explained that he was really a strange man, but suitable for the job—being so black he was not easily seen at night! While he was offering this explanation he suddenly found an opportunity to redirect suspicion towards Daniel. During the search for William, Burke had seen Daniel with the watchman on the beach, and he said as much to the inspector. He then related the events leading up to Daniel leaving the Manor House Estate, and essentially confirmed what Henry had told the inspector earlier. But he stressed the point that Daniel had good reason to dislike William; that Daniel and the watchman evidently knew each other, and both were in Annotto Bay during the night in question.

"Yes they were both there that night. I saw them several times. I don't know why Hutchings was there because he was not working for me or for Mr. Henderson."

"So what do you know about Hutchings?"

"I never worked with him, but I had some dealings with him. I can tell you this, he is a violent man." Burke continued, "he stoned me once and knocked me down. I only just got away in time—I'm sure he would have killed me!"

From his meetings with Henry the inspector already knew the answers to many of his questions, so all he was looking for were confirmations or contradictions in Burke's version of events. But this was something new—Daniel

Hutchings portrayed as a man with a violent temper. Burke presented a very different view of Daniel to that which Henry had given, and that was certainly of interest. He continued questioning Burke and noting his answers.

"Where is Hutchings now?"

"He is working at Chivers Estate for Major Thomson. You can find him there."

The inspector completed his interview with Burke, and then went over to Chivers Estate. Daniel was in a back segment when the officers approached and told him that the inspector was at the house and would like to see him. He rode on ahead and soon arrived at Henry's cottage.

In the meantime Henry had returned home, and had invited Higgins to have lunch with him. The purpose of his visit, he told Henry, was to question Daniel and to verify statements from Burke. They talked about the case, and Higgins admitted that very little progress had been made since they last met.

They were having drinks on the veranda when Daniel arrived and joined them. Henry introduced him and Daniel extended his hand. For several embarrassing moments Higgins hesitated, then he put down his glass, and half-rising from his chair, took Daniel's hand. To the inspector's surprise, Daniel then pulled up a chair and sat down beside them.

Higgins was taken aback and appeared uncomfortable. Here he was shaking hands with a man who was a possible murderer, and who he might be arresting in a few minutes. Besides that he was a colored man, an employee of his host, who blandly took a seat beside them and was behaving as though he belonged there! It took him more than a few moments to recover, and he began to wonder about the relationship between this man and Major Thomson. He was still puzzling over this when a short while later Opal brought a drink for her father, and said that the lunch was ready. The inspector had met Opal at the Barnham ball, but he did not know that Opel was Daniel's daughter. Through the meal, he mulled over the situation and decided not to probe.

After lunch they returned to the veranda and Higgins began to question Daniel. The situation to all appearances was far different to what he had expected and it threw him off track. Thomson obviously did not think that Daniel had anything to do with the murder—that had been made clear to him before, and Daniel too seemed genuinely anxious to see the culprit caught. But, thought Higgins, Daniel certainly had a motive. He still could not rule him out as a suspect, even though from what he observed it appeared to be completely out of character.

In a short while he was questioning Daniel about his encounter with Burke. The explanations given were reasonable and Higgins accepted it—that it happened at a particularly stressful time in his life, and Burke's provocation just pushed him over the edge.

"Who do you think committed the murder?" The inspector asked Daniel.

"I don't know," Daniel admitted. "Someone there that night did it, but one thing is certain—the watchman did not do it. He was with me during the night." He thought for a few moments and then added, "Take away the watchman an' who is lef? Only Burke and Rasta. Rasta was smoking ganga, an' they were into the rum too." There was a long pause in the conversation as the inspector listened. Then Daniel added, "Rasta carried a cutlass—the watchman never had a cutlass."

Henry agreed, but Higgins kept his thoughts to himself and did not comment.

Even considering that information, Higgins was still not convinced; the watchman had threatened William, and then he disappeared. Surely that was the way a guilty man would behave. It did not occur to him that the watchman might have only been afraid.

The inspector had lots to think about on his long drive back to Kingston. His visit had not produced much that would lead to the culprit—it had in fact complicated the case; there were now more than enough suspects to consider.

Jamaican Proverb—De man dat loose de mad darg is de rite man to tie 'im up.

CHAPTER 52

For the next few months nothing of interest or significant occurred. Burke had taken up residence in Daniel's house living alone and often visiting Harriet at the Manor House in the evening. There was nothing really unusual or strange about his visits; they were purely social in nature without any romantic involvement whatsoever. They would play cards, or listen to some of Harriet's records or just talk.

William's death seemed to have affected Harriet's sense of reality; she earnestly believed that one day he would return. She often said as much to Burke, even suggesting that she had seen and talked to him. Burke accepted this as fanciful imagination on Harriet's part, but said nothing to disillusion her; if she wanted to believe that William would return one day, that was fine with him. As Harriet became more absorbed with these fantasies, she suggested that Burke should take part in the spiritual contacts, but he was not about to partake in any ceremony that conjured up spirits of the dead. While he thought that Harriet was a little crazy, but harmless, he was not sure that spirits of the dead were harmless—they were better left alone—and he declined that invitation.

In a strange way Harriet had replaced William with Burke; she would lecture and correct him at times, treating him in much the same way she had treated William, but it was still a distant relationship. Even so Harriet had her moments of irritation and impatience, and would occasionally show her anger. William was not living in his mother's house when he was killed, and when he visited her he had a tendency to ignore the advice and lectures. Because Burke was an employee he was obliged to be attentive and considerate, more than William often was, and he paid attention to the lectures. From Burke's point of view, she was someone to converse with, and he enjoyed many privileges that otherwise would not have been available to him.

The Manor House was a very formidable country home having no less than ten bedrooms with sitting rooms on the second floor, several more on a third floor, and there were other floors and furnished rooms above those, none of which had been used for many years. This gave the house an air of mystery that never failed to arouse the awe and curiosity of any visitor. The house itself reeked with age, having been built by slaves in stages, taking at least ten or perhaps twenty years. Beneath the main floor there were foundations of solid stone and a labyrinth of passages, rooms and dungeons. No one ever went down there for any reason whatsoever; it was dark as midnight and extensively draped with ageless cobwebs in which one could easily be lost forever.

Burke, like most visitors, was facinated with the size and structure of the house, and occasionally wandered through examining various rooms and objects. At first Harriet accompanied him showing him places of interest, but later she let him roam freely wherever he wished. On the main floor there were several large disused rooms and a hallway leading to the front and far side of the building. Burke explored these over a number of days, and discovered an obscure trapdoor, hidden in a closet, leading to a passageway and steps to the dark dungeon-like rooms below. It was possible, he discovered, to enter the house from below, that is, if one knew the way through the dark passages and rooms below. Burke made it his business to learn the way; he used a long piece of string tied at the entrance to find his way back. After a number of visits, he succeeded in learning the route by memory; it was like the combination to a safe—so many steps forward, so many to the left, and then to the right, and so on. One just had to remember the combination.

A window in a top floor room gave a panoramic view to the front of the estate where it ended at the seashore. On clear days it was possible to see across the ocean for a hundred miles or so to the mountains of another country. Some evenings Burke went there alone and would stand for hours gazing out to the horizon, indulging his imagination. As a boy he had wanted to become a sailor and visit other countries; as a man he had not lost the urge. It was often getting dark when he decided to leave, and he would light a lamp to find his way down to the lower levels again. Over the weeks and days, these activities aroused the interest and curiosity of the servants; it became the subject of gossip and speculation. The maids and the cook on several occasions conspired together to spy on their mistress and her visitor, but the spies were disappointed, and soon ceased their clandestine observations with very little of interest to report.

One evening after the day's work had ended Rasta and Pedro visited Burke at his house, ostensibly to discuss some aspect of the field work. Rasta had visited him months before—actually two days after the murder—inquiring about his cutlass, which he had been unable to find in the car. He had been smoking 'weed' and was quite drunk on the night of the murder; he could not be sure where the cutlass had been put, even though Pedro assured him that it had been thrown in the back of the car. Burke denied all knowledge of the cutlass, insisting that he had not seen it. The subject was raised once again, and Burke kept to his story, but there was the sense that Rasta was suspicious and did not believe him.

During this visit the men remained longer than was necessary, and began talking about other things. A week later they visited him again with the same excuse, and again overstayed their welcome. As the weeks passed their visits became more frequent, more familiar and personal. They knew of Burke's frequent visits to Harriet, and they soon commented about it in a teasing and derogatory manner, implying there was some romantic connection—and every so often reminding him about the missing cutlass. Burke did not think his visits to Harriet was any of their business and he did not like them talking about it. He began to be concerned about the two men, and wondered what they were after—what their objectives were and what they sought to gain. Nevertheless, he allowed it to continue without stating his objections. He did not wish to appear aloof, and he wanted to remain on good terms with them, so he did not dissuade them.

Several weeks later on a Saturday afternoon after work they arrived each with a bottle of rum and they brought along a bottle for him too. Burke was not a drinker and protested, but in the end he accepted the gift. The evening started with a drink or two, but continued on into the early morning hours, ending when the men were drunk and he had imbibed far more that was good for him. The next day he did not feel well enough to visit Harriet.

The following Saturday afternoon the men appeared again, and once more Burke was persuaded to join them. They were becoming more and more persistent and familiar, treating him as though he was a close friend. Mistakenly Burke had not made his objections known or called a halt to the visits. He had known the men for years in his former position, and they had occasionally done things for him that were illegal. Mostly they had pilfered gasoline from the company for him to use in his car, and for which he had compensated them, but in so doing he had compromised his authority. They had never socialized before and now he wanted to put an end to the visits, but did not know how to do so without creating a bad relationship.

At work the following week he noted a change in their attitude; Rastaman did not like some instructions given and loudly mumbled his objections. Burke repeated his order and was again ignored. He was not used to the men questioning his decisions and not ever objecting to his instructions. He reprimanded him, but did not threaten him with dismissal, and Rasta grudgingly complied. It was now clear to Burke that his authority was being eroded; they knew too much about him and his personal affairs, and he decided to call a halt to their visits.

The Saturday afternoon following that incident they did not appear at his house, but a week later they again presented him with a bottle of rum, and were ready to imbibe through the night. They had already been drinking and Burke refused the gift telling them that their visiting days were over. At first they pleaded with him, reminding him that for the sake of the good times past he should join them. Burke was not in the mood to agree. Then they began to argue and after several minutes they were angry and started to swear at him. Several minutes passed in heated argument while the abuse continued, and then Rastaman, closely followed by his companion, pushed his way past Burke and the two men were in the house. He was going to drink with 'Brudda Burke' whether he liked it or not—they were brothers, he said, and he could not send them away. And Burke was powerless to get them out of the house

"Y'u tek y'u self up from us," he accused Burke. "But we'se brodder now, man. W'at y'u know an' w'at ah know mek us brodder!—Right man?"

"Yeah! Yeah man!" Pedro agreed.

The meaning was clear to Burke—by not telling all he knew about the murder at the right time he was now tied to them. William's murder had been most convenient for him; something he might have wished for but would never have done; he had never thought such a thing possible—not even in his dreams. The murder itself was very disturbing, but he could not change that, and since it happened he had tried to blank it out of his mind. He had retrieved the bloody cutlass from the back of his car and hidden it, and that he realized now was a bad mistake. By not going to the police right away he had tied himself to the crime, and he wondered now why he had not just gone and reported it. He had a great deal more to loose if he reported it now—the men would say that he was part of a conspiracy and had urged them—even paid them—to commit the murder.

They stayed for most of the night drinking, making fun of him and his friendship with Harriet. During the evening comments were made about their 'brodderhood,' the missing cutlass, and what they could do now that they were in partnership. Burke did not probe for details about the implied 'partnership'; he was wondering how he could rid himself of these men without implicating himself in the murder. He worried that they would draw him into some other criminal conspiracy. As the night went on he took several drinks to steady his nerves. Then he took several more hoping that it would help him to ignore the problems, and soon he was drunk. He left the men to their own devices and went to lie down, but he could not go to sleep. He got up as the men staggered to their feet about to leave in the early morning hours. Rastaman put his arm around his shoulders patting him on the back, saying that he would see him again—soon. It was an insolent demonstration of just how far they were ready to go to make sure that he understood and remained under their control.

For most of the night he lay in his bed—thinking, and very worried. He was full of regrets and blamed himself for letting his control slip away so easily. He could not tell Harriet—he could not tell anyone—there was no one he could go to and expect to get help. Yet he had to do something—he had to get rid of the men somehow without involving himself in William's murder.

Much of the talk between the men worried him—they talked about Harriet in a way that disturbed him; he knew they were dangerous and he knew that they might go to extreme limits. It seemed that Rasta was jealous of his relationship with Harriet, and the fact that she was not friendly with anyone else. Furthermore Rasta saw that she allowed Burke the use of William's motorcycle, and he was using her son's horse too. He evidently thought that Burke was in a position to obtain privileges for him as well. They suggested that he was sleeping with Harriet, even asking him how she was in bed. And then they accused him of lying when he denied it. Rasta seemed to think that he could share that benefit as well! All this was not mentioned in so many words, but the implied meaning was clear.

Not being able to sleep he got up early feeling quite ill and very depressed. He did not want to see either of the men that day as he slowly went about his usual Sunday morning activities. His dogs kept in the yard had to be fed and he cooked their food. In mid-afternoon he shaved and dressed, saddled the horse and left on his way to visit Harriet.

Harriet was reading her fortune with the cards spread out before her, looking intently at each card as she picked them up one at a time. She had been impatiently expecting him for almost an hour, and was somewhat peeved that he was late.

"What kept you so long?" she asked as he mounted the stairs and took a seat across the table. "Where have you been?"

He mumbled his answer watching as she concentrated on the message the cards were bringing her. Her expression began to change.

"Hummm!" she murmured to herself. "Not true! Not true!" After a while she shuffled the cards again. "Let me read your fortune," she said as she dealt the cards. He watched in silence. If she wanted to read his fortune he would not object.

Slowly she turned the cards over looking carefully at each one for several seconds. Then her expression became very serious. "I don't like this," she said after several more cards had been displayed. "It's not good!" More cards were picked up and she began to show her annoyance with the results. "There's a lot of evil here!" she said finally.

"What does it say?" he asked, leaning towards the table to see the upturned cards. His interest had been aroused.

"I don't like this at all," she said impatiently and before he could look she threw the cards face down on the table mixing them into a pile. "Let's play our game."

She dealt the cards and he picked them up one by one to spread them in a fan. Harriet did the same without speaking. Then again she asked, "What took you so long?"

He sat dejectedly and made no excuse. She lectured him as they played. His problems were weighing heavily on his mind, and he could not talk about them. There were several minutes of silence and finally she asked, "Is there something the matter?"

He did not answer right away. He would have to invent some convincing story that would disguise his hangover, and he needed an excuse for his depressed condition—something simple that he could enlarge on if necessary when he could think.

"I'm not feeling well," he said, being truthful for the moment. "Since yesterday—it must be something I ate."

Harriet was not really concerned, but she did not want anything to interfere with their card games.

"What did you eat?"

"Ackee and saltfish," he made up the lie. "Maybe it wasn't cooked well."

"You should get a housekeeper," she advised. "Then you wouldn't have to worry about cooking. Have you taken something for it?"

"I don't have anything to take."

"I have some soda—it's very good for settling the stomach."

She was up and returned in a few minutes with a small bottle and a glass of water. She opened the bottle and a teaspoon full went into the water and was stirred. "Here," she said, "drink this."

Burke took the glass and a small sip. He was thinking maybe he could play on her sympathy and see where it would end up. Slowly he drank the liquid—it tasted awful and did not make him feel any better—he thought he might vomit.

"Thank you," he said and he put the glass down.

"You must get a housekeeper," Harriet said again. "I could get you a suitable woman."

He remained silent but nodded his agreement with the suggestion. His mind was racing as his stomach churned. Various thoughts were crowding in one on top of another without time to sort them out. The salts did not made him feel better; he wanted to belch and relieve the pressure in his stomach.

The maid brought some tea and sandwiches and placed the tray on the table before Harriet. Burke was still mulling over his cards and his problems; his pay would allow him the luxury of a housekeeper, but he preferred to live by himself and save the money—nothing in the world could have persuaded him to employ a maid! Then he thought about the wretched men that kept pestering him—he must find a way to get rid of them—even to the point of killing them—if he could do so without getting caught! He did not have a gun and did not like the thought of shooting someone in cold blood, but there must be other ways. It occurred to him that every now and again they had to poison the rats to keep them out of the stored produce, and the poison was kept in a shed within easy reach. He would have to find a way to administer it—poison would be much better. The thought of killing the men was one way out, but really all he wanted was for them to stop blackmailing him and leave him alone. Then he realized they would never do that.

Harriet poured the tea handing him a cup and plate. He played several cards, took a few sips of the tea and ate a sandwich, hoping that the food would settle his stomach. After a while the sandwich was not sitting well, and he was beginning to feel quite ill. Several minutes later he was certain that he would vomit.

"I'm going to be sick," was all he could say before the contents of his stomach were in his mouth. He got to the edge of the veranda and expelled it over the railing onto a garden bed below. He hung on the rail, reaching violently. Now he was ill. He groaned as he reached again, the contents entering his nose and throat made him choke, gasp for air and vomit again.

Harriet brought a napkin and some water. She wiped his face and mouth as he supported himself unsteadily on the railing.

When he could speak again he apologized. "I'm sorry," he said. "I'm so sorry."

Harriet supported him back to his chair. She wiped the perspiration from his forehead with the napkin. "Never mind," she said, although her expression was one of disgust. "It's alright."

He remained quietly slouched in the chair for some time before he began to sit up. "I must be getting back home," he said. His stomach was beginning to rumble again and he knew that he would be sick again. Furthermore, he felt an urgent need to use the toilet.

"How are you feeling now?"

"Not well," he admitted. "I should be getting back home." He got up and staggered uncertainly towards the steps. His legs gave out beneath him and he collapsed on the floor, kneeling, his head resting on both his arms on the floor.

Harriet called for the maid. They helped him up and he went to the bathroom where he remained for the next hour. When he came out Harriet showed him to a bedroom that he could use, and he was just able to get to the bed by himself. Shortly after, Harriet knocked on the door and entered.

"You will have to stay here tonight," she told him. "You are too sick to go home and stay alone—in any case you would not be able to get there. I've had the boy stable the horse."

During the night he had several more attacks of vomiting and diarrhea, but in between he was exhausted and slept. By morning he was feeling better but quite weak. He got up and was pulling on some clothes when Harriet knocked on the door. He sat back down on the bed and called for her to come in. She had the maid bring a cup of tea and some toast. He was thirsty and drank the tea right away. He was only halfway through the toast when he began to feel the urge to vomit again.

"You must rest in bed today," she ordered him. "I will let the men know you are sick."

The food he had just eaten was again churning in his stomach. Just in time he knelt down beside the bed, frantically reached under it for the chamber pot and again began to vomit.

Several days later he was still in bed, but he had been able to eat without being sick. Harriet sent word to the foremen that he was still sick, and they would have to work on their own. They appeared several days later at the kitchen door asking if he was getting better.

Burke was too weak to be up and about, but he needed some clothes and personal items. Harriet sent Raymond, the yardman to his house to collect the items needed. When Raymond got there he was unable to get into the yard; the dogs had not been fed for several days and were in a wild and ferocious state. He did not dare enter the yard or open the gate and he returned to tell Harriet.

The dogs had to be fed and Raymond set about boiling a large pot of rice with scraps of meat. In the early afternoon the food had cooled sufficiently and he returned to the house. Again he could not enter the yard so he threw the food in large chunks over the gate. The dogs had gathered at the gate as soon as he appeared, and immediately began to fight among themselves, ignoring the food. The fighting continued for some time, first one pair and then the other. Even after the fighting had subsided it would break out again with incredible ferocity. The snarling and growling never stopped and he waited almost an hour until he felt it was safe to go inside. But he did not go in unarmed; he had brought along a long thick stick to defend himself if necessary. As the gate was opened the dogs rushed towards him snarling and barking, but he swung the stick and shouted at them, clouting one across the head to send it staggering away. He kept up the shouting and used the stick if any animal approached. Soon they backed off searching the ground for scraps. As he went into the house he noticed that one of the dogs was lying on the ground motionless. Blood and dust surrounded it, particularly about the head and neck and he was certain it was dead, but he did not investigate. He collected the personal items requested and was able to leave without being attacked.

A week later Burke was feeling better, more or less recovered, and was anxious to return to his house. He knew that somehow during his illness he had displeased Harriet, but he had not the least idea of what he had done or why. He told Harriet that he would be leaving in the morning and she was obviously quite glad to see him go. Although she had become used to having him there in the house—they had played cards the day before as he began to feel better—every now and again she had shown irritation and annoyance.

Staying in the Manor House with Harriet, even for a few days required adjustments; it was not quite the same as playing cards for a few hours on odd days of the week. When he sensed that he had somehow displeased her and was at a loss to know why, he hoped that it would pass, but Harriet was finding the adjustment quite trying and she was not sure that she had done the right thing to let him stay there.

Towards mid-morning he somewhat shakily prepared to go to his house; he still had not fully regained his strength, but was determined to get there. On arriving he was very upset at what he found; the dead dog had been partially eaten by the other starving animals, and the scattered remains were in an advanced state of decomposition. There was a strong, putrid odor about the place; vultures were perched nearby squabbling amongst themselves for the first opportunity at the carcass. Every now and again one or two of the large birds landed near by and were immediately chased away by the dogs. On the way back he arranged for the dead animal to be buried and for the other dogs to be fed.

He ate a light lunch and rode out to see how work had progressed in the fields during his absence. On inspection he found that little work had been done; it was as he had left it over a week earlier. He met both foremen who told him that the work had gone very well, but this he knew was far from the truth. He did not feel well enough to correct them and did not want to start off his return to work on a sour note, and there was little discussion between them.

Having to meet with them again made him nervous; they looked at him in a peculiar way—as though contemplating something. In fact it made him quite uneasy, even though sitting up on the horse gave him something of a dominant position and some feeling of security. In the future he decided he would try to avoid the foremen and give orders to the other workers directly. If possible, he would avoid meeting them, unless there were other people about.

A week later Burke had settled in again. For several days he had successfully avoided meeting the Rastafarian and his companion; if only he could find a way to get rid of them then he would be free, and he thought about it constantly. A few days later he worked up enough courage to go to the produce shed and remove some of the rat poison. He carefully wraped it in a piece of newspaper and put it in his pocket. Now, he only had to find a way to give it to them. Various ideas occurred to him over the next few days, but he did not think they good enough—they would have to swallow a fair quantity without tasting it, and he could not think how he could do that.

Burke's relationship with Harriet had soured and he had not the least idea of what he had done—thinking about it depressed him. Nevertheless he had quietly removed himself back to his house, and resolved not to visit her again in the evenings. Preoccupied with his thoughts he saw no reason to apply himself to any of the jobs at hand, and he spent large parts of the day at his house. He was unhappy with his employment, and for days he did little else but think about it, and think of a way to administer the poison. Then, for a while he thought about leaving the Estate, getting a place on a ship going to England or America. But as the days turned into weeks Harriet's irritation with Burke subsided, and once again she invited him to visit in the evening for a game of cards. Burke was pleasantly surprised and was happy to accept, resolving to let the earlier unpleasantness fade from memory.

Jamaican Lore:—Tek y'u time watch ant an y'u see how 'im mek nest.

CHAPTER 53

On the estates the months passed uneventfully and days dragged slowly by; in Kingston there was an earthquake that terrified many in the city but did little more than crack a few walls. In mid-August a hurricane passed over Cuba, brushing the north coast and drenching the island with torrents of rain. There had been no developments in the search for the Maroon, but the police had not given up their quest, and every now and again announced that he had been seen somewhere and an early capture was expected. So far he had eluded them for almost a year. On the estates it was still a subject of conversation and interest— it was of direct concern to the families.

Daniel was a sound sleeper in the early part of the night, but towards morning he would often lie in the bed half awake, dreaming, or mulling over the day's events. And then he would get up and prepare for the day's work ahead. Suddenly one night he was wide awake—something had startled him out of his deep sleep. He lay quietly in the bed not moving, listening quietly for any sound that might tell him what it was. For several minutes he lay still and then he heard the soft tread of footsteps just outside his door—someone was there. His heart started to pound and he heard nothing but the pounding of his heart, the blood surging thorough his head. He took a deep breath—another, and tried to quiet the pounding in his head. Someone tried the latch on his door, but it was locked from within. They tried it again, and Daniel prepared himself in the event the intruder broke in. There was silence for a while and then the footsteps went away to be replaced by the usual sounds of the tropical night. Slowly he got out of his bed and went to the door to listen—he heard nothing unusual for almost a minute. Then he quietly drew the latch and pushed the door open. He peered out, but saw nothing. The intruder must have left he concluded. He closed the door firmly latching it, and returned to his bed.

At the breakfast table he told Henry about the mystery visitor. Burglars as a rule avoided breaking into inhabited buildings—they avoided human contacts if possible—they were usually only looking for money or valuables. The mystery visitor it was concluded, was probably just a thief and not someone intent on breaking into a place where someone was sleeping.

The mystery did not remain so for long. About mid-morning Daniel rode towards a rear segment, in the distance he saw three men moving quickly through the bush up the hill. They were too far away to hear if he had shouted, so he turned his mule and rode in their direction. As he approached he could hear them shouting to one another in an excited way but he was too far away to hear the words. Then, to his astonishment there were four more men out on another stretch, also moving quickly through the bush up the hill. They appeared to be converging towards some undefined point on the hill. As Daniel drew closer he could see that some of the men were policemen in uniform, responding to the shouts from one of their number. He halted his mule to watch developments. The police quickly caught up with their quarry and subdued him with several blows from their truncheons. They lifted the man and dragged him back down the hill towards the open land and the pathway.

Daniel waited for the group to arrive, and to his surprise he recognized the man caught—it was Watchie—the Maroon. The police marched their prisoner down the pathway towards the great house and the other buildings. Daniel followed and quickly a crowd of curious spectators gathered to watch developments. They walked around gawking at the unfortunate prisoner who had been 'subdued' and was nursing his injuries, but still they kept a respectable distance. The constables surrounded him while his hands were bound behind his back, and he was made to sit on the ground with two men standing over him armed with their truncheons.

Henry arrived and joined Daniel. He had spoken to the sergeant in charge and was told that Inspector Higgins was expected shortly. The inspector had been to see Harriet at the Manor House to inform her of the expected capture. Within the hour the Inspector appeared. He had driven his personal car with several policemen from Kingston, and he was disinclined to transport the dirty, odoriferous prisoner back to Kingston in his clean expensive car. He instructed the District Corporal to keep the prisoner in the Port Antonio jail and await the arrival of the Black Mariah from Kingston. By noon the police had departed and except for excited discussions between workers and domestics, relative quiet returned to Chivers Estate.

As arranged the Maroon was taken to the Port Antonio jail. He had been held there a number of times in the past and was familiar with the cells, but because he was now an important prisoner he was placed in an older cell considered to be more secure. It was situated at the back of the building on a lower floor, out of sight from the road, thus depriving anyone held there of any human contact, save that of the jail keeper.

Inspector Higgins arrived back in Kingston that evening, quite triumphant and satisfied with the day's work. The following morning he issued orders for the immediate dispatch of the Black Mariah to Port Antonio to bring the prisoner back to Kingston. About the noon hour, the vehicle was ready and it departed with three officers aboard. They expected to reach Port Antonio some time that evening, and to leave with their charge early the following morning. However, on the way through the mountains in a torrent of rain, the vehicle drove into a washed out section of the road and broke an axel. It was stuck in a gully in the middle of the road unable to move or be moved, and as the rain continued to fall and wash away the road, the vehicle fell deeper and deeper into the gully. By the time the rain eased the vehicle was in danger of rolling off the road down a very steep embankment. When the word of the mishap reached Kingston it was two days later; the police there were in a state of high excitement, very concerned that the Black Mariah had not returned with the prisoner. A repair lorry was sent out to bring in the disabled vehicle, but the bad news was that the axel could not be replaced or repaired for several weeks—or perhaps months—and the prisoner in Port Antonio would not be brought back to Kingston until the vehicle was repaired.

It made little difference to the Maroon in which town or in which jail cell he was confined—prisons were all alike as far as he was concerned, and he settled himself into a tedious routine. There was little in the cell with which to amuse or entertain himself. At first he would lie on his board bed and watch the light move from one end of the room to the other as the hours passed. He had been relieved of all his personal possessions when placed in the jail, but several days later, after constantly pleading with his jailer, several articles were returned, including his pipe and tobacco. At last he was allowed to smoke!

One morning, standing on his cot to look through the small window, he discovered a crack in the wall between the large stones that made up the wall. He probed it with a small twig that had blown into the upswept cell. From the crack there emerged a swarm of enraged ants whose nest he had disturbed.

Stinging ants are not the best company at any time, but being deprived of all living contact made the stinging ants fine company indeed. It amused him to irritate the ants and watch them race about in search of the invader—they were so easily aroused! And there was no end to their fury and their numbers. It seemed impossible for so many to emerge so quickly from so small a hole. But these ants were not the common variety of stinging ants that usually nested in the ground. These ants were of a particularly ferocious kind that often nested in tree stumps and in built up places. They were a dark rusty-brown color and somewhat larger than the common variety, and considerably more venomous. And what made them so was that squashing them and getting the 'ant juice' on the skin was quite the equivalent to being stung—their body fluids were as poisonous as their sting or perhaps more so. They were generally known as 'ginger' ants or 'fire' ants, the latter name perhaps being the most suitable.

The following morning he again aroused the ants to fury, and then he scattered scraps of food near the opening. He watched, and as their anger subsided they began to collect the crumbs and carry them into their nest. For several days he played with the insects, occasionally getting stung and executing the culprits in reprisal. But he continued to feed them and watch their numbers multiply almost by the hour. There were many 'warrior' ants with large heads and huge nippers capable of inflicting a vicious sting. In less than a week the nest had enlarged itself to the extent that it took up a portion of the cell floor and part of the wall by the window, and that made it a place to be avoided.

As the days passed he got to know his jailer and they began to converse. The jailer, a police constable, was curious to hear about the murder, and Watchie did not disappoint him, telling all that he knew and the circumstances leading to his arrest. He described with considerable embellishment the condition of the body when it was brought to shore, and at the same time he firmly denied having committed the murder, suggesting that Burke's men were responsible. The jailer believed his story, and after a few days he was able to win some minor concessions that eased the boredom of his confinement.

During this time the corporal in charge, his sworn enemy, inspected the cell without prior warning every other day or so, to make sure that the prisoner was secure. These visits were also used as an opportunity to gloat over, to threaten, and occasionally to 'juck' the prisoner with his swagger stick. But Watchie was careful not to react, knowing full well that it would not better his situation. He did occasionally answer back just to keep the man talking—after all, even that kind of conversation was better than none at all.

These tours of inspection usually took place just before noon, and after a while Watchie was ready waiting for his arrival. One morning, however, he had been teasing the ants, and had aroused them to the extent that they were swarming angrily about the floor and on the wall by the window. He had been stung several times and was standing on his bed to be out of reach, but at the same time his interest had wandered somewhat from the ants, and he was looking through the window at the bright day outside. Just at that moment the corporal unexpectedly entered the cell. The sudden entry startled him and he jumped down from his perch to sit at the end of his bed away from the swarms. The corporal seeing the sudden reaction to his entrance suspected that his prisoner was somehow attempting an escape of some kind, and he went to investigate.

"Ah! Ah ketch y'u!" he shouted. "W'at y'u doin' dere?"

The corporal had been outside in the bright sunlight and was temporally blind in the darkness of the cell. He did not wait for an answer, but went immediately to the window, climbed on the end of the bed resting his hands on the wall to look through the window. He remained there looking about for some time before he was satisfied, and then he stepped off the bed to lean against the wall where the ants were crawling.

"W'at y'u doin dere?" he questioned again, still standing in the midst of the swarm, leaning against the wall.

Watchie returned a blank stare and did not answer. That was an admission of guilt, and he raised his stick, shaking it at the prisoner. "Y'u mek me mad y'u goin ketch me wrath!" He shouted. "W'at y'u doin dere?"

The Maroon kept silent; he watched as the corporal continued to threaten him unaware of the angry, swarming insects. He watched fascinated, expectantly; he was looking forward with considerable interest to the corporal's reaction when the first ant began to sting. The corporal brushed an insect from his neck and one from his arm, but paid little heed to the others that were clinging to his clothes. Again he brushed several from his neck. Ants have a way of crawling all over their victims before they start to sting, and then, as if responding to some given signal, they all start to sting at the same time, and this was no exception to that rule.

Suddenly the corporal was cut off in the middle of a sentence. His mouth opened and eyes bulged from his head. He was covered with the crawling insects and he began to frantically brush them from his clothes. He bent over while his hands beat at his body, his neck, his head, and at his arms and legs. He was beating at all parts of his body.

"Lawd a' mercy!" he bellowed. "Lawd a' mercy! Ant done tek me up!"

Watchie waited no longer. He seized the opportunity and bolted for the door, and was out of the cell before the corporal could react. None of the doors in the station were locked and he was out and away before anyone was aware of his escape. The corporal was too preoccupied to give chase; the ants had crawled into his under clothes and were stinging all parts of his body. He shouted to the constable who happened to be outside the station and did not hear, not until the corporal made his way to the main floor. When the constable finally understood what had happened it was too late—the prisoner was out of sight and no one knew in which direction he had fled.

The escape had not been planned—it was merely an opportunity seized, and it could not have worked better even if it had been planned, but the freedom that he won did not last long. While at large he was described in the newspapers as a dangerous and vicious killer, and even without a trial he was already a condemned man. There was no one willing to help him as many had done in the past. In his search for someone to help him he sought out Burke, who told him that although he knew who the murderer was, he was not able to help him. Within three weeks he was again taken into custody and this time he was transported directly to the Kingston Penitentiary to await trial. In the meantime, the corporal responsible for the escape was demoted to the rank of constable and transferred across the Island to the Black River station. Hearing about the demotion was of little satisfaction to Watchie—once again he was locked in a jail cell.

CHAPTER 54

Following his capture it was decided to push the trial forward; the Justice Department was satisfied that they had sufficient evidence for a conviction and saw no reason to investigate further or to delay proceedings, and the trial was scheduled for mid-November. The news was greeted everywhere with great interest, and especially on the two estates. Daniel resolved to appear at the trial; he was determined to give evidence that he hoped would save the Maroon. He was convinced beyond any doubt that the man was quite innocent. He did not think of himself as a friend, because he did not really like the man; Watchie was not the sort of person that one kept as a friend. But Daniel felt that the murder charge was based primarily on the threats the watchman made, and by a general dislike for Maroons, and a particular dislike for that Maroon. It was not based on the facts of the case as he knew them to be; justice would not be served by the execution of an innocent man.

A week before the trial there were heavy rains on the north coast; Daniel was obliged to spend a day outside in the downpour. He was soaked through and remained so for most of the day. The following morning it was still raining and he again ventured out to supervise some urgent work. The following day he did not feel well and returned home at noon, and by evening he had a fever and was forced to go to bed. The fever was much worse the next day and did not ease for the next five days. By the time he was able to stagger from his bed the trial in Kingston was over. The Maroon had been convicted and condemned to death. The sentence to be carried out on the sixteenth of December.

The news of the trial and sentence upset him, but in his weakened condition he could do little more than complain to his daughter and to Henry. They were far more concerned with the state of his health, fearing that if he ventured out it would lead to pneumonia from which he would not recover. They insisted that he remain in bed and then not to leave the house for the next week. Opal was there during the day and she made sure that he followed her directions. The fever had aggravated his boyhood injury, and he began to have bouts of severe pain.

As the sixteenth of December drew closer Daniel had regained some of his strength. He was feeling considerably better, but he was still very weak. He did little else but think about the approaching execution, and it disturbed him to the extent that he could not sleep at night, and the thought occupied every minute of the day. He agonized that he had been unable to appear at the trial, and thus would be responsible for the death of an innocent man. He prayed most earnestly, hoping that God would somehow intercede and reverse the court's decision. On the thirteenth of December there was no indication that the sentence had been squashed; he had to do what he could to save the man in spite of his weakened physical condition.

He collected all the money he could find about the house and took it to his room. That night he had his supper with Opal and Henry as usual, but shortly after he excused himself, saying that he wanted to rest, and was going to bed. In his room he dressed quietly, collected a few items that he would need for the next few days, wrote a brief note to his daughter, and then quietly slipped out of the house. He made his way down to the coast road and waited for the bus going to Kingston. It arrived less than an hour late. He boarded, was lucky to find a seat and settled in comfortably. It was a long journey; there were almost two-dozen stops on the way, and the bus finally parked in South Parade, in the center of Kingston a few minutes before eleven o'clock the next morning.

Dismounting from the bus he was hungry and tired from the long journey—it had been impossible to get much rest. During the trip he had thought about what he should do next; he would find a policeman and see someone in authority—someone who could tell him what to do and who to see. He bought a bun from a street peddler and while he ate he looked for a policeman. There was one in the middle of the street at the crossroad directing the traffic, but he looked to be too busy. Further along he spotted another and caught up to him. When he asked the questions the man gave him a queer look—it would not be possible to have an appeal, he was told—he would be wasting his time and efforts. Nevertheless he decided to go to the police station and talk to whoever was in charge—perhaps they could advise him. He got directions to the station, and spoke to the sergeant in charge. The man just laughed at him and was quite dismissive; it would be impossible to get the sentence changed, he told him. It could not be done, and there was no use in trying. Through it all he was being treated as though he was some kind of crazy person. Finally he told the sergeant that he had been there, with the convicted man the night of the murder, and that the Maroon could not have committed the crime. It was then that the officer began to take him seriously. He did not know what could be done or how anything could be done, but he suggested that only the judge could be of any help or make any decision affecting the sentence.

Who was the judge? Daniel asked. Where could he be found? The officer supplied that information, and Daniel went off to find the courthouse and the judge. The judge was not in court that day and he did not appear in his chambers; he was probably at his house. Where did he live? That information too was forthcoming—the judge lived outside Kingston, in a house up the Jack's Hill Road, at 'Billy Dun' an old estate house. If he wanted to get there he would have to take a tramcar to King's House Gate where the Governor's house was located, and then walk to the Judge's house, a distance of at least seven or eight miles.

It was nearly one o'clock in the early afternoon, and the day was oppressively hot. He bought some patties from a woman sitting at a curbside stand and ate them while waiting for the tramcar. He just finished eating when it came into view, it stopped and he boarded. He took a seat towards the back of the car on a long bench that extended the width of the open vehicle. When the conductor collected the fare he asked to be let out at King's House Gate. The conductor was a man who liked to display his knowledge to strangers and regular passengers alike; he was very obliging, expounding his knowledge about the countryside and the Jack's Hill Road.

Daniel had never been on a tram before nor had he ever been in a large town. On its way the tram rocked violently, swaying from side to side, leading him to cling anxiously to the handle of the bench seat. He wondered if the vehicle might not leave the tracks or turn over, but other passengers appeared calm and relaxed—some even sat with eyes closed, rocking back and forth with the motion of the vehicle. It might have been an enjoyable and interesting experience if not for the anxiety of his journey.

At King's House Gate he left the tram and took the road as directed by the conductor. The tramcar ride from Kingston had taken just under three-quarters of an hour. It seemed much longer but he had no idea of the time—he imagined it to be much later than it actually was, and he was anxious to find the Judge's house before it got dark. He had not given any thought to where he would spend the night or even if he would find a meal. But these were all secondary to his main purpose—he had to see the judge and have the sentence changed.

He arrived at a crossroad—the conductor had told him to take the road to the right, which he did. It was much like the country roads to which he was accustomed—unpaved and steep in parts, with large stones in the middle of the roadway, boulders at the side, deep ruts and sections where the road had been washed away into small gulleys. How any car could negotiate such a road he wondered—and this was Kingston! The center of civilization! He looked for a road sign to assure himself that he was on the right path, but there was none.

It was excessively hot and half an hour later he was forced to stop and rest. He sat on a large boulder at the side of the road, and mopped his face and neck. A mule dray came rumbling down the hill, the drayman hanging on to the reins, trying vainly to control the mule. He kept to the side out of the way, and then once again started off up the steep incline. Again he was forced to slow his pace—it was just too hot, his stomach ached, and the road was too steep. An hour later he slowly approached a bend in the road, rounding the bend he saw in the distance two large gray stone gateposts. As he got nearer he could make out the words—on one post was the word 'Billy' and on the other 'Dun.' At last—he had arrived—almost. The driveway, which led towards a large two-story wooden house, black with creosote, was almost a mile. On the left hand side was an open field spotted with a few large mango trees. On the right hand side was a fenced off wooded field, that had not been cleared of Macker thorn and Tamborin trees.

He slowed his pace and again wiped his face, head and neck; he wanted to make himself as presentable as possible. There was no one in sight so he followed the roadway. It did not lead to the front of the house, so he followed it around to the side of the house. There a man was tending a very dehydrated rose garden.

"Good afternoon. Is de Justice here?" he asked.

The man looked him over somewhat suspiciously, not answering until he had carried out his inspection.

"Well 'oo want to know?"

"It is important matters between 'im and me. If 'e is 'ere ah mus' see 'im."

"Go roun' de back an ax de maid," the man instructed him as he returned to his gardening. Daniel did as told.

The maid, dressed in a neat uniform, a sparkling white apron and cap, treated him to the same critical inspection and then replied that she would go and see. In a minute she returned.

"Justice can't see y'u," she told him.

Daniel showed his disappointment—a feeling of panic and desperation seized him—he had to see the judge.

"Please to tell de judge it is very important. It is a matter of life and death! Ah mus' talk to de judge."

The maid hesitated, but then sensed the urgency of the message. "Ah will tell 'im," she said and departed once again.

She returned shortly. "Justice will see y'u in a few minute," she informed him.

He breathed a sigh of relief and again wiped his face. There was a wooden box at the side of some steps and wearily he sat on it to wait for the judge to appear. It was not a long wait; the maid reappeared and told him to go around to the side of the house where he would find 'Justice' in the garden waiting for him.

At the side of the house he approached a white man sitting at a table in the garden quite some distance from the house. He had a glass in his hand from which he was drinking, and was smoking a freshly lighted cigarette held in a long cigarette holder. As Daniel approached he flicked the ashes from the cigarette and took another puff, slowly blowing the smoke up into the air above him. He was a small man, typically English, somewhat passed middle age and balding. He was quite deeply tanned showing a strong contrast on his legs where his shorts ended. This would not be a good meeting thought Daniel—a judge is a judge!

"Good afternoon," Daniel said, and then he added, "I'se sorry to disturb y'u, Sur."

The judge appeared to be in a relatively good mood—perhaps it was the drink, or perhaps the drink and the cigarette. This was not what Daniel had expected—not from his previous knowledge of judges; they had all been cross men, serious and severe, such as the one that sent his daughter to prison.

"How can I help you?"

Daniel introduced himself, and then stated the purpose of his visit. The judge listened without interrupting, puffing thoughtfully on his cigarette. When Daniel stopped talking, and stood awkwardly, fidgeting, anxious, the judge answered.

"Look, my good man," he said, "why don't you sit down." He pointed to an empty chair at the table.

Daniel hesitated unsure that he should do as directed. Then he decided to do as told. "Tank y'u, Sur," and he sat down. He was glad to be off his weary feet. He must have looked tired.

"You look like you could do with a drink," the judge said. He picked up an empty glass from the table and poured a generous quantity from a Johnny Walker whiskey bottle, and then, without asking squirted in some soda water. He handed the glass to Daniel, replenished his own glass and leaned back in his chair.

Daniel raised his glass. "Your good health sir," he said as he took a sip and then another. The drink made him feel much better and much more hopeful. The judge ignored the toast, and asked him to tell his story again, and then he asked questions: Why had he not appeared at the trial? Why was he not called as a witness for the defense? What was his connection to the defendant? And there were many more questions. Through it all Daniel insisted that the convicted man was not the murderer, and pointed out that an innocent man would be hanged for a crime he did not commit.

"Well," said the judge at last. "You know the matter is out of my hands. There is not much that I can do about it at this late date. It is up to the Governor—only the Governor can make that decision. But what I will do is this—I will speak to the Governor and tell him what you have told me. It will be his decision to stay the execution. I can't promise that he will, but I will tell him what you have told me, and suggest that the case be reviewed."

Daniel was relieved. "Thank y'u Sur." And he thanked him again. "God bless y'u, Sur. God bless y'u."

He got up to leave not wanting to encroach on the patience and goodwill of the judge any longer. But the judge was a man that liked his whiskey, and he liked to have company when drinking. He insisted that Daniel have another drink. The judge questioned him further about his connection with the Maroon and with the Henderson family. There was one more request that Daniel wanted to make, but he had been hesitant to make it earlier; he wanted to see Watchie, his imprisoned friend once more, perhaps for the last time if the appeal to the Governor failed. He had not broached the subject, but now that the discussion had progressed well so far he felt he could make that request. Could the judge arrange a visit?

That he could do, the judge assured him. He could give him a pass for the warden of the prison, and that should be sufficient. Again Daniel thanked him.

"Don't thank me," the judge told him. "People think that a judge's job is simple and easy, but it is not!" he said emphatically. "Sometimes I hate this work—especially when one must follow the law and sentence a man to death. It's not easy knowing that I will be responsible for this man's death. But it is the law, and it was my duty! It was my duty—you do understand that?"

There was a small bell on the table. The judge picked it up and rang it loudly several times. The maid appeared from the side of the house carrying a small tray.

"Yes Sur?"

"Bring me my briefcase," he instructed her. "It's beside my desk in the office."

A few minutes later she returned. He withdrew a fountain pen some paper and an envelope, he scribbled a note, signed it and placed it in the envelope. He handed it to Daniel without sealing it.

"Give this to the prison warden in Spanish Town. It should allow you to see the prisoner. You will have to do that tomorrow," he told him. "The execution is early on Friday morning."

Daniel thanked him again.

"You will not hear from me—you will only know if the sentence is to be reviewed by reading the newspapers. That does not mean that the sentence is changed, only that the execution is put off until there is a review, and perhaps appealed. I must have your full name and address in case there is to be a review, and you will have to appear as a witness. Do you understand?" The judge noted his name on a piece of paper and placed it in his briefcase. As he closed it he reminded Daniel that he would be called as a witness if the case was to be reviewed.

"Yes Justice," Daniel replied. "I understand, Sur." And then he said that he had to return to Kingston that night so must be on his way.

"Well, good luck, then," the judge said. "Good night." He remained seated, blowing the smoke from his cigarette up in the air, and sipping his whisky. He did not watch Daniel as he hurried away, across the lawn towards the long driveway and through the tall gray gateposts. On the long walk down to King's House Gate the dull pain in his stomach returned—it had nagged him most of the day, and he must be hungry—he had not eaten much for a full day, but the whiskey had dulled the hunger for a while. It was getting dark when he arrived, wondering where he could get something to eat and rest during the night. Kingston had the reputation of being a dangerous place, unsafe for visitors especially at night, and if he had to sleep outdoors he would prefer to be out of the city. At King's House Gate, a few steps further down Hope Road, there was a small shop, and he went to make inquiries and to buy something to eat.

The shop was open but there were no customers inside. It was dimly lit by single electric light bulb suspended from the ceiling, around which were buzzing millions of little moths and small ant-like insects with wings. The evening air was hot and still, and the light, even though quite dull, seemed to make the room hotter still. Behind a pinewood counter was a short, plump, brown skinned woman—most unusual, he thought. He had expected to see a Chinese man or woman; very few coloured people owned or operated grocery shops. She had been reading a newspaper as he entered, and she immediately folded it and stood up, smiling pleasantly.

"Yes, Sur," She seemed glad to see him, or perhaps she would have been glad to see anyone. "W'at me do fe y'u?"

317

"Good evening mam " He bought a 'hapony bulla,' and some sugar water, for which she provided an empty condensed milk tin. He sat at the counter on a high stool, broke the small bulla in two and ate slowly. He ate without talking, and as he did so he looked at the woman; she seemed to be looking him over too. She had a pleasing, cheerful face, and although she might be considered fat, she had a narrow waste and a shapely figure—'pleasingly plump!' Her breasts were not as he would have expected—large, floppy and shapeless. Instead, through her thin dress he observed, with some interest and satisfaction, that she was not wearing any support, and that her breasts were rather small and firm— considering her size—well rounded, beautifully shaped and pointed.

She wanted to know "from which parts y'u come?" He told her and explained that he needed a place for the night.

She did not immediately reply, and after a few minutes thought said "Well, me 'ave a room an' a bed, but y'u 'ave to share wid me son."

A shared room was far better than sleeping outdoors, or in Kingston, and he gladly accepted. But he would like to see the room.

"It fe me bed an' room," the woman explained, "but ah will sleep wid me sister te nite so y'u can tek de bed."

The woman picked up a lamp and lit it. She lifted the hinged counter and led him to the back of the small building. She opened a door to the side and walked into a small room. There were two beds and some sparse furniture, a chair and a crate that served as a table. The room was quite hot, but smelled pleasantly of kuskus.

"Dis is it," she said as she led him in, and placed the lamp on the table.

"Dat is good, mam," Daniel said. "An' how much y'u goine charge me?"

"For de nite, it is sixpence."

He fumbled in his pocket and withdrew a small handful of loose coins, all coppers. He picked out six pence and handed them to the woman.

"An' where y'u son?" he asked as she placed the coins in a small tin which she quickly tucked into her pocket.

"He jus' a lickle boy," she said. "He soon come back now."

They returned to the shop. "Me son is jus' six year now," she told him. "But he is a good lickle boy."

"Wher' 'im farder den?" Daniel asked.

"Lawd!" The woman exclaimed. "He done garn long time!" Then she sighed audibly and then took another deep breath 'Yes, 'im garn long time now," she said thoughtfully. "W'en 'im see I'se goin 'ave 'is chile, he pick up 'im t'ings same time." She paused again, "where 'im is me no know."

"Oh!" Daniel said—he was a bit embarrassed, and felt a little sorry for the woman. Why would a man leave her? He wondered. Even though she was plump, she was quite shapely, and she had a cheerful, attractive face. She was young, obviously a kind and good-natured person.

He resumed his seat at the counter, and they continued to converse while several customers entered, bought items and left. A tramcar passed going up Hope Road and it stopped at King's House Gate. As it started off again two neatly dressed men entered the shop, and suddenly the woman's expression changed from pleasant and jovial to one of anger or perhaps fear. She looked at the two men without speaking as one of the men settled himself on the stool beside Daniel, and the other leant against the wall, picking at his teeth with a broken match-stick.

"How y'u keepin' Miss Agoni?" the seated man asked.

"I'se doin' jes' fine," she replied. Her tone was defensive with no trace of friendliness.

"Well I'se jes lookin' in te see how y'u'se doin'," the man continued. "Y'u know I'se lookin' out fe y'u, Miss Agoni."

"Well now y'u look in an' see y'u can go look 'bout y'u bisnes," was the blunt reply.

The man sat for a few moments and said nothing, looking at her as if he had something more to say, but hesitated. The fact that Danel was also sitting at the counter hearing every word seemed to hold him back from answering as he might have wanted. He leaned towards her and swept his hand over the counter reaching out towards her's, but she quickly withdrew her hands off the counter, out of reach. He sat back against the counter for almost a minute without speaking, looking intensely into her face, while she defiantly returned his stair. Slowly he lowered his gaze, accepting rejection he pushed himself away from the counter and stood up, slowly turned about, and without another word left the shop, followed by his companion.

She watched the men leave and only when she was sure that they were out of hearing did the woman speak again. "'Im is a police," she said quietly.

"Uh?"

"'Im come after me many time," she continued. "Even w'en me husbin' was here. Many time 'e come after me. 'E is a fasty man!

"Uh hu."

"Many time 'e come tell me how we mus' lie down togedder!"

"An' w'at y'u sey?"

The woman ignored the question. "'E tell me I'se his pain an' suffering!" She was indignant, "I tell 'im dat I'se no man's pain an' suffering!" She paused again, "'e sey dat I'se 'is pain an' suffering 'cause me name is Agoni, an' 'cause me doant lie down wid 'im! An' same time 'e sey dat me husband was 'bout de place!" The woman was not only indignant—she was angry. For a while no one spoke, not until the woman stopped fuming.

"How come y'u name is Agoni?" Daniel asked.

"Well dat is de name me mudder name me. She sey dat it is a pretty name fe a girl child. An' ah did kno' dat she like it—many time she would sey to me 'Agoni! Sweet Agoni! Sweet Sweet Agoni!' Like she singing, an' it sound pretty. An some time she sing Sweet Agoni." The woman began to sing the words while Daniel watched and listened—she had a good ear for music and sang tunefully. The woman ended her song and then added, "She nebber kno' what it mean, she jus' sey dat it is a pretty name."

"It is a pretty name, an' y'u have a sweet voice. —Y'u can sing sweet. An' even if it mean pain an' suffering dat doant mean y'u is pain an' suffering!"

"No! No!" The woman protested. "Me doant sing sweet! Me mudder sing sweet—jus' like a bud!" And then she paused thoughtfully for almost a minute. "Dat was de fust time me fine out w'at it mean—w'en de policeman—de same man dere—did tell me ah was 'is pain an' suffering 'cause me no lie down wid 'im!"

"One time we was fren'—jus' fren y'u kno'," the woman continued. "W'en we first meet 'e was de policeman dat stan' guard at King's House Gate any time de Governor passin' by. An' den 'e become a plain-close policeman down Half-Way-Tree station. Dats w'en de trouble start. 'E come—quick time—bosie-bosie—like 'e is sometin' good, an' tell me dat he 'ave good news fe me—dat 'e is now plain-close police! Ah say to 'im, if dat is good news, me doant want to hear no bad news!" Again she paused. "One time 'e try to tek me from me husbin'—'e is a fasty man! 'E an' me husbin' ketch fight one time, an' from dat time 'e was out to get 'im. An' den 'e arrest 'im fe sell Pika Pow." The woman paused, deep in thought before continuing. "Me husbin' go to prison fe ninety days, an' w'en 'e come out 'e see dat I'se goin 'ave a chile, an' 'e leave same day!"

Just then a little boy entered the shop from the back door. "Hi y'u, Mumma," he said as he leaned up against her, placed his elbows in her lap and rested his chin in his hands, examining Daniel quizzically.

"Hi y'u Sonny! W'ere y'u bin?" she asked, throwing her arms around him and smothering him with a hug and a kiss, all of which he dismissed. "W'ere y'u bin? Y'u hungry now? Y'u ready te eat now?"

The little boy nodded without speaking, and continued to eye Daniel curiously.

The woman left the shop through the back door followed closely by her son. She soon returned with a plate heaped high with food, and a spoon, all of which she placed on the counter. The boy was put to sit on a high stool, handed the spoon, and the plate pushed towards him. She found another spoon and the two began to eat from the same dish. Daniel watched with interest from the other side of the counter. He could see what was on the plate; rice and ackees, and salt fish—he could see pieces of green scallions—and the smell was appetizing! The woman had taken several mouthfuls when she seemed to remember that Daniel was there. She looked towards him, her mouth full, with grains of rice sticking to her lips.

"Y'u want to eat?" she asked, wiping her mouth with the back of her hand. She did not wait for an answer. "Wait fe me," she said. "I get y'u food."

Again she disappeared through the back door and quickly reappeared holding a tin plate heaped high with the rice, ackee and saltfish.

"Come. Eat." She pushed the plate towards him and handed him a spoon.

Daniel was hungry; he had not had much to eat for a full day and the small bulla eaten earlier left him still hungry. A second invitation to join them was not needed. There was not much conversation while they ate, not until the plates were wiped clean, and for several minutes after. He thanked her and complimented her on her cooking. She withdrew a piece of cloth from beneath the counter, wiped her mouth and then her son's mouth and face.

They sat quietly for several minutes, and then the woman broke the silence, "It time fe y'u bed now Sonny. Go wash y'u han' an' 'member to peepee."

The boy departed with a kiss, and they resumed their conversation.

"Any time y'u want to tek up y'u bed," the woman said, "y'u can jus' go. Come ten I close de shop, but it not time yet."

"Me an' a bed will be good fren' te nite," he said. "Country bus doant mek a good place to rest."

His mind was really on getting to Spanish Town in the morning—finding the prison, and seeing his friend. There was only one day before the scheduled execution, and he had to be there. He asked for directions—the quickest way of getting there. As far as she knew, she told him, the bus to Spanish Town left Kingston about ten o'clock, and the fare was a shilling, she thought. But it was always late, and very crowded, and often passengers were left behind.

Daniel reached into his pocket and took out all the money he had left. It amounted to three shillings and ten pence. If he spent a shilling on the fare it would leave him without enough money to buy food or pay the bus fare back to Chivers Estate. He would have to walk to Spanish Town. How long would that take, he asked the woman. He learned to his dismay that she thought it would take a full day.

"Ah better get some rest, then," he said getting up and making his way towards the room. He thanked her again for the food, and prepared to go to bed. The little boy was already in bed, and seemed to be asleep; he did not stir when he entered the room.

The room was very warm so he removed his clothes and lay on the bed without covers. He could only allow himself a few hours rest—there was a long journey ahead and he had to be up very early, but he lay there thinking over the events of the day with his eyes open. People had been very kind to him that day, he thought—the policeman in Kingston, the tramcar conductor, the judge, Agoni, and he was grateful, quietly offering a prayer of thanks. Finally he closed his eyes and began to drift off. He was not asleep when he heard the door open and someone enter the room. Quickly he covered himself.

It was the woman. "Me sister bed is full up," she whispered. "She an' she husbin'" she explained. "Ah goin a'fe share y'u bed."

Daniel did not know if he should just get up and let her have the bed, but then he would need his clothes. He reached for them, but in a second she provided the answer.

"Mek little space fe me," she whispered, as she quickly removed her clothes and lay down beside him. The bed groaned with the additional weight, and as she settled in her arms went around him, pulling him close to her naked body. Her passion was without restraint, and they slept together in each other's arms.

He awoke having no idea of how long he had slept and with no idea of the time, but he felt very rested and was anxious to be on the way. The night was very dark, the air quite still and everything was very quiet. It must still be early morning, he thought as he withdrew himself from the woman's arms, and got up without wakening her. He dressed quickly while the woman and her son slept on. He took a sixpence from his pocket and left it on the box. Before leaving he kissed her on the cheek, gathered up his small bundle and quietly left the room.

The tramcars were not running at that time; he would have to walk to Half-Way-Tree to the junction of Hagley Park Road. The night was cool and he set out at a brisk pace. The clock in the tower at Half-Way-Tree told him that it was nearly half-past three and he had made good time, but there was much further to go. As directed by Agoni he took the turn to Hagley Park Road and kept up his pace. It was still dark when he got to Spanish Town Road. At Half-Way-Tree and on Hagley Park Road he had not seen anyone, but on Spanish Town Road there were signs of human activity. In the distance further along the road he could see the dim lights of some vehicle ahead, and he could hear the rumbling sound of a mule dray on the rough road still quite some distance behind him.

It took nearly five minutes for the dray to overtake him, so as it approached he stepped off the road to allow it to pass. Had he not done so he would certainly have been trampled by the trotting mule and run over by the heavy dray; the driver could not possibly have seen him—he was slouched over, his head resting on his chest; the man was sound asleep but still holding the reins. Fortunately, the mule was in complete charge and knew exactly where it was going.

As the sky became lighter another dray was heard approaching from behind, and as it drew nearer, Daniel again stepped off the road. If the driver was not asleep, in the breaking daylight he would be easily seen, but self-preservation is a strong instinct and he was not going to leave it to chance. He stood at the side of the road to let the dray pass. The driver was wide awake, but still that was no guarantee that he would not have been run over. As it passed the driver looked at him and waved. Daniel returned the wave, and a few yards further the dray came to a full stop. The man turned about and beckoned to him still standing at the roadside. He ran to catch it up.

"Wher' y'u goin dis time a' mawnin?" The drayman asked.

"Spanish Town. How far y'u goin'?"

"Me is goin to Cayman Estates. Come—tek a lif wid me," he offered.

It was a godsend and he did not need to be asked twice. Quickly he climbed aboard. The dray was bare except for some empty coconut sacks, and he used two to cushions the bumps from the ruts in the road. It soon became clear why the man was eager to have company on his way to work—he was the talkative kind and had a lot to say for himself.

He had worked all his life, he confided to Daniel, and he was making good money working at the sugar estate. It did not take him long to broach his favorite subject—his three 'wives' and seven children! All of them—his wives and children—were very dear to his heart he said, and he described their particular attributes in some detail. But it was his most recent 'wife' who was the subject of his concern; she had recently given birth to her first child, and the child did not in any way look like him; he doubted that the child was his, even before he overheard the whispers of a neighbour—"De chile not fe him pickney."

But she was the 'sweetest' woman of his three wives. Her faithfulness—or lack of it—worried him. There was never a time that she did not want him, he said, and he wondered if she did not have the same desires towards another man—or other men, for that matter. He worked a long hard day, the man said, and he made good money, and she shared with his other wives some of what he earned. Therefore, he reasoned, she should be faithful to him, and to him alone. Daniel was obliged to agree.

It was still early in the morning when they arrived at the Estate on the outskirts of Spanish Town. Daniel thanked him, wished him a good day, and made his way along the road towards the town of Old Harbour. He had been told that the prison ran along the Old Harbour Road and would be quite easy to find if he just took the Old Harbour Road. The road he traveled did not enter the town proper, and sure enough in a few minutes he could see the high brick walls and the south tower of the prison.

He walked around the wall until he came to the front of the institution, with a large, iron doorway at which a uniformed policeman stood sentry duty. He explained to the guard his reasons for the visit and showed him the Judge's letter. The policeman rang the doorbell, and shortly after he was let into the prison grounds and towards a small office, where he was told to wait.

A woman sitting on a bench against the wall was clutching a small bundle. Her expression clearly showed her distress; she was on the verge of breaking down completely with tears running down her cheeks. She ignored him as if crying was something people did shamelessly in public every day. They did not speak, even though he would have liked to offer her some kind of encouragement for whatever trouble she was in. He could not decide how the conversation could be started. Prisons are such very sad places, he thought. Just then a door at the side of the office opened and a guard appeared. He beckoned to the woman and she got up quickly and followed him. Daniel waited for over an hour before the guard appeared once again. Without speaking he approached Daniel, signaled to him to stand up, and still without speaking began to search his pockets and through his clothing. When he was satisfied that Daniel was not concealing any prohibited article he demanded the letter that the judge had given him. He examined it briefly and left the room without a word.

Five minutes later he reappeared. "Y'u come wid me," he said, and Daniel followed him across an open courtyard. At one end he could see a wooden scaffold with steps leading to the upper level—evidently the place of execution—the sight sickened him, and made him feel ill. The upper section was open, but the lower section below the platform was enclosed with a canvas curtain, not allowing any hanging corpse to be visible. They entered a large solid brick building across from the courtyard, in which there were numerous windows at all three levels, all heavily barred—the prison cells where convicts were housed.

The guard did not speak to Daniel as they made their way through an iron gate where another guard stood sentry, and then up a set of solid concrete steps to the upper level. At the top another iron gate and another guard. The man stopped to examine a piece of paper that he had been holding, and then he spoke to himself as if to remind himself of where he was going.

"Number forty-two," he said, and then repeated himself. "Number forty-two."

They continued along a concrete passageway lined from one end to the other on both sides with iron bars. The place was strangely quiet; some inmates watched him curiously as he went past. They continued to the end of the passageway and then up a second flight of stairs, another guarded iron gate to the third level.

"Forty-two. Forty-two. Forty-two—" The guard kept repeating to himself as if he would forget where he was going. At number forty-two he stopped, found a key and opened the door.

Without speaking he motioned for Daniel to enter. Inside the prison cell the iron door closed behind him with a clanging sound that echoed through the empty passageway—a surge of panic passed through his mind—he imagined for a momment, that he was being locked in too. For several moments he could not see anyone. Then he looked at the bed—there was a man lying there. Again he thought that some mistake had been made because he did not recognize the man—he was not the man he knew. He was expecting to see Watchie—the Maroon, the man with the thick mass of black hair, the dark piercing eyes, and the heavy set chest and neck. The man he saw had his hair cut short in the way for all convicts—and his hair was chalk white.

"Hay man! Is dat y'u?" he asked nervously, bending down to take a closer look. "Is dat y'u?"

The man turned to face him and then he saw that it was indeed the right cell—the man lying on the bed was Watchie. His whole appearance had changed; he was not the man he expected to see. The shock of his changed appearance left him without words, and he gasped in amazement—he could not find words.

"Yes man, it me—same one—Watchie." A feeble answer came back.

"Lawd 'a mercy! W'at dey do y'u? Dey tek off y'u hair and it tu'n white!"

"Dey goine heng me in de marnin' Dan. Dem goine heng me." He sat up on the bed and held out a hand to Daniel. Daniel took hold and held tightly. He could see that his legs were chained together—like an animal Daniel thought. What a dreadful way to treat a man!

When he could find words all he could say was "Yes, man. Ah come te see y'u." And then in a low voice, almost a whisper, "how y'u doin man?"

"Bad. Bad, man. I'se doin bad." He paused and took a deep breath. "Dem goin heng me in de marnin'."

"I'se not so sure 'bout dat," Daniel said. "Ah go see de Judge, an' 'im tell me he would see de Governer te day. Ah tell de judge dat y'u was wid me de whole time and y'u never kill no one."

"Dey condem me Dan, and dey goin heng me fe sumptin' me neber do."

Daniel took a deep breath. He was searching for something to say that would help and console the miserable man, or at least give him strength. "Well if dem goin heng y'u, y'u mus' pray to God, man. If de Lord doant save y'u life, den He will save y'u soul. Y'u mus' seek salvation in de Lord."

"Me do dat all de time now," replied the man, obviously in the depths of despair. "Me do dat all de time, now."

Y'u mus' mek y'u peace wid de Lord if dey goine heng y'u, so dat y'u spirit will rest in peace. Y'u doant want y'u spirit to wander 'bout de eart' an' fine no rest."

Watchie nodded his head in agreement. "Me nebber kill Mister Henderson— y'u knows dat?" he seemed to be seeking reassurance. "W'en ah bruk out'a de Port Antonio jail ah go fine Mista Burke to hide me, an' ah tell 'im dat ah neber chop up Mister Henderson. 'E say dat 'e knows who chop 'im—'e knows dat it was de Rasta man, an' dat de Rasta man hide 'im cutlass, an' dat de Rasta will chop 'im if 'e tell any one man. So 'im is too fraid to give testimony an' stan' as witness in court. An' 'e sey 'e can't hide me—'e sey it is too dangerous—'e sey ah mus' go fine hiding place far away from 'im."

Watchie was in a desperate state; he had been deserted by everyone and refused to believe there was any hope. Daniel persisted, trying to instill some hope and give the condemned man some comfort. When the guard returned Watchie had not changed his expectations—he knew he was living out his last day.

"Pray to de Lord," Daniel said, and those were the last words spoken between them. Daniel left him as miserable as he had found him, and when he was let through the prison doors back out onto the street, Daniel too, was similarly depressed. The visit had disturbed him deeply. The vision of the changed man, his white hair, his miserable condition, and the leg irons on his feet—things he could never forget.

Outside the prison on the street, there were people about. They seemed to come and go, waiting, expecting something to happen. There were several groups of two or three gathered about, and he wondered what they were waiting for, if it was the sign of an execution—the black flag hoisted on the prison flagpole. If there was to be one it would rise at about seven o'clock the next morning, but he desperately hoped that it would not—then he would know that his mission had been successful. He would not leave until he knew the outcome.

Among the people outside the prison walls was a ragged looking younger man—his shirt was quite dirty and torn in several places. He did not appear like the others, to be waiting for someone or for some event to take place—he moved restlessly about from one place to another. He seemed to be examining the faces of those standing about, and had looked over at Daniel several times, but Daniel had not paid him any attention—his mind was on other things. Shortly after the noon hour the man approached him where he was leaning against the prison wall.

"Marnin," the man said as he took a position beside Daniel.

"Marnin," Daniel replied, but did not start a conversation.

After a while Daniel left his place, and walked about to stretch his legs. The man followed him and was soon walking beside him. Daniel was somewhat surprised by the man's presence beside him, but he did not object and did not speak to him. Some time later he resumed his position against the prison wall, and the man did the same. As the day wore on he was getting hungry and began to feel very tired—as though he could lie down and go to sleep. It was not so much the hunger that drove him—it was the thirst and a nagging pain in his stomach—the perishing thirst. He had to find water.

He left the prison walls deciding to find his way to the center of the town where he could get drinking water. The man followed closely and finally asked, "where y'u goin man?"

A'h goin' fe look drinking water,"Daniel told him.

"A'h show y'u," the man said, and Daniel accepted the offer. Soon they were in the square standing before the Nelson Monument, and a fountain without any water flowing in it. But there was also a public standpipe from which anyone could get water. He drank heavily even though the water was brackish and did not sit well in his stomach. A food vendor near by supplied him with two patties, and some sugar water, which he ate sitting on the edge of the fountain. The man sitting beside him never took his eyes away from him as he ate. Finally, he could stand the stares no longer, and he bought a patty for the man too, which was devoured within seconds. There was no conversation between them as he rested by the fountain before returning to the prison walls again. As the afternoon came and passed, it began to get dark, there still had been very little conversation between them, and Daniel was wondering if the man would be hanging around through the night. Finally the man spoke to him.

"Ah afe go now," he told Daniel as he evidently prepared to leave.

"Good, good," Daniel answered.

"So y'u afe pay me now," the man replied.

Daniel was surprised and did not reply immediately. "Pay y'u fe w'at?" He demanded.

"Ah was wid y'u from de marnin an' y'u afe pay me."

"Y'u was wid me fe de marnin, but me nebber tell y'u to stay."

"Ah was wid y'u fe de marnin an' ah show y'u where to fine water, so y'u af' te pay me."

"Y'u was wid me fe de marnin, but me nebber tell y'u is to fine water fe me."

"Ah was wid y'u fe de day an' keep y'u company like a fren, so y'u mus' pay me"

"Look qua' boy," Daniel said angrily. "Y'u is not me fren, an' me nebber pay me fren to say 'marnin' or to stay wid me. So y'u is jus' go 'bout y'u bisness an' doant bodder me."

"Y'u is to pay me," the man grumbled, evidently realizing that his plan had not worked, but still keeping to his position.

Daniel ignored the remarks and the man drifted slowly away, still grumbling. He watched until he was out of sight, but wondered if he might not return after it was dark. He turned his thoughts to the immediate problem; where he would spend the night leaning against the proson wall, uncomfortable as it may be. He sat leaning against the prison wall and watched the people come and go from the prison. It was a busy place, he thought, with people constantly going in and coming out, and the small crowd outside—always waiting.

As the sun went down the air seemed to be drier and more comfortable, and feeling so tired, he wanted to find a quieter place where he might be able to sleep. He walked away from the gate around a corner, and closly followed along the high redbrick prison wall. It was indeed a quieter place, but there was a putrid and disgusting smell about the place. He examined the ground against the wall and found that it had been used as a latrine, possibly for many years, hence the unpleasant odor. He returned to his former place near the prison gate, and disregarding the people about sat down with his back against the wall, closed his eyes and dozed off. He awoke during the night to find the place quiet and deserted, and he quickly fell asleep again.

The sun was just rising when he opened his eyes. He was immediately wide awake, got up quickly, dusted off his clothes, and made his way to the gate, anxiously looking up at the prison flagpole. There was no flag there, and he breathed a sigh of relief, but it was still early, and it may yet deliver its dreadful message. For about thirty minutes he could not take his eyes off the stout mast, and then there seemed to be some movement of the rope that went to the top of the pole. He watched, transfixed; the rope continued to move; he watched expectantly, and then was horrified to see the black flag hoisted. It did not rise smoothly but in short jerky movements until it reached the top. For several minutes he was not able to move—he was frozen to his position with the realization that the watchman—not even a friend, but an innocent man he had come to know—had been hanged.

It was as though he had been injected with a powerful drug that immobilized his body and dulled his mind. His head swam—he was filled with anger, frustration, sorrow, and self-incrimination.

How long this mindless state of confusion lasted he could not say; he had no recollection of his return to Chivers Estate. He could not tell how he had made his way home some three weeks later. It all came back to him as he trudged his way along the coast road towards Chivers Estate, and the two large gateposts, leading to the great house.

Jamaican Proverb—It hard to keep the devil out, but even harder to drive 'im out.

CHAPTER 55

Across the Island the news of the execution was greeted with considerable interest—from some with great satisfaction. 'It serve 'im good' came from many quarters as most agreed that justice had been done. This was no less so than at the Manor House Estate. Harriet took in the news with mixed feelings; sadness at the thought of her son's murder—glad that his killer—or so she thought—had paid the price for his crime.

The news of the execution reached Manor House Estate the day following, on a Saturday morning. Rasta and his friend Pedro were elated and spontaneously decided that it should be the occasion for a celebration—to be held as usual at Burke's house. Burke, for his part was not sure what the execution meant for him; he knew that the man hanged in Spanish Town Prison was not the man who killed William Henderson, and that knowledge did not give him much satisfaction. He did not care about the Maroon, and was not really concerned that an innocent man had paid with his life for a crime that he did not commit, but he was relieved that as far as he could see the whole matter was closed, and the investigation was over. Rasta and Pedro agreed that they could no longer be considered suspects, and Burke believed that he was also exempted. He hoped that the whole unpleasant affair would now be put to rest, and he could get on with other things. He had a rude awakening from Rasta.

"Oh, no-no man!" Rasta told him. "Y'us not free like we. Y'use de man dat tell Watchie to chop 'im. Y'u mus' 'member dat man!"

The plot was obvious, and it struck deeply—it made him feel sick. He had suddenly realized that they intended to use this as a threat to keep him under their control. It made him think again of ways in which he could administer the rat poison, and rid himself of these men. But he knew he did not have the stomach for murder.

In the afternoon they appeared at his house, bringing with them several bottles of rum. They had been drinking from the early afternoon and were already almost drunk by the time they arrived, while Burke was still quite sober.

They sat around the table drinking. Pedro was singing a song imitating some popular American crooner, and Rasta was smoking his 'weed.' Burke was being urged to 'take a draw' but he did not smoke at all, and declined the offers. Finally he took one puff and returned the cigarette stub.

"Tell 'im who y'u is now" Pedro said to his friend. "Tell 'im how y'u tell me. How y'u is de mighty man!"

"Ah am de king!" Rasta responded. "See me 'ere—I'se de king!" He stood with raised hands above his head, turning around slowly in a complete circle.

"How y'u de king?" Pedro asked, as if following the lines of some rehearsed play.

"Ah slay de Satan!" And they both laughed. "Ah slay de Satan!" He swung his hand as if cutting with a sword—or machete!

They were playing a game between them, a game that they had evidently played before, but were repeating for Burke's benefit.

"Tell 'im like y'u tell me," Pedro urged again. He sat on a box grinning at Burke, relishing the tail that he soon hoped to hear again. His eyes were fixed on Burke—he watched him keenly to see the effects, if any, that it would have.

"De nite was dark—dark," Rasta began. "An' ah watch 'im tek de breeze. 'E lif 'im shirt so," and he demonstrated as he loosened his shirt in his trousers. "Ah watch 'im look 'bout de place, an' ah follow 'im close. 'E doant se'me, man. I'se too slick fe 'im. Same time, man, ah have me cutlass wid me. 'Im walk on de pier, lif 'im head like so," and again he demonstrated lifting his chin upwards. "Me was right behine' an' same time ah chop 'im! Wham!"

As Rasta paused, Pedro was grinning and laughing, enjoying the tale once again. "Wham!" he repeated, watching to see how Burke reacted.

"'E turn 'imself like so, to hold me an' open up 'im mout to call out, and me cut 'im troat." He made a motion with his hand again as though he was slicing some object at face level. "E mek a noise like 'trrrush'! De blood in 'im mout' choke 'im, an' ah cut 'im troat an' chop 'im one more time!"

Pedro, grinning from ear to ear, was squirming with delight like a child enjoying a favorite bedtime story.

"Same time 'im drop down an' ah push 'im into de water." Again he demonstrated how he pushed the body off the pier into the sea.

"Look 'pon me now," Rasta crowed. "Look 'pon me—I'se de king!" Again he raised his arms up above his head in a triumphant gesture. "Ah slay de Satan!"

"'E'se de king!" Pedro repeated, still with the silly grin across his face.

A minute or two passed as Burke adsorbed the story with all its gory detail. He had a serious expression that he simply could not disguise even though he had tried not to show any emotion during the telling—he sat subdued and numbed. He did not enjoy hearing about it. It was the cold-blooded manner in which it was described, and more so the obvious pleasure that they found in the telling that sickened him. He took a mouthful of his drink and put the glass down on the table. He did not know what to say—words seemed to have left him. A few minutes went by as the two men continued their 'celebration' and Burke sat quietly thinking.

At last he found words, "Tell me this," he said to Rasta. "Den why y'u do it?"

He was just curious to know the reason why he had killed William Henderson. As far as he knew William had never had much to do with the man—probably never even spoken to him. So why would he have killed him?

"Why y'u kill 'im?" he asked again.

Rasta fell silent for a moment; he looked at Burke incredulously. He could not understand why anyone would ask that question. To him the answer was obvious, and yet he could not find the words to give a reason. He looked from Burke to Pedro, spread his hands in a questioning gesture, searching for an answer.

"Why y'u do it? Burke asked again.

This time Rasta found the answer. "Every man did want 'im dead! Ah do it fe everyman."

No one spoke and Pedro continued his inane grinning at Burke.

Rasta continued his explanations, "'E was a wicked man an' everyman want 'im dead! 'E call de watchie 'dirty nigger!' 'E was a Satan, an' ah slay 'im, an dat mek me de King! No man can touch me!" He was getting very excited, Burke thought, and perhaps it was time to change the subject. He kept silent not knowing how best to divert their attention to some other topic.

"Look 'pon me now, man," Rasta shouted at Burke, who had diverted his gaze. "Ah sey look pon me! I'se de king!"

Burke glanced up at the man's face—it reflected rage—it scared him and he looked away. Rasta was within arms reach and he grabbed Burke by his hair jerking his face towards his so that Burke could only look at him.

"Look 'pon me man. Y'u lookin' at de king!" he shouted in Burke's face. "Ah can chop y'u up and dem can't touch me!" He held Burke's hair tightly and shook Burke's head, looking into his face as if he were contemplating just that! Burke was beginning to squirm, partly the discomfort of having his hair pulled, but mostly in fear.

"Ah goine chop y'u!" Rasta announced. "Ah goine chop y'u!"

Pedro was no longer grinning at Burke. Things were going too far and were getting out of hand. He intervened. "Give de man a break," he said to Rasta. "Y'u doant af te chop 'im." He put his hand on Rasta's shoulder to calm him down. "E knows dat y'use de King!"

Rasta did not let go his hold. "Who is de king?" he said to Burke. "Who is de king?"

"Y'u is de king," Burke said quietly, and then he repeated, "y'use de king!"

Rasta slowly let go his hold and Burke gave an audible sigh of relief. Rasta sat down again in his chair, picked up his glass, drank the contents, and refilled it as though nothing unusual had occurred.

"Drink wid me, Brudda Burke," he said, raising his glass towards Burke and smiling as though they were the best of friends. But Burke knew just how close he had come to having his throat cut. He poured himself another drink and sat back to watch as the revelry continued.

Pedro was singing at the top of his voice and clowning for the amusement of the other two men, but Burke was not amused. Urged on by his friend, Pedro began to prance and to dance about and remove his clothes piece by piece. Soon he was completely naked and he began to imitate various positions of copulation, all with a running commentary, for the entertainment of his Rastafarian friend. Then he tucked his genitals between his legs to hide them from view and strutted about as if he was a woman, while Rasta clapped his hands and roared his approval. When this activity no longer seemed to amuse, Pedro left the house completely naked, to cool off outside in the yard taking his bottle of rum with him, and occasionally breaking into song. During a quiet moment he heard voices—voices coming from the mountain road that went past the house. He stopped his crooning and listened quietly. He heard the voices of women—market women on the road returning home.

Market women survive—even thrive—under the most difficult conditions; they cultivate the plots, they bear the children and nurse them, they cook and keep house every day of the week, and then on market days they trudge many miles to and from the markets carrying heavy loads of produce. Each Friday morning they leave their homes on the way to market with their heavy loaded baskets, carefully balanced on their heads, and then they return on Saturday nights, walking the many miles home into the hills and mountains. The single benefit from this life is that they develop beautiful bodies built like the fabled Amazon

Women. And they are very strong. These two women trudging up the roadway were no exception, and were, under most circumstances, able to defend themselves against any attack. Quite able—that is, except for the fact that they were very tired after the labour of the past few days.

It did not take Pedro more than a few seconds to leave the yard and place himself in the middle of the road to await their arrival. The night was quite bright with a half-moon shining in the sky, but the two women, intent on making their way home, did not see the naked man in the middle of the road until he was right upon them. Suddenly they were face to face—a naked man appeared in front of them, one hand reaching towards them and the other hand clasping his erect penis, gyrating his body towards them.

The women screamed and shouted as they attempted to get past and he grabbed at them. He caught the first woman as the second woman slipped by. He quickly wrestled the woman to the ground, and climbed on top of her. When her companion returned to help he was astride his victim, groping at her breasts and tearing at her clothing. Her companion tried to grab his arm but could not keep hold of it, and in desperation she started to grab at anything within reach. She got her fingers into his hair with one hand and then with both hands. She curled in her fingers and yanked it violently jerking his head backwards. His hair, usually slicked back with generous amounts of coconut oil, was slippery and she lost her grip. Her efforts were in vain—he continued his attack and was removing the woman's clothes in strips. As another piece of her clothing was torn away, her companion searched desperately for some way to subdue the attacker. From between her feet she found a fist-sized stone picked it up. With all her strength clouted him across the head. The blow cracked his skull like an eggshell, but she did not stop with just the one blow, she delivered several more, each with the same deadly force. When he neither moved nor groaned she threw the bloodied stone to the side of the road and helped her friend get up.

"Y'u dirty fucker!" the woman shrieked. She stood and pulled down her skirt, and as she did so she stomped hard on his genitals that lay exposed. "Y'u will never fuck no more!"

The women dusted themselves off and assessed the damage to their bodies and clothes. The woman thrown to the ground was bruised and battered, and her companion helped her to the side of the spring where she washed her bruises and regained her breath. They collected their scattered possessions and strips of clothing, casting nervous glances at the still, naked body, blood oozing from several open wounds on his head. He did not move and he made no sound. They took one final look at the body and then hurriedly continued on their way. They were sure he was dead—a fact confirmed some days later when they heard about the naked body found on the mountain pathway. They said nothing about their involvement.

The bloody naked body on the mountain road created a great deal of excitement at the time, but the police never solved the case. In point of fact they never tried very hard, and never took the murder very seriously. They concluded, quite rightly from their investigations, that the man was killed because he had attacked someone on the road, and in that case it was justifiable manslaughter. Furthermore the case was very difficult to investigate and in all likelihood could never be solved, so they made some inquiries, got nowhere and then let the matter rest.

Burke arranged for Pedro's burial, and Harriet gave her permission for a grave in the old cemetery on the estate, the one reserved for such occasions. The only persons present were Rasta and Burke and four workers from the estate who had dug the grave, and were needed to transport the coffin and fill in the grave. Not even the curious, that as a matter of habit always attended these affairs were present at the graveside.

Pedro's demise was a great relief to Burke—there was one less to deal with—but he held back as much as he could on showing his real feelings. At first Rasta was unbelieving—he could not accept the fact that his friend, his henchman, an admirer, was dead. Following the initial shock, anger replaced his disbelief and sorrow—he became very angry—anger and sadness enveloped him and he swore to see his friend's death avenged. Several weeks later there had been no resolution of the case, and the disinterest of the police further enraged him. The police treated him with total disrespect; they were not working for a Rastafarian even if it involved a murder, and they let him know that in no uncertain terms. Not knowing who had killed his friend, Rasta did not know on whom to vent his revenge, and he began to direct his anger at everyone, including Burke.

Pedro's death delivered a message of mortality—no matter how invincible one is—or thinks one is—death will overtake everyone. But in spite of that Rasta was still a swaggering boastful man, and infinitely more dangerous; he was violent and volatile, and believed he was invincible. But in order to sustain his bravado Rasta needed an audience—an admiring audience—someone to fill the position that Pedro had filled so well—someone to feed his ego and remind him that 'he was the king!' The need did not die with Pedro, if anything it intensified, and Burke became the chosen audience.

Burke was anything but an admirer; he had come to fear and to hate the man, and that made Burke a very bad choice. The day of the burial Rasta was overcome with grief, and had tearfully begged Burke to let him stay in his house. He needed consolation and someone to talk to—to help ease his sorrow, and for pity's sake Burke could not refuse. Out of fear of the man and against his better judgment Burke agreed to let him stay there for a few days, and Rasta moved into Burke's house.

Rasta would only talk about Pedro's death, continue to swear vengeance against everyone, and keep Burke constantly on edge. Burke wanted to put the whole matter behind him—he wanted to live without thinking about William's murder or about Pedro's death, but Rasta was now constantly with him, and Burke, try as he could, found it impossible to avoid him and to forget those unpleasant events. After a few days the obvious lack of admiration and disinterest began to irritate Rasta, and he began to curse and to swear at Burke. Burke was so intimidated that he could not find the courage to tell the man to leave. Furthermore, during those days it became clear that Rasta had designs on Harriet. Part of his relief from sorrow, he said, would be to take Harriet—or any of the women living in the estate houses, including those living at Chivers Estate. It would be a form of revenge.

At night and even during the day, Rasta roamed the garden and places near the Great House hoping to encounter Harriet. He imagined that Harriet liked him—she looked at him in a peculiar way the few times that she had seen him, and he took this to mean that she desired him! He was sure that her expression indicated a liking for him. Had he known the truth, it was the look of utter revulsion tinged with fear that made Harriet look that way. Nevertheless he continued to speculate on what would take place between them when they met under the right circumstances. If she fancied Burke, as he thought, she would be enraptured when she encountered a real man!

As the days passed Rasta's anger subsided somewhat, but it was still there, simmering below the surface and easily aroused. The renewed relationship between Harriet and Burke was well and jealously observed by Rasta. He took this as a sign that things were once again back to where they were—and indeed they were—at least on the surface—Burke and Harriet were playing their card games again.

A few weeks later when Burke went to the Great House, Rasta appeared on the driveway in clear view of the card players on the veranda. He stood there looking up at Burke as though he had something to say, but did not speak.

"What does that man want?" Harriet asked Burke. "Does he want to see you?"

"I don't know. I suppose I'd better find out."

Burke left the table and descended to the driveway beside Rasta. "Is there something you want to see me about?" he asked.

"No! No! Mister Burke," he replied, "Ah jus' come fe watch y'u play."

"Well you can't do that. Missus Henderson doant like y'u watch. Y'u better go."

The man grumbled his objections at being sent away. He held his ground and argued the point. "Me is only watchin', an' not doin'no harm."

"Y'u can't do dat," Burke insisted. "De Missus doant like y'u watch. An' y'u af to go."

He continued to grumble but he turned about and slowly walked away. Burke watched him for a few moments and then returned to the game.

"What did he want?" Harriet asked.

"It wasn't anything important," Burke told her, as he picked up his cards.

"I don't like that man," Harriet said. "I don't like the way he looks. He's so dirty."

"He keeps the workers busy," Burke said, "and he's good at that. That's why I keep him on."

Harriet returned to her cards, apparently satisfied now that the man was out of sight.

The following week a similar event occurred. Rasta appeared walking past the veranda where the card game was in progress, and several minutes later he returned. It was not five minutes after that he returned once again, and each time he passed by he was leering and smiling at the card players on the veranda. After the third pass Harriet was visible agitated, and as soon as he was out of sight she angrily demanded that Burke find out what he wanted, and if he did not need anything, to get rid of him.

"If he comes back again I'll find out," Burke replied nervously. He was not relishing the encounter, and his nerves were getting the better of him. Beads of sweat appeared on his forehead, and he wiped his head and neck with his handkerchief.

Sure enough, several minutes later Rasta was slowly passing by, again leering and smiling at the card players. He was scarcely past when Burke left the table descended to the driveway and started after him. He caught up to him a few steps further on, putting his hand on his shoulder to walk further along the driveway, hoping that Harriet would not hear their conversation. In a low voice he again repeated Harriet's objections.

"Missus Henderson doant want te see y'u here," he said earnestly. And then his voice took on a tone of urgency. "Look 'ere man," he said, "de missus will say ah mus' fire y'u. Y'u doant want dat to happen. Ah doant want dat to happen. Jus' walk on an' doant come back—jus' do dis t'ing fe me," he pleaded.

Rasta was not about to agree, and the argument got stronger and louder—his voice was being raised.

"Me not doin' any harm—I'se jus' watchin' an' dere's no harm in dat!

When Burke finally succeeded in getting him to leave he was obviously very angry; he was glaring at Harriet, occasionally lifting his hand and pointing in her direction. But he did finally turn and walk away. Burke watched him until he was out of sight and then he returned to the card table.

Harriet was furious. "What is he arguing with you about?"

"Don't you have any control over him?"

"He should not be contradicting you like that.

"Why do you stand for that?"

"I want you to fire him—do you understand me?"

"I don't like the way he looks at me, and I want him off this property—immediately."

"I can't do that," Burke blurted out in panic, not having thought out the consequences of contradicting a direct order from Harriet, but knowing too well the consequences of firing Rastaman.

"I mean, not right away," he added quickly.

"Oh yes you can!" Harriet corrected him. "And you will! He is to be off this property immediately. Do you understand me? Immediately! Do it now. Right now."

Burke took several moments to collect his wits, looking at Harriet quite speechless. He was trying to find a way out, but Harriet's order left him no room. Then he said meekly, "Very well—as you wish."

"The insolence of that dreadful man! I don't want to see him ever again! Get rid of him!" She shouted as he departed.

Burke placed his unfinished hand on the table and left; he was almost in a state of panic; his hands were shaking, his heart was throbbing wildly and he could not think clearly. He hoped that Rasta had not heard Harriet's shout as he left. He took the pathway towards his house—he had not ridden the horse that evening—he had used the animal all day and it was showing signs of being lame. Furthermore he had removed the saddle in the late afternoon and was not about to replace it just for the afternoon. The walk back to his house was like a dream—he was deep in thought, so much so that he could not have recalled a single thing about it, not even if his life depended on it. He decided to leave matters until the following morning—he could not fire Rasta that night. He would be in better control of himself in the morning when he had thought it over.

Rasta was not in the house when he arrived there, but throughout the night he worried, and when the morning came he was still quite undecided about how he would handle it. He was very afraid of the Rastafarian—he did not know how violently he would react—that he would be very angry and threaten him was a certainty, and it could very well get out of control. He did have a plan though, he would continue to employ the man on condition that he kept away, and Harriet never caught sight of him. He would have to make sure that Harriet never saw him, and he would tell Harriet that he had been fired. But he did not know if this would work—the Rastafarian was unpredictable and he wished he had something to protect himself—even a gun.

Early the next morning Burke went looking for Rasta who had not returned during the night. He went to saddle the horse and discovered that it was quite lame and could not be used for a few days. He would have to find Rasta, and prepared to search for him on foot, but he did not want to find him alone. He was somewhat relieved to find him at the produce shed where there were a number of men working. As he got nearer he called to him.

"Marnin'," he said, "how y'u doin man?"

Rasta grumbled. "Marnin.'"

"A bad-bad t'ing happen last nite," Burke began. "A bad-bad thing, man." He took a deep breath, and paused for 'the bad t'ing' to take effect. "But I have to tell y'u Rastaman—I have to tell y'u that Missus Henderson sey I must fire y'u. She say y'u not to be here no more. She say I must fire y'u to day."

"Y'u doant fire me, man!" Rasta exploded at the top of his voice. "Y'u fire me man, an ah tek y'u down wid me. Y'u fire me an' you'se a dead man!"

"I have a plan—listen to me man." Burke was trying to explain, but Rasta was not listening—he had heard the first few words and that was enough for him.

Burke had expected as much, but as long as it did not get any worse, he was going to push it through. Again he tried to reason with the man—if he would only listen.

"Missus Henderson say y'u is fired, but we can work out something between us. See wid me man," he pleaded.

Burke's words were not getting through—the man was in a violent rage. He was shouting, waving his arms about, and swearing. He would not stand still—one minute he was storming off towards the shed only to turn about and storm back again, pointing his finger at Burke, shaking his clenched fist, and hurling volumes of abuse. He was beyond reason—not listening to a word, and because of the shouting, Burke could not even hear his own words. The workers gathered about to watch, curious to know what had triggered his dismissal and enraged him to such an extent.

Rasta ran to the shed once again; he searched briefly and reappeared with his cutlass, shouting threats against Harriet and against Burke. This had an immediate effect on Burke; he knew the man was crazy enough to carry out his threats, and there would be little that he could do about it.

"Ah goine chop y'u up!" He shouted. "Ah goine chop up all una white people!"

Burke knew it was time for him to leave. He backed up a few steps and then took off as fast as he could run towards his house. The men watched in amazement.

"Doan't sleep in y'u bed te nite!" Rasta shouted at the departing figure. "Doan't live in y'u house—ah will fine y'u! Ah goine chop y'u!"

Burke entered his house breathless and in a state of panic. He had to find somewhere to stay where he would be safe until the man calmed down and he had time to think clearly. He thought again about going to the police but that might make the situation much worse for him—Rasta would accuse him of murdering William, so seeking their protection was not the answer. He searched desperately about the house wondering what he could take with him—some food? Some clothes? He could not make up his mind. He picked up a sack and began stuffing it with clothes. Soon it was nearly full and too bulky for him to carry, much less run with, so he threw half the contents out onto the bed. Then he decided that he would need the food. He went to the shelf and dragged the contents into the sack. Now it was too heavy—he began taking items out that were heavy, or that he could do without. One of the bags burst in the sack and soiled the clothes, so once again he began to sort the clothes trying unsuccessfully to find the unsoiled garments. Finally, in desperation, he took all the clothes out of the sack and angrily threw them on the floor; none were fit to wear. He had little time to collect his things before Rasta could get there.

The dogs in the yard suddenly started to bark; someone was coming—it must be Rasta—he had to leave without a moment's delay. There was nowhere for him to go, and no one to help him. He looked outside to see who it might be—he saw no one, but the dogs were barking. He dropped the sack and left the house as he had entered—with nothing, and ran off to hide in the bush.

CHAPTER 56

Burke had not been seen for several days—neither had the Rastafarian, but in the meantime gossip had spread the word that Rasta was going to 'chop up Mista Burke!' Henry heard about the threats, and he took them seriously, but most had dismissed the tirade as just an empty threat. Burke, they thought, had just run away, and would soon return when things calmed down. Henry went to his dresser drawer and took out his service revolver. He checked the action, loaded the chambers, and replaced it in the holster. He had little doubt that the Rastafarian was quite capable of carrying out his threat, especially if he had made it openly with people about. He decided to report the matter to the police in Port Antonio.

The following day Henry left for Kingston on business, and was expected to be away for several days. Having concerns for the safety of the people at Chivers, he handed over the revolver to Daniel who put it in a drawer in the pantry, where it could be easily reached if needed. Later that afternoon Daniel instructed Opal on its use. He did not think it would be needed, but he was not about to take any chances.

The next morning a constable appeared at Manor House Estate to investigate the matter and to speak with Harriet. The threats against Burke were news to Harriet—she had not heard the gossip circulating through the estates, and she was very alarmed. Burke was the only person on the estate on whom she could depend, but she had not seen him for two days, so she tried to get the constable to remain there throughout the night, offering him a bribe and all kinds of rewards. The constable had been told to investigate, and then to report back at the station, which is exactly what he did. He left Harriet in an agitated state, very anxious to get someone to stay with her in the house.

Burke spent the day in the bush, not far from his house, keeping a watchful lookout for Rasta. Towards the evening he was very hungry, and decided that he must get something to eat. He waited until it was quite dark, and then cautiously made his way through the bush to the Manor House. He went into the underground passageway trying to remember the combination that would get him to the hidden doorway and gain him entry to the house. At the opening to the passages he had left a candle and some matches, which he found, and he lit the candle. He slowly crept his way along the walls, brushing the dusty cobwebs from his head and face as he went. In his anxiety he could not remember the combination, and it took almost two hours for him to find the doorway, and start up the steps leading to the main house. The door at the top was not locked, and he was quickly in the house.

In the house there were no lamps burning, and it was deathly silent. He knew Harriet would not be about as she usually retired early, and she would not hear his movements through the house. He went to the drawing room and looked about as much as the faint light would allow. He left the room and went to the pantry where he found some bread, milk in the icebox, and some jam. He was sitting at the pantry table quietly eating when he was startled; there was a noise that alerted him; someone else was in the house! He literally froze and listened intensely, his heart throbbing in his ears and his pulse racing. He blew out the candle and went to the door, looked out and saw no one. And then there was the strong odour of smoke that wafted into the room—someone was smoking—or had been smoking. It was a smell he knew very well—the person in the house was Rasta! He remained quiet as he slid down behind the pantry door to sit on the floor, just listening. For several hours he remained quiet, during which there were the faint sounds of movement, and long periods of total silence. As the hours passed he closed his eyes but did not fall asleep. Then suddenly he heard a scream! And then another scream that continued for several long seconds. Rasta must have found Harriet—he was petrified as the screaming continued—hiding behind the door he covered his ears. He did not have the courage to investigate much less help. When he uncovered his ears the house was silent once again.

Burke remained in the pantry not daring to move into the rest of the house. His head swam with the thought that Rasta had raped Harriet—or even killed her—but he was not going to investigate, and also perhaps be killed. He would wait until it was getting light before he tried to leave the house—he had to see where he was going and avoid Rasta. As the light broke he got up and looked out to see if anyone was about. He would leave the house the quickest way— by the front door—he could not risk going through the house to find the back steps where he had entered. In the half light of the early dawn, he made his way past the drawing room, and from there to the front door. It was locked and bolted—it took him a minute to cautiously loosen the bolt, but as he drew it back it made a loud squeaking sound. He pushed against the door to open it, but it was double bolted and it did not yield—the door would not open. He found the other bolt and drew it back, again pushing against the door. Rasta was almost behind him as the door opened and he ran out with Rasta in hot pursuit.

CHAPTER 57

It was a very busy time of the year for Henry to be away in Kingston, and not a good time for Burke to be absent from the Manor House. At Chivers Daniel was in charge of the work there, but no one was overseeing the work at the Manor House. Someone would have to take charge. In spite of Harriet's preferences in the matter, Daniel decided to take over in Henry's place, or until Burke reappeared.

Daniel was up early in the morning to organized the work at Chivers. By midmorning he was on his way to the Manor House to get the work started there. The men had not expected him; some had scattered when Burke did not appear, and some were already out in the fields, so it took much longer to get the work started. He found that the Estate was in bad shape; much of the work done over the past weeks was unsatisfactory—it had to be done again. By the late afternoon he was on his way back to Chivers, and it was quite dark by the time he fed and stabled the mule, and he was on his way to the Busher's cottage.

There was a lighted lantern hanging from a rafter over the broad walk and Daniel went to fetch it, but before he could take it down a figure appeared from out of the darkness right in front of him—it was Rastaman, and he was holding his cutlass, swinging it from his hand. For a split second Daniel froze, and then he cautiously continued towards the lantern, and towards the pantry. He could not get into the pantry without passing in front of the man with the cutlass, but he continued to approach him. Rastaman appeared to be puzzled by this—not what he expected, and he did not react—he stood his ground, but watched as Daniel drew closer to him.

"Evenin'" Daniel said, calmly. "A'h goin tek down de lite."

Rastaman did not answer. He was breathing heavily, almost snorting, like an enraged animal, but he did not move to bar the way. As Daniel passed he could smell the liquor and smoke on the man's breath. Apparently Daniel's calm reaction to his presence did not alarm him, and Daniel took down the lantern and continued on to the pantry. He was wondering where his daughter was—it crossed his mind that the Rastafarian could have found her. He entered the pantry and quickly opened the draw to get the revolver. As he turned about the other man was at the door, standing in the entrance, glaring at him, snorting in anger, and swinging his cutlass—he had changed his mind about letting this man go!

He stood in the doorway glaring at Daniel. He changed his grip on the cutlass holding it ready. Daniel could see the angry expression, the dreadlocks half covering his face, and he knew the man was about to attack him. With a loud growl Rasta rushed at him, raising the cutlass aiming it at Daniel's head. Daniel drew the pistol from the holster, pointed it and pulled the trigger. There was a flash, and a loud explosion as the bullet entered the chest, knocking the man backward and off his feet.

For several minutes Daniel remained still, holding the pistol at his side, looking at the man he had just shot. He was in a state of shock—his head was spinning. He looked at the man sprawled on the ground bleeding from the wound in the chest. Rastaman must be dead he concluded, and as he regained some of his senses he was not going to spend time examining him. Where was his daughter? Had she been harmed? He went into the house calling her name. There was no answer. He went out the front door down the steps and on to the driveway, and then to his great relief Opal appeared out of the darkness, running towards the cottage.

"What hapin?" she asked. "I heard a loud noise. Are you hurt?"

"No, no. I just shoot Rastaman," breathlessly he told her, "he come after me with his cutlass an' I shoot him."

Daniel was still in a state of shock when the police arrived from Port Antonio. He had returned to the cottage and helped himself to a hefty swig of Henry's whisky in an effort to steady his nerves, but it had not helped much. It was a long night as the police carried out their investigation, and a much longer day when Harriet appeared in the early morning, battered and bruised. Mrs. Barnham took her to the hospital in Port Antonio, driven there by Joseph.

When Henry returned a day later the excitement had almost completely dissipated. People were still talking about what had happened, but everything appeared to be normal. The police were still investigating and they expected Daniel to be charged with manslaughter, but they also expected the charge to be dismissed in court, and they held off laying the charge.

Burke's absence did not alarm them, and the police decided that a search was not necessary. They were sure he had just gone away of his own free will, and would reappear in a few days. How wrong they were! The vultures, circling high in the sky over the mountain ridge led them to the headless body in the bush.

CHAPTER 58

Good things were happening in Jamaica; it made the island better, a more comfortable place for all its inhabitants. New roads were being constructed, and old ones improved. Dams and reservoirs were nearing completion, and these would bring electricity and clean water to many of the smaller towns and villages, where previously they relied on kerosene oil for light and fuel, and on pans of water, carried great distances. Telephone lines were being strung to the outer regions, and Montego Bay was connected to Kingston, where the residents already had electricity, and soon to have telephones too. On Christmas Eve that year the Government Buildings in Kingston were all aglow with colored floodlights, and people came from all parts of the island to view the spectacle. The island celebrated the Diamond Jubilee of King George V and Queen Mary, and many festivities were held throughout the island.

Following the death of the Rastafarian, life returned to its old ways on both estates. Burke was given a proper funeral and buried on the Manor House Estate; there were no mourners at the crowded burial; most had just come as curious onlookers. Harriet was a long time recovering from her ordeal, and moved to her house in Kingston to be away from it all. She never returned to the Manor House Estate, agreeing to put the management of the Estate in Henry Thomson's hands, and within the week Daniel was made the Busha.

It was a Friday afternoon and Pre was on her way home from the school in Port Antonio. She sat in the front seat beside Joseph as he drove, and she chatted about the events at school during the past week. It was the weekly exchange of news that everyone looked forward to on Friday afternoons. Joseph told her that her grandfather had been made the 'Big' Busha, to manage both Chivers and Manor House Estates. And Pre told him that someone placed a pin on the teacher's chair, for which they were all punished. But it was funny to see the teacher jump, and they all had laughed! As the car rounded the corner off the coastal road and turned up the long driveway towards the great house, Joseph slowed down; there were some people on the driveway in front of the house. They got closer and could see it was the nursemaid with Jamie, Bridget's little boy.

"Stop! Stop the car Joseph," Pre ordered. "Stop and let me out."

The car slowed and stopped beside the nurse and the little boy. Pre jumped out leaving the car door wide open for the nurse to close. She bent down to pick up the little boy, standing there with outstretched arms. He threw his little arms tightly around her neck and kissed her fondly on the cheek. She in turn kissed him, and carried him up the steps to the veranda where the rest of the family, Mrs. Barnham, Bridget and Opal were having afternoon tea.

"See! See Mummy!" Jaime said excitedly. "Pre come home!"

"Yes," Bridget said with a smile. "Pre's come home!"